YEAR'S BEST
HARDCORE
HORROR
VOLUME 1

EDITORS:
RANDY CHANDLER
CHERYL MULLENAX

COMETPRESS
WWW.COMETPRESS.US

First Comet Press Trade Paperback Edition
June 2016

Cover and interior by Inkubus Design www.inkubusdesign.com

ISBN 13: 978-1-936964-58-1

Visit Comet Press on the web at: www.cometpress.us
facebook.com/cometpress
twitter.com/cometpress

WWW.COMETPRESS.US

ACKNOWLEDGEMENTS

"Worth The Having" by Michael Paul Gonzalez, from *Chilling Horror Short Stories (Gothic Fantasy)*, Flame Tree Publishing (Sept 2015)

"Awakening" by Jeff Strand, from *Splatterpunk Zine 7* (Oct 2015)

"Readings Off The Charts" by Adam Cesare, from *Splatterpunk Zine* (Oct 2015)

"Reborn" by The Behrg, from *Not Your Average Monster: A Bestiary of Horrors*, Bloodshot Books (Oct 2015)

"What's Worst" by David James Keaton, from *Stealing Propeller Hats From the Dead*, Perpetual Motion Machine Publishing (Aug 2015)

"Dead End" by Kristopher Triana, from *Chilling Horror Short Stories (Gothic Fantasy)*, Flame Tree Publishing (Sept 2015)

"What You Wish For" by Lilith Morgan, from *Murderlust*, Comet Press (April 2015)

"King Shits" by Charles Austin Muir, from *18 Wheels of Horror: A Trailer Full of Trucking Terrors*, Big Time Books (Sept 2015)

"Clean-up On Aisle 3" by Adam Howe, from *Thuglit 19* (Aug 2015)

"Bath Salt Fetus" by Jorge Palacios, from *Blood For You: A Literary Tribute To GG Allin*, Weirdpunk Books (Oct 2015)

"Bored With Brutality" by MP Johnson, from *Blood For You: A Literary Tribute To GG Allin*, Weirdpunk Books (Oct 2015)

"Exposed" by Monica J. O'Rourke, from *Cut Corners Volume 2*, Sinister Grin Press (Oct 2015)

"Eleanor" by Jason Parent, from *Dead Roses: Five Dark Tales of Twisted Love*, Corpus Press (Mar 2015)

"The Scavengers" by Tony Knighton, from *Happy Hour And Other Philadelphia Cruelties*, Crime Wave Press (Jun 2015)

"The Most Important Miracle" by Scott Emerson, from *Diner Stories: Off The Menu*, Mountain State Press, Inc. (January 2015)

"Hungry For Control" by Clare de Lune, from Zombiegasm.com (Sept 2015)

"Clarissa" by Robert Essig & Jack Bantry, from *Creepy Campfire Stories (For Grownups)*, EMP Publishing (Sept 2015)

"Where The Sun Don't Shine" by Pete Kahle, from *Not Your Average Monster: A Bestiary of Horrors*, Bloodshot Books (Oct 2015)

"Blackbird Lullaby" by George Cotronis, from *Thirteen Stories of Transformation*, Underland Press (Mar 2015)

CONTENTS

INTRODUCTION: THE YEAR THAT WAS

It was a year full of horror. Wherever in the world you were, you knew it was there, even if it didn't touch you directly. You knew it might be reaching for you at most any moment, from any direction, coming at you as an 18-wheeler with a dying driver at the wheel or as an innocent-looking suicide bomber pushing a baby-less pram packed with explosives. With the world sinking deeper into chaos and wars raging round the world, refugees fled into bordering countries, inadvertently creating more chaos as they went. War, famine, pestilence and paranoia set the table and we were all invited to the feast of fear. While the Doomsday Clock ticked ever closer to Apocalyptic Midnight.

There is, however, a different breed among us. They are aware of the real-world terrors but they make it their business to explore horrors as yet unseen and to gaze into the deeper darkness of the soul. They may appear normal enough but their outward appearances cloak the horrors happening in their heads. Their imaginations take them places most of us would never dream of going. Yet they go, driven by personal obsessions or pulled by mysterious forces within the darkness, and they chronicle what they find there and make it available to those brave enough to retrace their incursions into taboo territory. You know who we're talking about. We've gathered some of the best of that hearty breed within these pages and proudly present their tales in our Year's Best Hardcore Horror Volume 1.

We did our best to find the best. We put the call out to horror writers and editors of extreme stories, the hardcore stuff that breaks boundaries and trashes taboos, the transgressive tales you can't "unread" (as Chuck Palahniuk says). We staked out our territory and nailed this to the wall to guide us:

YEAR'S BEST HARDEST HORROR
Not your mama's best-of horror annual.
This stuff comes from the edge of the abyss,

stories you read at your own risk
because you feel the abyss looking right back into you
through the tainted lens of each twisted tale.

Thanks to the authors and editors who submitted their work, we believe we have succeeded in finding tales that live up to Year's-Best standard. Odds are, we may have missed some that could've been included, but that's the nature of the beast. We trust that those working far afield will in years to come find their way to us with new twisted tales.

Some of the stories you'll find here are loaded with very graphic descriptions of violence, sex and depravities, while others may contain only one shocking moment of brutality. In others, the hardcore aspect may be less graphic and subtler than you might expect. Some of these quieter tales offer the reader some time to recover from the more disturbing ones preceding.

Most of the stories collected here are from small and specialty press anthologies, with a few from periodicals, like the prestigious *Splatterpunk Zine* in the UK and *Thuglit* here in the US. Bizarro is also represented with a couple of tales from the unlikely anthology *Blood For You: A Literary Tribute To GG Allin* from Weirdpunk Books. (If you're not familiar with the late GG Allin, you can find snippets from some of his outrageous and obscene punk shows online, which will increase your appreciation of those two tales.)

So for now, forget about that neighbor you suspect is a serial killer, don't worry about the drunk driver that could take you out on your next trip to the store, push those troubling news stories to the back of your mind and immerse yourself in the imaginary horrors at hand.

But don't be surprised if you sense something dark staring back at you from between the lines. That is to be expected when you enter these forbidding realms. With any luck, you may find something useful to help you survive the approaching Apocalypse.

Cheryl Mullenax & Randy Chandler
February 2, 2016

WORTH THE HAVING
Michael Paul Gonzalez

How does it feel?

It asks this as it cuts deep into the inner thigh, flesh and fat zippering apart, its tongue probing into the fresh wound.

How are you doing?

The thing wouldn't want an answer even if there was one. It only wants screams.

This is going to be worth it. You're going to love next year. This will make it worth the having.

I used to wonder what could be worth this. The heat of its palms pushing legs apart. The cold, slow rivulets of saliva dripping down like icy syrup, washed away with slowing pulses of hot blood. That single tooth in its lower jaw, barbed and curved, that awful knowing smile from the puckered sphincter of its mouth. This year, I finally understand that phrase, *worth the having*. This year, the final year of our horrible agreement—the thing still uses that word, *agreement*, as if I wanted any of this—I understand it all.

Twenty-two years ago, I was cutting across the backyard of Mikey Slater's dad's house. This was the night before Halloween; the night, I'd later learn, that the thing would stretch its legs and go for a walk. The thing was the reason for the season, the whole tradition of Halloween had started because of it. Masks, costumes, disguises, none of it for fun. All of it primal camouflage to help the prey hide from the predator. Nobody remembers that part of the tradition anymore. Not even the thing itself. It just knows to walk the night before Halloween. And it walks to me. I don't ask where it goes when it leaves me, or what it does on Halloween night. I'm just glad it's gone.

Anyway, Mikey Slater. His parents had been divorced a few years, and I still treated this, our original hangout, like a second home. The other bonus was that it was a quick end-around the neighborhood when I needed to get home fast. I was on my way home from checking out Mikey's Halloween costume at his mom's house, and had about two minutes to get home before dinner was cold and my ass would get spanked. We'd made a pact to dress as characters from this cartoon about interstellar knights. We had some great things rigged to our costumes, lights and fake swords, the whole works. We expected that tomorrow night, we'd barely be able to do any trick or treating since we'd be mobbed by admirers wondering how we obtained these amazing costumes.

I vaulted the six foot wooden slatted fence, landed soft in the garden, not caring if my presence was announced or not, since Mikey's dad never cared if I cut through.

And then I saw him there, lying in the grass near the backdoor, naked. Another person was straddling him, pinning his arms down. Pale skin, soft curves, it looked like a woman. The back did, anyway. The head was too small, and bald with a Mohawk of downy feathers. This thing, this silhouette was dipping down, the head bobbing just above Mr. Slater's crotch. I was young, but not so young that I didn't have a small clue about what I might be seeing.

I heard a whisper, *Almost done, almost done. Next year is going to be fantastic. This will all be worth it.*

And Mr. Slater was replying "No, no, no. No more. There's nothing I want. Everything I want is gone . . ." and occasionally hissing his breath, stifling a scream. Pleasure wasn't part of this. "No more! No more, please!"

You must want something. It's you and I forever. If you don't want anything . . .

And here the thing yanked a hand back from Mr. Slater's thigh, and that's when I noticed the blood, and the flap of flayed skin that I'd initially mistaken for underwear pulled down. I tried to turn around, grabbed the fence to bail out. I wanted to get out of there, wanted to be home.

You . . . want?

It whipped its head around at me, and I felt its voice in my head more than I heard it.

"Take him! Take him!" Mr. Slater cried out, pointing at me.

I can't explain any of what happened next. Can't explain the face that I saw when I locked eyes with the thing. Can't explain the speed with which it moved, crossing the yard in three hitching strides, seizing my ankle as I tried to get out of the yard. I flopped my upper body over the fence and struggled for anything to grab, to pull, to get free.

I heard a whisper . . . no, felt it.

Mine.

One quick bite on my ankle. A burning pain, searing, electric.

Make a wish before you go to bed. Think about what you want next year more than anything. We have an agreement now.

It wasn't a question or an offer.

I was released and dropped to the ground in the alley behind the fence.

I reached to my ankle. There was a fading flash of pain and burning, but no blood. No cut. Mikey's dad came stumbling around the corner, wearing nothing but a pair of shorts, holding a handgun.

"Is it still here? Is it?"

I said nothing. What could I say? What the hell was happening?

"My God, if you hadn't shown up . . . I'd . . . I'm free," he smiled at me and turned away. There was a flash in his eyes, a moment where he was teetering between life and death, that gun the fulcrum between finishing something very bad or starting something new. His hand raised slowly.

"But, don't, Mikey . . ." those were the only three words in the mess behind my lips that could break through. It was enough. His hand swung free and heavy.

"I'm sorry. I'm so sorry. Try to . . . just . . . try to think of good things for yourself." He looked at the gun again. "Heh. What the hell was I gonna do with this thing? Don't ever think about trying to kill it, whatever you do. Just take what you have coming and then think of good things for yourself."

I barely remember getting home. By the time I was through my front door, the details were hazy. My ankle was fine. No cut, no scab, not even a scratch. I slid into bed, trying to remember the thing, the face, the hands, anything, but it was all gone. A haze. My gaze drifted over the shelves around my room, the random toys scattered around, the baseball bat leaning against the corner. I hopped out of bed and brought it close by, feeling like it would keep me safe, not knowing from what. And as I drifted off that night, my last thought was about Little League and wishing I wasn't too damn fat to play shortstop.

That's good enough. A whisper, shot through the center of my brain.

Cold sweat broke over my upper lip, then calmness, then sleep.

When I woke up the next morning, I'd forgotten the previous night completely. I was full of energy, light on my feet. I felt ready to take on the world. Things felt a little darker in the afternoon as I walked by Mr. Slater's house on my way to Mikey's, but I couldn't quite peg why. I saw him sitting on his porch, a strange smile on his face. I kept moving, and that night was a Halloween much like any other.

The following year I dropped a lot of weight. Got faster. Made the team. Didn't think of how or why, just attributed it to hard work and eating right.

Then early October came and I found the postcard on my pillow when I got home from school. I'd like to say I got cold chills when I picked it up, or that it felt like flesh or leathery hide, but no, just plain, cheap cardboard. Typed in a neat white font on one side, it read:

Halloween is almost here. Did you have a good year? What do you want next year? Think hard! Make it worth the having.

I wanted to show the card to my mom, but by the time she'd gotten home from work, it was gone. It was an itch at the back of my mind, every time anyone brought up Halloween, this icicle of dread would rocket down my spine, and then disappear in a haze of thoughts about candy and costumes.

The night before Halloween, laying my costume out before going to bed, my only thoughts were on candy and sneaking around in the dark. It was two in the morning when I woke to a great weight on top of me, pushing the blankets down tight and cocooning me inside. I opened my eyes to see a silhouette, slight shoulders that were a bit too sharp, full breasts that seemed too round, slender arms that pinned me down. It was too dark to see details. I tried to cry out for my parents, but the thing lifted a hand to my mouth, cold boneless fingers clamping down. The palm spread like cold jelly as the thing drew its palm back, forcing one, then two fingers into my mouth. There was a texture to the bottom of them, something between a snake's belly and octopus suction pads.

Shhhhh . . .

The whisper in my brain.

Have you thought on it?

Thought on what?

The postcard I sent. What you want for next year.

Who are you?

It doesn't matter who I am. It matters who you are. You are mine.

How did you—

Just as you hear me in your mind, I hear you in mine. You are mine.

What does that mean?

It means you are mine.

I felt the thing rock down with its pelvis, grind into my stomach.

The agreement is not without benefit to you.

I didn't agree to anything.

Does a fish agree to feed a shark? Does a tree agree to be struck by lightning? You are mine.

The thing drew closer to me, and I squeezed my eyes shut. Everything grew bright, until I could make out shapes, then colors. Then I could see it in front of me.

You don't need your ears to hear me, nor your eyes to see. You are mine.

It was mottled and grey. The torso was curved and sensuous, but the head, that too-small head. The puckered sphincter of a mouth that prolapsed in and out, exposing that single jagged tooth. The two giant eyes, bulbous and red, shot with veins but no pupils, the two smaller green eyes in between. No ears. No nose. The tuft of white feathers in a stripe over the shining bald skull. Squeezing my eyes shut tighter only seemed to draw out more clarity.

You need to understand how this works. I will show you. Think of a woman you desire.

I couldn't. I was twelve. There wasn't desire yet, only a strange fascination. An occasional stirring if I saw a woman on TV in a swimsuit or that time I sneaked a peek at my dad's private magazine collection—

And the thing on top of me changed. Hair grew, the head filled in, the face melted and morphed into the perfectly sculpted features of that lady from *Beach Patrol* that had just done the cover shoot for Playboy. Bronze skin. Swaying breasts. A sculpted collarbone, skin coated in a sheen of sweat, just as I'd seen her in the centerfold.

Better?

It hadn't changed the feeling of the fingers in my mouth, cold like snails, twitching and probing around my tongue.

Every year on this night, I'm going to find you. I must feed. In exchange, you will tell me something you want, and over the course of the next year, you shall have it.

But I don't want—

You are—and the fingers extended slowly, pushing against the back of my throat, gagging me—*mine. Understand it. Tell me your desire. Make it worth the having.*

I want you to leave.

Not part of the bargain. Not your place to ask. You are mine.

The fingers pushed deeper still until I could feel them sliding down into my throat. I couldn't breathe. Instinct kicked in and I began to thrash. I needed to escape. I bit down hard on the fingers, breaking the skin, cold peppery ichor oozing into my mouth.

The thing didn't draw back. It moaned. Reached up its other hand and caressed itself.

More.

It pushed hard on my mouth, wanting me to bite. I let my jaw go slack. It sighed, the kind of sigh I was too young to understand as sexually frustrated, and its fingers pulled back. I felt my lungs suck in air. I thought I was going to die. Thoughts of school crossed my mind. Thoughts of family trips I'd never get to take, that I'd never get to see Disney World—

Is that something you desire?

I nodded in spite of myself. The thing on top of me slowly morphed back to its original form, spinning around on my body so I could only see its back. I felt it pulling at the sheets covering my feet.

I want you to think harder next year. Make it good. Make it worth the having. This is scarcely worth a toe, let alone two.

"What, what—"

And I felt the cold fingers of one hand clamp down on my ankle while the other fingers slithered between my toes, constricting them, spreading them apart.

"No," I said. "Nononono please don't—"

Next year you will remember this and understand what it means when I say make it worth the having.

Its head lowered down and I felt its lips wrap around my big toe, felt it suck once, twice, then clamp down with a force I can't describe, that single tooth razoring into the meat of my toe and flicking, cutting, tearing. I screamed. I had to have screamed, but there was no sound. I could feel the blood pumping out of my toe, feel the vibration of serrated tooth on bone; clamping, twisting, pulling, until it was all electricity and cold air, the thing turned to me and pursed its lips. It showed me my toe, sucking it so it would bob in and out of its mouth before tipping its head back and swallowing. The opening between its legs pulsed and shuddered, cold slime pooling onto my sheets. It sighed.

One more.

This time I did get a scream out, a small yelp as it latched onto my second toe and began chewing again. Its leg cracked and bent around at an impossible angle until its foot was over my mouth, spreading like taffy, covering my nose and lips so that no sound could escape, no breath could enter. There was no smell, just electric pain, vibrant agony.

A crack, a tear, and more cold air. The second toe went much easier than the first. It arched its back and swallowed, ripples shivering down its back as it came again. It spun, bringing its face close to mine. I squeezed my eyes shut to no effect.

Enjoy your trip. Next year, think harder.

And without moving its torso, it raised one leg, stretched it toward my windowsill, gripping hard. It pulled itself up and out into the night. I stared down over my soaked sheets at my foot, the silhouette in the dark room dancing through the purple lightning of pain. It didn't seem to be bleeding. It didn't hurt. I didn't pass out from the pain, I passed out when I tried to count them and had to stop at three.

I awoke screaming as I felt someone shaking my shoulder. Unbidden, I saw that face, round and leathery and purple, hovering inches from mine.

"Honey, it's okay!"

When I opened my eyes I saw my mother's face.

"Are you feeling okay? Your bed is soaked. Did you wet the bed?"

I burst into tears, kicking at the sheets until they came free. I could feel the burning sensation in my toes still, the raw wound scraping at the fabric.

"No!" I shouted. "Look what it did! Look what it did!"

I held my foot up. Five toes. Had I not already been crying, I might have started then. Or possibly even wet the bed out of sheer joy. I wiggled my toes. Jumped out of bed.

"What's gotten into you?"

My big toe was a bit red. My second toe had a definite hard ridge beneath the skin like a scar, but they were there. They were back. I was whole. My toes were—

Mine

Mine.

"Did you stub your toe last night?" My mom grabbed my foot, poking at my toes.

No pain.

"No, I'm . . . Ow!"

There was a scab on the underside of my big toe. Damp sheets. No blood. Five toes.

"You need to get up! And be more careful. You get a cut like that, you show me, okay? Otherwise it could get infected and you might lose your toes. You wouldn't want that, would you?"

I blanched.

"You need to get up. It's Halloween! Big breakfast to fuel up for a big night, right?"

Her hand sank into the dampness on my sheet, the essence that the creature had left behind in its ecstasy. Her eyes became vacant, distant, as she pulled the sheet off and bunched them on the floor.

"Well. I'll wash these later. You go run along." She absently licked at her fingers as she left.

By the time I made it downstairs for breakfast, I'd forgotten about my aching toes. By the time I was out the door, my sheets were in the wash and my mind was on Halloween. The events of the evening never returned to traumatize me. I don't remember much of the school year that followed, but I remember our vacation. The best time we'd ever had as a family. I remember years later, my parents telling me that trip had been a new beginning for them, bringing them out of a rough patch that I had been blissfully unaware of.

The next year when Halloween drew close, I got another card, this time in my lunchbox at school.

Matte black, this time bearing only the reminder: MAKE IT WORTH THE HAVING.

Reading those words instantly sent a spasm of pain through my foot and up my spine. I couldn't see the creature in mind, but it was omnipresent, that assault, that pain, and the reward it brought.

The night before Halloween that year, I asked if I could sleep in my parent's room. And as soon as the question left my mouth, a whisper buzzed through my brain—

Oh no, don't make them watch. Why would you do that to them?

So I didn't. I slept in my closet that year, thinking it might not find me, but I was wrong. I could explain this to you. Break it down year by year and tell you what happened, but that's not why I'm telling you this. It's about that phrase, *Make It Worth the Having.*

That second time, it stood at the door of my closet, towering over me, taking on features it must have thought looked friendly, the face shifting from Santa Claus to Jesus to cartoon mice and rabbits.

I don't want you to go through this for nothing. This is why I want you to think big. If it's physically possible, it will happen for you. If your only wish is for me to stop, I can only say that I'll stop when I'm full and finished and I'll still come back next year. Don't wish for toys. Don't wish for things for other people. Think of yourself. Remember our meeting last year, and know that what's about to happen will be far worse than a few toes. Don't let this happen for nothing. Make it worth the—

I screamed hard, muffled by the gelatinous glob of fingers it had forced into my mouth again. I just wanted it to shut up. I never wanted to hear that phrase again, but I knew I would. I knew this, all of this, would be happening again, and again.

That's a big burden to put on the shoulders of a child, right? Have almost anything you want, in exchange for giving the thing what it wants. That's not accurate. In exchange for the thing *taking* what it wants. I mean, what can a child think of that would be worth that? The second year, all I could think of was sports cars. It made me try again—why ask for something I couldn't legally use? Millions of dollars? Same thing. It had to be personal. So the second year, I wished to be the fastest, strongest kid in my school.

Done.

And in exchange for that, for the next 60 minutes, the creature flayed my arms and legs with that horrible tooth, peeled back my skin so my muscles were visible, and chose three strands of tissue from each limb, snapping them near one tendon and pulling them out like spaghetti, lifting it as high as it would go before placing the strand in its mouth and sucking it down greedily, biting off the other end at the tendon. Its gelatinous foot on my mouth the whole time, tiny suctioned footpads inhaling the screams that never made it into the night. Blood everywhere. Pain like I'd never felt, to that point anyway.

When it was done, it left me there, wide open like a biology class project pinned to a tray, trying to sleep and failing miserably. I passed out at some point and woke up in the morning, mildly sore but fully intact, testing out my newfound strength on my dad's weight bench by the end of the day. By the end of the week, I was running home from school without breaking a sweat. By the end of the school year, I was medaling in every sport I chose.

When October rolled around, when the black postcard fell out a library book I pulled from the shelf, the sinking dread in my stomach was almost matched by the excitement of the next thing to ask for.

That night, it ate half of one my kidneys. Once it managed to pull the organ free it wasn't so bad, but getting there was sheer hell. Fourteen years old, I made the wish any hormonally rampaging boy would, and that year I got every girl I was interested in. Was it worth it? Hard to say. But that year I came to understand that I was addicted. That I understood what *worth the having* meant, and that my life was going to improve.

I thought I had it all figured out. I had to try something new, and something new, despite seeing the thing lick its lips, despite seeing the horrible tongue dance over that single stupid tooth in the puckered maw it called a mouth, something new was too enticing to resist. Year by year, piece by piece, I was going to become a better man.

Everything that's happened in my life is a bit of a blur, but not those nights. Those, I have perfect clarity on. Better-than-perfect eyesight was the year it spent hours working my eyeballs free from the sockets after using one jagged nail to cut my eyelids off. More length and girth downstairs (it was my first year in college, after all), that year was sheer torture. It changed its shape to a calendar girl, arousing me, bringing me to climax orally in spite of myself, the soft supple features of the woman's body betrayed by the cold, slimy oatmeal feeling of the thing's mouth and throat. And then came the pain, my member first peeled like a raw potato with that single hooked tooth, then the soft tissue torn free, then the tongue probing into the open wound at my crotch until my testes were pulled free from my body and eaten—no, nibbled, slowly and exquisitely—until they were gone. That night I was on a camping trip, so the thing didn't even need to muffle my screams, and I obliged it until I was choking on my own vomit and my throat was raw. Physically, I was fine the next day, but it took me a few weeks to get the feeling of it all out of my mind. Once I did, I quickly developed a reputation as Big Man on Campus in every way imaginable. By the end of the year, every man and woman on campus worth having knew my number.

After college, everything became career-oriented. Real Estate. Stock Market. Passive income. I wanted to be rich while having as much free time as possible to research, because I needed to know how to finish this thing. Mikey's Dad, all those years ago, had simply begged the creature to stop, and when it saw me, it did. I asked it one year if I could do the same thing. It only replied *You are mine.*

I researched it, through college and beyond, and when I had enough money to hire people, they researched it too. I couldn't be very specific with them about my reasons, of course, but I could offer grants to religious studies students, hire paranormal investigators, demonologists. Six solid years of research yielded nothing. Not a damn thing. Every ancient society, every dead culture I could study I did, end to end, to the extent that there was some buzz that I'd be nominated for a Nobel for advancing the studies so far. Nobody had heard of the thing. In college, I'd had the idea to go back and ask Mr. Slater about it, but he looked at me like I was crazy.

And I wondered how much time it had spent with him, since his life wasn't so great. What if that was the first night he'd encountered it? What if the thing had been with him for years and was on a down-swing, taking things away instead of granting them? I'd never know.

I was thirty five now, with another Halloween approaching, a wife I loved and my first child on the way. And that was the final straw. I couldn't have this thing in my life with a child in the house. This year I was going to ask it for an exit.

This year, I received something worse than a black postcard in the mail. This year, the afternoon of what I'd come to think of as Visitation Night, we had to rush to the hospital. Complications. Our baby was lost. It made no sense. My wife was perfectly healthy, and everything had been going fine. But there was no heartbeat, no sign of life. My wife was inconsolable. She had to be sedated, and even as they were putting the IV into her, she was crying out, asking *Will this hurt the baby? You can't give me these drugs, it'll cause complications . . .*

My wife refused treatment, insisted that they were mistaken. We went home, the doctor pulling me aside to suggest that we let her rest a few days, then discuss inducing labor to finish the procedure.

Finish the procedure. Just like that, our baby had somehow progressed from human being to benign growth. A mole to be scraped off, a boil to be lanced. All of those cardboard pumpkins hanging on the wall, smiling, calm, that stupid friendly skeleton on the door, they were the only witnesses.

That night, it came. Slow, silent, and sad-eyed. It sat at the foot of the couch, where I was sleeping. My wife wanted to be alone, and I didn't know what to do. I didn't notice that I'd drifted off to sleep, but one minute it wasn't there and then it was, laying a hand on my calf. I didn't feel fear. I only felt empty.

I am ready—

Just take something and go, I said.

I am ready to end our bargain.

I was speechless. It felt strange, another gut-punch, another loss, another branch pruned form the tree of my life. I wanted to dictate terms. I wanted a safe exit, but once the baby was gone . . . I wanted it back. I wanted it to continue. I needed it, this thing, this surety.

I will give you your child.

What?

I will give you your child. I will take it. I will be the surrogate. Tomorrow, you will be a father.

It wasn't a question or an offer.

"But my wife can't—"

She will remember nothing.

"I don't want this. You can't have it—my child. You can't. It's done."

Have I ever asked your permission for anything? The bargain ends because I say so. You are mine. Tomorrow you will be a father.

It led me to the bedroom. Made me open the door. Made sure my wife . . . I can't describe the look I saw on her face, how she instinctively curled her arms over her stomach, a feral glare that burned through me until *it* came into the room. Then she froze, and softened, and looked at me, her lower jaw working, trying to get out a question, to ask me what was happening.

And it mounted her, stretched its arms out and wrapped those rubbery, cold fingers around her wrists, pinned her legs down, didn't bother to cover her mouth, because there was nobody to disturb with her screams. All I could do was watch. I knew what it felt like, I knew *exactly* what she was going through. I chuckled in spite of myself that she'd never be able to hold the pain of this childbirth over my head.

That single tooth tearing her nightshirt open to expose her. That sphincter mouth tracing kisses down her collarbone, between her breasts, suckling at her nipples until milk started to flow, then moving lower, elbows and shoulders dislocating so that it could keep her pinned down. Not that she was fighting at this point, only staring at me with wide eyes, panting for air until the thing's mouth reached her thighs.

How does it feel?

It asks this as it cuts deep into the inner thigh, flesh and fat zippering apart, its tongue probing into the fresh wound.

How are you doing?

The thing wouldn't want an answer even if there was one. It only wants screams.

This is going to be worth it. You're going to love next year. This will make it worth the having.

Its head stretched thin, narrowing impossibly at the mouth, the entire face a tubular beak, a hard proboscis that poked at her vulva until it found its way inside. She screamed then, my wife.

I could do nothing but watch it root, the heat of its palms pushing her legs apart. The cold, slow rivulets of saliva dripping down her sides like icy syrup, washed away with the regular and slowing pulses of her hot blood.

That single tooth in its lower jaw, barbed and curved, that awful knowing smile from the puckered sphincter of its mouth as it comes up for air, slowly retracting its head to stare at me, neck bent round the wrong way, slime coating its face, it made that hideous ring-mouth into an imitation of a smile.

It's a boy.

Then it plunged the beak into her stomach, slicing through skin, and fat, and muscle, splaying her open as that cold grey slime oozed down her, mixing and pooling with her blood and that ringing, that ringing in my ears isn't ringing it's her screaming, screaming for the baby, screaming *no*, screaming my name, cursing me, damning me, cursing the thing, even as it lowered its face to her flayed abdomen and forced its head inside.

Its back lurched up once, twice, as if taking great gulping swallows, and then it came, orgasmic shudders rippling through its spine as it straightened and stood from the bed, staring at me, one hand cupping its swollen belly. It caressed my cheek, pushed a finger inside my mouth, kept pressing until my knees buckled and it lowered me onto the bed beside my wife, tears streaming from her eyes, her organs warm and wet against my stomach. I reached out to her, stupidly, tried to cradle her in my arms.

The thing stood above us and arched its back, convulsing, straining, eyes swelling until the veins that laced them began to burst and bloody tears flowed. It straddled her, crouching lower until its vagina was positioned above my wife's open torso and it pushed, pushed until it came . . . until . . . you came. A membranous sac, sliding out of its dilated opening and landing inside my wife. I saw through the pale pink membrane your face, calm and serene, sleeping.

Sleeping.

I woke to her screams, my wife clutching my arm, saying "It's time! Holy shit it's time, they were wrong! My water broke! Do you feel it?"

I climbed from the bed, soaked, but not in her blood, but amniotic fluid. Aside from that, the sheets were clean in a way my memory could never be.

And we drove to the hospital, and I strode through the doors like a champion, pushing her wheelchair through the throng gathered there, staring down the confused faces of the nurses and doctors, telling them it was time.

They checked signs. They double-checked charts. They made me sign waivers promising not to sue over all of this stillbirth confusion, these things happen sometimes, we will of course be paying you for your pain and suffering in exchange for—

I told them to shut the fuck up and do their job. We could discuss it later. There would be a later. There would be a rest of our lives. That's all that mattered. *You* are all that mattered. Our son. My son. Mine.

I'm telling you all of this now before you understand it, because I never want you to hear it again. I never want you to know about any of this. It's gone. It's gone and it won't come back. It always keeps its promises. You're in my arms, with your perfect eyes, your ruddy cheeks, and I love you. More than anything. More than everything. I'm laughing at your gurgles, your tiny nose twitching, your perfect little ruby lips when they stretch into that smile, that same kind of goofy smile your mother gets. Your happy little gummy mouth that looks perfect. Perfect and normal except for that one thing that confused the doctors.

That single, smooth tiny tooth breaking through your lower gums. Doctors say this isn't unusual, they call them natal teeth. I know better. You yawn wide, showing me that tiny ivory blade, and you stare at me placidly, and I can only think, *worth the having.*

AWAKENING
Jeff Strand

When I discovered that I was the Downtown Dixonville Dismemberer, I took that shit seriously. It was something I'd suspected for a couple of weeks. The blackout periods. The blood stains on my jeans. The dismembered body in my garage. It wasn't until I found a live body in my shed, not yet fully dismembered, that I had to confront the truth.

"Who did this to you?" I asked the man with no legs.

"*You* did, you psycho son of a bitch!" he wailed.

I looked at the hacksaw in my hand. I tried to convince myself that the scraps of flesh dangling from the blade did not belong to this man's leg. They could've come from somebody else's leg. Maybe they weren't even *from* a leg; it's not like I was a forensics specialist.

I'm not saying that it wasn't pretty damning evidence that I was holding a bloody hacksaw over a guy with recently sawn-off legs. It was. You'd have to be a fool to think otherwise. But, in the moment, I did try to brainstorm other possibilities.

Maybe I'd *saved* the legless guy. I could've stumbled upon a psycho killer, kicked his ass, dragged him to another room, taken his hacksaw with me to ensure that he wouldn't have it handy if he regained consciousness, and was now standing over the victim to assure him that everything was going to be fine.

"Am I a hero?" I asked.

"No!" the legless guy screamed. "You're a monster!"

"I'm not calling you a liar," I said, "but clearly you've had a traumatic experience, and maybe you're not remembering things accurately. Hell, it's entirely possible that you've been hallucinating.

I think I'd be hallucinating if I had that much gushing blood. Are you *sure* I'm the one who did this?"

"Yeah, I'm sure!"

"All right, I guess you'd have no reason to lie."

So, yes, I was the Downtown Dixonville Dismemberer. What an awkward name. Hard to say out loud. When I was a child, dreaming of one day becoming a serial killer, I'd always thought that I'd end up with a really cool nickname. Slashy Jim or something.

"What are you going to do to me?" the man asked.

That was a good question. Lots of possibilities. I could, for example, just leave. The man would presumably bleed out, and I could go on pretending that there was some alternate explanation for what had happened. If I let him die, he wouldn't talk to the police, unless the police propped him up and jiggled his head around and spoke for him in a high-pitched funny voice, which was unlikely.

Or I could saw off his arms. That would put me on low moral ground, obviously, but I never liked letting a job go unfinished. Like if a neighbor was mowing his lawn, and he stopped halfway through because it started to rain, I'd look through the window and think, "Dude! Finish your damn lawn!" I wouldn't actually mow his the second half of his lawn for him, because mowing lawns sucks, especially in this heat.

"What do you want me to do?" I asked the man.

"Let me go!"

"But that's kind of impractical, don't you think? Where are you going to go?"

"Just stop hurting me!"

"I've already stopped. What you're asking is for me not to resume hurting you. I understand that you're under a lot of trauma, but communication skills are important."

"Please, give me a phone!"

"If I give you a phone and let you call for help, they'll be able to trace it back to me. That wouldn't be very smart of me, now would it? It's kind of disrespectful that you would suggest that I'd do something so stupid. Come on, man, I'm standing over you with a hacksaw; why would you insult me?"

"I'm sorry . . ."

"I don't think you mean it."

The man began to weep. "I'm really sorry."

Now I felt bad, because it seemed like this conversation was turning into something where I was taunting a victim, but I swear I wasn't. Everything I was saying was sincere. I didn't have a wicked grin or anything. Nothing would've made me happier than if we could work this out in a civilized manner.

"You're bleeding pretty bad," I told him, even though I was sure he already knew.

He didn't answer.

"Do you know how to make a tourniquet?"

He still didn't answer.

"Are you dead?"

"No."

"You were acting kind of dead. Please respond to my questions to avoid further confusion. You do *not* want to get buried alive. Goodness, no. It's never happened to me, but you don't need first-hand experience to know that it's not pleasant. Now what were we talking about before I thought you were dead?"

"Tourniquet."

"That's right. Do you want one?"

The man shrugged.

"I'm going to have to look up how to make one online. Do you think you'll live long enough? That pool of blood underneath you is pretty big." I resisted the desire to splash my shoes around in it. That would be undignified.

The man closed his eyes.

That rude piece of crap. Well, we'd see if having me saw off one of his arms was motivation for him to pay attention to the conversation.

It wasn't.

I checked to see if he was breathing. No breath. I checked his heartbeat. No heartbeat. I checked his pulse. No pulse. This lack of breath, heartbeat, and pulse, combined with the fact that several pints of his blood were no longer in his body, was a pretty clear indicator that he'd passed away.

To cut off the other arm of a man who was already dead was an extremely deranged thing to do. You couldn't exactly stand in front of a jury and have them nod their heads and say, "Yeah, that's probably what I would have done in similar circumstances."

I really, really wanted to cut off that arm. I'd missed out on the legs because of the blackout period, so I was feeling kind of cheated. Getting to saw off his last remaining arm would go a long way toward resolving that feeling.

Only a sick person would do that.

But in contemporary slang, "sick" meant "cool," and I wanted to be cool. So I'd do it. I'd saw off his arm.

I sawed off his arm.

It was kind of disappointing. Like when you have two slices of chocolate cake, and you eat the first one, and it's sooooo delicious, and then you think about how great the second piece is going to be, but then you're full after the first couple of bites, and you wish you'd saved it for later.

Then I cut off his head. Also disappointing. Not as disappointing as the second arm, but not nearly as fulfilling as I would have hoped.

I thought about cutting his head into several pieces, but, no, that would be going too far. I settled for just cutting off his ears. He had very soft earlobes.

I realized that somebody was watching me.

I turned around and glanced at the police officer. His arms were crossed over his chest and he looked quite stern.

"I, uh, didn't know anybody was there," I said.

"Obviously."

"Am I under arrest?"

"I think you know the answer to that."

"How long have you been watching?"

"Long enough."

"But how long?"

"That is none of your business."

"You would've had to open a door to come in here, and while I was cutting off his ears, I wasn't absorbed enough in my work not to hear a door open. It would've had to happen while I was sawing off his head. And I started to lose interest while I was doing it, so it would've had to happen when I'd just started sawing off his head. You just stood there and watched me saw it off!"

"So?"

"So, why didn't you stop me?"

"That, also, is none of your business."

"I think you were getting some kind of deviant pleasure out of it. No officer of the law would stand there and just watch a decapitation if he wasn't enthralled by the sight. You disgust me, sir."

"Oh, is that how it is? A man who saws off the head of an innocent victim can judge the spectator? Maybe I feared for my life."

"You've got a gun. I've only got a hacksaw."

"You could also have a gun. I haven't searched you."

"All the more reason to diffuse the situation instead of watching it. If I'd seen you out of the corner of my eye, I could have taken out the gun—which I don't have—and shot you."

The police officer nodded. "Busted. I was watching because it made me tingle."

"So now what do we do?"

"I don't know. Suicide pact?"

I shrugged. "Yeah, all right."

I let him go first. He blew his brains out, but instead of taking the gun and doing the same, I kicked it aside. Yes, it was a dick move. But by then I'd accepted that I was the kind of person who would back out of suicide pacts.

I cut up the police officer's body. It felt great.

I was invulnerable.

I was God.

It turned out, I was not invulnerable and/or God. My next victim had a Tazer and two brothers who were unhappy with me for trying to kidnap her. I'm in their garage now. Ironic.

Anyway, I suppose these are the last words of the Downtown Dixonville Dismemberer, which they were kind enough to let me write down in my own blood. (Excuse the typos.) I probably won't talk to you soon, so enjoy the rest of your evening.

READINGS OFF THE CHARTS
Adam Cesare

Three dates into our relationship and it's hard to tell if she likes me for me. Or because I own a car and a GoPro.

We pull up to the agreed upon meeting place—a stretch of road where a busted streetlight provides the most cover for the car—and park.

Sitting in the passenger's side, Trish looks great in the glow of her phone's screen. Unlike a lot of girls, her profile picture doesn't do her justice.

She looks so good that I don't give a shit *why* she likes me.

Then I look at the guy approaching my car. He's a heavyset dude with a chinstrap. I think maybe this guy, Bobby, *is* her boyfriend and they are using me for my car and equipment.

It's the same thought I've been having all day.

Last night Trish told me that she wanted me to come along on one of her hunting expeditions, which sounded cute, harmless. And it was only this morning that she let spill we would be meeting up with her "investigative partner" when we got to Kings Park.

"Bobby doesn't need a ride from you, though. He lives within walking distance of the site," I remember her adding, as if anticipating what I'd been thinking.

Kings is an abandoned insane asylum that the government has been in the process of dismantling for over a decade. I've driven by it hundreds of times growing up, but I don't live on this part of the Island so I never snuck in as a kid.

Around six o'clock I packed up my camera and a flashlight, then we stop by Trish's parent's house so she can pick up her equipment.

While she was doing that I was parked in her neighbor's driveway.

I'm not quite ready to meet her parents.

"Good to meet you, dude," Bobby says, holding his hand out and then giving me one of those alpha-guy shakes. I don't get the impression that he's trying to be protective of Trish, just that this is the way he shakes hands with every "dude" he meets.

He crushes my hand. He's probably been carrying his extra weight since high school and this is the way he thinks the cool kids greet each other, all these years later.

He's wearing black cargo shorts and a black t-shirt, with a black and white bandana pressed across his forehead. All those black clothes would be great for stealth, but his exposed shins are so pale that they're practically phosphorescent.

Even in the low light of the abandoned stretch of service road, I can see that his bandana is mottled with sweat. The accumulated crust makes me think that it's a permanent fixture on his head. To make myself feel better in the throb left by the handshake, I imagine his head rag is hiding early onset baldness. He's maybe a year or two older than me, thirty, I'd guess.

"Has Trish explained what we plan on doing tonight?" he asks, crossing his arms, his tone immediately becoming faux-professional.

It's going to be really hard to maintain my composure if this guy starts lecturing me about spirits and orbs.

"Trespass on government property?" I ask, smiling back.

His laugh is polite, more acknowledging that I made a joke than telling me he finds it funny.

"Well, that too, but what we're doing," he starts.

Trish interrupts Bobby, tapping on the trunk of my car with one of her many rings. She's indicating that she needs to get her duffle bag. I take the dongle out of my pocket and hold the button to pop the trunk.

"Trish tells me you have no experience," Bobby begins again, "So let me break it down, because I can already tell that you're skeptical."

I start to make an excuse. I want to say something to reassure him that I'm not going to be a sarcastic asshole the entire night, but the only thing stopping me from engaging in that sarcasm is that

I want to get back in Trish's pants. I could give less of a shit about their "investigation."

I nod for him to continue and he does.

"You know, on those reality shows they call it ghost *hunting*. But that's gives the wrong impression to the public about what it is we do. We hold ourselves to rigorous scientific standards. We don't hunt, we perform experiments, set up controls, and then document."

"With GoPros."

"Yes. The better the camera, the higher the clarity of the recording and the more likely we can be to get confirmation of an observable phenomena. Likewise, the more cameras we have fixed on one area, the better chance we have of catching the phenomena from multiple perspectives."

I have to admit, I'm taken aback by how well Bobby speaks. I was expecting him to be barely able to string a sentence together. It didn't make his subject any less bullshit, but his semi-rehearsed lecture does make him seem more legitimate.

I decide I like Bobby.

As long as he and Trish don't bonk me on the head and take off into the sunset with my car.

Trish crosses to the front of the car, unzips her duffle bag, and begins to take inventory.

"EMFs, two, spectrometers, remote and handheld, audio recorders," she says as she peers into the bag. I hear metal and plastic clanging around and I hope whatever she's stirring up inside that bag doesn't leave a dent on my hood, there seems to be a lot of it.

Yeah, rigorously catalogued inventories of shit all thrown into one ratty Everlast duffle.

While she's doing that, Bobby slings a small camera bag from his shoulder. The bag is something I didn't see in the gloom because it's black on black against his shirt.

I feel a mosquito bite me on the neck and I wish I'd remembered to apply bug spray. Who knew how long we were going to be out here.

"And you've got your camera?" Bobby asks, taking a small camcorder with a flip-screen out of his bag and holding a button on the side until it chirps to life. The camera has an extended lens almost as long as the body and there's a mechanical whir as it starts itself.

"Full spectrum," Bobby says, sensing my interest, "not just night vision but *everything*," That's the first thing he's said that sounds like complete gibberish to me, but he's clearly proud of the attachment. "Fuckin' thing costs more than the camera itself. I'm still running MiniDV, it'll be great to have some HD footage from tonight's experiments."

I get what he's implying. I open the rear driver's side door and scoop my small camera up from under the seat. The GoPro came packaged in a polyester drawstring bag and I've seen no reason to upgrade to anything fancier.

It's not like I use the thing. I received it a couple years ago as a gift after making the mistake of telling my sister that I'd taken up mountain biking.

"Now you can record your bike rides!" she told me then.

I should have just returned it. I meant to, but time got away from me. Hey, if it gets me lucky, then thanks, sis.

"Do you need to do anything to get it ready?" I ask Bobby, holding my own camera out in front of me. "Like in the settings?"

"We can up the contrast and mess with stuff like that in post." Bobby says. "All our lights are external. Nothing has to get done now except you pointing and shooting. White balance and all that crap doesn't really matter for our purposes."

My camera came equipped with ghost finding capabilities right out of the box, who knew?

"Ready?" Trish asks, coming up behind me and snaking her fingers around my free hand. Cool and tacky in the autumn chill, her touch still reassures me. Her holding hands gets me thinking that this may even be fun, bug bites and all.

Bobby lifts up a break in the chain-link fence surrounding Kings Park and the material lifts neatly, like a curtain.

He knows exactly where to pull to let us in, which makes me wonder how many nights he spends slinking around abandoned psychiatric hospitals.

It's a little bit of a hike to the site and we pass a row of partially demolished buildings on the way there. There must be workmen here during the day because there's still heavy machinery around. Driving up, I could tell that the campus isn't as impressive as it once was, a few more years and the demolition will be complete and there will be no Kings Park.

"What happens if the cops come?" I ask, less afraid then I am interested in how many times Bobby and Trish have been escorted off the premises.

"They post all those No Trespassing signs so they don't have to patrol. You'll see, once we get into Building Three, you've never seen more graffiti in your life. Don't have to worry about cops."

That was true, Suffolk County police were among the highest paid in the country, I doubt they were going to venture very far into Kings Park to shoo away drunk teenagers or delusional guys with "full spectrum" camcorders.

"So, best-case scenario, what are we looking to find tonight?" I ask to cover the soundtrack of our footfalls on over-grown lawn. Where I assume we're going, Building Three, looms on the horizon.

Bobby makes a noise like he's going to continue his verbal diarrhea, but instead Trish speaks up.

"You would think that we'd be looking for the spirits of inmates, but these buildings that are still standing weren't residences, they were administrative buildings and infirmaries. As cool as the old gurneys and operating light fixtures seem, there weren't many documented deaths here. Not many people die of root canals," she says.

"True, I would imagine any critical care would be outsourced to a hospital."

"Indeed. But these buildings have been standing empty for twenty years now. You know how many junkies have kicked it in there?" She points to Building Three, we're much closer now, like I've been walking on autopilot. There are no doors on the doorway, it's a rectangle of black shadow. There had been a piece of plywood nailed over the opening, but that's been pried off and set to the side of the threshold, it's covered in police tape.

"We're junkie ghost hunting?" I ask and Bobby scoffs.

"A lot of, we'll call it the paranormal tourist industry," even she can't keep the sarcasm out of her voice and she owns all this equipment, "that focuses on stories of Civil War sprit sightings and ancient Indian hauntings, but there's a theory in more serious circles that, well, fresher is better."

"Sounds legit." I say.

"Think about an echo," Bobby says, igniting a small LED flashlight that he's taken out of one of his many cargo short pockets. He points the flashlight inside the doorway, I catch a glimpse of molding drywall, vinyl tiling, peeling paint, and a giant full-color cartoon cock. The dick graffiti ruins the ambiance.

"Anyone in there? Time to clear out, this is the police!" he yells into the entryway. His voice echoes, he looks back at me and he smiles, his ear cocked to listen.

I don't hear any movement inside, if there are junkies they're either lying low or conked out for the night.

"Ghosts are just energy. Energy like that echo," Trish says. "They're louder and then they dissipate. And if the apparition was filled with a large amount of negative energy at their time of death, say a relatively younger person, dying before their time because they're an addict . . ."

"I getcha," I say, taking out my own flashlight before we go inside. Trish does the same.

I don't want to admit it, but this tag team of investigators has succeeded in creeping me out. Combine the long walk from the car with the fact that there very well could be live, violent junkies living in Building Three and I feel *less sure* that this will be a fun night.

We enter Building Three, the three of our flashlight beams giving me some kind of idea about the large foyer we're standing in, but leaving dark shadows in the room's corners.

There is a built-in desk against the far wall and above that outcropping is a Plexiglas enclosure. The glass is no longer translucent but instead opaque with spray-paint.

On the Plexiglas is layers and layers of graffiti, and if there was ever anything as elaborate as the Technicolor cock on the east wall, it's been buried under a wash of unimaginative tags. Words like "Blaze" and "STiNKBOI" were probably put there by burnout kids traveling into Building Three on a dare.

"Cool, huh?" Trish asks.

"Very," I say, passing my light behind us, checking my corners. I was expecting more debris, shopping carts, maybe? A trashcan fireplace? But the room is spare except for two swing doors to the east and west. "What now?"

"We find a room to set up in, lay the equipment out, and wait," she says, shifting her duffle bag between hands.

I notice and feel like a real doofus.

"I can carry that if you need," I say, aware that the only thing I'm holding is a polyester bag filled with a camera that's the dimensions and weight of a deck of playing cards.

"I've got it."

A girl wants to carry something, you don't press it. Chivalry edges over into chauvinism so easily these days, for some girls.

"Hope you're okay with climbing stairs," Bobby says to me, smiling. There's a joke there, about one of the two of us being in shape, but it's not the time or the place. And Bobby shouldn't be the target.

We go through the east door, past a few rooms. One in particular was either meant to be a bathroom or is just doubling as one, my eyes tear up from the stink. I don't poke my flashlight inside, but instead quicken my tread to the stairwell at the end of the hallway.

Bobby goes first and I'm thankful for that. If the steps are sturdy enough to hold him, Trish and I will be a breeze. I'm a little underwhelmed by the second floor. I figured that would be where all the good stuff was kept, the creaking antique wheelchairs and hydrotherapy equipment à la *One Flew Over The Cuckoo's Nest*, but there's nothing in these rooms save for the occasional beer can and discarded sleeping bag.

We step into one of the few rooms in the hallway that still has a door, no glass in the window, but at least a door. It also has a row of file cabinets pushed against one wall, the drawers are dented but intact.

"I'll do lights?" Bobby asks Trish, but there's no conversation that ensues, they simply move to separate corners of the room and get to work.

The flashlight he was using before wasn't alone. Like the world's most nu-metal clown, Bobby unpacks an unending supply of small LED lights from his many pockets and spreads them around the room. The lights all have different hues, some are blue and red, some are pure white crystals, but if there's a reason to why he puts which ones where, it's lost on me. The best I can tell is that he's trying to eliminate as many shadows as possible.

While he does this, Trish unpacks her duffle. I ask if she needs help, she says no and leans over the opening to the bag. Like I'm going to steal her trade secrets.

She lays out and switches on different meters, most of them are silent but one shouts back shrill feedback and she switches it back off.

"I forgot. You've got to turn your cell phone off. It would have been better if we left it in the car, but . . ." She trails off.

I take my phone out and look at the time. It's nearly ten. I wonder how long we're going to be here.

"All the way off," she says, smiling but her tone not a joke. "Not airplane mode. It fucks with the readings."

When she's done with whatever she's doing to calibrate the equipment, she passes the bag to Bobby who stows it atop the file cabinets.

Bobby's already set up his camera on the ground using a small tripod he took from his, you guessed it, shorts pocket. It's a low angle and the camera's pointed up, I imagine to reduce the glare from the LEDs.

He looks at me expectantly and I realize that my GoPro is the only piece of equipment not accounted for. He helps me turn an old nail on the wall opposite the file cabinets into a hanger and we affix my camera about four feet off the ground. There must have been a picture or diploma hanging here at some point. Maybe this was someone important's office.

"Do we know what this room used to be?" I ask, looking to get some flavor for the ghost story now running in my own imagination. Was this the office of a depraved administrator or doctor who took advantage of patients, maybe did a few illegal experiments?

"It doesn't matter, only the present matters, remember?" Trish says.

"Well, the near past, right?"

"Are we good to go?" she ignores my question and asks Bobby. Behind me I can hear the familiar chirp of my own camera as he sets it to record.

"All good," he says.

"Good, the levels are neutral," she says, looking down at the small device she's holding and moving back to the file cabinet and her duffle bag.

"So now we just wait?" I ask.

That's when Bobby hits me.

On the follow-through I feel my entire scalp shift atop my skull but I don't lose consciousness.

I spin with the blow and can see that he's got a small hammer. The tool's got a broad flat head and the metal has no sheen to it, it's a well-used carpenter's hammer.

Inexplicably, my first thought is: *he had that in his shorts, too? Or did he take it out of the duffle when I wasn't looking.*

I can see from his eyes that he's surprised I'm still standing.

"Goddamn it," Trish's voice comes from behind me, floaty. "You have to do it in one. Make sure you're not blocking it."

The starfield of LEDs seems to dim and her words seem like they're coming from far off. And they echo.

I feel one of her small, clammy hands press against the skin of my neck, and a second one push my left ear flat against my head.

It feels good to be held.

Bobby winds up for a second blow and hits me on the left side of my head.

The crack over my temple is the last thing I hear and make sense of.

There. Play it again. The glint isn't from the hammer, see?

And look! It's in the exact same position on the second camera.

Now go back. Frame by frame. Do you see the blink on my EMF?

It coincides with the exact moment of the flare.

This is it, babe.

It's the exact moment of conception.

I can't believe it worked.

I can't believe after all this time we have *proof.*

REBORN
The Behrg

"I used to believe in God, then I believed in the Devil.
Now I laugh at both and only believe in Evil."
—Diary of Darius Maggiolini, Archbishop,
spoken on his deathbed

In 1974, the Catholic Church sent out a declaration to every bishop, presbyter, and deacon who resided within a sanctioned diocese. This formal document, which you will find (though partially torn) at the end of my tale, has since been repudiated, as have all official communications regarding the Sancto Saepes Motu Proprio. Ask any secretariat of the Church about the rumored incursion and you will receive only shaking heads or drudged denials. You will however find that the mandates held within this clandestine document are stringently, if quietly, upheld to this day.

The following is taken directly from the declaration:

From this day . . . forward . . . no infant child abandoned on or before [a Church-affiliated domicile] shall be admitted within said domicile by a member of the clergy. This sanctioned decree is to be upheld without exception.

My tale, and those unfortunate souls who experienced similar trespasses, will provide more than enough evidence as to why.

It was an April evening in 1971, a day that had been muddled with a constant downpour. It is important to note that this was a time when I still believed in a Higher Power. At twenty-three I was young to have been chosen as chaplain of the Sacred Heart Basilica of the Immaculate Conception. So young, in fact, that I still believed

I was doing God's work.

Evenings in Bridgeport, Connecticut were quite dull, and with the hellacious storm our evening services amounted to a dress rehearsal, only vacant pews and the occasional scurrying mouse in attendance—the rain always drove them inside. Sister Bedford, a motherly nun in every sense of the word, had taken to mopping the nave, humming an amalgamation of hymns that no choir would recognize. She was deaf in one ear and tone deaf in the other, but her jovial cheeks and maternal charm warmed the soul (not to mention her chocolate chip cookies which were absolutely divine!). I hurriedly gathered the hymnals pew by pew, ready to call it an early night.

There was a chill in the high-ceilinged halls and Father Maggiolini, an old-world coot and the attending Bishop, had gone off to check the pilot of the furnace which was always blowing out. If I recall correctly I believe that rainy season we had a leak in the basement. The water pooling against the outer walls of the church seeped through the porous stones rotted with age. It made for an eerie walk through those long corridors below ground, as if the very walls were weeping.

As we mindlessly went about our evening duties thinking only of the warm wool comforters awaiting our shivering bodies—or at least such were my thoughts—a shocking boom resounded from the outer cloister doors. Sister Bedford dropped her mop, her hands going to her ample, yet covered, bosom. The teetering, towering pile of hymnals which I had collected were sent scattered across the hard marbled floor, pages bristling and book bindings breaking. Who would be out at this hour in such conditions? And why a single knock and nothing more?

My heart seemed to answer the resounding thud with a steady knocking of its own. Please remember, I was but twenty-three, at an age where imagination could still conjure demons from shadows and redemption from a statue of a man on a cross.

Footsteps echoed from the west wing, Sister Nettle appearing, a small candle cradled in her hands. "You're not going to open it?"

Her British accent tugged at the strings of my heart which was no good, considering she had already tied them into a jumbled knot.

She was adorable, Sister Nettles—a tiny thing at only five foot two. A small crook for a nose, long neck and bony chin and eyes which were much too large for her face, but the disjointedness came together like a tightly woven collage creating something far more magnificent than the sum of the individual parts on their own. While I would not have admitted so back then, I see no harm in doing so now; I was taken by her, and despite my vows there were many nights when she visited me in the lucid realms of sleep.

Before I had a chance to gather my thoughts, Nettles swept past both Sister Bedford and me, cupping her hand around the flame so as not to let it die.

"Allow me!" I shouted, hurrying after her.

She, of course, did.

The ornate iron doors, crested with scenes from the bible so analogous each square could represent your pick of stories, were set in the floor with heavy pins that dropped down latching them closed. The pins, each a good eighteen inches in length, required an inordinate amount of effort to free from their catch not only due to their weight but the levers within the flooring that had to be turned just so. Once I wriggled the damnable pin free, I pulled the door open, sliding the pin beneath as a doorstop, as we commonly did at the time.

Heavy rivulets poured down just beyond the alcove of the porch, the night black beyond the stoop. I swallowed hard, noting that no one was there—no gust of wind could have come at the doors with that much alarm, and then Sister Nettles was crouching down, her little bottom pursed out towards me. With reddened cheeks almost as rosy as Nettles', I quickly glanced away. The sound of that sweet Sister cooing brought my attention back, her soft voice answered by a piercing wail.

A baby.

Someone had dropped it at our porch. Like a bag of groceries or an advert for the local theater. And whatever depraved soul left it, had failed to turn it from the stuck position of *ff*—FORTISSIMO.

Nettles motioned for my assistance, gathering up her skirt and glancing out at the darkness. I noticed that despite the lack of a breeze, the candle's flame had blown out. I took in the woven reed basket and infant swimming within a sea of churning pink cloth. Her face was the color of a plum and I marveled at how much anger something so small and innocent could manifest. Oh, if we had only known.

After carrying the bundle inside, I placed it on a raised bench. Sister Bedford crowded in beside me. Her heavy jowls curved her lips downward in a permanent frown though it was apparent she was beaming inside.

"Oh, she's such a sweetheart!" Not surprising—I did mention she was partially deaf.

While Nettles still hovered out on the stoop, Sister Bedford reached down taking the screaming infant, blankets and all, and brought her up to bounce against her . . . well, bouncy chest. "Shh, shh, shh, you are a sweet thing, aren't you?"

"You should wait for the Olfac," Nettles said.

"Huh?"

I knew the name by which Maggiolini was called by the attending nuns, Olfac or Factory, in reference to the persistent body odor which always accompanied the man, redolent of a wet and hirsute dog. It was said that the Archbishop Alcote had once nearly fainted in Maggiolini's presence and, while he had attributed it to his fasting, we all knew the true offender. *'If thy right eye offend thee, pluck it out, and cast it from thee.'* Not so simple with the pungent musk of one's own pores.

Knowing that Sister Bedford was just as habituated with the name, I presumed she just hadn't heard. "She said you should wait for Father Maggiolini," I said.

"Nonsense. We used to see this sort of thing all the time at the Rectory on Forty-Second—young girls knocked up by married men who should exchange their wedding rings for chains, if you ask me. And besides, a man—even a Father, Sister Nettles—lacks the proper equipment. Now close that door! It's drafty as a turnip field in Poland in here."

"I'll get it." My enthusiasm this time wasn't for aiding Nettles but rather born of sheer desperation to escape the gales of the child's cries.

"Here, here, you sweet thing. Now when they haven't a teat

to suckle you can slip them a finger and most times they'll pacify themselves to sleep."

"That's disgusting," Nettles crooned.

"That, my dear Sister, is biology."

I always wondered what Sister Bedford heard next. Whether, for instance, the rending of flesh and snapping of bone and cartilage, melded with the sickeningly frantic slurps and bellicose sucking noises, came to her as something other than what it was. I'm quite certain, however, that she heard her own screaming.

The baby dropped from her arms as Sister Bedford backed away, a smear of gristly red coating its small chin. Somewhere along its descent I realized, it was no longer crying. A stream of blood flowed from Sister Bedford's finger like the curved spray of a drinking fountain. Hysterical and dazed, she tumbled against the back pew, falling onto her considerably padded behind with a loud harrumph.

I braced myself for the thud of the child connecting with the marbled floor but watched with fascination as it adroitly righted itself in the air, landing delicately on outstretched fingers and toes. With the blankets torn off, you could see the rippled muscles in its tiny arms and legs as it held itself in a pushup position. Shoulder blades extended, triceps and deltoids flexed—it was like watching some freak carnival showing off a grown man the size of a baby.

Until I saw its tail.

It slithered out the top of the cloth wrapped around its waist, the appendage ending not in a point but a four tendon knob. The digits gripped the cloth diaper at its posterior and tore it free, twirling it once before casting it aside. Then the tail dropped to the ground, its four tendons spread out like talons, the fleshy knob raised slightly above.

The tail started vibrating. Then the creature was launched into the air.

Sister Bedford, who at this moment was mid-scream, grappled for anything nearby with which to ward off her attacker. Unfortunately we were in a church, not a junkyard or garage or office where miscellaneous items could be quickly requisitioned and repurposed. The hymnals, while scattered on the ground, were several rows up, and all of the wall hangings and architectural ornamentation had been anchored to walls and pillars long ago.

The creature landed between the crux of Sister Bedford's outstretched legs, the skirt of her dress bowing inward and drawing up with its weight. Beyond the tethered muscles which rippled beneath its pale flesh, and of course, the tail, it was difficult not to see a helpless infant propped awkwardly between the nun's quite hairy legs.

"MotherofMercysendthisdemonbacktoitsprisonandblessuswith yourholylight." The words came out in a single gasp and must have struck the infant beast like a psychic blow. It began wailing a piercing and heartrending cry.

"BytheFatherandtheSonandtheHolyGhostIcommandtheetoleave thisholyplaceatonce!"

The creature let out a burp. A chunk of what must have been flesh or maybe a nail dislodged from its mouth, skipping with a wet slap along the floor. The crying immediately stopped. It hadn't been Sister Bedford's words that had caused its panic; just an upset stomach.

The beast's tail shot forward, puncturing a slit in Sister Bedford's dress through which it promptly disappeared. A moment passed in which only our breathing was heard, then Sister's Bedford's eyes tripled in size and she cried out with renewed vigor.

"Get it . . . out of me!" Her legs kicked wildly and she doubled over, a strained consternation coming over her face. "Get it out!"

Whatever paralysis had held Nettles and I bound was lifted, incredulity replaced with a need to act, to save. Though we were accustomed to believing in that which could not be seen, we had little experience with doubting that which was directly before our eyes.

I slid to the floor on my knees, reaching through the slit in the fallen nun's gown, the fabric tearing further beneath my weight. The baby was not on the ground between the Sister's legs as I had hoped. No, the atrocity before me was so unimaginable, so damning to both spirit and body, that I quaked at the sight. As a virgin, this was the first time I had ever seen the workings of a woman. But what should have been a curious fascination was vilified by the sight of two extended feet slithering upward into the cavity of Sister Bedford's vagina, the pronged tail sticking out, pressed deep into the flesh of her inner thigh, leveraging its ascent.

This was not the rebirth I had read of in the Holy Bible.

Sister Bedford's screams by now filled the entire chapel and let me tell you, no choir had ever sung so loud within our humble halls.

Nettles fell against me, frantically clawing at Sister Bedford's dress. "Where is it?"

"It went . . . up," I said, "where a baby comes out."

Elocution had failed me.

I stood, unable to watch as Nettles plunged her arm in after the creature. I don't remember consciously going back to the open door; perhaps I had wanted to leave, to escape the insanity that had stumbled onto the doorstep of our lives, but instead I shoved that heavy door closed, gripping the metal pin in my hand. The feeling that came over me next was what some might consider, revelatory. I felt like a vampire slayer, divinely called to rid the world of evil, armed with only righteousness and a holy wooden cross—or in this case, an eighteen inch bar of ribbed steel.

"No, no, no, no, no!"

Nettles' arm and neck were slathered in blood. She now knelt atop Sister Bedford, pressing both arms against the older woman's torso where a pronounced mound beneath the skin continued climbing northward. The off key screaming had subsided, a milky substance bubbling from Sister Bedford's mouth. I moved back toward the two women, the pin gripped like a miniature baseball bat. A firm calm and determination had settled over me; I knew what had to be done.

Before I crossed the threshold, Sister Bedford's neck bulged, her jaw dislocating with two distinct mercurial pops. And then, from within her gaping lips and saggy cheeks, the top of a head began to crown. Like a bubble blown from chewing gum, the pink head expanded until, with a sickening suction sound, the creature's full head popped free of Sister Bedford's mouth. The rest of its tiny and slime covered body wriggled out, slipping down her face to the marbled floor.

The creature leapt off the ground just as I swung the metal pin toward it, my calculated strike instead slashing open the side of Sister Bedford's face from lip to jaw. Another misplaced swing sent fleshy pulp splattering upward, disfiguring the poor motherly Sister even further, though by this point she was quite dead. When the infant scrambled over Sister Bedford's body toward Nettles I acted only as any gallant knight might, but the creature avoided each assault with an uncanny dexterity. Its tail suddenly plunged down against a thick bony knee, vibrating ferociously, then it launched itself at the thin nun weeping over Sister Bedford's body.

Footsteps echoed from the hall, Father Maggiolini's raspy voice lost behind the blood thrumming in my ears. The creature was in Nettles' arms, tangling itself in the tassels of her white smock, trying to scale her. I brought the pin back, leaping forward with my thrust. The chiseled tip of the pin sunk through the creatures flesh as if I had been wielding a sword. It shrieked a piercing cry cut short as the metal rod slid through its small body, puncturing both organs and life.

I exhaled a deep breath, an inner peace coming over me. I had exterminated this foul monster, this infernal beast that had risen from the seventh circle of hell. Then I heard the clatter of a small box of tools dropping to the ground behind me.

"My God, what have you done?"

Father Maggiolini stood at the end of the arched hallway, his eyes giant saucers within murky ponds of wrinkles. His jaw hung open, a puppet no longer in use.

I turned back to Nettles, pulling the pin free from the vile creature in her arms. It slid out with much more difficulty than it had going in, ruptured organs and stringy tissue clinging to the inanimate object. I looked for confirmation on Nettles' face, the corroboration of my innocence, of the true culprit of the massacre we had just witnessed.

Without a word, the child slipped from her hands. It smacked the marbled floor with the heart-wrenching thud I had anticipated earlier, when it had caught itself on fingers and toes. While I could still see the hint of wiry muscles beneath, its taloned appendage had withdrawn, tail somehow retracting into smooth, if wrinkly, skin. The blood leaked from its two gaping wounds in its torso like an overturned jar of ink.

And where the baby once had been, Nettles held a pool of

crimson blood cupped within her hands. Dangling from the hole in her gown was the creature's tail. It had speared right through her stomach, ripping into her intestinal track. Liquid feces, mixed with blood, spilled from the puncture wound.

Her legs gave out just as I turned back to Father Maggiolini.

"Look—it's tail!"

I never heard him coming. He struck me with the end of a candelabra and I followed my Nettles down.

I was convicted of triple homicide. Life, with no chance of parole. Thanks to our corrupt legal system, and untraceable bribes from the Vatican, a plea of insanity landed me, thankfully, in a more hospitable residence than a federal detention facility. They claimed, of course, that the tail was merely mangled flesh, a part of Nettles' intestines. That I suffered a psychotic relapse, remembering my own abandonment as a child, and was caught up in a schizophrenic hallucination. And the creature—well, dead, it looked as innocent as a newborn. With no biological family to press for an autopsy, it was quietly swept under a very thick Italian rug. What's one cover-up in the history of a Church that is riddled with them?

But I know the truth because I'm not alone. There are others just like me. A nun in Tampa, Florida, who set an infant child on fire; a priest in Tacoma, Washington, who threw a baby from the top of a bell tower; a groundskeeper in Southern Utah, who buried a trowel through an infant's skull. They've seen what I've seen. They know.

And they're not the only ones.

There's a reason that Motu Proprio was sent out to every church and domicile under the authority of the Pope. And if you don't believe me, ask around. You'll see—they'll all say they don't know why or when the practice of bringing abandoned infants into the church was abolished. But if you look closely while they're giving their answers, you'll notice a bead of sweat trickle down a forehead. Nostrils flaring, when their sinuses were fine before. They will quickly excuse themselves to other matters while apologizing that they couldn't give you more of their time. And then you too will know.

Evil walks amongst us. Or crawls. Cries. Screams.

And we are the ones who must stop it.

Sancto Saepes Motu Proprio:

The Second Vatican Council, in adherence to the infallible truths set forth by the Magisterium, has ascertained the need to set forth, in divine promulgation, the ensuing statute, requiring the immediate and universal assent, both in faith and by works, of all magistrates whose ministries extend to any sacred domiciliary station including, but not limited to, cathedrals, churches, convents, oratories, monasteries, rectories, or any other place of worship or sanctioned tutelage:

From this day, the 22nd of May in the year of our Lord 1974, forward, and ever looking backward, for God is the same today, yesterday, and tomorrow, no infant child abandoned on o before the holy grounds of an aforementioned domiciliary station, or any analogous edifice, shall be admitted within said domicile by a member of the clergy. This sanctioned decree upheld without exception.

In the event that such a circumstance should arise it is advisable in the establis which said domicile should subscribe, namely in relation to the governin contact the local authorities. Such an outreach should be made w wherein the presiding council will convene to determine th file, in the Church archives, both the discovering p with accordance to the doctrines of the eve and His Holy Word in which all m Further council should recording names without th apol

WHAT'S WORST
David James Keaton

"Whenever it was taken outside, some officious person
was always pointing out that it was in danger
of being left behind."
—Edward Gorey—*The Beastly Baby*

Jason drove past a dead baby on the side of the road.

He drove on a few more seconds, until he slowly realized what he'd seen, foot easing off the gas as he stared in his rearview mirror, engine revving down. Nothing back there except the vanishing point. He turned down the stereo as he coasted. He was driving slow enough to count ten white lines sliding under his car between heartbeats, and he felt the warmth of the crackling speaker behind his head. He'd mounted the speakers in his headrests, despite his mechanic's warnings, gutting the cushions like his old teddy bears, like a kid forced to play doctor all by himself, and he forced the speakers to fit inside, even though they really didn't, then black-taped it all shut. This gave the headrests too many sharp corners to ever rest his head on them again, but he figured it was worth all the sweat and middle-of-the-night tinkering with those hordes of mosquitoes drawn to his dome light. He never rested his head when he drove anyway.

Hell, speaker magnets shouldn't be too *close to the skull, right?*

With the balance turned all the way to the right it gave him someone to talk to, and the vibrations under his arm were comforting. And after enough miles, he even started talking to it a bit. Nothing crazy. Just thinking out loud really. Until one night after a particularly good song, a speaker finally blew. Lately, the ruptured music was popping and sparking so badly he had to turn them down a bit. The right side was a little better, and he figured one would be enough though. Especially since he didn't have enough money to replace them, but mostly because he couldn't see himself ever going through the effort of cutting them open again even if he did have the cash. Although he was sure the static couldn't be that bad for his brains, he'd wrapped at least seven rolls of black tape around those headrests. That meant forever.

"Was that really a dead baby back there? No freaking way." He titled his head, rolling it around on his shoulders until it cracked. His eyes never left the rearview mirror as he slowed down to about 10 miles an hour. Still no cars anywhere around.

"A dead baby. Not just something pink that looked like a dead baby. I know that's what I saw. Please, let that be what I saw . . ." He said that last part almost to himself, leaning over even more, the fuzz on the seat tickling his ear. "I should go back, huh? I know it wasn't an animal. There was no blood, no fur. Nothing red, just pink. That means no one threw a baby out of a car. Now that would be worse. You'd be a little red comet, and I'd still be driving next to you, if that were the case."

A couple seconds went by, about ten white lines sliding under the car while he thought about it, then he leaned over again and explained himself to no one.

"You know, there's something to be said about someone like myself who sees something that horrible and just keeps on driving. Doesn't even phase him enough to go back. I know what you're thinking. That I'm scared. That I don't want to touch it or see it up close or something. That's ridiculous."

He turned the stereo off. It was stuck in the static between stations anyway. Second ticked by with his engine. Suddenly he had both hands on the wheel, both arms locked, both feet on the brake, subwoofer popping.

But what if someone else sees it and thinks they found it first?

Jason went back for the baby. Fast and backwards. When he got up next to it, he opened the passenger door, stretched across the seat on his stomach with his head in his palms and stared at the thing, with the car rumbling under his body. It was right there by his tire. His hands trembled a bit, and he told himself it was the low idle from the car. Not the fact that this was definitely a dead baby.

No flies, no blood, no smell, nothing, he thought. *No bugs, no red . . . just dead.*

It was on its stomach, too, and he studied the smooth, pink head and thought about rolling it over to see if it was a boy or a girl. Then he decided he liked not knowing. He considered drawing three lines on the back of its scalp so he'd never have to turn it over. Three lines, that's all you need for two eyes and a mouth. Then he could pretend he found an alien instead.

Now that was a dilemma, he thought. *What would you rather find on the side of the road? A dead baby or a dead alien? Alien. What about a live baby or a dead alien? Live baby, definitely. I'd be big hero. Dead alien and you'd end up on the slab in Area 51 right next to it.*

A strange sound came from the car, as if it was thinking hard along with him, and he grabbed it by its swollen ankle and picked it up fast before he changed his mind. It was heavier than he expected, and he thought of stuffed toys left outside to soak up the rain. He flung it into the seat beside him.

"Damn, what you been eatin'? That must be how it died," he explained to the static. "First, someone lost the thing, maybe while they were changing a tire, and when it got left behind, there was no one around to stop it from putting things in its mouth. And everyone knows a baby on the side of the road will eat rocks all night long if no one is around to stop it . . ." He trailed off as he noticed something else in the roadside gravel as he was closing his door. He leaned out, reaching out slow so his back could crack, but also hoping someone would come along. It was a toy. Or it had been a toy at one time. It was smashed now, many times run over, and Jason couldn't decipher what it had been. He knew what it was supposed to do though, and that was rattle. Babies liked things that rattled. This was a toy that had rattled once, then burst open under a wheel, all the popcorn kernels that had made those noises now scattered in a star pattern around it. He thought maybe it was homemade, sewn together from some dying stuffed animal. He counted the extra eyes and ear on the rattle and decide it was a bunch of animals, by the look of it. Something tightened in Jason's chest, something about the toy affecting him in a way the baby hadn't, and he shook his head hard, like a dog that got thrown in the pool or a cat reacting to a surprise gunshot, and he slammed his car door to get moving. He guessed his reaction was just from being down there at exhaust level, the fumes or something. He clicked the volume knob off, then reached over and strapped the baby in while the hiss of the stereo static faded away again. He didn't want the thing rolling over onto his side of the car when he took any hard turns. He still remembered how important it was to stay on your own side when he was on a long drive in the backseat with his brother.

When he clicked the seat belt over its distended belly, he noticed that he'd placed it onto the seat perfectly, carefully, just like any child. And right before he pulled back onto the road, his eyes took a snapshot of its face before he could stop himself. It was a boy.

"So what?" Jason said, looking straight ahead. He played with the rearview and drove on, then leaned over and whispered to it without looking.

"Hey, here's a good one. What's easier to unload? A truckload of bowling balls? Or a truckload of dead babies? Dead babies! Because you can use a pitchfork."

Jason sighed, satisfied he'd broken the tension.

"So, you from around here? No one threw you out of the car, did they? You'd have been a little red comet if that had happened! You run away? Someone give birth to you in that ditch? No, there's no cord. Can you imagine that? Some girl pulls over to have a baby and leave it behind, only she forgets the cord, right? Then, miles later, she gets pulled over 'cause the cops see the baby bouncing behind the car. Now, that's a worse ticket than not having a baby properly restrained in the car seat, ain't it?" Jason's smile dropped a little. "I should probably take you to the police now, shouldn't I?" But an hour later, Jason was still driving, telling himself that he'd done nothing wrong. He worried someone would take it to a lab, cut it in half, count the rings to solve the mystery, then wonder what the hell he was doing driving around with it for so long. He honestly just wanted someone to scratch their head and ask him why he'd hauled a dead baby around the highways, and he imagined himself on TV, symbolizing detached youth everywhere or some such nonsense. This was right up there with those headlines about teens leaving babies in the toilets then heading to prom. No, this was worse. Nobody ever did what he was doing. He'd be the boy who drove around with a dead baby, telling it dead baby jokes.

He leaned over again, still not looking.

"Okay, what's worse? Killing a baby, or driving around with it like it's nothing? Hey, you remember those 'what's worse' jokes? You know, what's worse? Fifty dead babies in a garbage can or one dead baby in fifty garbage cans? That's a tough one, ain't it? I wonder what someone would say if they heard me right now. I am a true mystery." Jason's eyes got wide. "Holy shit! I wonder what someone would say if I took you to a movie! Do you want to go see a movie! It would have to be a drive-in though. I'd get in trouble if I carried you into a theater, especially if it was rated 'R.' They check I.D.'s these days."

He tilted the rearview to pretend someone was in the back seat listening to him.

"Hey! What's worse than finding a dead baby in the back seat of your car? Realizing you fucked it! So nasty." He wished for a train or a red light so he'd have to slam on the brakes at least once. He leaned over and unhooked its seat belt, always without looking. He wanted to hit the brakes while he was talking to it, then act shocked when it bounced off the dashboard. He thought that would be hilarious and edgy as fuck. Especially if anyone saw it. But there were still no cars around. No one at all. He wondered if he'd missed the end of the world. This was a depressing thought, as he couldn't imagine finding a dead baby then having no one to show how unimpressed he was by such a discovery. Then he had another idea. What if he turned the baby in to the authorities, but then the cops found out he went through a car wash before he surrendered it?

They would be confused, suspicious as hell, but couldn't do anything about it. He'd be pretty mysterious if he did that. *Maybe they'd think I was washing blood off my car?*

Jason drove faster, looking for a car wash. He looked hard for one, needing desperately to find one, even wishing so hard that he visualized blowing the candles off a birthday cake with this wish and extinguishing every candle on his first try. And what the hell, he found one.

+ + +

It was one of those crazy car washes where you drove through the mouth of a monster clown or something equally sinister. Not that he thought clowns were sinister.

"Don't be afraid of clowns," he said. "Aren't you sick of people saying they're afraid of clowns? You will be. They're all like, 'you know what's scary? A killer clown with sharp teeth. Who kills people. Oooh, I'm so weird being afraid of clowns! You know what else is scary? Alligators with nine heads! Keep them away from me!'"

He'd seen car washes before where the garage-door entrance was painted to look like a dragon, or a dinosaur, depending on if it was a Creationist state. Whatever monster the starving-artist graffiti ~~artists~~ employees had come up with in-between wiping down cars, that was the theme. He was still far outside any town and surprised he found it, at least there was still no sign of highway life. This made the gyrating mechanical gorilla out front even more unnerving. The ape was painted green and clutching a bundle of deflated Valentine's Day balloons with "$5" scrawled on each one in black marker. The balloons swung around, lolling lazily in the dry wind, while the metal gears within the gorilla's shoulder creaked and strained. Wires protruded around the joints where the fur had worn away, leading to a spool of cable and a power outlet behind the human-like feet. The gorilla stood grinning through green teeth, waving Jason in. He heard hissing and clanking inside the wash, but there were no cars exiting the back. Never any cars anywhere today but his own.

Car washes were scary enough when you were little, Jason thought. *Children must shit their pants when they take a wrong turn into this freakshow.*

He looked around as he pulled closer to the entrance, and seeing no one to take his money, and an "Out of Order" sign taped to a busted "Change Machine, he put a five-dollar bill in the mailbox by the door. The box was painted up as another smaller clown, with the inside of the flip-up painted like a tongue. Jason slammed it shut, and a loud bang made his heart jump. He looked up to see the garage door retracting and this monstrous tongue disappearing into the clown's maw. A flashing green light beckoned him inside, and Jason gave the car a little gas to accommodate.

"Now, I know babies get scared in car washes," Jason whispered soothingly to his cargo. "I used to get scared in these myself, I'm not afraid to admit. But I'm sorry, I'm not going to close your eyes."

Something thumped under his seat as the car wash took control of the vehicle.

"I heard that dogs go bonkers inside these things. Hey, that reminds me, what do you give a dead baby for its birthday? A dead puppy!"

There was another jerk as the wheels found the sweet spot in the tracks and now the machines had taken over completely. Jason took his hands off his steering wheel and the green light flashed red. Water started trickling down the windshield as the tongue rolled closed behind him and his car was drawn the rest of the way into the dark. Jason stifled a laugh, some of it snorting from his nose to betray his nervousness.

"You ever wonder where dead baby jokes come from?

Wait, no, you ever wonder where dead babies come from? Dead stork brings 'em! Just teasing. Hey, who comes up with all those jokes? Maybe you really need a dead baby around to get the best ideas going, to get the real funny stuff . . ."

Something rocked the car hard, and Jason bit his tongue.

"Ow. Hey! Why did the dead baby cross the road?

Because it was nailed to the chicken!"

The car lurched like a bronco as the water pressure increased, and he sat up a bit straighter. He jumped at a wet slap on the glass and watched an octopus of purple fingers dance down to his wiper blades. That part always scared the shit out of him as a kid—the way the tentacles squirmed there for a second, then lazily dragged themselves up and over the car, leaving a steaming white trail of bubbles and slime behind them. And when the two huge, green scrubbers started slowly moving up and down his doors, his heart may have skipped and he coughed a bit in panic, bringing both feet down hard on the brake pedal. Then he sighed and scratched himself hard behind the ears in disgust. For some reason, whenever those scrubbers moved past the car, he always thought the car was moving instead of the machines. The optical illusion never failed to make him stomp the brakes like a dumb shit.

The heavy soap started spraying, and Jason looked down at his crossed arms, watching the pattern change as foam and water marbled the light across his skin. He adjusted the rearview mirror again to see how the dance of light looked on his face, then his eyes. But he saw the toy again in the back seat, and before he could hypothesize the species of stuffed animals skinned to create it, there was the blur of a tire flashing over it in his mind, and the popcorn kernels bursting, dancing, then rolling away to pop on the heat of the asphalt. Another tire rolled through his mind's eye, and the popcorn on the road popped and boiled up higher in the heat. Then another tire as the popcorn sprouted wings like blowflies as the rattling sound magnified . . .

But something didn't sound right outside the car, outside in the wash. He looked down the hood and found the problem. The rattling was the sound of the antenna on his car getting hammered by a particularly angry green scrubber. It was bouncing back and forth way too hard, bending much too far, wiggling dangerously fast. Jason sighed. He'd forgotten to unscrew it before he went in. And even though he hadn't seen the sign, he knew neither the clown nor the gorilla would be "responsible for anything lost or broken." He wondered what someone would say if he complained, "Your evil-clown car wash scared my baby to death. You owe me a new rattler. At least!"

The scrubbers were up and spinning on the side windows now, pounding away at the glass and filling the car with strobe lights and vibrations. He never saw them move like that before, never that high anyway. He could feel the tendrils almost touching each other on the roof above his head. Every sound in the wash seemed too loud, and he clicked on the radio and put his arm around the dead speaker in the passenger's side headrest, listening for his soothing lullaby of static.

"You know, I remember more jokes about killing babies, instead of jokes about babies that are already dead. Like, what's red and squirms in the corner?"

A fleet of scrubbers surrounded his car. He hadn't counted them, but he was sure they were multiplying. The antenna was batted back and forth between two of them like Pong on the fastest level.

"A baby playing with a razor! Okay, what's blue and squirms in the corner?"

Now the antenna was being slapped around harder, and under the splashing and the rattling, his radio was making a noise he'd never heard before.

"A baby playing with a garbage bag! And what's green and *doesn't* squirm in the corner?"

The antenna shook and wiggled so fast that it vanished, then it snapped and was gone for good, flipping end over end into a chaotic blur of chrome, water and suds.

"Same baby! Three weeks later!"

Dead air on his radio now. Seconds passed. Then minutes. His car had stopped moving forward, though it was still being washed. It felt like he'd been in there a long time. A lot more than five bucks worth anyway. He leaned over to talk to the speaker in the passenger-side headrest, only to jerk back his arm as if he'd been burned. He'd heard something strange, more of a feeling in his head than an actual sound. But something was very wrong. He crawled out of his driver's seat and into the back to squint through the defroster lines to see if anyone was in the wash with him. It was hard to see through the steam and foam, and his breath fogged the glass. He was sure someone had to be working on getting the tracks moving again.

Maybe they got distracted refilling the soap, blowing bubbles. Or blowing up more balloons, feeding the robot monkey.

"Nothing to worry about," he lied to the dead baby. "This is just like when you're stuck at the top of a Ferris wheel. That never hurt nobody."

A frozen Ferris wheel, he thought. *Now* that *meant forever.*

The car started shaking violently, and he wiped the fog rolling off his skin from all the windows, checking every direction for someone inside working on repairs. He saw no one and adjusted a side mirror to watch the scrubbers down beating on his wheel wells. He wondered what they were made of, if they would puncture his tires if they cleaned the same spot of rubber long enough.

If a hundred moneys washed a hundred tires for a hundred years, they wouldn't need to shake a spear . . .

He figured anything could cut through anything if it worked on it long enough, and he remembered a picture he'd seen depicting the aftermath of a tornado. It made no sense at the time, but the photograph revealed a sock monkey stuck half in and half out of tree trunk, its soft head buried in the wood.

If something gets spinning fast enough, he decided.

Anything can happen. Is that what's going on in here . . .

He climbed back into the driver's seat, then leaned over to the passenger's side, not sure whether he was talking to the static or the baby, wondering again how easy it would be to not notice the end of the world.

"What's worse than running over a baby with your car? Getting it out of your treads." He scratched his scalp hard in frustration. "Didn't like that one? Fine. Why do babies have soft spots on their heads? So you can carry them ten at a time. Like a six-pack! Hey, you know what?"

He squeezed the headrest under his arm affectionately. "I really don't like those kinds of jokes. The 'what's worst' ones are better. Remember the little kids and their 'what's worst' jokes? Or 'what's grosser than gross'?" A strange smell rolled his eyeballs down to the passenger's seat before he could stop himself.

"Phew, someone's baby needs changin'! Changin' back to *alive,* mean."

Change machine out of order . . .

Jason tried giggling, but he'd already made the mistake of looking. And he could have sworn the baby had been staring back at him before he could pinch his own eyes shut.

And its mouth was open, too.

He shook his head to erase the image, then his back was stiff and straight in his driver's seat again, both hands on his window, pressing his nose against the glass. He wished he would have looked closer when he first found it back there on the road. Then he would have known if the eyes and mouth were already open. Then he'd know for sure if anything on the baby had changed. Or needed changing.

What's worst? he wondered. *Open eyes or open mouth?*

At first he thought maybe the eyes? But now he wasn't so sure which would be worse. But he was pretty sure the open mouth was where the smell was coming from.

But what about that sound?

He looked at digital clock in his dashboard, trying to remember what time he'd entered the wash. Then he tried to remember the make and model of his car. Or where he had been going. Or how long he'd been inside. He had none of these answers. And the clock seemed to be displaying military time, or something equally impossible. And his odometer was creeping backwards. Something about the wash was affecting things, this he was sure of. Maybe it was as simple as the heat and moisture and pressure of a car wash's ecosystem, like a miniature storm over the Bermuda Triangle.

How long could you be stuck in a car wash without someone noticing? he thought. *Would I even want to know the record?*

He squinted out through the bubbles again and decided that the washing stage should be done by now, at the very least. He thought it should definitely be time for some different machines to come crawling over besides these scrubbers. He knew there were more machines out there. And people. He could hear them all. He crawled into the back seat again, and smeared his hand through the fog to peer out toward the mouth of the clown. A new machine lowered onto his trunk, and between the rhythm and bounce of this cylinder of shredded beach towels, Jason could see some light through the garage-door's windows, and then, past that, the shimmering dark outline of the empty road. He had to keep wiping away his breath to see, and he told himself that maybe there was a long line of cars filing past, that maybe cars were going by unseen, every time his hand cleared the steam from the glass. He climbed into the front again and sucked in a deep breath, preparing for his space walk. Then he gently pulled up on his door handle and cracked his car open like a soda. Hot needles of white water peppered his arm, and he was ready to make a run for it when one of the green scrubwheels suddenly lurched towards him and slammed his door back shut. He forced a laugh and opened it again. But the door stopped against the scrubbing wheel and bounced violently under his hand. The noise of the wash was impossibly loud now that the seal had been broken, and his head ached with the tidal sounds of the machinery. He leaned his shoulder against the door and pushed. The door would only open a crack, vibrating so hard he bit his tongue from the force. He put all his weight against the door, gaining a few more centimeters, but not enough for even his shoe to hold it open. He pushed harder, then threw himself against it in a tantrum, worried for a moment that he might lose control of his bowels, like a baby. He thought about a video he saw once where a woman was giving birth and defecated at the same time. It had made him sick, and at the time he thought it was because it had made him realize humans were mere animals. But now he knew it was so disturbing because of the possibility of raising the wrong one as your child.

He shoved hard and a jet of hot water filled his mouth and his drowning reflex kicked it.

How do you make a dead baby float? Take your foot off its head. How else do you make a dead baby float? One can of root beer and two scoops of dead baby. How do you spoil a baby? Leave it on the side of the road . . .

The door slammed shut, and as he coughed and spit out the fluids, he was suddenly worried that fighting a door to the death might mean he'd be discovered in a car wash with shit in his pants, never mind the dead baby. So he stopped pushing and forced himself to relax. All the windows and mirrors were fogged, even the chrome on the radio knobs. He couldn't see the whirling mechanisms surrounding him at all anymore, and he started work to control his breathing, slowing his exhales so that all the glass would clear and he could see what was holding him captive, so he could work on getting out.

"You know what you never hear?" Jason practically screamed at the dead baby over the static and the bashing hurricane of the wash.

He worried the speakers were broadcasting the beat of the machines, maybe even before he got there. Maybe that's what he'd been tapping his foot to for hours.

Can you hear a car wash through your radio? If it was loud enough. I swear I heard a hockey game once that wasn't being broadcast. No one believed me, but how did I know it went to a shoot-out and had six fights? In the parking lot.

"You never hear someone make up a joke. No one's ever around to see it happen. Just like you can smell a skunk on the road but never see it. Just like you hear the tires squeal and never hear the crash. And even though we know the dead storks bring the dead babies, don't you ever wonder where jokes come from?"

For the first time since he'd picked up his tiny hitchhiker, Jason forced himself to look directly at it. Its eyes and mouth were looking at him, just like he knew they would be. But it was much worse that he'd feared. He stared at the thing long and hard, until the baby blurred and finally faded from his vision. Jason knew that this always happened when he stared at things too long, and this was the first time it had ever happened as a defensive measure, but he told himself it was really just the impenetrable steam inside the car that had mercifully swept the baby away.

"So let's make a dead baby joke! Right here, right now. You know, just to pass the time. Now, how do jokes usually start?"

He blinked and his vision cleared, and the baby was back in his head, burrowing behind his eyelids. He waited until it faded again.

"So, a dead baby walks into a bar . . . shit! That doesn't work, does it?"

He slapped himself upside the head and vigorously scratched the back of his neck to focus.

"The best jokes always start with the words 'what's worst.' This we know. I once heard this little girl telling dead baby jokes and she kept saying the words "what's *worst*" instead of 'what's worse,' and it's so much better that way. So what's worst? Driving over a baby on the road or . . . getting the baby out of your . . . fuck, we already did that one. Okay, what's worst? Trying to get the dead baby off the hood ornament or . . ."

Jason closed his eyes to keep it together.

"What's worst? Trying to get a dead baby out of your grill? Or trying to get it out of your head?" Jason looked around for answers, his spit drying and foaming on the back of his tongue. He looked at the baby and saw its mouth was closed. Then it blinked. It was time to go.

Jason slammed his back against his driver's seat and pulled his gear shift down hard. His foot stabbed the pedal and he straightened his arms to brace against the dash, waiting for the crashing and sparks and sunlight as he broke through the clown's mouth and splintered its metal tongue, bouncing and scraping his car out into the road in a shower of fireworks.

Nothing.

He pushed the gas down flush against the floorboards, stomping so hard he felt the pedal actually bend to the curve of his foot. He heard the engine screaming with all the power it had and he wished he could remember what kind of car he drove so he could visualize maximum performance in the commercial. He still wasn't moving.

Are my wheels off the ground? That's not how these things work. You ever notice how you never see a hockey fight during overtime? Time to focus. Let me the fuck . . . out.

He tried to remember what had happened when the red light flashed on and the car wash first pulled him in. There was no way it could be holding him up with his wheels up in the air. There was something very wrong, and he was leaving. He shoved himself back in his driver's seat even further, grunting and punching the horn with his fist, then his feet, walking his legs up and over the steering wheel onto the glass of the windscreen. Then Jason started jack-hammering the with his heels. He kicked hard, then harder, then faster, almost running in midair, hearing the rubber on his shoes squeaking and watching the crazy patterns they were smearing in the vapor. He thought of a kaleidoscope, one that he'd had and loved as a boy, a toy that he just had to break open, and how two rolls of black tape couldn't fix it after he cracked it open to see what was inside. Nothing really, nothing like what he seen through the hole anyway. He tried refilling it with sand and bugs and screws and apple juice and marbles, and even after all that labor, it still never worked again. He shook the image out of his head, cracked his neck in both directions, and pushed the muscles in his legs faster and harder than he ever had before.

His sneakers kick-started a spider web of cracks between the steaming bubbles and wax splashing across the glass, and his frantic heels squeaked and spasmed. He imagined an army of spiders on the outside of the windshield, in a furious competition to finish their design first, all while he drove off down the road, RPMs redlining on the curves, trying desperately to find a straightaway long enough to gather the speed to blow the passengers off.

His ankles ached, one of his shoes slipped, and a flailing knee turned the radio back on. Static and voices fought for his attention, even without the antenna, distorted singing and crying rising up from the passenger's seat that couldn't be coming from the speakers, and Jason kicked the windshield with everything he had left. And finally, his legs locked straight behind the knees, both feet went smashing through the glass.

Coming out breach, he thought. *Got no choice, doc.*

His hands came up to protect his head.

Just don't let the cord wrap around the neck . . .

Then a snowstorm of safety glass cubes splashed his crossed arms and showered his face. The roar of the wash and the hot water riding in with it, dragging the shards across his nose and forehead. A shard stung him over the eyebrow, then another bee sting under his nostril. He fought the urge to wipe them away, knowing this would make the cuts deeper. Then he pulled his feet back inside and surged forward, trying to exit head first, eyes pinched closed, ears getting the worst of the scalding wax. His shoulders got stuck, and he sliced through his shirt working his way free, grinding the sand of the windshield into his chest and stomach as he strained and contorted his body to widen the hole. Eventually it was big enough, and he exploded out, rolling across the hood and flopped onto the ground gasping for air.

He stood up tall outside the car, watching the machines dancing and spinning around him, seemingly keeping their distance now as the pink, blood-streaked water pooled on his dashboard under the jagged hole where he'd come from, crimson and foam running down his throat, past his legs, and gathering between his toes. He turned, and the clown's mouth started to open for him, just like the baby's had, and he finally stepped out into the sun.

It was only when he saw the boy lying there outside that Jason's heart started to slow to a normal speed. Gray, soggy rags wrapped around his arm, mouth frozen in a yawn, and stretched out in a grass-angel he'd worn into the ground around him. Headphones covered his ears, and the boy was slowly sitting up on his elbows and realizing that Jason was there.

The boy squinted and pulled the headphones down to his throat, absently picked dirt and stones out of the skin on his arms, then checked his watch and shrugged with a

"What the fuck?"

Jason turned to watch his car exit the clown's mouth behind him, safe, wheels locked on the tracks, windshield gutted yet gleaming, and right on schedule. That's when Jason knew his car had been in neutral the whole time he was gunning it in there, that he hadn't been inside the wash any longer than normal.

So he went back for the baby. And this time, when he strode out through the scalding foam and the sting and the Turtle Wax snapping, a dead baby clenched tight against his chest, soft translucent head under Jason's chin, brittle snakeskin like an accordion around its neck. He covered the open eyes and open mouth with a loving, protective hand when the blast of the last machine came down over both of them, blowing the water out of his ears like they were candles, and he didn't hesitated to look anymore. It was his baby now.

He stopped to let the machine finish, feeling the tiny single rubber wheel on the blower rolling down the back of his neck, the hot wind filling up his eyes and roasting away any bad memories, evaporating the pools inside his ear and turning the static back to music.

What's worst? Finding a dead baby on the side of the road? Or wanting to?

He walked to the boy in the grass and yanked the headphones from his head, surprised they weren't connected. He used the rattle in his hands to lead the boy's eyes around like a drunk test, imagining how powerful he looked after his rescue. Even if he'd only gone back in to get the antenna.

DEAD END
Kristopher Triana

With the body securely locked in the trunk, all Jake had to do was shatter the mirrors and he would be ready to leave. It didn't matter where to. It never did. The only important thing was to keep moving.

Perpetual motion. Keep the body strong by pumping blood.

So much blood.

Some was even speckled across the high heel he now used to shatter the side mirrors of the car. Getting in, he broke the rear view in the same fashion, the cracks bursting like lightning across the reflection as he averted his gaze. He pulled his bandana from his jeans and used it to wipe the shoe of any prints before throwing it out the window. It landed in the gutter of the motel lot, swishing in the rain swill, adrift with so many cigarette butts and condom wrappers.

Old Vegas. A candy colored monument to wretchedness.

The motel was like so many on the outskirts of the city, shit-sandwiched between bail bond joints and discount wedding chapels. This was the side of Vegas they didn't advertise, far from the expensive glamour of the main strip. To Jake, that whole stretch was so soft-boiled you could sop it up with a biscuit. The true exploitive sleaze was to be found on Fremont and beyond, down where the buses stopped running. He'd drifted around here for a few months, pushing his own disciplined time limits because he'd been enjoying himself perhaps a little too much.

Don't stay in one place. Don't show a pattern. Don't allow yourself to have an M.O.

As the exhaust belched to life the car shuddered forward. The trunk gave a soft thud as the bar whore's corpse flopped about before settling. Jake wondered if when the whore had first gotten this car if she had thought *anyone* would have ever ended up in the trunk, let alone she herself. It was an uncommon stroke of luck for him that she had one at all. When he'd finished with her he'd rooted through her purse and found the keys. It had one of those beepers on it to unlock the car. He'd gone outside and hit the button and the Dodge honked, identifying itself. It made sense. From the lived-in look of the motel room it was obvious that she'd been living there. It was a foreign concept to Jake. Not living in a motel room, but living anywhere. He knew, just as surely as he knew he would kill again, that there was no such thing as home.

+ + +

Jake was a misogynist, but that wasn't why he primarily murdered women. He chose them because the act of killing was so intimate and emotional. The methodical taking of a life was the one act that made him feel connected to the human race in any way. It almost felt homoerotic for him to kill a man unless it was out of blind rage, which had occurred on a few occasions in his wasted youth. He chose to kill women just as straight men would choose to sleep with women; it was an instinctual, sexual impulse as natural to him as eating or taking a piss.

Not that Jake could explain it or put it into words. The dollar-store education of a renegade orphan didn't get him much further cognitively than his bad genes and the mild brain damage he'd suffered in the womb from his mother's drug use.

The world had been cruel to Jake from the beginning.

He'd gone from the dumpster they'd found him in right into the hands of the state, allowing apathy and bureaucracy to further poison his future. He was shuffled through orphanages, never fitting in or getting along with even other abandoned children like himself. By thirteen his bad behavior and petty crimes led him to a reform school that was really nothing more than a juvenile detention hall; a sort of pre-prison. It was there that he learned to be a much better fighter and thief.

It was also where he'd learned to hate mirrors.

He'd always been uncomfortable with his own reflection because whom he felt he was never looked back at him in a mirror. His image haunted him, always looking so alien and never matching the image he felt was imposed upon the mirror. He was like a dog seeing its own reflection in a sliding glass door and barking, never seeing the image as itself. As he reached his teens the identity denial worsened, and so did the mirror image: pimples, uneven facial hair, and an awkward body struggling through growth spurts. The greasy hair never settled right, the skin always oily and inflamed, the chest birdlike and freckled. He didn't think of it as a body so much as an inescapable shell, a prison that had him bound in a manner far more debilitating than the bars of any jail.

He hated what he saw in the mirror.

But he hated what others saw in it more.

+ + +

"You're looking kinda pretty there, boy," Larry had said from behind him.

Jake wore only a damp towel around his waist. He'd just finished in the shower room and was standing before the sink where the long mirror stretched from one end of the bathroom counter to the other. As usual, he had been avoiding looking into it, so he hadn't seen Larry walking up behind him.

Larry was one of the bigger bullies in juvie hall. At eighteen, he had a few years on Jake then to boot, years that packed on meanness as well as size. Jake had felt his hand on his shoulder before Larry spun him around. He'd watched Larry's nose crinkle in confusion as he looked at Jake, then at Jake's reflection, and then back again.

"How come you look so pretty in the mirror when you look so ugly in real life?" Larry had asked him.

Jake was silent. Larry got so close to him he could smell his morning cigarette breath. Fear made his legs tremble, and that just seemed to excite Larry. He'd spun Jake back around to make him face the mirror.

"Your reflection makes you look real pretty don't it?"

Larry had grabbed him by the jaw then and made him look at himself, but Jake only saw the same ugly boy who always greeted him. He couldn't see what Larry meant. But that hadn't stop Larry from bending him over the sink.

The whole time, Larry had stared at Jake's reflection in the mirror.

+ + +

He drove through the Nevada desert now, excited by what unseen curiosities might lurk within the tangerine haze beyond. Red sandstone formations were all that lined the sides of the state road now, the dilapidated ghetto of Vegas's outskirts far behind. The rocks were magnificent in color, bleeding orange and forming psychedelic swirls of lavender upon their jagged edges. On some of them Jake could see the rock art petroglyphs that an ancient race had left behind some three hundred years before Christ. While Jake didn't know or care much about history, he'd heard many whispered ghost stories during his time in Old Vegas; the tall tales of the old tribes of the valley that were said to practice ritual sacrifice so to be favored by the things that lurked in the core of the basin. Things that were said to make a man go mad at the sheer sight of them. Because of its haunted history, the locals regarded it as some sort of Bermuda Triangle where any kind of supernatural nightmare could become reality. Now the high walls of the desert told a similar story with their carved images of stick figures splitting one another in half, impaling each other, and even feeding each other to horned serpents. The engravings were ominous, titillating Jake's vicious psyche. They were images of a Hell on earth, etched into a landscape that looked as if it could be quite the happy home for Satan himself. He gnawed on his thumbnail as his blood throbbed beneath his sweaty flesh, the horrible summer heat making him and the desert boil together.

Gotta love a little Twilight Zone thrill.

But he didn't just want to explore these demonic stomping grounds. He also needed to dispose of the dead whore in the trunk. What better place than in the bowels of a devil's canyon?

He exited unto a side road and then another, winding through the plains, hoping for even further seclusion. He hadn't seen another car in a while but he wasn't careless enough to stop on a road that was adjacent to the interstate. He found a fork that had one path leading to a dead end. A rusted cattle gate blocked it off and a bullet-hole riddled road closed sign hung crookedly from one hinge. He pulled up close and got out, leaving the car running.

The dry heat was even more intense outside. He could feel himself baking in the blinding sun the moment he stepped out. It was more than just hot, it was downright blistering; a heat that bordered on otherworldly. He needed to use his bandana to open the trunk. It felt like a damn oven rack.

The comforter had held together fine, tied together using the whore's nylons. There was a bit of seepage from her head still. He'd drained her in the bathtub and had been meticulous about it, working her arms like pumps. But a few drops always remained.

No such thing as clean.

He hauled her out and let her drop upon the pot-holes with a wet thud. Upon impact the flap covering her face came loose and her lifeless eyes looked up at him, into him, through him. She wore mascara tears like graffiti. She looked even older now in the daylight. Her face bore the scars of many broken dreams and her dyed hair was matted with blood, sticking to the gash he'd made in her forehead.

"Love is a burnin' thing," he said, quoting the song that'd been playing when he'd taken her.

+ + +

After a few bourbons in the casino, Jake had come with the whore back to her motel room. It had been several weeks since his last kill—a twenty-something runaway whose guard he'd lowered with fast food and cocaine. He'd felt the old itch burning inside him, the beast within howling and gargling blood. When the lust for murder flushed him it was impossible to ignore for long. Only his sensibility and desire to not return to prison kept him in control. Armed robbery had given him a long enough stint. He sure as Hell didn't want to go up on a murder rap and spend the rest of his days rotting on death row. He had to be careful, but he also had to give in. There was temptation and then there was need. The act of killing fell under the latter for Jake; it had since he'd strangled his girlfriend when he was nineteen.

In the motel room, Jake could feel the black murk of murder enveloping him as the whore began to do what she'd been paid for.

It was like the same sinking feeling he'd always get in his gut when a rollercoaster dropped. It felt like that at first, and then the gooseflesh would hit him as his eyes glazed. It was almost like a meditative state. There were no voices in his head, no split personalities or any of the other horseshit he'd heard about in relation to serial killers. There was just the darkness, warm and sweet like molasses and just as thick. It was a high he'd never been able to top with drugs and booze, exhilaration far greater than sex, beyond religious and beyond transcendence.

He'd heard a weird word once that he felt summed it up right.

Euphoria.

That was the essence of creating death.

When he'd finished getting his money's worth out of the whore he'd slipped into his jeans and gone to the bathroom to freshen up. He could feel the hard bulk of the folded knife in his front pocket, nudging him more seductively than the whore's breasts when they'd pressed against his bare back. She had come up behind him. Her lips grazed his ear in a soft nibble.

"Fantastic, baby," she'd said.

"Yeah, right."

He hated when women played up how great the sex was, lying to him and every other man they met. *They're all whores,* he often told himself, *except the ones who say they aren't; they're lying whores.*

"Is there anything else I can do for you, sugar?" she'd asked.

"No. I'm broke now."

"Well, maybe after pay day then. Want me to pencil you in for sometime next week?"

"You won't have time."

"I can make time for you, baby."

She'd run her nails across his scalp and through his thinning hair.

That's when she'd caught his reflection in the mirror.

He had known then what was coming next. It had happened so many times before. Her head had cocked to one side, revealing her puzzlement. She'd peered closer into the stained mirror, looking at Jake's image.

"I must have had too much to drink," she said. "You look so

different in the mirror."

He was glad she'd left the old country station going on the radio at such a high volume. It would drown out some of the noise. *I fell into a burning ring of fire, I went down, down, down, and the flames went higher.*

"You look pretty," she said and snorted a laugh, "why you almost look like a . . ."

Her words fell into a gasp as he'd forced her skull into the mirror. It exploded all about them as her head cracked. The sink became an instant blossom of blood. She had still been conscious as he threw her into the bathtub. He'd planned to use the knife, but a large sliver from the mirror felt right as he picked it up. She'd begun to stand on her wobbly legs, hyperventilating in her sudden thrall of fear as she reached out blindly, her own blood obscuring her vision. More of her blood misted the air as he'd plunged the shard into her for the first time, and then again and again in movements just as fluid.

He lived for this.

The frantic look in their eyes when they grasped what was happening, and the even more frantic look when they knew it would soon be over along with everything else they had ever experienced. They had eaten their last bite, had their last screw, spoken to their loved ones for the final time, all without knowing it. Animal-like, they would shudder and writhe against his embrace as he ravaged their torsos with his weapon. Anything that could enter and exit would do. He had evolved from strangulation, to rage killing, to sickly sensuous stabbing. He thought of it as sensuous not because of the penetrating nature of the stab but because he knew he would be their last goodbye, and in that essence he claimed ownership. It was post-mortem husbandry to Jake, and each fresh kill left a notch on his heart like on a gunman's revolver.

The whore had slammed backward, breaking a tile. Her eyes had dilated with the twist of the shard in her stomach, and that old acidic stench hit Jake's nostrils making him bray like a horse. He'd let his jaw give in to his trembles, making his teeth chatter closer and closer to her as he inhaled her final breaths, savoring them.

They were always so beautiful in the end. They were open to him, without judgment of him. They were free of anxiety and self-consciousness, limp in their expired carcasses.

The dead never treated you like a creep for looking when they'd been taunting you with high heels and lipstick to begin with.

The dead never talked back.

The dead never said no.

+   +   +

With the whore's body tossed into a gorge of forgotten rock, Jake lit up a cigarette in a small toast and got back into her car. It was midday now, the sun was merciless, and the a/c unit only wheezed out a little whiff. It was about as helpful as someone fanning an ice cream cone at him.

He's thought he'd taken the fork right back, but he must have made a wrong turn somewhere. Perhaps he was getting snow-blind in the middle of all that red dust. The desert seemed to heave in the haze, the invisible heat lines distorting the alien world around him. He was having trouble finding his way back to the main road. The one he was on seemed endless but he pressed on, delving deeper into the canyon's heart.

He continued to hum Cash's *Ring of Fire*. It had been stuck in his head to the point of annoyance.

A good hour passed before he saw another sign of life.

There'd been nary a vulture in the sky or a lizard baking on the asphalt when the hitchhiker appeared. He hadn't even seen a road sign for the last thirty miles, just endless, unrelenting rock and sand. At first he mistook her for a cactus, the only green in this god-forsaken badland. But the swivel in her hips gave her away.

Well look what we have here.

She may as well have been a mirage out there in the haze. She was a busty brunette in a wife beater and a pair of tight jean shorts. A pair of cowboy boots completed her outfit. She had no backpack or water bottle. She didn't even have a purse.

This bitch must be out of her mind. He laughed at the sight of her. *Maybe someone got sick of her shit and threw her out of the car.* Just passing her by and leaving her alone out there would be enough to kill her. It was an interesting death sentence, but not one that satisfied him the way a personal tango of violence would.

She turned around to wave him down and he slowed. There wasn't a nearby rock that an accomplice could be hiding behind and if she had a gun on her he didn't know where she could possibly be hiding it, except in one of those boots. Being that he had just come from Vegas, he was still in a gambling mood. He pulled up next to her and got a better ogling. Sweat had made her clothes cling to her and her nipples pushed through her top like she was in a dirty magazine. She leaned down to greet him.

"Thanks for stopping," she said.

She had smooth features and smoother skin that was flushed in the cheeks. Her good looks were only slightly spoiled by the crazed and frantic look in her eyes. Even her eyelids twitched as if struggling to contain them. She was like a centerfold with a Manson family stare.

"Get in good lookin'," Jake said, and she did.

He knew the vinyl of the seat must have felt like lava, but it didn't seem to bother those long, tan legs of hers. She closed the door and they took off.

"What's a pretty thing like you doing all alone out here?" he asked.

Her stare was locked on the road ahead even as she replied.

"Car broke down."

He nodded and there was an awkward silence.

"Where you headed?" he asked, not caring.

"Just had to get out of Vegas, I guess."

He looked at her face more closely now, sizing her up. Her left eye had a hint of a bruise and he wondered if she was running from an abusive boyfriend. He'd been so focused on her body before that he hadn't looked at her face as much. On top of being beautiful, there was something familiar about her. Something he couldn't place. But she wasn't much for conversation, even though she seemed like she had something to get off her chest. She was twitchy and seemed anxious, squirming slightly in her seat. She picked at her cuticles while still staring out at the endless desert.

"I'm headed west," he said. "Following the sun."

He was trying to joke based on how hot it was outside, but she

didn't seem amused. Instead she seemed deep in crazed contempla-
tion, as if she was struggling for words that just wouldn't come.

"What is it?" he finally asked. "What's going on?"

She looked at him now. Her eyes were not only frantic, he saw,
but bloodshot and dilated.

*Probably stoned out of her mind. Probably came out here to
trip out on the colors of the rocks.*

"I'm okay," she said. "I'm just not sure what to say to you."

She turned her head away again and began to make little noises
under her breath. At first he thought she was sighing. But as she
continued, he realized she was humming a song.

She was humming *Ring of Fire.*

Something cold moved inside of him despite the heat.

"How about a little music?" he asked, trying to shake off the
creeps.

He flicked on the radio, half expecting dead air. He didn't expect
to hear screaming and the sounds of breaking glass. He wondered
if it was some sort of radio play like *War of the Worlds*, but then he
recognized the bar whore's whimpers from the night before, the soft
cries of a woman in the throes of dying. He switched the station in
a sudden panic and the next one had similar sounds. These screams
were of the runaway he'd slain after they shared a night of cocaine
and rough sex. Her recognized her repeated cries of "*no*". He switched
the dial once more and heard another woman, gasping and gagging.
It was the girlfriend he'd choked to death all those years ago.

He turned the radio off and looked at the hitchhiker. Her eyes
were crazed but they had been that way since he'd picked her up. She
seemed unfazed. She was still humming Johnny Cash.

Had she even heard any of that?

He wondered if he was cracking up, starting to hear voices like
all those other serial killers he'd read about. He shook his head as if
to get the memory of the noise out of his skull. He hoped it was just
the heat fucking with him. But if he was going nuts he wasn't alone.
He noticed the hitchhiker wasn't just picking at her nails. Now she
was peeling one off. Blood had pooled around the rim of the nail
as she picked it, making a clicking percussion for her humming. He

watched her tug with each flick of the nail, seeing the connecting flesh begin to shred.

I'll be doing this pretty mess a favor.

He didn't want to admit that he was lost, but when the check engine light popped on he began to worry. He didn't want to be one hundred miles from the nearest gas station with nothing but this sexy voodoo zombie for help. He figured the car was just overheating, but that didn't improve his situation. He was getting frustrated; with the car, his own mind, the hitchhiker's odd behavior, and the whole goddamned desert that just stretched out before him in a horrible infinity.

"Do you know how to get back to the highway from here?" he asked her.

"There's only one way out."

He waited for her to go on but she went all crazy mute again.

"Well," he asked, losing patience, "how the Hell do I get out?"

"That's what I've been having trouble telling you. I'm not sure what to say. I want you to take it right."

He didn't understand but tried to act as if he did.

"I'll take it right," he told her.

"You didn't last time."

"What?" he asked. He wasn't just losing his patience now. He was losing his temper. "Look, you psycho bitch, do you know the way out or don't you?"

Her mad eyes left the desert and fell upon him.

"The only way out," she said, "is to not kill me."

Jake spun the wheel and rode the brake, sending the car hurtling off the road and into the plains. He was overcome with fury and paranoia, and he vented by riding deeper into the desert, pumping the gas again, shaking the car about to rattle his passenger. He sneered with sadism as her body thrashed about the interior, knocking into the dash and back. He then slammed on the brakes and the hitchhiker went face first into the dashboard. Her nose exploded in a burst of dark blood, broken in an instant.

He put the car in park and got out. He reached in and dragged her out too.

"Who the fuck are you?" he demanded.

He threw her against the car and hit her in the stomach. She flopped about like a wet doll.

"You'll never believe me," she said, spitting blood.

He put his hands in her armpits and threw her up on the hood. He could actually hear her exposed flesh sizzle like an egg in a skillet when she touched it. He pushed her all the way down and realized their crotches were grinding together. It excited him and she must have felt it.

"Fuck me if you want," she said, "just don't kill me. Otherwise we'll never get out of this Hell."

He drew the pocketknife from his jeans and flicked it open.

"You stupid son of a bitch," she hissed.

He saw that her eyes had dilated further somehow, the blackness taking up more space than the whites. She bore her bloodied teeth like a mad beast, rage flushing her face.

"You moron!" she screamed, "it will never end because of you!"

She lunged at him, punching him in the eye before he got the knife in her. Even then she kicked and bucked, furious and surprisingly strong. Her madness seemed to give her the strength of a man. He snatched her by the throat and held her up, silhouetting her against the white sun as he slid the blade in and out of her in quick, hot thrusts. Jets of red splashed across his cheeks in little gore geysers. He could feel her shudder into dying. He could smell the gutting and taste the kill sweat bubbling on his upper lip. But there was no euphoria in it, hardly even a thrill. It felt filthy to him somehow, off kilter and unnatural, unlike all of the others. It was suddenly alien and repulsive, something about it feeling like a form of incest.

He let her bleed out.

Disgusted, he pushed her limp body off of him and let it fall into the sand.

The car quaked as it stalled out. In his rage he'd just left it running and now it had finally farted out one last puff of exhaust before croaking. He turned to it grimacing.

Ah, man, I am screwed.

He took his bandana out of his pocket and wiped off his knife.

He held it in the light to make sure he'd gotten all of the blood off and he caught a glimpse of himself reflected in the blade.

Only it wasn't him.

He peered closer, finally seeing what so many others had seen in his mirror image.

He had smooth features and smoother skin that was flushed in the cheeks from where the blood had sprayed. His good looks were only slightly spoiled by the crazed and frantic look in his eyes, one of which had a small bruise from where she'd hit him. His lips were fuller and his hair wasn't just longer, *it was still growing.*

He gasped and dropped the blade, turning to his bigger reflection in the windshield of the car. Breasts and curves greeted him with effeminate menace. For a moment he'd been so focused on his body that he hadn't looked at his face as much. On top of being beautiful, his new face was all too familiar. He could place it now.

He stumbled backward in crazed shock and stumbled over the hitchhiker's body.

It was now his own.

His old male face stared up at him, into him, through him.

+ + +

The road was what he stuck to, having no other destination.

His clothes were lighter now but the desert heat was wicked. That was one of the reasons he was sweating rain barrels. The other reason was the terror that boiled in his veins, for he was throttled now in the unrelenting stranglehold of insanity.

He walked on, trying not to look up at the engravings in the nearby rocks. The petroglyphs were no longer just morbid depictions of ancient bloodshed. They were fresher now, updated. Each of his own murders was depicted in stunning detail, the gruesome slayings illustrated with macabre artistry upon the crimson walls of the devil's canyon. He avoided them as if they were mirrors and waited for the stolen Dodge to appear on the horizon. When it did, he waved it down, wondering how he was going to approach things from this end.

The car slowed to a stop and he leaned down to see the driver, knowing who it would be, wishing there was some other way out.

"Get in good lookin'," his old self said, and she did.

WHAT YOU WISH FOR
Lilith Morgan

Someone had once called New York a city of strangers. Perhaps many people had. But it was true, and every one of those people . . . it was impossible to know for sure what was going on in any of their minds. Matt liked to think about what was on the minds of strangers. It was part of his work, in advertising. He wanted to predict where any set of eyes would land, and what they would want to see there. He wanted to know what people wanted. To start, there was the girl eye-fucking him on the train.

Well, eye-fucking might be a little strong. Matt had caught the girl staring at him three times on the subway ride. Every time he met her eyes she quickly blushed and looked away. He was surprised. She was gorgeous. She didn't seem like the type to be shy. She seemed more like the kind of girl who would walk over and give him her number if that was what she wanted, but then if his career had taught him anything it was that sometimes appearances could be deceiving. He could tell that she was giving him that bedroom gaze, though. She just was. She wanted him, and he wanted her too, but it was clear that nothing would happen. As much as he desired her, there was no way he could approach her without seeming like a creep, and her shyness was not encouraging. It was going to be a frustrating train ride. Suddenly, the train stopped. The passengers froze, and Matt was left in utter silence.

"Do you want her?" Matt whirled around. Sitting to his left was a man who hadn't been there before. He was dressed in a slick suit and tie, hair slicked back. He looked like he belonged in some noir film. His smile was almost too white.

"Who are you?" Matt asked. "What's going on?"

The man leaned back and nodded toward the woman across the aisle.

"Her name is Emily," he said. "Do you want her?"

"How do you know her name?" His mind was scrambling for answers. It was as if time had frozen around him, and now some mysterious figure was offering this strange woman to him. "What do you mean 'do I want her'?"

The strange man got to his feet and walked across the train to sit next to the girl he called Emily.

"She wants you too," he said, smiling. "She wants you, but she's worried about the consequences. She has a fantasy she's cycling in her head right now. She'll be running through it all night." The stranger pointed to her. Her face was flushed and one hand was pinned tightly between her knees. "See?"

There was a long moment, as Matt tried to understand what was happening.

"What are you offering me?" he asked finally.

The stranger smiled.

"I'm offering you the chance to live her sexual fantasy," he said, "consequence free."

"Consequence free," Matt repeated.

The stranger nodded. "For both of you," he said. "You'd do it outside of time. When you're done, and only then mind you, you'll both slip back into the time it was when I stopped it. Like it never happened. Are you interested?"

There was a long moment as Matt thought it over. There had to be a catch. There was always a catch. But then again . . . this was an extraordinary situation.

"You never have to see her again," the stranger crooned. "Or you can, but you'll have to hurry. The stop after next is hers."

"Alright," Matt said. If it was true, why not? Clearly something was going on.

Time had literally stopped all around him. If the supernatural wanted him to fuck this girl, then he might as well do so. He had no reason to believe it wouldn't be consequence free. "I'll do it."

The stranger smiled. In an instant, the train was empty except for Matt, Emily, and the stranger. Emily blinked.

"Who . . ." she gasped. "What's going on?"

"Good afternoon, Emily," said the stranger. "Matt here has offered to let you live your greatest sexual fantasy." Her eyes widened, but she did not look happy, she looked frightened. "Consequence free."

"What do you mean by that?" she gasped. She turned to Matt. "Did he tell you—"

"I didn't tell him anything," the stranger cooed. He put an arm around Emily and a hand in his pocket. "That's your job. That's part of it, isn't it? Telling him?"

Matt was watching this exchange in confusion. Why was she so upset? If she really did have a fantasy that she was dwelling on so steadfastly, why wouldn't she jump at the opportunity to play it out? But it seemed as if she weren't jumping. She seemed terrified.

"What if I say no?" she said softly.

The stranger smiled. "As I already told him, I'll only put you back into time once you two are done," he said softly. "You can take as long as you want, but you have to do it, or stay here indefinitely."

Emily closed her eyes and took a deep breath.

"What's wrong?" Matt asked. Emily looked at him, seemingly unable to speak.

"Here's something for you," the stranger said smoothly, handing her a small box. "And I'll leave you two alone."

His last word was still ringing when he was gone, and Matt was left with only Emily and the little box on her lap. She looked close to tears.

"Hey, it's okay," Matt said softly. She looked up and met his eyes. "You don't have to worry. Consequence free, remember? We can go back to reality and pretend it never happened."

"I don't want—" She broke off, her voice cracking under the strain of anxiety. A tear trailed down her cheek.

"You don't like me," he said, more a statement than a question. He knew there had to be some catch to the offer. That was it. Good for him, bad for her.

"No!" Emily gasped. "No, that's not it at all. You're perfect, I just . . ." She stopped, chose her words carefully. "You won't like it very much."

Matt arched an eyebrow. "Won't I?" he asked, trying his best to appear politely flirtatious. "I'm the one who asked for it, didn't I?"

Emily nodded, a wry smile touching her face. "You didn't know what you were asking for," she said.

Matt got to his feet and walked to the other side of the train. Sitting next to her, he spoke calmly. "Whatever you're worried about, don't," he said. "I won't judge you, whatever your fantasy is. Trust me, I'm pretty open-minded."

Emily looked at him. Her face was serious, intense, a little frighteningly so. "There's something wrong," she said. "Something got fucked up in my wiring, Matt. I don't have regular sexual fantasies." Matt shook his head.

"What do you mean by that?" he asked. "You can tell me, it's okay." She moved down the bench away from him, then opened the box and placed its contents on the seat between them. Two zip ties and a scalpel. Matt just stared.

"I wasn't thinking about sex," she said. "When I looked at you, I thought about murder."

"Whoa, whoa, hold on," Matt said, getting up. "Hold the fucking phone. Do you mean to tell me you kill people?"

Emily's head snapped up. "No! Never!" she gasped. "Never, I just . . . think about it. I never killed anyone. I never will." A guilty look. "I never would have."

Matt's mind was racing. He had royally fucked up. Why hadn't he thought to ask the stranger what her fantasy was? Because she was a slender, pretty girl. Girls weren't supposed to be homicidal. They weren't even supposed to be aggressive! But obviously, this one was. There it was. Appearances could be deceiving.

"So you think," he began. "That cutting people is sexy?"

Emily nodded, face red with embarrassment. "I hate it," she said. "I wish I wasn't that way, but I am. I deal with it. I watch horror movies. I look at people with beautiful bodies in public places." She shook her head. "I hate it when they look back. I feel like shit."

Matt was shaking his head.

"You can't do this," he said.

Emily was calming down, but still visibly upset. "I think I have to," she said. "If we ever want to leave this train."

There was a long silence then, stretching on for several minutes. The girl was right. Matt had set himself up for this. But consequence free, for both of them. So he would survive his murder. But still, he had to be murdered. He sat down on the opposite bench again, running his fingers through his hair. Emily was sitting quietly, staring at her knees. This slender, delicate thing had been sitting across from him on the train, thinking about cutting him.

"How?" he said softly. "How do you want to do it?"

Emily looked up. "I, uh," she began. Her face was a deep crimson. Was it embarrassment only? Or . . . "I was thinking about how you have a perfect . . . stomach . . ." She swallowed hard. "I'm sorry. I'm so sorry." Matt swallowed hard.

"You want to cut my stomach?" he asked.

"I don't want you to suffer," she said.

"But you think cutting me open is sexy," he retorted.

Emily nodded, beginning to sob again. "I don't want to hurt you!" she cried. "I don't. I swear to God I don't, but I think . . . if I did . . . it would . . ." She trailed off.

Matt finally understood. "It would turn you on anyway?" he asked. Emily slowly nodded. "That's fucked."

"I know," she said. "I hate myself a lot of the time."

Matt took a deep breath. He was going to be murdered. He was going to be murdered, but then wake up as if it never happened. He was going to suffer, but at the same time he would fulfill this woman's impossible sexual fantasy. He slowly nodded.

"Okay," he said. "Okay, let's do it."

Emily looked at him in shock. "What?" she asked.

"Go ahead," he said. "Kill me."

Emily was squirming in her chair. This time, though, there was something in her eyes other than discomfort. "Are you sure?" she asked him. He nodded.

"It's not gonna count in the real world, right?" he asked. "And it's the only way we ever get out of this train car."

There was a moment of pause, then Emily spoke. "It's going to hurt," she said. "A lot."

Matt felt a knot of fear forming in his chest. He nodded again. "I know," he replied, voice shaking. "I did a stupid thing, made a stupid wish, and you shouldn't beat yourself up over it." Emily's knuckles were white, fists clenched in her lap. Matt's heart was pounding. It was the only way they could get out of the train car, it was true, but still it terrified him. She was right, it would hurt. A lot. But he had to endure it, or be trapped there indefinitely.

"I'm sorry," she said.

"It'll be okay," he said, to himself as much as to her. "It'll be over, and then it'll be like it never happened." He forced a smile. "Consequence free." Her eyes were wide and her breathing was quick. It was clear that she was intensely excited, and that left Matt simultaneously aroused and terrified. She was going to cut him, kill him, and that knowledge turned her on. She got shakily to her feet and walked over to him, sitting beside him, the scalpel and plastic ties left behind. Her hands remained awkwardly on her knees.

"Can I . . ." she began, then faltered. "Is it alright if I touch you?"

"I'm all yours," he said.

Emily took a deep breath, then reached out toward him. She gently touched his chest with her fragile fingers, tracing lines from his chest to his stomach. His breathing was quick, nervous. Her fingers hovered at the top button of his shirt. "Is it okay?"

He nodded, and she began to unbutton his shirt, exposing his bare torso to the empty subway. Matt closed his eyes and let himself feel the gentle touch of her fingertips as she explored him. She spent a lot of time touching and caressing his stomach. The places she would cut. His eyes opened with a gasp and she drew back. "I'm sorry," she said, almost an automatic response. Matt was shaking his head. He was terrified, but it was necessary.

"Maybe . . ." He swallowed hard. "I don't think I can do this, Emily. Maybe you better tie me up."

"Okay," she said. "Okay."

With a sudden and unfathomable need to comfort, Matt reached out and touched her face.

She turned aside, biting her lip. "You can if you want. It's only fair."

Matt drew back. "What are you talking about?"

Emily was having trouble meeting his eyes. "If you want to fuck me, you can," she said. "Before I tie you up."

Matt stared at her in surprise. Since the revelation of her actual fantasy, he had been too anxious to give sex a second thought. Did he want her still, even knowing what she really wanted from him? His body gave him a resounding affirmative answer to that question. He nodded.

"Okay," she said softly. Her hands were moving slightly, as if unsure of where to settle themselves. There was a long pause. "Tell me what to do."

"What?" Matt asked, startled by her soft plea.

Emily couldn't meet his eyes. "I don't know what to do," she said. "I've never . . . you know."

"You're a virgin?" he asked, trying not to let too much of the shock he was feeling bleed into his voice.

Emily stared intently at her knees. "I was never really interested in sex," she said. "Per se."

Suddenly, everything was crystal clear. To this girl, death was sex. Intercourse had never mattered to her. Sex was not a turn on at all. He entertained a thought of guilt, but then he realized the other half of the circumstance. Murder was not a turn on for him, it was the worst thing that he could imagine. It was only fair.

"Take your clothes off," he said softly. Shaking, Emily got to her feet and began to undress. She was beautiful, her plain undergarments adding to her overall innocent charm. She hesitated briefly before unhooking her bra and letting it fall to the floor, followed by her underpants. There she stood, naked, in all her perfection. This was what he had wanted. He got to his feet and removed his jacket, spreading it out on the floor. Then, he simply pointed. Emily's teeth were chattering, with some combination of cold and nerves. She settled on her back on his jacket, hands folded self-consciously over her stomach. Matt got onto his knees, reached out, and gently parted her legs.

"Do I have to look?" Emily asked, her voice weak.

Matt thought for a moment, then shook his head. "You don't have to look if you don't want to," he said.

Emily closed her eyes and bit her lip, clearly trying to relax and failing utterly. Matt was struggling with his empathic instincts. He wanted her so badly, but he didn't want her scared. As much as it suited his sense of justice, or fairness or whatever he chose to call it, to just fuck her, there was no chance that he could do so unless she was in the state where he wanted her. That state was one of pleasure. Her fear did nothing for him. Matt breathed deeply and began to caress her legs gently. Emily's hands were balled into tight fists and pressed into her stomach.

"I'm going to make it nice," he attempted, then shook his head. The phrase was lame at best.

"You don't have to make it nice." Her response was immediate, and not what he had been expecting. Matt moved closer to her and took her hands from her stomach, unfolding them carefully.

"I want to," he said. He traced his fingers over her arms gently. Her breathing was growing deeper, but her eyes remained shut.

"Why do you want that?" she asked. "I can't do you the same favor."

Matt felt a chill at that remark, but didn't let it show. He stopped what he was doing and took her hands. "Look at me." She slowly opened her eyes. They were a stunning shade of green. "I know you want me to hurt you so you'll feel better about yourself or whatever, but I'm not like you. I can't get it up unless you're enjoying yourself." Emily's mouth opened in shock, her face turning bright red again. "So let me make it nice." She closed her mouth, lip trembling. "It's what I want. Then you can do what you want."

"I'm sorry," Emily whispered. Matt shook his head and moved his hand from hers, placing it instead on her stomach, pressing gently with his fingertips. She closed her eyes again. Carefully, he leaned over her, kissing her neck. That got a moan out of her. He moved in a little harder, nibbling a little, licking a little, until he found something he thought she liked. Then, he raised his head slightly and spoke into her ear.

"Where do you want me to touch you?" he asked. Emily shook her head.

"I don't know," she whispered. Matt slid his hands over her shoulders and onto her breasts. She gasped. Her hands moved as if to stop him, but then she forced herself down again.

"You don't like that?" he asked.

"I do," she said. "I do." He resumed what he was doing, slowly building her pleasure, and building himself up at the same time. Her eyes were still clamped tightly shut, but her hands were now open, fingers digging into his jacket sleeves. He decided to make the leap. Keeping one hand on her right breast, he pressed his mouth to the left one and slid his right hand between her thighs. "Oh!" she gasped, shock in her voice.

"Okay?" Matt asked, petting her gently.

"Yeah," she said. There were tears trickling down her cheeks. Matt slowly began probing with one finger.

"What's wrong?" he asked.

Emily just shook her head. "I don't deserve this," she whimpered.

"Deserve what?" he asked.

"I don't deserve for it to be nice."

Matt took a deep breath and let it out, blowing on her already damp nipple. She shivered.

"Do you really want it to hurt?" he asked.

Emily was nodding before he had finished his sentence. "It's what I deserve," she said.

Matt's right hand remained between her legs and his left moved to open his fly. "Okay," he said. "Okay." He lined himself up, then hesitated. He understood what she wanted and why, but it just wasn't in him to hurt her, even if it was outside of reality. He moved slowly and carefully, checking her responses, until finally, he had managed to get there. "Are you okay?" he asked when he was finally inside her.

Emily groaned in frustration and wrapped her legs around him, hands reaching up and clasping at his arms. "Stop being so nice to me!" she screeched. "Stop it!" Slowly at first, then with building intensity, he began to thrust into her. Her cries fell silent, changing to soft, shallow breathing. Her legs were still clinging to him, but her hands began to move over his shoulders and onto his chest, around his waist and to his back, pulling him closer. His entire body pressed against hers, he could feel her heartbeat, hear her breathing. He froze as he finished and Emily sighed, fingers still digging into his shoulder blades. When he had recovered, he pulled out and sat up. He was still breathing hard as he cleaned himself with his already soiled jacket and tucked himself back into his pants. Emily was sitting up as well. She looked embarrassed, her arms crossed over her breasts.

"Are you alright?" Matt asked quietly. Emily nodded. She reached up and brushed back her hair.

"Was that okay?" she asked. Matt very nearly laughed.

"Beautiful," he said. "You're beautiful." She gave a small and diluted smile, but said nothing. Her eyes turned back down toward her knees. It wasn't too long before the afterglow faded enough that Matt was able to remember why. They weren't done. He still had to die. Slowly, he got to his feet and extended a hand toward Emily. She looked at it, but didn't take it.

"I don't know if I can do this," she said.

"We're stuck here if you don't," he countered. "Hey look, just do one thing for me, okay?"

She nodded and got to her feet without his help. "Yes?"

Matt tried his best to smile. "Don't get dressed?"

Emily stared at him for a moment, then laughed. "I won't," she said. "Get your fill." He laughed and sat down on the bench again, trying not to feel the fear that was building inside of him. He tried to tell himself that it wasn't real, but the more he thought about it the more panicked he became. Emily saw it on his face. She did not walk to the other side of the train, instead staying where she was, standing on his jacket. "Do you still want me to tie you up?" she asked softly.

"I . . ." Matt trailed off, staring at the scalpel, glinting, across the subway car. "I think maybe you have to." Emily nodded and went for the zip ties. She left the scalpel on the opposite bench. She sat next to him. He was squirming inside of his own skin. She was about to cut him. She had to. "What do you want me to do?" he asked. Emily shook her head.

"Get comfortable," she said. "With your hands behind your back and toward the bars."

"You've really thought this out, huh?" He tried to laugh, but it sounded false and strained.

"You do a lot of thinking when you're like me."

Matt did as she said, placing his wrists against the lowest bar. He could feel his heart starting to race. Emily went behind him and bound his wrists to the bars.

"Emily?" he asked. She walked around in front of him.

"Yes?"

He tugged against the ties to make sure that they were tight, then took a deep breath and spoke again. "Look," he said. "I know you're freaked out right now, and I'm freaked out too, but please try to enjoy this." Emily's eyes widened, but she said nothing. Matt continued. "I don't mean hurt me more than you have to, I don't really want that, but I'm pretty sure this is your only chance to live this fantasy. Don't kill me for nothing, okay? I'm not going to judge you if you let yourself like it." Emily looked like she might cry again.

"I'm so sorry," she said. "I'm really sorry." He nodded. She went to get the scalpel. Matt was trying not to start screaming. That would probably just spook her. He couldn't spook her if he wanted to get out of this train car. He closed his eyes and listened to her as she slowly walked back and sat down beside him on the bench. There was a long moment of silence. Relative silence. There was the soft clicking as Emily uncapped and capped the scalpel.

"Emily?" he asked.

"Yes?"

Matt opened his eyes. The knife was clutched in her hand, capped. "I . . ." He trailed off, shifting uncomfortably. His stomach felt too exposed and his arms were straining to escape their prison.

"I know," she said. She uncapped the scalpel and started to touch his stomach with her free hand. Matt was starting to feel lightheaded. She moved the scalpel closer.

"Wait, wait, wait!" he said. Emily stopped. "Wait just a minute. Please wait?" Emily took the knife back and waited. "I'm sorry. I just . . ."

"If you keep stopping me," Emily said. "We're going to be here forever."

Matt was breathing hard. "I know," he said. "I know, but I can't help it."

Emily thought this over for a moment, then spoke again. "I'm going to stop listening to what you say now, okay?" she said. "So say whatever you want."

Matt gaped at her. "What do you mean?" She was reaching toward him with the scalpel. "No, wait please!" Emily shook her head. She touched the blade to his stomach.

"I'm gonna press hard," she said. "I don't want to have to do it again."

"Oh my God oh my God," Matt was panicking. She took the blade off briefly to change her position so that she was sitting on his legs, trapping him. He bit his lip and whimpered. Emily pressed the blade hard against his stomach. It went in easily, but the pain was worse than any that Matt had ever experienced. He wanted to scream, but it went beyond even that. He looked up into Emily's face. She was staring at the wound in his stomach with an incredible mix of emotions in her eyes. She grabbed his side with her empty hand and began to drag the scalpel across his stomach, cutting a perfect slit from one end of his abdomen to the other. "Ahhhhhhh . . . nnno," he moaned. He still couldn't muster a scream. His every breath was agony. Emily pulled out the knife and tossed it aside. It clattered across the floor of the train car. Matt's head slumped forward and he watched as blood oozed out of his open stomach. He gave an anguished groan. She'd cut him, sliced his belly all the way across. Why wasn't he dead?

"This might take a little bit," she said. Her voice was apologetic, but overshadowed with fascination. "Stomach wounds . . . they don't bleed like other places." Her fingers delicately touched the wound. "Can I?" As her fingers toyed with the gash he realized what she wanted.

He swallowed hard, barely managing to find words around his pain. "Yes," he gasped. Emily's lips parted and she wrapped her arm around his neck, kissing him hard. While his focus was there, her fingers entered his abdomen. "Aaahhhhh!" Matt turned his head away from her mouth, burying his face in her shoulder. She held his head with her arm.

"Don't look," she said. Her voice sounded ecstatic. "You don't want to see this."

Matt didn't need to see. He could feel her fingers weaving around inside of him. He felt their grip in places he had never actively felt anything before. She was exploring his insides, and she was more turned on than he had ever seen any woman in his life. Suddenly, a new sensation.

"Ohhhhhh . . ." he moaned, digging his face harder into her shoulder. She was pulling them out. She was pulling his intestines out. He could feel it. He was awash with pain and nausea the likes of which he had never experienced before. She pulled them away from their proper place and pressed them against her skin, letting the blood touch her breasts, her stomach, her sex. He gagged, spitting a mouthful of blood onto her shoulder. "Em," he breathed. She leaned back and looked at him, something glowing in her eyes. As soon as she locked eyes with Matt, the glow faded and her face filled with horror. She turned over her shoulder, then gasped.

"Matt," she hissed. "The knife is gone. I'm sorry." Matt was sobbing, shoulders lurching. Her eyes flickered with guilt, landing on resolution. "I'm so sorry for this." Before he had time to react, Emily had forced her hand inside of him again, tearing out more of his insides and piling them onto his lap. He screamed horribly, but the next time she reached, it was with both hands. He could feel the destruction that she was causing both in and out of his body. He could feel her tearing out his internal organs with two fists. He could feel himself getting lightheaded. Her right arm jammed inside him to the elbow. He felt the air forced out of his body. He felt incredible strength and suffering pooling in his chest. Suddenly, a crushing pain that seemed to engulf him, black spots in front of his eyes, Emily's gasp of pleasure . . .

"This is Fourteenth Street, Union Square," a mechanical voice said. "The next stop is Astor Place." Shaking, Matt drew one unbound hand to his perfectly intact stomach. He closed his eyes and sighed. When he opened them, they met with those of Emily. Dressed, but pale and close to tears. She got to her feet and walked to him, leaning over as if to read the subway map.

"I'm so sorry," she whispered. Matt nodded. Then, he handed her his business card.

"This is Astor Place," the robotic voice said. Emily got off of the train. Matt watched her go, a strange sense of wonder overcoming him. He was alive. They were both alive, and they were both forever changed. She had acted on a fantasy she had thought impossible, and he had seen something in her that she had thought no one could see. There was incredible beauty in the danger of her, not just in spite of the risk but because of it. He had given her the means to contact him because of the look on her face when she had seen inside of him for the first time. He knew, however, that she would never do it. She was too powerfully shy, too ashamed. She wouldn't throw his card away, no, she would hold onto that forever. But she would never use it.

It was just over a week later that he was proven wrong. He was out of the office, at lunch, when the phone rang. It was a number he didn't recognize, and came up as Denver, Colorado. Matt didn't know anyone in the entire state, but his curiosity got the better of him. Still, he waited until the third ring to answer.

"Hello," he said. It was not his usual phone greeting, but it would have to do. He somewhat disliked the idea of giving his name to strangers who called his cell. There was a long pause. He could only just hear breathing on the other end of the line. "Hello, can I help you?"

"Matt?"

His heart leapt into his throat, but he tried to keep his voice steady. "Emily?" he asked.

"Yeah," she replied. "Sorry, I didn't know what to say when I called so I didn't call."

Matt switched ears. "Are you in Denver?"

Emily laughed. "I never got a new cell number when I moved here for college," she said. She sounded so calm on the phone, so even. Matt felt like he might explode at any moment.

"Oh, when was that?" he asked.

"About three years ago," she replied. Matt cringed. He had a good eight years on her, at least. "Matt, I just wanted to say again how sorry I am. I never would have—"

"I know." Matt ran his fingers through his hair and checked his watch. Only ten minutes before he had to be back. "It was my fault, really."

"You could never have known—"

"I'm an ad man," he grunted. "It's my job to know." At this, Emily laughed.

"Okay, ad man," she said. "What am I thinking now?"

He decided to take a risk. "You're thinking dinner," he said. "Tonight." The phone picked up the smallest hitch of breath on her end of the line.

"You're good," she sighed. "Six o clock?"

"I can make that," Matt said. Truth was, even if she had asked him to be there in ten minutes he would have found a way to make it work. Although he couldn't understand why, he was desperate to see her again. They decided on a place and hung up, Matt feeling like he'd won something. Something infinitely valuable and just as dangerous. Five hours until he saw her again, the woman who had killed him.

Five minutes until he saw her again. Matt approached their agreed upon meeting place with a slow and meaningful stride. There was still something of worry in him. He knew in his heart that she was not dangerous, not now, but she had killed him only a week before. Brutally. And liked it. True, they had known that none of it mattered in the real world, but somehow it mattered anyway. They both knew what it would be like now . . . the murder. He wondered if it had sated or ignited her need.

When he walked into the cafe, he saw her immediately. She was sitting in a corner booth, dressed as a high schooler might dress for a date. Modest, a lavender dress and white cardigan. A hardcover book was open on the table in front of her and she seemed lost in it. There was something so beautiful about her when she was relaxed, her features calm and smooth, but engaged. What would it be like to glance up from his own reading at home and see that on the couch next to him? He shook the thought out of his mind with a twitch of his head.

"Emily," he said. She jerked to attention.

"Matt!" she said. "I . . . I thought you might not come." She snapped the book shut and stuffed it into her backpack, which was resting under the table, but not before Matt got a look at the title. *Misery*. Fitting. He had seen the movie and it made his skin crawl just thinking about it. Kathy Bates with her hammer. That was the kind of thing that turned this girl on.

"Why did you think that?" He sat down and opened his menu, but didn't look at it. He had chosen this place because he already knew his order. Less to think about. If he felt up to eating anything at all.

Emily just shrugged. "I guess . . . I don't know." Matt took a sip of his water and waited. "I killed you."

"I'm still here," he replied.

"But why?" she asked. "If I were you, I'd have run for the hills. I don't even understand why you gave me your card." Matt opened his mouth, but the waiter had made a silent approach during her last sentence.

"Can I get you two started off with something to drink?" he asked. Matt turned his face to the menu, but Emily looked up.

"I'm fine with . . ." She trailed off. It was a long moment before Matt looked up, but when he did he saw that her eyes were still on the waiter. Her mouth was still open. He glanced up and immediately saw why.

Standing alongside their table was the man from the train. He was still wearing his suit, a white apron the only addition. In his hand he held the same small box that had held the ties and the blade. Out of the corner of his eye, Matt saw Emily's hand reach up to cover her mouth.

"I'm sorry," the stranger said, a sly smile on his impeccable face. "Did you two need a few minutes to decide?"

"I don't think we do," Matt said, surprising himself. The world around them had gone uncomfortably silent. He didn't look, but he felt sure that if he did he would find them alone in the restaurant with this man.

"No we don't," she snapped. When she spoke again, her words overlapped with his. "Please leave us alone."

"We'll do it," Matt said. Emily gaped.

"What?" she screeched. "He can't make us do that again. He can't make *you* do that again!" Matt swallowed hard. His mouth was dry, but he felt oddly calm.

"No one is making me do anything," he said. He reached out and took the hand that was still resting on the table. "It's what you want, isn't it?" She was shaking her head before he had even finished the sentence.

"I don't want to hurt you," she said. "I told you that."

"But what if I wasn't real?" he asked. "If I didn't matter? If I was just an illusion?" Emily was chewing her lip. "You'd do it, wouldn't you?" She extracted her hand from his and smudged out a tear as it began its journey down her cheek. Then she reached for him again. His thumb traced a little circle on the back of her hand. "Would you do it, Emily? If I wasn't real?"

"Yes," she choked. "Fuck. Yes I would. I'm sorry." Matt chanced a look at the stranger standing tableside. His hand, with the box, was still extended and there was an amused look in his eyes. "I don't want to hurt you."

"You just . . ." Matt trailed off. He didn't want her to hurt him either. Not really. But how could he express what he did want? Why he would let her hurt him a million times over? "You have no idea how beautiful you look when you see blood, do you?" She looked at him as though his words had thrown the floodlights on in front of her eyes. Her breathing was quick and shallow, with either arousal or panic. She wanted it as much as he did. More than he did. He had only to convince her that he wanted it at all.

"Which is it then?" the strange man asked. "Will you or won't you?"

"Can you please give us a minute?" Matt asked.

The man smirked. "Look, Matt," he retorted, his voice dripping with oil. "I'm on your side, and hers."

"You're not on my side." Emily was close to tears again.

The man turned to her. "Is there any other way you could have gotten what you wanted?"

Tears were flowing freely down her face. "I. Don't. Want it!" The tablecloth slid an inch or two toward her. She was grasping it under the table with her free hand. Matt gave the other one a squeeze.

"Nobody thinks you're evil," he said. "Least of all me." Her eyes locked onto his. There was something of ice in them, glossy and frozen.

"I think I'm evil, Matt," she said. "I think that every day." For some reason, he felt chastened. Who was he, really, to come into her life and blindly pardon a lifetime of her perceived sins? He was no one. He was a stranger to her, and her struggle was alien to him. Certainly, he was willing to go through it, but there was no guilt in it for him. It was not something that had kept him up nights since he had hit puberty. Not something he had watched on film and touched himself, fearing that someone might walk in at any moment. This was not his difficulty, as difficult as that was for him to admit. This was hers.

"That must be so hard for you," he whispered. "I'm sorry." She lifted her napkin and dabbed at her nose. Her mascara was running and she was still exquisite. "But I meant what I said. I want you to do it. I want you to take that box and use whatever is inside of it. I want you to let yourself be the person you're afraid of becoming, just for a few minutes, huh? Do you think you can do that? Don't you want to give it a try?"

Eyes never leaving his, Emily reached out and took the box. Matt turned to dismiss the stranger, but he was already gone. "Thank you."

"No," she said, pressing her lips to the back of his hand. "Thank you." He nodded and caressed her cheek.

"Just remember," he said. "None of this is real." She nodded and opened the box. She gazed into it, her face revealing nothing. Then she looked up at him again. Something had changed in her eyes. There was something behind them that he had never seen before, some snarling and smoldering hunger. Slowly, she got to her feet. She took the box in her right hand and, using only her left, turned the table on its side. Matt choked out a gasp. Glass shattered and their bread bowl scattered its contents across the empty tiles. Out of the box, she drew an impossibly large hunting knife. The blade itself had to be at least ten inches. How had that fit inside such a small box? But then, wasn't he asking that question from somewhere outside of time?

Her heels were crunching on broken glass as she walked toward him, kicking silverware out of her way. The box was cast aside and the knife was raised. In a blink she was at his throat, her fingers closing around his tie. She pressed the hilt of the knife into his side, hard, then kissed him harder. Her tongue darted into his mouth and then snapped back as she closed her teeth around his lower lip, making him moan. The pressure on his lip increased to painful levels and his moan rose in pitch. When she pulled back, there was blood on her chin. His blood. He could feel his breath hitching, catching, coming in panting waves. He could feel the pressure of the knife handle still against his skin and, strangest of all, he could feel his slacks tightening between his legs. It wasn't the pain, he had no interest in being hurt, it was something that he saw in her when she hurt him. Something sensually exquisite and miraculous. He didn't want her to hurt him, but she was so beautiful when she did it.

"What are you smiling about?" The knife dug in harder and he gasped. "What's so funny? Don't you know you're about to die?"

"I wasn't smiling," he murmured. Her hand moved from his tie to his throat.

"What was that?"

"I wasn't smiling!" His voice was shrill, panicked. Matt didn't like the way he sounded, but evidently Emily did. He could feel her body squirming against his. He reached for her, but she twitched out of his way.

"Don't touch me," she said. His hands fell to his sides. "Get on the ground."

"The glass—" he started. Her palm had connected with his face before he had registered her releasing his neck.

"The glass is the least of your worries," she said. "Get on the fucking ground. Now." With panic rising like bile in his throat, he did as she said, falling to his knees at her feet. He could feel several pieces of his bread plate digging into his shins, but he didn't want to make any sudden movements. Her face was set, determination in the hard line of her jaw. The knife was glinting in her hand, her knuckles white where she clutched it. Her empty right hand shoved his left shoulder and he reeled back, arm shooting out behind him to stop his fall. A sliver of glass dug into his palm and he let out a hiss of pain. She didn't stop, forcing him onto his back, straddling him just below the waist. When he reached for her, he found his hands crushed beneath her knees.

"Aah," he yelped. Her every movement was pressing him into the broken glass on the tile floor. It couldn't have been comfortable for her either, but she seemed too lost in it to care. Her knife settled on his throat and she watched him, waiting. What was she waiting for? He swallowed hard, feeling the minute change in pressure as his Adam's apple bobbed against the blade.

"Tell me what you're thinking," she said.

"I'm scared," he replied. The words came out of his mouth without a second thought, and they were the correct ones. He could tell by the light in her eyes, the way she was rubbing up against him, pleasuring herself on the fabric of his pants. How he wished she would take just a moment to unbuckle his belt, take down his fly and . . .

"I could do anything I want to you," she was saying. "Anything. I could fuck you, or I could kill you. I could do neither. I could do both at the same time. What do you think of that? I could hold the knife against my body or tuck it into my belt and every time you sink into me I sink into you." Matt suppressed a shudder. He wanted to give her what she needed, but everything he gave away was another clue she could use against him. "Do you like that idea, Matt?" He was already shaking his head.

"Please, I—Aah!" She had lifted herself up onto her knees, bones digging into bones, glass digging into flesh. Her skirt was up and over her head, cast across the room. Her shirt and cardigan and belt stayed on. Matt noted briefly that he thought she had been wearing a dress, then he saw her take the knife and slice off her panties. It was then he realized that even under all of this duress, his cock was still standing at attention, extending desperately toward what he feared he would soon have at a terrible cost. With the underpants gone, she turned the blade toward him.

Matt tried his best to breathe through his nose. Deep, calming breaths. But this woman was about to literally fuck him to death. Certainly, as he had said, none of it was real, but it was really going to hurt. The handle of the knife slipped upward, between the belt she wore and her skin. It extended a solid four or five inches down between her legs. Once her hands were free, one rested on his chest and the other began to unbuckle his belt.

"Don't," he gasped. She had finished the belt and was moving on to his fly. Never had he been so thankful for the hindrance caused by a button fly.

"You don't want me to fuck you, Matt?" she asked. His cock was in her hand now, the only part of him that was grateful for her touch.

"Not like this," he said. He didn't regret his choice, not exactly, but he didn't expect it to go the way it was going. He expected her sensual beauty, the incredible, lustful way she looked at him when he was bleeding out, but he did not expect her to turn so cold. She was still far from ugly, but he was beginning to see a bit of what it was she saw in herself. The hand that was on his chest lifted to his face and caressed it, a blackened mirror of his earlier gesture.

"This is the best you get," she said. His entire body lurched. He felt as if he was about to experience the first and highest drop on a roller coaster too large to exist. She guided him toward her opening and sank down on top of him.

As the blade of the knife plunged into his body, the agony was too great for sound. He watched, open-mouthed and silent, as she lifted herself and followed the first thrust with a second, equally powerful one. She had come, loudly, by the conclusion of the second thrust. He had gone flaccid by the third. She abandoned her attempts at intercourse, but left the knife where it was, twisting it in the wound as she leaned her body toward his face.

"Had enough?" There was nothing of malice in her voice. It was an honest question. Matt nodded and then winced as she sat back up, withdrawing the knife from both her belt and his body. She draped herself over him, inching her knees off of his hands. With some hesitation, he wrapped his arms around her.

"Emily please," the words came out bloody, bubbling up from somewhere deep and destroyed. The knife, already coated generously with his blood, traced across his throat. There was a great and terrible rushing in his body as his own unfaithful pulse carried the lifeblood out of his veins. He could see Emily, her face covered in a spray of it, leaning in to kiss his dying lips.

"Hi there, my name is Krissi and I'll be taking care of you today," a chipper voice shattered them awake. "Can I get either of you started with something to drink?"

It was over. Christ, it was over.

"I think we may need a minute," Emily said. Matt looked up at her. She was pale. He could only imagine what he must look like.

"Okay," Krissi was saying. "Just give me a holler if you need anything at all!" As she skipped away, Matt looked up at Emily. Her blanch had turned to a flush.

"Emily . . ." he started, but wasn't able to finish. He didn't know what to say to her. He didn't know what he felt anymore.

"You've met her now," she said. "What do you think?"

"Her?" he asked. It was all he could think of to say. He couldn't bring himself to admit that maybe, in spite of all of the pain and suffering he had endured, he had liked what he had seen.

"The girl I don't want to be," she said. Matt nodded. He reached for his water glass, but did not lift it. Moments ago fragments of it had been opening his palms. "When I was in high school, I gave her a name. I named her Wesley Rose, after Rose West . . . some serial killer I read about." Emily was carefully studying her hands, watching as she picked at her cuticles. It was all Matt could do not to grab them, make them hold still. And, in doing so, touch her skin again. "I guess I sort of tried to dissociate from her? Like, I wanted to make myself believe that I was a split personality or something. Sharing my body with a serial killer. Like I was some kind of hero for keeping her locked up."

"You're a hero for keeping her in check," Matt said. "But you don't have to keep her locked up."

Emily looked at him as if he had sprouted horns. "You mean if that man comes back?" Matt shook his head. "I don't understand."

"What I mean is . . ." He trailed off. What did he mean? He didn't mean that he wanted her to become this other woman, not even on a temporary basis. "Would you like to come over for a drink?"

"Yes," she sighed. There was gratitude in her voice. "I can't help feeling like someone's listening here, you know?"

"Believe me," he said. "I know." Matt glanced around, then reached into his pocket and fished out a couple of dollars. "Let's go." As they walked out of the restaurant, Matt took a moment to observe the people sitting at tables around them. No, it was reasonably certain that there was nobody listening to them. This was New York City. Center of the universe containing eight million more centers of the universe. There was not a single person in the area with a concern greater than his or hers. And yet . . . all it takes is one eavesdropper.

Matt lived three blocks away from the cafe they had chosen, but he wouldn't admit to having done that on purpose unless pressed. She had been the one to suggest Italian food. It was a nice building, but not overwhelmingly nice. Simple, with a doorman. Not too far from where he worked either. He rarely took the trains. Frankly, it was pure chance that he had run into her on the subway when he had. He had had a meeting on the upper East side that day. He wondered briefly if it had been predestined somehow. But that was ridiculous. He hadn't known himself he would respond to her the way he had, how could anyone else? But then, how had they stopped time?

Or, the real question, why?

They got off the elevator on the sixth floor and walked to his apartment. It was a true one-bedroom, which Emily noted the moment they walked in. It was nice. Clean. He had no maid service, but tried to keep it reasonably well maintained. He had scoured it the evening he had met Emily, though, in the vain hope that she might call him and come by. It seemed silly, impossible, but here she was. The first woman he had had over in almost a year, and he'd had to let her kill him twice to get her there.

"I'm glad we came here," Emily was saying. "I've got three suitemates and they all think the reason I don't date is because I'm a closet lesbian. I'd sort of like to keep the answer that simple."

Matt snorted. "Is this a date?" Emily said nothing, just sat down on his couch, perched on the edge of the cushion like she might fly away if given the chance. "I see." He walked to the kitchen and opened the fridge. "I've got beer and I've got whisky. I might also have some vodka in the freezer if—"

"Beer is good," Emily said. "I mean, I don't really drink, but I think if there was ever a time to start . . ." He pulled two bottles out of the fridge and set them on the counter, beginning his usual search for his bottle opener. The thing had feet. It never stayed in one place.

"How old are you, anyway?" he asked. He didn't want to know, not really, but the question had come and it was too late to take it back.

"Twenty," she said. He licked his lips. "You?"

"Twenty nine," he replied. The bottle opener was where it was supposed to be for a change. The bottles were opened and Matt made his way to the girl on the sofa. "Sorry it wasn't someone closer to your age."

"Matt," she said, accepting the beer he offered her. "If it had been anyone else, he and I would still be on the train." At this, Matt couldn't help but laugh, but she only gave a watery smile. She was right. He knew she was. Perhaps not *anybody* else, but the chances of her being paired with someone willing to die for her were slim. If the pairing was accidental.

"Do you do this often?" he asked. "I mean, stare at people on trains?"

Emily shrugged, then nodded. "I try not to, but sometimes . . ."

Matt took a long pull of his beer. "Maybe he's been waiting for someone like me," he said. "Maybe the guy knew I'd be . . . I dunno. Whatever it is I am."

"How would he know?" she asked.

"How would he do any of whatever he does?" Matt replied.

"So what are you then?" Emily was peeling the label off of her drink, but not drinking it. Matt glanced at the ABV and wished it was higher.

"I'm not sure," he sighed. "I don't have a death wish. I'm not even a masochist." At this, Emily took her first swallow of beer. She winced. "Okay?"

"I'm not used to it," she said. Matt nodded. She was a kid. Not even old enough to drink. He was giving booze to an underage girl. "If it's not masochism, what is it?"

"I think it's you," Matt said. Emily choked on her second sip.

"Me?" she asked, wiping a dribble of foam off her lower lip. She used her wrist, then glanced at it like there might be something there other than a little liquid and a slight smear of pink from her lipstick. The leak made her lips shine. "What do you mean it's me?"

"It's hard to explain to someone who's never seen it," he said. "I mean, I know you can't see it. But when you're that . . . um . . . on . . . it's just . . . I mean, you're beautiful." Her face was flushing and her eyes were on her wrist, which was in her lap. She carefully rubbed away the lipstick smudge with her thumb. "Not that you're not beautiful otherwise, just . . . it's hard to explain."

Emily spoke softly, without looking up. "Try?" she said.

Matt glanced at his beer, wishing they had opted for whisky. "Well." He set it on the coffee table. "Do you remember how I said I uh, was most interested in you enjoying yourself?"

"That's one way to read what you said." There was a faint smile playing at the corner of her mouth. Now it was Matt's turn to look away.

"Yeah," he said. "Well, I mean, watching you watching me when I was . . . I mean . . . it was the most *on* I'd ever seen any woman get."

"To use your language," Emily said carefully. "It was also the most *on* I had ever been." She set her drink down and turned to face him. There was an urgency in her features that made her look even younger. "You have no idea how much I wish that wasn't true, but it is." She set her beer next to his and began picking at her cuticles again. This time, Matt decided to make the leap and take her hand. Her fingers were pale and clammy. Probably because every drop of blood had just rushed to her face. "Matt," she said.

"Emily," he replied. Unable to fight the magnetic pull drawing his lips to her neck, Matt simply gave in, kissing lightly along the line of her throat. She gasped, but didn't pull away.

"You don't want to get involved with me," she sighed. "I'm

messed up. No one knows that better than you."

"I know how much you wanted to kill me," Matt breathed into her collarbone. "And how much I had to beg before you did it. Do you think that means you'll hurt me now?" Her fingers were plucking at his suit jacket like harp strings.

"I won't," she whispered.

"I know," he said. "You're not—" Her mouth found and silenced his, chasing all thought of words away with her kiss. Matt let his hands wander over her waist, her back, not daring to go further . . . but longing to. Unlike all of their previous encounters, this was real, and he did not want to overstep his bounds. Neither did she, as she kept her tongue in her mouth and her hands above his waist, kissing him with careful desperation. When she finally pulled away her face was still flushed, her brow furrowed. "What?"

"I think," she began, then took a gulp of air. "Technically I'm still a virgin." Matt felt his heart lurch.

"You want me to—" he stopped himself. She was already nodding.

"I can't think of anyone in the world I trust more than you," she said. "Isn't that the most important thing? Trust?"

"More important than love?"

Emily smiled down at her knees.

"I'm not ready to talk about love just yet," she said. At this, Matt almost laughed.

"Okay," he said. "What are you ready to talk about?" His fingertips touched her wrist, tracing just under her sleeve. Her shuddering inhalation gave the same answer as her words. "Okay," he said. "Okay, but we're gonna do it right this time." He kissed her lightly, hand in her hair. "This time it's for real."

"You're not helping my nerves any." Her voice was soft, an admission.

"We don't have to do anything," Matt said. "We could just talk. Whatever you want." She took his hands in hers and drew them up to her face, kissing each one before placing them on her waist. Her hands traced up his arms to his shoulders, then his neck, his face. Matt turned his head and kissed her palm.

"I want you," Emily murmured. "That's all."

Matt nodded. It was the only reply he could muster. She was so beautiful. He traced his palms up her sides and spread his fingers, letting his thumbs graze her breasts. Her back arched and her hands moved to his shoulders. Her fingers were tense against him. When he leaned toward her, her hands paused before letting him come. Nerves. It had to be. She had said in no uncertain terms that she wanted this. But if that was true, then why was she moving with such uncertainty?

"Are you okay?" Matt asked her, letting his lip trace her jawline.

"I'm sorry," she murmured.

"For what?"

"I can't stop thinking about it," she said. "I'm sorry." Matt sat back. There were tears in her eyelashes, but none on her cheeks. There was a funny sort of resignation in her eyes. They were eyes that had decided she was better off a virgin. This gave Matt a small flutter in his chest, something like dismay.

"Do you want me to stop?" he asked.

"I'm not normal."

"That's not really an answer."

Emily was staring at the floor, but her hands were still on him, fingers gripping the hem of his shirt. "I don't understand why you don't want to stop," she said, so softly he had to lean in to hear her. "I don't understand why you're not asking me to leave."

"I don't want you to leave," he said. He tried to kiss her cheek but she drew back, meeting his gaze. Her eyes seemed darker, a forest green compared to the previous spring.

"But why?" she asked. "You should be running. You should. You have no reason to try anything with me. Nothing will ever change."

"What needs to change?" Matt sat back on the couch. He thought about reaching for his beer, but he just couldn't find it in him. "You're perfect."

"I'm one lapse of conscience away from being a serial killer," she retorted. Their bodies were no longer touching. Somewhere along the line they had both pulled away.

"If your face when you killed me is any indication then that makes your conscience a very impressive one."

Emily didn't smile. "What if it breaks?" she asked. "Where does that leave you?"

Matt got to his feet. The girl he was looking at now was the same, scared girl he met on the train. Though she contained traces of that other girl, the one he had met briefly in the restaurant, that girl was not here now. He didn't take time to consider his next step. He couldn't, he knew, or he'd change his mind. Without a word, he walked into the kitchen. He came back out with the largest kitchen knife he owned.

"Let's find out," he said. A little noise escaped her throat then, not quite a scream but not far off. Her hands rushed to her face, and then to her lap, clenched tightly together. This was not a defensive pose. With a shock, Matt realized that she truly was more afraid of herself than she was of an armed man. He set the knife on the coffee table in front of her and sat back down.

"Matt, don't," she said.

"You don't have to do anything you don't want to do," he replied. His breathing was shallow, tense. He forced himself to take a deep breath.

"I don't want to hurt you," she said. Her eyes had settled on the handle of the knife, carefully pointed in her direction. He could see the telltale flush returning to her face. It took everything he had not to touch her.

"Then don't." Matt heard her breath catch and felt his heart stop. Emily's right hand crawled forward with all the grace of some delicate insect, extending, almost floating, toward the weapon he had placed in front of her. He knew he had made the right decision. He hoped he had made the right decision. There was a twitch in her hips as her fingers closed around the knife. He imagined that she was feeling the same electric jolt that he felt in his body when she met his frightened eyes with her terrible greens. She turned those green eyes on him now, uncertainty and arousal boiling together behind them. He couldn't speak. He could only nod and hope against hope that he wouldn't regret the gesture.

First, Emily slipped off her shoes. Her feet weren't bare under her heels, as he had expected, but covered by very short socks, ones that did not even reach her ankle. Black. She pulled her knees under her body and turned to face him. Matt didn't move. The knife was still in her hand, her knuckles white against the black plastic. The thumb of her left hand traced over the blade, testing its sharpness. Her tongue darted over her lip. She reached for him and it took everything in him not to flinch, but she just took his hand onto her lap.

The blade made its first contact with his palm. He gasped, but kept still. This was real. Unlike the previous times, this was real. Emily mumbled something comforting, but it was too soft for him to make out. It hardly mattered anyway. Her face spoke more loudly than her voice ever could. She was lost in it, the lines she was tracing on his body. She didn't break the skin, not yet anyway, but his body was alive with the power of the contact.

She could.

That was all that mattered. She could. She pulled the knife away and they both started speaking at once.

"Can you—"

"Are you—" He stopped himself. "I'm sorry, go ahead."

Emily bit her lip. "Can you turn and face me?" she said. "Like on the train?"

"Sure," Matt said. The request surprised him, but he complied, doing his best to keep his movements even. Not too fast, and not too slow. But she was on his lap before he had fully settled. The knife was at his throat and her right hand was untying his tie. His left hand was pinned to the couch and he was uncertain what to do with his right, desperate to touch her but afraid to do it.

She managed to get his tie off and shirt unbuttoned with one hand, the other pressing the blade against his skin just hard enough to threaten. Her fingers dug into his freshly bare stomach with enough force to make him moan. When she pulled her hand away he saw that she had left him with a few pink marks where her nails had been. Her face was pinker, flushed with some combination of arousal and shame. Matt felt himself quaking under her blade, and hoped she felt it too. His fear was something he wanted her to have. He offered it to her as a gift. And she took it, with gusto.

The knife traced over his body, bloodlessly devouring every

108 WHAT YOU WISH FOR

inch of skin it could find. She traced the pointed tip over his neck, which remembered being slit, and his stomach, which recalled that it had twice been torn apart. The memories of the pain he had felt were almost sensations themselves. The desperation he felt to never experience that pain again became an ache in his chest. Right hand still pressing the knife against his throat, Emily moved his one free hand to her waist. Then she took him tightly by the chin.

"Emily . . ." His voice sounded garbled as he tried to work his jaw within her grasp.

"Touch me," she breathed. Matt's hand slipped under her shirt and up her side. His hand was not on her breast, not yet, not without permission, but it was high enough that he knew she was not wearing a bra. She forced his head back and he moaned. It was very nearly a moan of pleasure. Her blade traced the underside of his jawline up to where her hand held his face. Her shoulders rotated, placing her breast in his palm. It was almost too much, the cacophony of sensations she was handing him, but still his body reached for more, squirming under her and pressing his hips into her thigh. She felt him there and matched his movements with a rhythmic undulation of her own. The blade in her hand traced down the center of his throat, his chest, ending at his stomach.

"Emily," Matt groaned. He did not know what it was that he wanted to tell her. Perhaps he wanted only to remind her that he was still there. She placed the cool flat of the knife against his skin and leaned in to kiss his neck, pressing the weapon tightly between their bodies. Her body was still in motion, rubbing herself on his pants. Matt let out a breath. He needed to hold it together, at least until she was done with him. He couldn't just lose it right there like some teenager. But the stimulation, coming from all sides and in all types, was not making it easy. "Emily," he gasped her name again as she tugged at the skin of his neck with her teeth.

"Is that okay?" she murmured into his ear.

"God, yes," he managed. She bit him again, harder this time. Matt could feel his pulse straining against the grip of her teeth. He thought about her sinking her canines into his soft flesh and tossing back her head like a wild animal, tearing his throat open and bleeding hot red all over her body and his couch. He should have shuddered at the thought. He wished he could return to a time when that kind of thought made him shudder. She released her hold and he felt her body curl against his. The knife was still against his skin, but her other hand was tight around his shirt and her movements were catlike.

"Okay?" she asked. Matt nodded and watched as she stepped out of her panties, leaving the rest of her clothes on. The urgency in that small detail nearly put him over the edge. She couldn't even wait long enough for them to get undressed. She mounted him, but before he was allowed to enter her she pressed the knife to his throat again.

"What if I told you," she said. "That if you come I'll kill you?" Matt looked up at her. There was something in her eyes now, an earnestness that he recognized from the subway, from their first meeting. He swallowed hard, feeling the bite of the metal against his skin.

"I'd believe you," he said. Emily nodded, but she didn't say it. As she fucked him though, one hand on his chest and one on the handle of the knife she had not removed from his skin, he could not forget those words. What if she meant it, even though she'd only said it in the hypothetical? What if she meant to kill him when he finished? There was fear in his eyes. He could feel it there like a mist in front of his pupils, clouding her face and softening her beauty to something even more otherworldly. He let it float there for her to see. Because even through the haze he could see what his look of terror did to her.

By the time he felt close to finishing, she had come three times. The little cry of panic he gave as he neared his climax was enough to drive her to a fourth. He had forced it down, held it back for so long that when it finally did come it was one of the most powerful orgasms he had ever experienced. She stopped not long after, and waited until the afterglow faded to move again. He knew she was waiting for him to come back down, so that he would know what was happening to him. Her fingers laced through his hair and her blade pressed to the underside of his jawline. The sound that slipped between his lips was a high whine. Without any further contact, Emily came for a fifth time. Then she let him go.

Matt's body sagged back and he almost laughed as he heard the knife clatter to the floor. He was alive. He had managed to get through it alive. *She* had managed to get through it and leave him alive. She leaned into his chest, nuzzling and kissing at his neck gently. Every once in a while he felt teeth, but they were always quickly withdrawn, as if she was reminding herself to be gentle. After a while, he took her by the shoulders and pushed her upright.

"You didn't kill me," he said. He meant it to sound triumphant. But there wasn't an ounce of self-righteousness left in him. He was too tired, too spent, too relieved.

"I didn't," she said. There was pride in her voice, but there was disappointment there too. How long could she keep it up? How long could she go on fucking without killing?

Matt smiled and kissed her softly, turning a laugh into a pained cough as she bit his lip.

How long?

That, strangely, was something he was willing to find out.

KING SHITS
Charles Austin Muir

1

For Clay Haller, pain was another delivery. Like anything else he transported across thousands of miles of open road. It was a job, like driving 11 hours or calling his dispatcher or backing his 53-foot trailer into a tight dock. But unlike his other deliveries, pain was a secret load, a shadow operation within the one he got paid for.

His war against King Shits.

According to the Internet, a King Shit was someone who overestimated his importance. The seven men across the street were real big shots, if muscle defined importance. The blazing sun painted their torsos pink and copper, ridges and bands of armor forged with gym machines and steroids. To passersby they made a startling sight, quaffing from plastic cups and 40-ounce bottles in front of a bungalow. Not even old ladies and minors escaped their drunken taunts.

On the sidewalk, a hulking bald man from whom the others took their cue intercepted a black teenager. "What up, NEE-gro?" His mock jive-ass falsetto shrilled across the street. Whatever the kid replied, Chrome Dome spat beer in his face.

Clay munched on a gummy bear, watching inside his truck cab. He had been waiting on the light at the head of the street when he decided to investigate these Mr. Universe wannabes. They made quite a spectacle. Since parking on the side street catty-corner to the bungalow, he had seen them harass a woman in Daisy Dukes, menace an old Vietnamese lady and yank the American flag off a drooling man's mobility scooter. But what he saw at the traffic light prompted his surveillance.

A scrawny, Jesus-bearded dude stumbled down the driveway, coughing blood. One of Chrome Dome's buddies—a Filipino who looked like Rufio from the Peter Pan movie, but with twenty-inch arms—tossed Jesus Beard in the bed of a pickup truck parked on the street. Three rounds of rock-paper-scissors ensued between him and a mop-headed kid wearing a lifting belt. Rufio beat Mop-head, paper over rock.

As Mop-head drove off in the pickup, someone shouted a line from the movie *Road House*:

"PAIN DON'T HURT!"

And Clay recalled another line about pain as he circled the block to his present position, a motivational saying, *pain is something*. He was still trying to remember it when the black kid stalked away, passing a dude wearing a scarf in the ninety-degree heat. Scarf Ace stopped before the Great Wall of Chrome Dome.

Clay zoomed in with binoculars. Chrome Dome gesticulated like a hard-sell personal trainer. Scarf Ace, ashen, shook his head, then pinched up a smile. He followed the others up the driveway through a tall wooden gate. His view cut off, Clay nibbled on gummy bears and waited.

Grabbing the binoculars again, he saw Scarf Ace stagger through the opened gate, sans neckpiece and bleeding from the forehead. Right behind him, Chrome Dome swept him up in a bear hug and dropped him into the pickup bed where Jesus Beard had been. Once again, Mop-head lost to Rufio's paper. Minutes later he returned—wherever he dumped Chrome Dome's victims, it was nearby.

Pain is weakness leaving the body. That was the saying. Marine Corps ad or something. Since King Shits were made of weakness, Clay thought, what would happen if he tested the axiom on Chrome Dome and Co.'s magnificent bodies?

He got out and crossed the street. A breeze stirred his hair as he walked past the neighboring houses. Eyes straight ahead, he felt the group push without touching him, a psychic bum rush of liquid courage and testosterone. They allowed him to pass, belching and carrying on, waiting for their leader to command respect. Finally a tank of thinly veiled muscle stepped in Clay's face.

"Hey man, wanna stick fight?"

Chrome Dome stiffened like a point man sensing danger, despite his hundred pounds over the thin, middle-aged nobody reflected in his gold Elvis sunglasses. To feed the man's beast of self-satisfaction, Clay shrank back a step.

"I, uh, well, I'm afraid I'm not really into blood sport."

Along with his buddies, Chrome Dome snorted. "'S'not like that. Gentlemen's rules. No head shots, no groin shots, no hitting when a man's down. Just for fun."

Fun.

As in, *pain don't hurt.*

"I'll even give you a free beer. Come on, Jim Carrey." Chrome Dome felt his alpha maleness now. Though people often mentioned Clay's resemblance to the actor, they didn't also chuck him in the arm with a gap-toothed grin.

"I do like beer . . ."

"Good man."

Clay followed Chrome Dome through the wooden gate onto a covered patio. He pretended not to notice the scarf folded in a corner, the abstract floor art made from Jesus Beard's sputum and Scarf Ace's head wound. Grabbing beers from a cooler, Chrome Dome launched into a prolegomenon on the art of stick fighting. "Have you ever watched the opening scene from *Rambo III* . . . ?" Clay imagined his predecessors withering inside while Mop-head and another bodybuilder slapped each other with rattan sticks. The sight of the seven bare-chested, sweat-oiled beefcakes brought to mind a 'roided reenactment of the beach volleyball scene from *Top Gun.*

"No blood, no foul," Chrome Dome said. "But don't try anything funny. We go for arms and legs only. And if you spill any of these I get a free shot and vice versa." He swept his arm at the drinking containers bordering the patio. Clay gathered the "free shot" wasn't for refreshment.

"Not having second thoughts, are you?"

"Well—"

"Get us those sticks," Chrome Dome shouted. Taking his pair, Clay weighed them in each hand as if awestruck by their virility, dildos of impossibly manly proportion.

Chrome Dome flashed gap teeth again. "Ding-ding." Backing into a corner, he stared Clay down while a crony removed his Elvis sunglasses. Clay glanced at the eager-eyed behemoths crowding around the patio. He wondered how many men waylaid by Chrome Dome had had second thoughts and still wound up in Mop-head's pickup truck.

The kid threw down a fist and lost a third time to Rufio's paper. Mop-head cursed and stepped between the two fighters. He removed his lifting belt and raised it like a start flag. "Begin."

Twice, circling the ring, Clay flinched in anticipation. But he redeemed himself sidestepping a wild swing and tapped Chrome Dome's log-like upper arm. The big man retaliated with a backhanded strike that should have caved in Clay's skull. But Clay dodged the stick and smashed his against Chrome Dome's nose, spraying both men with blood.

"Carrey's a ringer," someone said.

Gurgling a war cry, Chrome Dome raised his stick, but the smaller man hooked around behind him.

Knifing his stick between Chrome Dome's legs, Clay ended the fight.

Chrome Dome fell on his face, convulsing around his sudden vasectomy. A hollowed-out, miniature watermelon filled with red liquid skidded onto the grass as his size-11 Adidas kicked out.

A phantom, a flicker of temperature behind Clay as someone charged in. He took Rufio out with a liver shot, then wheeled amongst the onrushing bodybuilders. Sticks arcing in the sunlight, Clay taught Chrome Dome's crew that pain hurt immensely. Mop-head fell last, beaten by wood instead of paper. When he was done, Clay drank in the sight of weakness leaving bodies, the suits of living armor now scattered and broken around the yard.

As the groaning men fell silent, other sounds arose. Birds chirping, dogs barking, children laughing down the street. Clay was always amazed at how tender the world could be in the aftermath of violence. He despised men like Chrome Dome who profaned life's sanctity, forced their will down the world's throat like some orally obsessed rapist. For their viciousness surpassing all other animals, he felt *they* should be raped. Yet Clay couldn't perform that function—his sex organs weren't wired into his will to break King Shits.

Instead, he found other methods of punishment.

Clay dropped one of his sticks and rolled Chrome Dome on his back. Then he took the hollowed-out, miniature watermelon from the grass and cupped it to the injured man's drooling, gap-toothed orifice. Red margarita dregs spluttered from under the cup and mixed with crimsoned vomit. Holding the cup in place, Clay drove the other stick through the rind, impaling Chrome Dome's soft palate with blood-soaked rattan. He stopped when he had punched through the first cervical vertebra.

"My free shot," he said, and departed.

2

A mile or so from Chrome Dome's bungalow, Clay stopped at a restaurant. He entered through the bar side and ducked into the restroom. He cleansed his face and hands. Then he waited. Moments later his bowels seized and he slammed the toilet seat back. Brownish, chunky liquid shot from his mouth and filled the bowl. He flushed and returned to the sink. He was lucky. Once he pulled off the highway and barely clambered over the passenger seat to splatter the roadside. The last shadow jobs, he puked afterward even though he didn't eat much. It was as if conscience struck through his digestion, rejected his vigilantism through his gorge.

What puzzled him was that it tasted earthy, like mud. Clay washed up again and frowned in the mirror. He sat at a booth in the restaurant.

Since his Rebirth, he needed little food. But he still enjoyed the ritual, sitting down to a meal and "playing" at eating. Ensconced among objects dedicated to a single task. The plastic menu stand, votive candle and salt and pepper shakers on his table were like the knobs, gauges and caution stickers inside his truck—a microcosm where chaos didn't reach. As a young man he became a trucker to escape the world's noise, tumult and disorder.

While he nibbled burnt toast and watched pigeons out the

window, Clay forgot his gut problems and his war against King Shits. Then voices rose behind him.

"Yo cunt, I'm talkin' to you."

"Shhh, T, she'll hear you."

He barely noticed them when he came in. The restaurant's only other patrons, two booths behind him. Talking about the waitress, the Kim Kardashian lookalike arranging silverware by the bar. The man was black and the blonde white woman wore short-shorts. A second woman at the table muttered something inaudible.

Then: WHAAAP cracked a fist on the tabletop. "I said, hey, BITCH, I'm TALKIN' to you."

The first woman said: "For God's sake, T, I'll get us some napkins. Just leave her alone, will you?"

"Fuck off, Iris. Sitcher ass down 'fore I smack you into next week."

Iris sighed.

Clay laid his butter knife next to the toast. He pitied Iris and the other woman. And he pitied the waitress. No wage was worth dealing with venomous shitheels like T. She deserved Employee of the Month for the way she endured his goading. Clay admired her swelling backside as she bent over utensils, moving so minutely she looked like her celebrity twin's wax double. Maybe she'd found the best way to handle men like T was to freeze like a squirrel before a large dog.

"The ho hears me," T said. "Right, ho? You hear me. Been hearin' me for the last five minutes and actin' like you Helen Mirren."

"I think you mean Helen Keller," Iris said.

"Whatever. Bitch better serve us."

"I think I've got some toilet paper in my purse," the second woman said.

"The hell for? Jesus, Betsy. Aiight. If that bitch don't come in ten seconds I'm goin' over dere and give her some a' big T."

Betsy said, "Actually, I've got tissues too."

"Ten—"

"T," Iris said.

"Nine—"

"Who wants some tissues?"

"Eight—"

"I promise they're not used."

"Seven—"

"T, please . . ."

"That was a joke. Come on, T, just take my—"

WHAAAP! cracked the fist again, this time on bone.

"Damn it, T!" Iris.

"Not a peep from you tricks. You wanted to use them tissues, girl, use 'em."

Betsy sobbed.

"Oh, NOW I got your attention," T shouted at the waitress. "Don't look at me like that, you deaf-actin' bitch. You stay right where you are. You just keep playin' with that silverware while I tear dat fat ass *up*."

Clay got up and marched toward the table. T, on his feet, wiped his knuckles on his jeans leg and scowled. "The *fuck* you want, you Jim Carrey-looking motherfucker?"

He was Clay's height, but beefier. Wearing a sleeveless tee-shirt. A lifetime of urban desolation and rage exuded through his pores. Clay had read about pimps: Confused, desperate young girls fell for their promises of protection and prosperity and wound up drug-addicted, sexually battered and often pregnant from their coercions.

Iris, the blond, turned in her seat and gaped up at Clay as if he'd punched in the code for a nuclear missile launch.

T was out of the booth and swinging when Clay stepped inside and drove his fist in T's sternum. T's legs meant to wheel him back ten feet but the wall absorbed the impact and he slid to a sitting position on the floor. Iris yelped when Clay pushed her gently back to her seat. "But he can't breathe," she said. Guppy-eyed, T sucked at air as if fellating an under-endowed john.

The waitress said, "Holy shit," as Clay bent T over the table. He twisted the pimp's arm back and nodded at the puffy-eyed Latina between Iris and the wall. "Cover your eyes." From the plate of chicken fried steak under T's belly, he extracted a steak knife slathered in sausage gravy. He drove it into the base of T's neck, paralyzing him.

Iris shrieked. The waitress shrieked. Betsy shrieked, peeking through her fingers at T's blood leaking onto her French fries. Without use of his legs, the pimp was like a 200-pound dead fish.

"Napkins," Clay snapped. The waitress quieted down and did as told. Clay tore a hole in the napkins pushing them down the knife in T's neck.

"Here's your damn napkins. Have a nice day."

Iris gaped. Betsy shrieked again.

Clay left a hefty tip.

3

The town was called Wanting. Population 94, a gas station, a general store. Nearest post office was twenty miles north, in Dayton.

The Hallers and family dog lived in the old Wanting fire station. Mr. Haller, fresh from the military, worked in Dayton and dropped Clay at Dayton Elementary each morning.

This was Clay's first year there. Seventh grade. One day at recess, Chris Kezzlewick, an eighth-grader and the biggest kid in school, challenged Clay to a fight. When he refused, Chris made to tackle him and slipped. The nimble new kid dodged him all around the playground until a teacher stepped in. How he finally caught Clay came a week later, after school.

It happened on the forest road that led to the bus stop. Backed by buddies David and Quinton, Chris jumped Clay and dragged him into the forest. David and Quinton braced him against a tree in crucifix position while Chris pummeled him. A low blow dropped Clay to his knees. The sight of him kneeling, wet with tears, inspired the bully to relieve himself. Clay gagged on blood and Chris's copious piss, still in his captors' clutches, in Christ pose.

Dusk in those woods, pencil beams of sunlight stabbing through the murk of old growth. Next they turned Clay toward the tree and laid him face down. Dirt and pine needles sandpapered his cheek. "I said hold him!" Chris barked, behind him. Quinton's hand clamped down on Clay's wrist. The other boy, David, grabbed the other. "Don't move, Clay," he whispered, and it sounded like advice, like how Clay's father advised him where to place his thumb when he drove a hammer. "Hic," Quinton said, Quinton who always had hiccups because he ate like a famished dog, "hic."

Clay heard Chris unbuckle his overall suspenders. He was like some fat snake crawling over Clay now, breathing hotly. His hands found Clay's fly, pulled pants down, underwear next, cold earth kissing his shriveled penis and indrawn testicles. Time stretched Clay on a rack of pain and humiliation. Then finally the nerve ends in his broken boyhood granted him mercy and he passed out.

He didn't tell his parents what had been done to him. Only that three classmates had beat him. His torment snowballed over the next few weeks when Chris Kezzlewick spread a rumor in school that Clay was a "homo." Even teachers looked at Clay like some sort of pervert.

How hateful some of the boys called him names, Clay wondered if they, too, had been taken to those woods.

He grew so despondent that finally his parents moved from Wanting, population 94, to Los Angeles, population two-million-something. The Hallers took an apartment in a neighborhood where white, undersized, timid boys were singled out on the street. After so many Band-Aids and ice packs, Clay's dad enrolled him in a Kung Fu school in the building where he worked.

"You won't like it here," the pudgy Chinese man warned Clay. "Children want action—" he whirled around and snapped a side kick over Clay's head—"big movement."

"All I want is to be left alone."

"Then I'll show you how, but you must honor the teachings."

A year later, Clay stopped coming home bruised and bloodied.

From then on he avoided conflict. He treated others with kindness, compassion and restraint. As his skills developed so did his ability to find peaceable solutions. Trucking seemed a natural entry into the real world, a life of solitude and purpose. Sealed in the bubble of his semi, he reduced his chance of running into Chris Kezzlewicks and street toughs. Of course, he could never completely avoid bullies.

He was between shifts at a bar in Butte, Montana. Rowdy place. Friday night. A big man, like Chrome Dome but more fat than muscle, bumped Clay in passing. He turned on Clay and shoved him off his barstool. Clay reseated himself. Felt Big Man watch him. Didn't see

Big Man's friend come up from behind and crack a glass stein on his noggin. Next thing he knew, two Big Men had him on the floor, working him over with steel-toed boots.

Visions of Chris Kezzlewick and his buddies flashed through his nerves. Chris pushing inside him, becoming part of him. Hic. Hic. Something in the brutal touch of his attackers awakened memories buried in his cells. Flipped a switch. Pain sloughed off Clay like old skin, and the kicks to his skull and rib cage, the commotion around him, passed through him like light through water.

Training took over. He rolled to his feet. Jabbed his fingers in each man's throat. Slipped outside them, gave one a liver shot and the other a knee breaker. Dragged them by the wrists out the front door. Training turned into something other than self-defense. Clay pierced eyeballs. Broke fingers. Stomped scrotums. As the men screamed, he no longer saw pain as an end to conflict but as the beginning of a conversation. A lesson in how much can be broken if he plowed the body deeply enough.

Brutalizing those men, Clay felt nothing. No rage or hate. He followed a script in his muscles, the way a predator takes down its prey. Witnesses gaped when, with an air of punctuality, he urinated on his victims. Even then he felt no pleasure, no satisfaction beyond a job well done, like delivering a load to his next receiver. Pain and humiliation, right on time.

"You're a monster!" Someone shouted.

Clay got the hell out of Butte, Montana.

Next night, walking down quiet back streets, he followed his shadow. And he realized he felt no rage or hate because he *was* those things, a negative incarnation of the principles he had lived by. Clay Haller died under a rain of steel-toed boots. His body now was like the shadow at his feet. A resurrection, a Rebirth of opposites. Like the men he had beaten, shadows of power driven by fear and weakness. The world, nothing but shadows.

Time to stop running from them.

Realizing that, Clay shed biological imperatives like food and sleep. One night he watched a TV show about a golem. A magical entity formed from clay, like his name, unstoppable pursuing the mission it was made for. He'd never heard of such a thing, but here he was, like that golem, a monster created from pain and humiliation to give the self-crowned kings of the earth—King Shits—a taste of their own medicine.

But how would he find them?

How could he reach so many?

Then he realized the answer was parked right outside his motel room.

4

Surfing the Internet on his laptop, Clay came across an item on cop killer Clint "Herc" Walker. Herc was well over six feet and resembled his granite-jawed, movie-actor namesake, at least in the mug shot. He was a hard drinker with a vicious temper. One night a deputy called on him, responding to a disturbance call. Heated by drink and bad poker hands, Herc bludgeoned the lawman with a bronze sculpture.

Paroled after 25 years in prison, Herc was back in his hometown, the article said. Grimsbo, population 1,100, on the way to Clay's next pickup.

A temper like that, Herc might need talking to.

The temperature was in the nineties when Clay rolled into Grimsbo the next day. He checked into a motel. After weeks of napping in his truck, a private bed called to him. Curtains closed, A/C whirring, crisp sheets beneath him. Normally he didn't need but an hour of rest, but the bodybuilders and T had drained him. Drifting off, last thing he saw was Chrome Dome's gold Elvis sunglasses and gap teeth. *Come on, Jim Carrey.*

Next thing he knew he was sitting up straight throwing punches in the dark. He kept on going till he realized he was hitting air. Shadow boxing.

"Clay!" The voice so close, like Chris Kezzlewick at his neck while he ran the shower. Dripping wet, Clay shot into the bedroom, found no one.

He peered through a gap in the curtain: Dusk out. He got dressed. Stared at himself in the bathroom's cracked mirror. He threw back the toilet seat, puked mud and conscience.

"Clay!" Calling him from the door of the town watering hole.

Where he thought he might find Herc, or get a lead on him. The sort of place where peanut shells littered the floor and deer heads lined the walls. Business was good. Clay sat near some old-timers and scanned the bar's patrons. Was someone stalking him, or was he getting twitchy after so long at war?

"Smashed a bottle on a guy's throat, Herc did," an old-timer said, wiping beer froth off his mustache.

Minutes later the legend himself walked in. He reminded Clay of rock stars who hadn't seen the limelight in decades, a jarring contrast to yesterday's portrait. Herc looked old, stooped and milk-pale, with wispy white hair and pinkish eyes. "Kidney cancer," a Stetsoned old-timer said. Only his height and granite jaw identified him as the hard-drinking juggernaut who beat a peace officer to death twenty-five years ago.

Grimsbo's drinkers, they patted him on the back and made way for him. Herc smiled through the welcome reception, eyes downcast, edging through the crowd. He nodded at Clay, the small-town courtesy, as he brushed past and joined a frumpy redhead sitting in back. A waitress served him ice water.

While this went on the old-timers talked about how Herc became an ordained minister in prison. Clay was about to leave when Herc's spitting image—from the mug shot—lumbered through the door.

"Even worse than his old man, back when," the mustached old-timer said.

Herc Jr., it seemed. Slightly shorter, but beefier. A few more steroid injections and he could be with Chrome Dome's crew. He looked in his mid-twenties, wearing a baseball cap turned backward and a skintight tee-shirt that said "Dick Diesel." Grimsbo's drinkers, they greeted him and his entourage with a scant nod.

"Them dogfights up at Sin Mountain," the Stetsoned old-timer said.

"What up, Meat!" The shouter had fewer pounds on him than the gold chains he wore over his Yankees baseball jersey. Meat gave Pencil-Neck a fist bump and led his entourage to the bar.

Clay guessed none of them could fight. Not Meat, who measured toughness in biceps peak. Not the tousle-haired Frankenstein's monster showing Pencil-Neck some karate block. Not the mutton-chopped beach ball rolling his head around like a boxer and shrugging to a twenty-year-old rap song he picked on the jukebox.

A row of shots was set before them which they raised toward Herc. "Welcome home, dad!" Meat downed the shot and slammed the glass on the bar top. His father, at the rear of the bar, nodded gloomily.

The buxom waitress drifted over to Clay, smelling of gum and perfume. "Sorry to keep you waiting, hon. Can I get you anything?"

"You can get *me* something, Maria," Meat shouted before Clay could speak. "Name of that fake casting agent who creampied up your slit. Nice video on Jizzhub!"

Maria made a face like she was counting to ten, then stormed off crunching peanut shells underfoot.

Clay had seen enough. He nodded to the old-timers and went back to his truck. He parked in a lot across the street facing the bar. An hour later Meat and his boys climbed into a black Escalade. Clay tailed them through side streets and turned off when they entered a cul-de-sac. He cruised the area a few minutes, then parked on the street facing the cul-de-sac. The turnaround was packed with SUVs, pickup trucks, vans, motorcycles and hoopties.

Rap music boomed from the biggest house on the dead-end street.

Somewhere behind the house, dogs were crying.

5

The party raged into the early dawn. All night people went in and out of the house, drinking and smoking. No one seemed to notice the black 18-wheeler parked down the street. Clay saw nothing of interest until just before noon, when a van cruised past his truck and stopped on the lawn.

Meat came out to greet it. Through his binoculars Clay watched the van's side door open and a Mr. Universe wobble out with two leashed pit bulls. The driver, a gorilla in a cutoff army jacket, went to the back of the van, grabbed a bucket of 5/8-inch steel chain and followed Meat and the dog walker into the house.

Clay wiped his binocular eyecups on his shirt and mopped his brow. Hot as hell out.

Hotter in his chest, where an old memory caught fire.

Old Man Gardner. He was why Jimmy, Clay's dog, his twenty-pound Boston terrier, never made it to Los Angeles. Clay wanted to blame his father for not mending the fence where Jimmy escaped, but in the end it was Old Man Gardner who pulled the trigger, who blew the back out of Jimmy for crapping in his yard. Jimmy and his butter-soft coat, how he leaned on Clay's chest and rolled his eyes up for attention. Old Man Gardner left the dead dog on the road outside his gate. This he declared on the Hallers' front steps, reeking of cheap whiskey and self-satisfaction—Chrome Dome's granddaddy with a shotgun.

Clay sweated in the cab, thinking about Jimmy.

About the pit bulls.

What the old-timer said: "Them dog fights up at Sin Mountain."

He'd read about dog fighting. How so-called "dog men" beat and starved the dogs to make them more aggressive. Set them loose on "bait" animals, like cats or smaller dogs, to sharpen their taste for blood. Chained them in cages or steel drums. Drowned, strangled, shot or beat against the ground the dogs who lost or were severely injured. He'd seen pictures of dead dogs in trash bags, blood-spattered walls. One image, the combatants locked like Kama Sutra lovers, bleeding all over each other, the bottom dog staring at the camera, infinitely rueful.

The pit bulls from the van, they looked like they'd survived such a contest—barely. Faces like meat tossed under a lawn mower.

Clay's dad didn't let him see the body when he picked it up, but that didn't help. For weeks he kept picturing Jimmy raped by Old Man Gardner's shotgun. Post-traumatic stress disorder, he didn't know the term back then, he only knew that what happened to him in the forest transformed how he would see life forever. Every show of strength, every flaunting of power, extended the Rapist's will, thrust a knife through the core of him.

These trailer-trash King Shits, these gangster-wannabe King Shits, these muscle-bound King Shits with their chains and cages and fight rings. They were rapists of the animal kingdom, Old Man Gardner with a god complex.

Thinking about Jimmy, Clay realized his war was only his boyhood self still searching for redemption. A mask he hid behind, like the truck he spent so much time inside, a mask he couldn't take off.

He should have driven away, he should never have followed those men from the bar. What he had seen today, written on those pit bulls' faces, was the end of every King Shit in Grimsbo, population about to drop. Even Meat's three-story headquarters looked like a King Shit house.

Blue sky, a day promising to top a hundred, a day for glaring sun and bug splats on the windshield while he tore up the interstate, and Clay sat in his truck picturing the .50-caliber Desert Eagles he kept in a briefcase. Nasty way to send a man to the underworld.

Little by little, like dawn breaking over years, Clay had made peace with death. He knew that for every man he hunted, he brought death closer. Chasing down foes in his 18-wheel King Shit chariot, Clay the ultimate King Shit, a King Shit killer of King Shits. That, he'd learned in his forty-one years, was how the universe worked. When shadows peeled back the world and all you saw were your sins, reflections of reflections, mirrored to infinity. Whether he died in the next few minutes or lived to fight another day, a King Shit killer was coming for him.

So bright the sun-baked asphalt, so sour-sweet the gummy bears he chewed while he stared at the opened side of the van where the pit bulls had been. Thinking about them, about Jimmy, voices from the past chattering in back of his mind—and then:

"Don't move, Clay," David, still thirteen years old, making Clay wait after all those years. Some wisp of foreknowledge sampling from his worst memory, guiding him into another dark forest.

Minutes later, Meat pushed out the front door.

"We're heading out," he said to someone inside.

So that was why Clay's subconscious urged him to wait. Meat would lead him to Sin Mountain.

Clay watched over twenty people stream out of the house and disperse into vehicles. Beach Ball and Frankenstein's Monster and

Pencil-Neck. Van Driver and Dog Walker, minus the dogs. All dudes except for a skinny blonde in a Jeep convertible, turning out of the cul-de-sac onto the lane intersecting with the dead-end street. Clay started the truck and followed the procession to a freeway onramp. A mile out of town Meat's Escalade turned right onto a rural road and led the convoy up a steep, golden hill. Clay followed, hanging back so he'd have plenty of room to pull over when they reached their destination. This turned out to be the gravel drive of a big white farmhouse.

The only house within miles, atop a blaze of arid land known as Sin Mountain.

Through his binoculars he scanned the trees and fence obscuring the property. Place like that, they didn't want you crapping in their backyard.

"Well, Jimmy," Clay said, "looks like we're finally gonna pay back Old Man Gardner."

6

Over-the-top didn't begin to describe them—the hand cannons under his armpits. Bought from a guy on the Internet at a reasonable price, if your tastes included signed Picassos and rare Scotch. Over four pounds each, ten-inch barrels, titanium gold finish, custom gold-plated grips featuring a black dog with glowing red eyes. Hellhounds. The seller gave them funky names from Welsh myth, but Clay just called them Jimmy One and Jimmy Two.

So far, the Jimmies had only shot pumpkins. The exit holes so big Clay could put his fist through them.

Truly a King Shit weapon, how a shotgun blast must have felt to a twenty-pound dog taking a crap. Clay's "Rebirth-day" gift to himself, came with the custom double-gun shoulder holster and leather briefcase. The seller had a flair for the cinematic.

Long shot of Clay driving across open field, his big rig black as dreamless sleep, a shadow growing under the eye of the sun.

No plan, just jump down, point, shoot. Dumb as Chrome Dome's stick fight technique, but it was now or never, he should've been on the road by now.

The Jimmies hungered for more than pumpkin seeds and pulp.

Anyway, probably the whole town knew what Meat's gang was up to and all they worried about were law agencies spread too thin for some Podunk animal abusers. Last thing they'd expect was a battle with a long-haul truck driver.

Sin Mountain: Dead land ready to catch fire and a King Shit party at the far end. It could have been some farmer's family picnic, people drinking beer and standing around or sitting in lawn chairs. But then there was that pavilion-type thing back by the trees, like a wooden carport built around a large, empty sandbox. Cars parked around it, except where a wooded trail sheltered some dozen dogs chained to overturned barrels, some lumped on their sides, not moving.

Now Meat kicked something in the sandbox—the fight ring— something too small to see over the low wall. He went after it and kicked it again, while a buffed shirtless dude in a doo-rag jerked the chain on a pit bull in one corner.

Those Hellhounds, they were the most decadent purchase Clay ever made, but he knew someday he'd need them.

His last delivery: Pain and humiliation, right on time.

He rolled in slowly, honking thunder as if the crowd were kids pulling on an air horn. By now everyone was watching him. The skinny blonde grabbed something from her Jeep, and Meat vaulted from the ring, striking his best college bouncer pose in a gap between parked cars.

Clay killed the engine. Jumped down from the cab. Heat and parched grass smells hit him.

Meat's sleeveless tee-shirt said, "Do you even lift, bro?"

"Jesus," Meat said, "it's Jim Carrey—"

BAWWWWMMM!

That was Jimmy One, and the blonde on Clay's right fell behind the Jeep, shotgun pointed skyward.

BAWWWWMMM!

Jimmy Two barked left at a redheaded guy reaching down the back of his jean shorts. Blood and entrails showered the tree behind him. He collapsed next to a dog lump.

Someone screamed. People ran for cover. Jimmy One followed

Pencil-Neck around back of the ring, turned his face into a menstrual explosion. Guy in a feathered pimp hat made it to the trail when Jimmy Two turned his chest into a porthole, flashing a gap in the trees ahead.

Hellhounds.

Silly, Clay knew, giving his guns personalities like he was a hit man in the movies. But then, they were his muscle, weren't they, like Chris Kezzlewick had David and Quinton? And this was *his* rape stage, *his* forest.

These metaphors of male potency, extensions of the Rapist's will, forcing themselves on people where holes weren't supposed to be.

Clay heard screaming inside the ring. Doo-Rag had let the pit bull loose, and instead of charging Clay it seized in its teeth the thing Meat had been kicking. The small, fawn-colored dog thrashed in the pit bull's jaws. Flopped behind the low wall and swung up again, its cries so shrill Clay felt his blood turn to crushed glass. Jimmy Two put down both animals with a bullet through the pit bull's muzzle.

To the right: *Chakk-chakk . . . BOOOMMM!*

Beach Ball with Blonde Girl's shotgun, nicking a corner post of the ring.

Jimmy One and Jimmy Two tore into him, his third-trimester gut.

The spent cartridges whipped past Clay's face.

Hellhounds.

"Anyone else?" Clay pointed them, side by side, at the crowd. "What about the house," to Meat. "Anyone in there?"

"No, man."

BAWWWWMMM!

Jimmy One saw Cell Phone Guy before Clay, scalped him with his sunglasses sitting on his head. He crumpled out of sight between a Corvette and a Buick.

Where he fell came a ring tone: *Wocka-wocka-wocka-wocka-wocka-wocka.*

Pac-Man, eating.

Meat hit a biceps shot palming his forehead.

"Everyone put their hands up," Clay said. "No one uses cell phones. Sure there's no one in the house?"

"No, man. I mean yes. Fucking yes."

Then, "What is this? You were parked back at the house, right? What the hell do you want?"

"I want your people to get in back of my truck."

"What for?"

Jimmy Two pointed at Meat's chest. The part that said, "bro."

"Everyone but you."

Meat scowled. "You got six rounds left."

"That's right."

Not including the magazines in his cargo pants pockets.

"Anyone want a piece of my Jimmies?" Clay shouted.

Wocka-wocka-wocka-wocka-wocka-wocka

Meat said, "You're something, man."

"Someone should answer that phone."

"But you said no—"

BAWWWWMMM!

"Five rounds left," Clay said, Doo-Rag, still in the ring, pulling his hand back from his right boot.

"You want something to do, big man, open the trailer door on my truck. Let's go, people, form a line."

Doo-Rag went to the back of the truck. Meat next, everyone else filing after him, hands raised, the Jimmies tracking them. "Used to drive long haul myself." Doo-Rag, arms akimbo, stared up at the empty trailer. "It's going to be hot as hell in there."

"Like those dogs you got chained."

Doo-Rag turned to Clay. "Man, those are dogs, four-legged things, this is what they do." Nodding toward the ring. "You, you're killin' *people*."

"People, huh?"

"Heat stroke, starvation, whatever you got planned—it's *monstrous*."

Doo-Rag was a monster himself. Chiseled, in olive-drab fatigues and black boots—Clay hadn't forgotten the piece hidden in the right—tattoos on front and back like giant monk script, illegible against the dark canvas of muscle. Knife scar where the right pectoral tied in with the front deltoid. Bad dude, but he had a point. Clay with his Hellhounds and trailer-cum-death-chamber, like some King Shit Nazi . . . he hadn't thought what to do when the shooting ended.

"Two-legged things," he said finally. "Okay, here's what we do. First, everyone else gets in the trailer. Then you shut the door and go to the ring. You, too, *bro*," Jimmy Two pointing at Meat, "and you three, Frankenstein." Jimmy One waving at the sleepy-eyed brute near the back of the line. "Let's go, people, this isn't a spectator event."

Dog Walker, last inside the furnace, glared down at Clay. "You're gonna get your ass whupped."

Doo-Rag shut the trailer door.

Meat, Doo-Rag and Frankenstein's Monster went to the ring. Clay approached from the trail side, the chained dogs eying him, ears forward, brows furrowed. He kenneled his Hellhounds, removed the shoulder holster and laid it at his feet. Stepping over the low wall, he took a spot behind the dead dogs, conjoined at fang and face. The warning he'd fired at Doo-Rag through the low wall had ripped a hole in the pit bull's underbelly, pooling guts and sticky stuff on the killing floor.

Lined behind the dog mess the three men exchanged glances.

"Two-legged things," Clay said. "This is what we do."

The ring was infernally hot, miasma of old contests and fresh kill. Adrenaline gripped the men in place, unsure how to triple-team their opponent.

Two-legged things, doing what four-legged things do.

Outside the ring, two-legged and four-legged things dead or dying under the eye of the sun.

Hop-stepping around the dogs, Clay threw a shield up—elbows and front knee covering groin and midsection—and blocked Frankenstein's Monster's roundhouse kick. He chopped the man's windpipe, then bent his arm back so that Doo-Rag, knife flashing from the right boot, bayoneted a corpse. Doo-Rag threw a hook around the human obstacle in his face. Clay straight-arm blocked it, released Frankenstein's Monster and stabbed his fingers in Doo-Rag's eyes.

For an instant he felt a phantom, a flicker of temperature behind him as he finished Doo-Rag with an elbow to the temple. For an instant he became a child again, back in the nightmare forest. Chris

Kezzlewick snaking over him, breathing on him. "Don't move Clay," David's ghost, freezing him.

For an instant. Then he felt a death grip on his shoulders, and teeth tear into his earlobe. Clay twisted with elbow out, knocking Meat off balance.

Stepping around the dog mess again—now a heap of four- and two-legged things—he thrust his fingers into Meat's mastoid process.

Clay didn't fight people, he dissected them.

But now training turned into something other than self-defense.

Like his Hellhounds, he hungered.

A four-legged thing descended on Meat's sprawled body. A digestive tract in the guise of a man, boiling with pain and blood lust. There was a script to it, the feeding. Clamp hands around prey's neck. Smell its fear. Bite off piece of prey's upper lip, like tearing open a bag with your teeth. Create an entry point.

Clay spat out the chunk of lip—Meat wouldn't be able to pronounce "lip" after that—and bit off pieces around the mouth. Speech, what two-legged things do. Then he bit off part of the tongue—Meat wouldn't be able to pronounce "tongue" after that—chewing, rending, working through the eyeballs, ears, nose cartilage. Meat kicked and flailed under the onslaught, shrieking like the little fawn dog. He tried to whip Clay with the chain around the pit bull's neck. Clay slammed Meat's arm down, then dug his fingers in the nose holes of the face beneath Meat's face.

Monstrous.

It was a red skull Clay left when he walked back to the truck. "An eye for an eye," an ear for a face—a face for every animal that had perished where Meat now lay screaming.

Meat, he hadn't even bitten all the way through Clay's earlobe. Mistake like that would have cost him if he'd been one of his own fight dogs.

Clay started the truck.

He hit the gas, Meat crawling toward him, at the front of the ring. One arm over the low wall, teeth gritted in that anatomy-chart face—at the last instant he jerked up and seemed to blink his lidless, eyeless eyes. Then the semi plowed through him and the low wall and clove the roof down the middle, slamming to a halt on the jumble of dead men and dead dogs in a cloud of dust and falling wood debris.

Clay dropped down from the cab, sunlight pouring in where holes weren't supposed to be, yelling and pounding and bumping inside the trailer where people weren't supposed to be, and the floor around the tractor unit streaked with gore. Meat's body laid out in a smeary contortion of limbs and spine and what looked like a raw ham hock with hair and, "lift, bro?" more identifiable than the rest of him sticking out under the fuel tank. It reeked of slaughter.

End of the line.

Clay staggered out of the ring where he'd entered, strapped on his shoulder holster. Doleful eyes watched him. He was always amazed at how tender the world could be in the aftermath of violence. Odor of gunpowder, corpses and spent cartridges strewn around the field and the chained dogs gazing at him like sad mothers. Sun blazing down on the rape he'd made of man and earth.

Sin Mountain, Clay's masterpiece.

I'm everything I hate, he thought.

He wandered through the carnage.

I've turned my truck, my sanctuary, into a weapon. I've turned Jimmy into a weapon. I've turned my body into a weapon. I've disgraced my teacher, my art. And I've walked on four legs, I've tasted the flesh of my enemy.

For the second time that day, Clay dropped to all fours.

His bowels seized, and conscience shot from him like it would never stop. It erupted with the force of weeping held back for years, racking gut-sobs of inestimable loss. His body wept for itself, every monstrous thing he'd made it do and remember. A river of death, sludgy and putrid, flooded from his mouth, bounteous and indifferent to his torment. He clawed the earth, hands soaked in mud and the pain of men, until only drool came and he fell on his back. Blue throbbed in his vision, death sky-written where no birds soared.

Then he slipped into dreamless sleep, black as the prison where Meat's people cried out.

Wocka-wocka-wocka-wocka-wocka-wocka

The Pac-Man ring tone jerked Clay awake.

Wocka-wocka-wocka-wocka-wocka-wocka

He got to his feet and drew Jimmy One.

Something caught his eye near the trail. A figure fleeing toward the woods. He had the impression it wasn't clothed, and didn't know how to run. Arms flailing, feet slapping down like clown shoes. Body of a lanky, undersize youth, how Clay was when he was twelve, swallowed by another forest. Only this stranger seemed eager, even desperate, to plunge into the woods.

No visible musculature, no butt crack, no hair even. The dogs saw it, too, watched it dash past, this live mannequin. They looked at Clay then. Their eyes said, *What are you going to do?*

He holstered the gun. Whoever it was could have attacked him and opted for escape. His gut—what he hadn't puked, what was left of it—told him he had a mess to clean up.

Morbid curiosity made him check the mountain he'd heaved, only to find the ground was clean. Not a scrap of Clay's moral bulimia remained in the puke-yellow grass. Like the first time Jimmy barfed and when Clay brought paper towels it was all gone, Jimmy licking his paws.

The chained pits, still staring.

What are you going to do?

The sun was still high in the sky. He hadn't been out for long.

He had five rounds in the Jimmies and four magazines in his pants pockets. Thirty-three rounds left, and seventeen people he'd counted climbing into the trailer. Some pounding the wall now. They would be his last kills. Then his war was finished. The massacre here, it would expose him and he deserved to die as he lived, by his own vengeance. Jimmy One would get the privilege, nasty way to send a man to the underworld.

Sin Mountain, Clay's self-portrait.

His swan song.

He fed the Hellhounds fresh magazines and went to the back of the truck.

Then he heard tires and saw a car coming toward him. He stepped out to meet it, Jimmy One drawn. The pounding in the trailer doubled. People shouted. Through the cracked, dusty windshield, Herc met his eye.

Clint "Herc" Walker, the cop killer, the minister. "I'm unarmed," he said, ducking out of the Trans-Am. Eaten by disease, he looked like a dweller in darkness, not meant to stand in the sun. Eyes even pinker and more rat-like, skin like the transparent membrane of an onion.

"You'll want to raise your hands," Clay said.

Herc did.

"You shouldn't have come here, Herc."

"I recognize you. You were at the bar last night."

He'd gone to the house to talk to Junior again, he explained. Son thought he was just another born-again, a Bible thumper. Which he supposed he was. Finding the place empty, he drove out here, a place he swore he'd never visit.

"I've heard what my son does." Herc glanced at the chained pit bulls. "What I saw at the house was bad enough. Is he in there?" He nodded at the trailer.

Clay shook his head.

Herc peered past him, into the ring. Swallowed.

He wanted to try one last time with his son before he called police, he said. Kept calling Scott, Junior's childhood friend. Scott usually answered.

"I don't suppose he's in there, either," Herc said.

"Try him again."

Herc dialed a number.

Wocka-wocka-wocka-wocka-wocka-wocka

He sighed.

"I was hoping I could save him. My son. But he didn't want to be saved. Him, Scott, the whole gang, they were headed for a reckoning. And you gave it to them. What you've done here, it's . . ."

"Monstrous," Clay mimicked Doo-Rag.

" . . . something I might have done, if I hadn't spent my youth busting heads in bars." Herc smiled with one side of his face, the way some men smile after crying.

"I used to be a vindictive SOB. You may have heard I killed a man. A deputy. I was drunk that night, but I'd been fixing to kill him anyway. He stole the woman I loved."

Every brawl, Herc said, was practice for when he would finally kill that man. Then all that rage, all that vengefulness, caught up with him. God forgave him for what he did, but his body wouldn't. That was God's price, he said, giving us vessels that can't sustain our darkest impulses.

"God will forgive you for what you've done," Herc said. "Even I can forgive you. It's not too late for you, if you stop now. Let those people go. Kill me instead. I'm dead anyway. Take my car. Disappear. With your health, the sky's the limit. Save yourself. Be born again. All that rage and vengefulness, it doesn't have to kill you."

"Maybe, not yet," Clay said, approaching Herc. "Still, you've given me an idea."

He pressed Jimmy One to Herc's forehead. Kidney cancer, nasty way to send a man to the underworld.

"Maybe not even the sky's the limit," Clay said.

And pistol-whipped him unconscious.

Herc, the born-again, saving people.

Offering them redemption.

Clay got in the Trans-Am. Keys were in the ignition. Rosary draped over the rearview mirror, Christ on a chain of death and rebirth. And Clay's face in the glass—a mask of puke and gore, a mask he couldn't take off.

Monstrous.

7

Flight 1580 to Athens landed right on time.

Dressed in the airline's new blue uniform, Shem Steward rolled his luggage through the jet bridge into the airport terminal. He bought coffee and gummy bears and took a table in the nearest food court.

Not that he needed caffeine, but he still enjoyed the ritual, sitting down with a cup of joe and "playing" at drinking.

In his down time, sightseeing, Shem learned something about Greek myth.

This ancient king of Thebes, Laius, gets rid of his baby because an oracle told him he's going to sire a son who will kill him. Years later he's traveling to Delphi in his chariot when he encounters a young man walking toward him at the crossroads. Young man won't give way, so Laius tries to run him off the path. Young man gets so enraged he kills Laius. Young man turns out to be Laius's grown-up son.

Moral of the story: Don't be a King Shit like Laius.

The young man, he's got troubles, too.

When he gets to the crossroads, he's already upset. The oracle tells him he's going to kill his father and marry his mother. And because he's a King Shit like his dad, because he won't share the road even with a sovereign, he fulfills the prophecy and doesn't realize it till way after.

Moral of the story: Don't be a King Shit like Oedipus.

For some of you, life's a Greek tragedy: You can't accept how things are, but if you think you're the one to fix them, you're begging for a beat down.

You're a King Shit.

You're doomed.

And doom followed Shem from city to city. Guts, Shem called him, born of horror and disgust, the shadow of the shadow of a man named Clay Haller. Shem sort of looked like Haller, only bald and mustached, his co-worker was sure he resembled someone famous but couldn't place it. Guts knew, though, Guts who stalked Shem across oceans, who needed no food or rest. Guts, like that golem Haller became long ago.

That day on Sin Mountain, pointing a gun at a dead man's head, Haller saw he would take his war to the skies, where no birds soared.

Since then the puking stopped and Shem Steward felt strong as ever. Like Guts, biding his time, studying his adversary, a creature of rage like his creator, waiting to give the King Shit a taste of his own medicine.

Till that day of reckoning, Shem had work to do.

That job in a bubble thirty-thousand feet in the air, a microcosm where chaos didn't reach. Annoyances yes, but only the occasional Laius type. Like the guy in 26C, wouldn't stop texting while they readied for takeoff. Ignored Shem's request three times, finally said he'd stop when he finished his message and not a moment before.

His skintight tee-shirt said, "Contents of this shirt may cause choking." Woman next to him, staring at something across the aisle, had a dime-sized bruise on her throat.

Sitting at the table, Shem popped a gummy bear in his mouth and watched people go by. His co-worker waved and rolled her luggage over.

Her name was Absolut, like the vodka, like Shem's attitude toward guys like 26C. Cocoa-skinned, big dark almond eyes, men rubbernecking when she sashayed down the aisle. His partner in coach sashayed toward him now, back from the deli with a mountain of curly fries she placed between them.

"That's right, you don't eat," she said, "except for those things." The gummy bears. "How do you do it?"

"I put one in my mouth. Then I chew it."

"Haha. I mean, how is it you never get tired or hungry?"

"I'm just made funny."

While Absolut dug into her fries, Shem noticed someone watching them across the food court. Guy his size, wearing black jeans and a matching hoodie. He slunk off behind the magazine rack, and Shem knew from experience he was gone, like a shadow into a shadow, the shadow of Athens, the shadow of a chariot waiting at the crossroads.

26C walked past, pausing mid-text to give Shem the stink eye. The woman next to him on the plane trailed after him, hauling their carry-on's.

Shem watched 26C go into the men's room.

"That jerk," Absolut said. "The whole flight he kept looking at me like I was naked. Where are you going?"

"Restroom," Shem said, standing. "I have a delivery to make."

"Eww, Shem. Too much. You've just put an awful picture in my head."

Shem smiled with one side of his face, the way some men smile after crying.

"Tell me about it."

CLEAN-UP ON AISLE 3
Adam Howe

Donnie sat in his beat-to-shit Pinto with the heater on full, huddling for warmth beneath the driver's-side window that wouldn't quite shut. An icy wind whipped through the half-inch gap, numbing his hands as he checked the .38 Special. He shoved the piece in his coat pocket, and then stared across the street at the mini mart, the neon KWIK STOP sign flashing red and blue in the night. It was the only store on the downtown strip still open this late. All the other stores had their shutters lowered, tagged with graffiti like tribal markings. Through the window he saw the scrawny Arab storekeeper perched behind the counter reading a magazine. Donnie hadn't seen any customers since he pulled up outside. The guy was alone in there. Just him and the cash register.

Checking his reflection in the rearview, Donnie gave a pained sigh. He looked and felt like stepped-on shit, sick with whatever bug was going around. Last thing he needed was to be pulling a job. But he was already late on this week's vig. He didn't pay what he owed and the flu would be the least of his problems.

He reached across the car to pop the glove compartment, fished out his lucky ski mask. Black wool, trimmed with red around the eyes and mouth. Dusting off the mask, he yanked it down over his head and then rolled it back up in a beanie hat. Donnie honked his nose into a snot rag, stuffed the hanky in his pocket with the piece, pumped himself up with a few wheezy breaths, and then he clambered from the Pinto and started crossing the street to the KWIK STOP.

The bell above the door tinkled as he entered. The cramped little store was divided into three narrow aisles, the shelves stockpiled like a doomsday prepper's bunker. Loud ethnic music was playing: trumpets and drums and off-key warbling like a cat being castrated. The storekeeper glanced up from his magazine. Leathery olive skin and a gray goatee beard, his bald pate polished to a gleaming shine. He wore a white collarless shirt and a ratty old cardigan. The guy reminded Donnie of the limey actor who went blackface to play Gandhi.

On the counter beside him a *No Checks, No Credit* sign was taped to the back of the register. Donnie cut a glance at the security camera above the cigarette rack. The very latest model . . . from the 90s. If the damn thing even worked, the playback would be a blizzard of static. It was probably just for show, to scare off amateurs.

Not taking any chances, Donnie bowed his head and shielded his mug from the camera's gaze as he sloped to the beer cooler opposite the counter. At the front of the store was a discount DVD bin, and a half-price arsenal of fireworks for New Years, the boxes all stacked in a pyramid like one giant rocket.

Donnie glanced down the three aisles for customers or other employees. He didn't see anyone. Just a lonely-looking mop and bucket in Aisle 2. The storekeeper was clearly no neat freak; the shelves were dusty, the goods caked in grime. The place could've used a good airing. It reeked worse than Donnie's fleapit apartment, and that was smelling something. At the back of the store was the liquor display, a few ragged cobwebs clinging to the bottles, and a steel door marked STAFF ONLY. Donnie couldn't hear anything behind the door, but it was hard to tell over the blaring music. Maybe the storekeeper lived back there with his wife and their litter of kids? *The hell with it.* He'd be gone before anyone even knew it.

With his back to the storekeeper, Donnie tugged his lucky ski mask down over his face and then reeled towards the counter, whipping the .38 from his pocket.

"Okay, asshole!" he shouted above the music. "You know what this is!"

The storekeeper glanced up from his magazine as if Donnie had only asked him to price check an item. Seeing the revolver in Donnie's fist, the man's dark eyes narrowed. He rose slowly from his stool, raising his hands. Unlike Donnie's they were steady as a rock. The guy looked so calm, Donnie wondered if he even spoke English.

Then he said, with a heavy accent: "Oh yes, my friend, I know what *this* is."

"Just open the register and gimme the money, you won't get hurt."

The storekeeper gave a curt nod, well versed in armed robbery etiquette.

Lowering one hand, he reached slowly towards the cash register and pressed a button—

And suddenly he wasn't there.

Donnie blinked in surprise.

The fucking guy just disappeared.

Peering over the counter, Donnie saw a trapdoor—the door still swinging where the storekeeper had dropped down into the basement onto a mattress. Splayed out on his back, the man glared up at Donnie with a hateful grin. Then he slashed a finger across his throat, before rolling off the mattress and out of sight.

"The fuck?" Donnie muttered—

And then steel shutters crashed down over the front door and window. The power went out, the store went black, and the music and even the hum of the refrigerators shut off, entombing the place in sudden silence.

It took a moment for Donnie's eyes to adjust to the gloom. He rolled his ski mask back up into a beanie. Stood gaping at the shutters in disbelief.

He'd never seen shutters *inside* a store before. He banged his fist against the shutters—thick steel, like the treads of a tank. Donnie lashed out with his boot until his knee buckled, and he hobbled back in pain. Feeling his skin crawl, he glanced up at the winking red eye of the security camera above the cigarette rack, shuddering as he pictured the storekeeper silently watching him.

He scurried behind the counter, ignoring the register, the cash now forgotten. Careful not to fall through the open trap, Donnie searched beneath the counter for a button or something to raise the shutters. What the hell had the storekeeper pressed to drop the trapdoor? Donnie couldn't even find a panic button. And now that he thought of it, why wasn't any alarm sounding?

Crouching warily above the open trap, he peered down into the dingy basement. All he could see was the mattress where the storekeeper had landed. "Hey!" Donnie shouted down, panic in his voice. "Open these fucking shutters!"

He could hear the storekeeper cursing in Arabic, like a camel clearing phlegm from its throat. The guy sounded pissed, like this wasn't the first time his store had been held up, but by Allah, it would be the last. Then came the unmistakable *shick-shuck* of a pump shotgun being racked. Donnie darted back from the open trap.

That's why there wasn't any alarm.

The guy planned to take care of business himself.

Donnie looked despairingly at his .38. He never worked with a loaded gun. If the threat of being shot wasn't enough, then the job wasn't worth it. Better to walk away, find some other place to stick up. Ideally with an owner who had enough sense to do what they were told when you stuck a gun in their face.

Until now, he'd thought he was being smart.

Shoving the *useless fucking gun* back in his coat, Donnie scuttled down the aisles towards the STAFF ONLY door at the back of the store. If it was locked, he was screwed. He'd have to take his licks and beg the storekeeper not to kill him. He was almost at the door when he heard the jangle of keys on the other side.

Donnie dove into Aisle 1 and crouched low behind the shelves, cloaking himself in the shadows as the door clattered open. The storekeeper emerged from the back room, clutching a shotgun bigger than he was. He paused to yank the door shut behind him, locking it from a key hoop clipped to his belt.

There was something funny-looking about him. In the gloom, it was hard to tell exactly what. Then the storekeeper turned his head, and Donnie thought he'd lost his mind. A giant frog was sweeping the shotgun left to right across the aisles. Donnie tried to blink away the nightmare. Then he realized the storekeeper was wearing some kind of mask. No . . . Not a mask. Night-vision goggles, the lenses protruding from his head like bulbous amphibian eyes.

Tiny jewels of sweat glittered on the Arab's scalp. He began to sidestep slowly along the end of the aisles, his cheap leather shoes squeaking as he crabbed along—the shotgun steady in his hands as he moved methodically towards Aisle 1—towards Donnie, crouching in the shadows.

Panicking, Donnie snatched a jar of coffee from the shelf in front of him, and then lobbed it over the aisles like a grenade. Glass shattered as it exploded on the far side of the store. The storekeeper pivoted with a squeal of his squeaky shoes. The shotgun roared, the blast punching a hole through the aisles and scattering stock, the deafening noise drowning out Donnie's scream.

This guy wasn't fucking around. He wasn't going to rough him up or make a citizen's arrest. Donnie wasn't talking his way out of this shit. There'd been no hesitation as the storekeeper turned and fired. That blast was intended to cut him in half. The man meant to kill him.

This should've been a quick dollar stickup. Donnie wasn't going to play cat-and-mouse with a shotgun-toting maniac. Let the cops deal with the crazy bastard. He'd take the arrest if it meant he left the KWIK STOP alive.

He dug in his coat for his cellphone. No signal bars on the display. He waved the phone about frantically, searching for a signal. Had the shutters caused some kind of blackout? He raised the phone towards the ceiling. A single signal bar flickered weakly. He listened out for the storekeeper. On the far side of the store, he heard Arabic cursing as the man found the shattered coffee jar and realized he'd been duped. The storekeeper racked the shotgun and started back along the aisles, his shoes squeaking urgently.

Donnie monkeyed up the shelves in front of him. The flimsy wooden shelving boards sagged beneath his weight. His ears were still ringing from the shotgun blast. He could only hope that the storekeeper had also been deafened; that the guy didn't hear him as Donnie slid on top of the shelving unit, disturbing a thick layer of dust that swirled around him in a cloud that prickled his fluey nose.

The storekeeper sprang into the aisle directly below him. When he saw the aisle was empty, the Arab muttered a curse, lowering the shotgun, and then adjusted the sweaty strap of his night-goggles. He was breathing hard. Maybe even excited. Enjoying the thrill of the hunt. He started stalking down the aisle towards the front of the store.

Flattened on top of the shelving unit, Donnie didn't dare move, holding his breath and fighting an almost overwhelming urge to sneeze. From the corner of his eye, he watched as the storekeeper crept along the aisle below him. The man left his line of sight, but Donnie was still able to track him by his squeaky shoe.

He checked his cellphone again, and gave a silent prayer of thanks when he saw there were now *two* signal bars on the display. But before he could dial 911, he inhaled another thick cloud of dust that set his nose ablaze—

The sneeze echoed through the store like a karate cry.

The Arab turned and fired without hesitation, the shotgun belching fire.

Donnie sprang from the shelving unit, shredded cereal boxes exploding behind him, a shower of Kellogg's raining over the store. Slamming into the next shelving unit, he crashed down into Aisle 2, landing heavily on his back next to the mop-bucket, his cellphone shattering on the floor beside him.

The storekeeper racked his shotgun and charged up the aisle towards him. Woofing for breath, Donnie could only flail his legs, kicking over the mop-bucket. Sludgy gray water spewed across the floor. The storekeeper slid on the muck like an Arabic Chevy Chase. He thudded to the floor and fired another deafening blast, plaster raining down from the ceiling.

Before the man could recover, Donnie scrambled to the nearest shelving unit. He slithered across the bottom shelf, clawing through a crinkling wall of potato chip bags, emerging into Aisle 3. Bracing himself against a deep-freeze refrigerator chest, he hauled himself up onto rubbery legs, sucking for breath.

Through the gaps in the shelves, he could see the storekeeper in the center aisle, wobbling to his feet like a prizefighter trying to beat the ref's count.

Racking the shotgun with a grunt, the Arab began limping around the aisle after Donnie, careful not to slip on the sludge-slick floor, one hand clutching at the shelves for balance.

Donnie was still slumped against the deep-freeze, trying to catch his breath. The small of his back was screaming with pain where he'd landed on it. His legs could barely support him, let alone carry him away. Before the storekeeper rounded the aisles and spotted him, Donnie hauled up the lid of the deep-freeze.

Hardly thinking about what he was doing, he slid inside the chest and buried himself among the frozen food packages. As he cowered inside the icy coffin, peering up in terror through the frosted glass, listening to the storekeeper's shoes squeak closer, it occurred to Donnie that as far as dumb fucking ideas went, this was right up there alongside robbing a store with an unloaded gun.

The storekeeper paused next to the deep-freeze. Wheezing for breath, he steadied himself against the refrigerator chest. Donnie stifled a scream as a hand thudded down on the glass lid. For a moment it seemed like the man was staring right down at him. Then he dragged his hand from the glass to wipe the sweat off his forehead. Frowning, the Arab glanced back down the aisle, maybe fearing his prey had circled behind him. Then he moved on to the back of the store.

Donnie waited until he heard the distant jangle of keys as the storekeeper checked whether the STAFF ONLY door was locked. Then he palmed up the glass door of the deep-freeze, and eased himself out, crouching down beside the refrigerator and listening intently. It sounded like the guy was doing another lap of the store.

This time, Donnie would be waiting for the crazy fuck.

He scuttled to the liquor display at the back of the store. Forced to squint in the gloom, Donnie scanned the shelves for firewater, saw a picture of Speedy Gonzales on a dusty label, and grabbed the bottle of *Arriba* 100-proof tequila.

Nodding to himself, he crouched behind the Aisle 2 end-shelf, and then peeked around the corner, waiting for the storekeeper to appear at the front of the store. He unscrewed the bottle cap, wincing at the screech of twisted metal. But the storekeeper didn't seem to hear. Donnie listened to the guy's shoes squeaking as he continued his patrol of the store. Donnie necked a big swig from the bottle. For what he needed to do, and for courage. He shuddered as the tequila burned through him. Snatching his snot rag from his pocket, he began stuffing it into the bottleneck until only a little cloth tongue poked out. Then he pulled his Zippo lighter from his pocket and thumbed the wheel. *Click!*

The storekeeper's shoes stopped in mid-squeak.

The Zippo shook in Donnie's hand as he torched the snot rag fuse.

The shotgun roared. A tower of Heinz cans exploded on the shelf above Donnie's head. Spaghetti sauce sprayed down over him, nearly snuffing out the flame. The storekeeper reloaded, feeding shells into the shotgun like a degenerate gambler playing the slots. Donnie mopped the spaghetti sauce from his eyes and then leapt out from cover. They faced each other like Old West gunfighters. A tin of beans rolled like tumbleweed across the aisle between them. The storekeeper saw the Molotov cocktail in Donnie's hands. His mouth dropped open in shock. He started raising the shotgun.

Donnie Hail Mary-ed the burning bottle . . .

And then he watched in horror as it sailed harmlessly over the storekeeper's head.

The bottle shattered against the steel shutters behind him and burst into flames. The storekeeper stood silhouetted before a wall of fire like a frog-headed demon from hell. Oblivious to the danger behind him, the storekeeper sneered at Donnie as he aimed the shotgun, his finger teasing the trigger—as flames started licking the fireworks display.

There was a blinding white flash and then the fireworks boomed like Hiroshima. Instantly, the storekeeper became a human fireball, the blast blowing him off his feet and hurling him up the aisles like a missile. He sailed straight past Donnie and crashed into the STAFF ONLY door, thudding to the floor like a piece of barbecue you toss to the dog.

The front of the store was now an inferno. Rockets ignited and screeched from the flames, setting shelves ablaze, the sound deafening inside the steel-shuttered store. The place was fast becoming a death trap.

Donnie crouched beside the charred storekeeper. He took off his coat and smothered the flames of the man's burning cardigan.

Wrestling the key hoop from his belt, Donnie juggled the red-hot keys, yelping as they scorched his palms. Wrapping his coat around his hand like an oven glove, he unlocked the STAFF ONLY door to reveal another locked door marked DELIVERY, and stairs leading down to the basement. Donnie knelt in front of the second door and sorted through the jumble of keys, trying to find the key that would fit the lock—

Something squeaked behind him.

Glancing over his shoulder, he saw the storekeeper staggering to his feet. His face was flame-grilled hamburger. The night-goggles were melted onto his head like devil horns. He propped himself up in the doorway, smoke coiling from the scorched rags of his cardigan. Before Donnie could stand, the Arab lunged at him, slamming the shotgun across his throat, pinning him back against the door. The fire had fused the shotgun to his hands. The melted flesh of his fingers was webbed across the stock as he crushed Donnie's larynx.

Choking, Donnie grappled the shotgun and shoved the guy back. They stumbled across the landing, tumbling down the stone steps and thudding onto the concrete floor of the basement. Landing on top of Donnie, the storekeeper jammed the shotgun back across his throat and pressed down with all his weight. Donnie spluttered and bucked, the key hoop in his hand jangling wildly as he flailed at the man's face before he slammed a long mortise key through the left lens of the Arab's night-goggles, driving it deep into the eye socket. He then wrenched the key in the man's eyeball like he was forcing open a rusty lock.

The storekeeper gave a hog-like squeal. His head jerked back, the keys dangling from his face like bloody jewelry. Yolky yellow gunk gushed from the shattered lens of his goggles, spraying across Donnie's face. Gagging, Donnie hammered the heel of his hand against the key, burying it deeper in the Arab's eye. The storekeeper shrieked, lurching to his feet and staggering blindly about the basement. Donnie scrabbled back across the floor, spitting eyeball fluid and heaving for breath.

The Arab crashed against a stock shelf, cans and jars clattering and smashing on the floor around him. He reached up to remove the keys from his eye, before realizing he couldn't—not with the shotgun welded to his hands. His arms twitched pathetically. Once, twice . . . Then all the fight seemed to drain right out of him. His body sagged, and he slumped down on a camp bed parked against the cinderblock wall, the springs squealing like his squeaky shoes.

Huddled on the bed, the man glowered at Donnie with his one good eye, the other a ruined hollow of red and yellow slime. He slowly raised his left knee. Donnie watched in disbelief as the man planted the sole of his shoe against the length of the shotgun and sucked a few shallow breaths . . . before he flexed his leg and the melted flesh of his palms ripped free from the stock with a sound like Velcro tearing. The shotgun clattered to the floor in front of him, but he was too weak to reach for it.

With raw and bloody hands, the Arab grasped the hoop of keys dangling from his face. Donnie covered his mouth with his hand— nearly begged the guy to stop—but he couldn't look away. The Arab yanked on the key hoop. The key ripped from his eye socket with a wet popping sound. He gave a yelp and fainted dead away, flopping back on the camp bed with the keys clutched tightly in his fist.

Donnie almost fainted himself; his head was spinning as he staggered to his feet. He peeled off his ski mask and covered his nose and mouth to keep from choking on the thick black smoke belching down into the basement through the open trapdoor above them. Fiery ash rained down onto the mattress. It wouldn't be long before the fire spread downstairs. Already the basement was baking like a pizza oven.

He took a wary step towards the storekeeper, eyeing the keys clutched in the man's fist. It looked like the guy was out for the count. All it took was getting burned half to death, blasted into a wall, thrown down a staircase and stabbed in the eye. But Donnie wasn't about to take any chances. This guy was like the fucking Terminator.

He kicked the shotgun beyond the Arab's reach. It skidded across the floor and clanged against the legs of a workbench. Don-nie paused when he noticed some kind of photo shrine on the wall above the workbench.

The cluster of photos showed a young woman. The storekeeper's wife, Donnie figured. She was beautiful (even in a burning building, Donnie could appreciate a piece of ass) and very pregnant. Beneath the shrine sat a chunky security monitor—but it wasn't showing the store go up in flames. Instead it was hooked to an old VCR player running a short loop of silent film.

The grainy black and white footage was timecoded in the bottom corner, dated six years ago. It showed the storekeeper's pregnant wife as she stood in terror behind the shop counter. She was opening the cash register for a jittery punk wearing a stocking mask that mashed his features. He was clutching a pistol in a sideways gangsta-grip. The cash drawer slid open. The punk's pistol spat fire. The back of the woman's long hair flailed as her brains splattered the cigarette rack. Bloody cartons of smokes rained from the rack in a waterfall. The woman crumpled to the floor. Leaning over the counter, the punk raided the cash register, pocketing bills as he fled the store.

The footage looped and played again. And again.

Donnie looked at the cushioned chair parked in front of the monitor, the cushion cratered by the weight of the husband, and the weight of the grief pressing down on him. How long had the storekeeper sat here? Hour after hour . . . day after day . . . watching again and again as his pregnant wife was gunned down by a two-bit stickup man. A piece of shit like Donnie.

Before the footage could loop and play again, Donnie switched off the monitor. He saw his reflection in the blank TV screen, and was about to look away in shame, sickened at the sight of himself. Then something in the screen's reflection caught his eye. A sudden movement behind him.

He wheeled around in time to see the storekeeper swinging a fire extinguisher by the hose like a mace-and-chain. The metal butt of the fire extinguisher scythed across his jaw, smashing teeth and bone, and Donnie dropped like he'd been shot, like the storekeeper's wife, out cold before he hit the deck.

When he came to, Donnie found himself facedown on the cracked concrete floor. His ankles and wrists were bound tightly with duct tape, hogtied behind him. He raised his throbbing head weakly off the floor. A rope of congealed blood drooled from his mouth, puddling like black treacle on the concrete. His vision blurred in and out of focus, but he could see he was still in the basement.

The room was fogged with smoke that was starting to clear. The fire upstairs had been extinguished. The storekeeper must have doused the flames while Donnie was unconsciousness. Donnie listened intently for the wail of EMS sirens outside. Surely someone must have reported World War III breaking out in the KWIK STOP. But all he could hear was the sound of someone digging.

A section of the basement's concrete floor had been broken, probably by the sledgehammer propped against the wall, a slab of stone levered up to reveal the dirt below. The storekeeper was using a shovel to dig a hole in the plot of earth, piling up the dirt beside a steel drum with a skull and crossbones symbol and a label marked LYE. The Arab's wounded hands were swathed in bandages. He grimaced in pain as he worked the shovel. Whenever the pain seemed too much to bear, he would glance at the security monitor on the workbench, watching the footage of his dying wife again, and summon the strength to continue digging.

When he was done, he climbed from the hole and loomed over Donnie.

Donnie tried to beg, but his shattered jaw and blood-clogged mouth allowed only a pitiful choked whimper. The Arab planted a foot on him, his shoes giving the last squeak Donnie would ever hear, as he kicked him into the grave.

Donnie landed on his back, his bound arms and legs twisting painfully beneath him with the impact. He watched in helpless terror as the storekeeper began shoveling the dirt over him. The last thing he saw was what looked like another shrine on the wall directly above him. No photos, this time. Donnie thought this one looked less like a shrine than a trophy wall. Nailed to the cinderblocks was a stocking mask, a bandana, and three ski masks, one of them black wool, with red trim around the eyes and mouth, and not so lucky after all.

BATH SALT FETUS
Jorge Palacios

Being a pregnant teenager is hard; being a pregnant teenager in Puerto Rico can be downright infernal. This island is a shit-stain in the Caribbean, a hellhole seething with Catholic guilt, a judgmental attitude, and unfiltered sexism.

Maria was one of these teenagers. She came from a broken home, but found a family in the local punk scene. She explored every kind of experience she could find. She'd slept around since she was twelve. By fifteen, she was tattooed and pierced all over, and was sloppily learning to play bass so she could someday start her own punk band. For now though, she was forced to be part of normal society and was sent by her mother to the laundromat.

As she folded her laundry, she felt the eyes of other people in the establishment, staring at her huge belly, giving her looks, cursing at her in silence and laughing at her misfortune, a pure sense of satisfaction in them knowing they were superior to this underage hood rat.

Maria just wanted to throw the detergent at them with all kinds of swearing and hatred. She couldn't take it anymore, those stares judging every step she took, every breath released from her body. She wanted to return to normal. She wanted an abortion.

She begged her friends to lend her money for the abortion, but none of them wanted to give it, some out of catholic guilt, but most of them because they were broke, since they too lived with their parents, or on the streets. She even asked her mother. After her mother screamed at her and called her a murderer, the subject was put to rest.

As the clothing spun around and around, she wondered what she could do to get rid of this problem, this reminder of the loser she had let inside her body.

After a twenty-minute walk carrying a huge bag of warm, clean clothes, she made it to her low-income housing (which was also a notorious drug-selling area code-named Crackville).

"Mom?" she called. She waited for a response, but there was none, just the humming of the refrigerator. Maria walked in and looked around expecting to find her mother, who must have gone out. Good, Maria thought. The last thing she wanted was some speech about how the youth of today was going down the drain, save your soul before it's too late, blah, blah, blah. She dropped the laundry bag next to the refrigerator, grabbed an entire box of Oreos, and went to her room.

Her room was the only place she could get any kind of peace. The walls were decorated with posters from some of her favorite bands: Discharge, GBH, The Casualties, DRI, Gwar and The Mentors. Most of her wall space, however, was dedicated to her own personal Jesus, the only rock star she ever thought was genuine, the true King of Rock 'N' Roll (fuck Elvis!), Kevin Michael Allin, better known as GG. She had photos and posters from his young rock 'n' roller punk days to his last moments, when he looked like a beaten-up bulldog.

She turned on her stereo, blasting "Hated in the Nation" as she took her clothes off. Her pregnant body repulsed her. Stretch marks covered her huge belly. Her swollen nipples looked brown when they used to be pink. More upsetting was the fact that the nipple rings had to be taken out, and her stomach tattoos, which she loved to display, were stretched to the point of repugnance. She had tattooed the word "Mayhem" in bold, pointy black letters. Now it looked like it had been smeared on with a paintbrush.

She wanted to drown in the bottle of Jack Daniels she had been saving for the day she got rid of the fetus, the bottle that had been lying under the bed for three months now. As she grabbed it, her cell phone rang.

"Yes?" she answered.

"Hey bitch, it's me." Loca. The kind of friend you didn't like, but couldn't really get rid of either.

"Hey Loca, what's up?"

"You still trying to abort that baby?"

"Of course!" Maria shouted.

"Stay calm, I'm on my way."

Maria's mind raced as Loca hung up. What could she have meant? Did she have a way to get rid of the fetus? She paced the living room, eyes wide as a meth-head, throwing her phone from her right hand to her left.

The sun was going down by the time Loca reached Maria's apartment, and there was still no sign of Maria's mother. They greeted each other the way two old acquaintances would, shaking hands and awkwardly hugging, then sitting next to each other on the living room couch.

"What stinks, bitch?" Loca asked.

"What do you mean?"

"Don't you smell it?"

Maria shrugged.

"Well anyway," Loca continued after shrugging in unison, "I've got this great shit you have to try called Freezing Moon. It's a new kind of crystal meth, supposedly from Norway or some shit."

"Why should I try it?" Maria asked.

"Because, bitch, not only will it get you high as fuck, but you'll abort the baby naturally."

Maria never thought Loca's words could sound so beautiful, with her nasally tone and arrogant stance, but what she said was exactly what Maria wanted to hear.

Loca pulled out a bag of blue powder that looked like cleaning detergent. Maria felt disappointed. For some reason, she thought that this "natural abortion" drug would look more . . . epic.

"I hope this doesn't kill me," Maria said. She was only half-serious, as she was willing to die if it meant getting rid of this thing.

Loca said, "At least it's guaranteed not to give you an overdose."

After a half hour of gossip and drug talk, Loca left, leaving Maria alone with the blue powder. She stared at it, sitting on top of the living room table, almost as if it was staring back at her.

She really wanted a cigarette, but her mother had forced her to throw them out. Hey, where was her mother anyway? It was night and the crickets were in full swing. She shrugged it off. Her mother had probably found somebody from her church group to shack up with.

This was it, no more waiting around.

She rolled the Freezing Moon into a joint, lit it up, and took a deep suck. The power of this drug hit her almost immediately, and the usually warm Puerto Rican weather turned ice cold. It ran down her veins and into her extremities, and up to her brain, like an electric shock. Her eyes became completely wide. She felt the sensation of riding a roller coaster, the ride moving faster and faster until her own skin started to peel, and her eyeballs detached from her skull. She screamed, and realized she was still in her apartment.

"This shit is awesome!"

She blasted one of her G.I.S.M. 7 inch records, and moshed around her living room, screaming loud Japanese nonsense that she thought was the lyrics. Once in a while she could feel the child inside her, kicking as if begging for her to stop, but she simply ignored it.

After fifteen minutes, the record ended and she blacked out on the couch. As she slept, she imagined herself falling from a mountain, hitting all the rocks on the way down and laughing the whole time.

She woke up two hours later, expecting to be on the side of a snowy precipice, but was instead lying on her couch. She looked around, trying to recollect what had happened, but the room looked spotless, and the only sound was the record skipping. She called for her mother again, but there was no answer. Where the hell was she? She was supposed to bring home a bucket of KFC.

"I'm starving!" Maria screamed. She rubbed her belly. She looked down at it and her frown grew deeper. "Fuck, I forgot I'm pregnant . . ."

She scratched her belly, and everything came back to her, especially Loca and her Freezing Moon drug bullshit. Sure, smoking it had made her feel awesome for a while, but it hadn't done what it was supposed to do. She was still preggo. She should have known Loca's tall tales were too good to be true. The lying bitch.

She began to scratch her belly deeper and deeper until she realized she had broken the skin. She looked at her fingers, covered in chunks of meat, and felt a weird energy inside her. She licked her fingers, and that energy went into her mouth as well. She had heard some weird stories about what meth could do to your body, especially from reality shows, and she wondered . . .

She got up from the couch and grabbed a knife from the kitchen. She cut into her arm, and the sensation that she felt ran all over her body. She let out a moan of pleasure as the blade sliced into her flesh and blood dripped onto the floor. That's when she realized the second side effect from this Freezing Moon meth strain: all the pain she should be feeling turned to sexual pleasure.

She let out a laugh, took off her clothes, and went to town on her body. She cut across her arms, her breasts, her thighs, her legs and her face, turning her once beautiful body into a road map of scarification and bleeding that turned the light blue carpeting into a dark mix of red and brown.

Then, as if in defiance of every "sanctity of life" speech she ever heard, she began to cut a target into her pregnant stomach.

She could not stop laughing. The orgasmic pain made her masturbate nonstop. She had multiple orgasms, the most intense coming when she slid the blade across her right nipple. It was the greatest moment of her life.

She sat on the floor, letting the energy flow and the blood escape. She looked down on her belly. She knew now that her body would never abort her baby naturally with those drugs, but the pain just felt too good to stop.

She went to her room, leaving a trail of blood as she walked. She looked at the poster of a bloody GG Allin and smiled, knowing she looked so much like him that he would be proud. She grabbed a wire hanger from the closet, bent it enough so that it looked like a long hook, and grinned.

The bathroom was filthy and needed a good scrubbing, as there was a huge black mildew stain running from the showerhead to the drain, nasty and constantly wet. This was a bane to Maria's existence. She hated having to stand there and look at it as she cleaned herself. But today it didn't matter, as her blood was now darker than any bathtub shitstain could ever be.

Standing in the tub, she opened her legs, took a deep breath, and inserted the wire hanger into her vagina. As the metal hook entered, what should have been an incredible pain made her instantly wet. She prodded her insides with the hanger's tip and perforated her internal organs, achieving multiple orgasms and squirting twice before she finally hit something. It was hard and round, and it seemed to shift with her belly as she pulled on the wire. This had to be the baby. It wasn't fun pain, or orgasmic, or sexy. It was real.

As the thing inside her stretched her vagina and broke her privates apart, she moaned louder than any porn star. She orgasmed as she pulled out the head. The hanger's hook was buried deep inside the baby's eyeball. She counted one, two, three, and gave another big pull. Out slid the baby, blood, flesh, and umbilical cord all in one. It splashed into the bathtub with a loud thump. Maria screamed once again in pleasure, and her legs gave way. She collapsed.

For a couple minutes, she was in orgasmic ecstasy. She had never experienced anything like this with anyone, not with a man, or a woman, or a vibrator. Her heart pounded at a million beats per second, making her breathing quite painful. Her vision blurred, and she wasn't in control of her lips, drooling on herself like a panting dog.

"Hey, bitch!"

The voice was gruff and loud, like somebody with authority, or just a creep that had smoked way too many cigarettes. It called to her a couple times, but her ecstatic state prevented her from doing anything. After a few minutes, her eyesight returned to normal, and she could move just enough to look at the aborted fetus between her legs.

She expected it to be lying there, dead as fuck, purple and covered in flies. Instead, it was sitting down, umbilical cord wrapped around it's body like a fucked-up meat toga that lead to her vagina, clearly alive, and far more familiar than she could have imagined. It was shaped like a normal baby, with tiny but chubby features and a big clunky head, but it had fucked-up facial hair, was covered in bad tattoos, and it's penis was tinier than your typical baby dick. She recognized the creature immediately, but at the same time, she couldn't believe it.

"You're . . . you're . . ." Maria struggled to say it.

"Yeah, I'm GG Allin, bitch. Your drugs gave me the perfect opportunity to come back from the dead. Now I need you to cut that umbilical cord so I can be free."

The fetus pointed at the cord. Maria wanted to laugh out loud, more because of the absurdity of the situation than anything else. But she simply nodded. She grabbed the umbilical cord, and began to stretch it in an attempt to tear herself free of her child.

"No scissors, eh?" GG Allin said. "I guess you'll have to do it the old-fashioned way."

Maria laughed, lowered her head and bit into the cord. The meat and blood tasted foul, and she was disappointed that it didn't discharge the same level of orgasmic pain that her other mutilations had caused her. After a few big bites and some pulling, the chord detached.

GG Allin chuckled, and began to levitate, the umbilical cord wrapping around his tiny body.

"Thanks, you fucking slut!"

GG Allin grabbed the end of the cord, and inserted it into his anus. He pulled it in and out, in and out, and he moaned and groaned with pleasure.

"Oh yeah," GG said, "That's it. I love to fuck myself."

Maria laughed and nodded, remembering the song.

After a small ejaculation, which looked more like a mass of yellow pus and smelled like mayonnaise that had gone bad, GG removed the end of the cord from his anus, and wiped the shit that covered it all over his mouth. Maria just watched, fascinated. GG couldn't help but notice.

"What are you looking at?" GG screamed.

"I've always wanted to meet you," Maria said. "I'm your biggest fan. I've modeled my entire life on what you preach."

"Yeah?" the fetus replied. "Well, why don't you suck on my asshole?"

Maria thought about it, but GG interrupted her train of thought.

"Wait!" GG screamed. "Better yet, why don't we get some drugs?"

"It's really late."

"I don't give a fuck, you cocksucking cunt!" the fetus growled.

"I need heroin!"

Maria stood still for a few seconds, staring at the stain that covered her tub, and thought about where she should take the fetus to get high. She then remembered that she was high, and looked at the fetus, smiling at his crooked, scarred face.

"I have a friend called Loca who has excellent drugs. We could go to her!"

"Lead the way, whore!"

Men, women, and children watched in horror as Maria walked down the street, completely nude and covered in blood and cuts, laughing maniacally, a blade still in her right hand. She did not know if people were looking at her or if they could see the creature following her.

GG Allin floated behind, sucking on his shit-covered umbilical cord and singing some unintelligible song that sounded more like barking. For the ten minutes that it took her to walk to Loca's apartment, everybody stared, but nobody dared to say anything to her. She stepped on broken glass and other pieces of miscellaneous objects, and the pain gave her bliss.

She walked into Loca's building. An old Dominican lady saw her and ran away screaming, but Maria didn't even react. She got on the elevator and pressed the seventh floor button. She knocked on Loca's apartment door, quickly, anxiously.

Loca opened the door, her hair covered in rolls, and her face smeared in skin cream.

"What the fuck is wrong with you?" Loca screamed as she opened the door. Her attitude dropped immediately after she saw the state of Maria before her. "Oh my God!"

Maria pushed her way in. Loca fell back onto her apartment floor, too shocked to push back. Maria locked the door behind her, and raised her knife. She grinned, and Loca looked horrified at Maria's red eyes and teeth, stained from blood.

"What happened to you?"

"Never mind that," Maria yelled. "I need more drugs, like the one you gave me."

"Oh fuck, the Freezing Moon . . ." Loca said.

"Hurry up!" Maria screamed.

"I . . . I don't have anymore!"

Maria's smile turned into a frown, and slowly turned into anger.

"You lie!" Maria screamed.

Maria raised her knife, and ran toward Loca.

Loca raised her hands, trying to block the knife.

Loca's severed fingers splattered on the floor, her screaming continuing as Maria sliced and diced her body. Maria stabbed her repeatedly, until the forty-fourth stab, which went directly into the middle of Loca's chest. Loca collapsed completely, and pooped herself.

Maria struggled to take the knife out, but it seemed to be stuck. After a couple of tries, she laughed again, drooling in her insanity.

"Mommy!"

Maria recognized the voice behind her, and turned around. GG Allin floated above her, poop falling from him onto the floor.

"Did you get the drugs, mommy?"

"No, darling," Maria said, "but I know exactly what you need."

Maria grabbed GG's umbilical cord, pulled the fetus to her.

She bit into him.

GG screamed and called her "cunt" and "bitch" repeatedly as Maria ripped off body part after body part. Blood and organs splashed on the floor and the walls of the apartment. The carnage went on until there was nothing of GG but a mess on the floor, and she digested it completely.

That's when the police kicked in Loca's apartment door. The sight of Maria, with Loca's dead body and tiny body parts that could only belong to a baby on the floor, turned their faces pale white and made them raise their weapons, ordering her to lie down.

As they entered, Maria again tried to pull the knife out of Loca's chest, succeeding and swinging it at the officers.

When they shot off her hand, she felt the bullet penetrate, and saw, as if in slow motion, the meat and the fingers explode, splashing into the air and to her face. The feeling of warm meat and plasma was electric. It went the same way as the panic-stricken officers let out bullet after bullet, breaking into her body with splashes of gore flying across the floor. Each one was like a jolt on her vagina, a never-ending vibrator, her body a huge clitoris, charged completely.

Was this death? Wasn't it supposed to be more morbid? She laughed out loud, and had an intense orgasm.

BORED WITH BRUTALITY
MP Johnson

Bored with everything, GG Allin decided to take a new approach to life.

He'd punched. He'd pooped. He'd bled. He'd fucked. He'd fucking rocked. He'd spent a decade outraging to the fullest extent possible, and now it just made him yawn. He couldn't even shoot heroin and shit in some whore's mouth while jerking off two faggots without falling asleep. To be fair, it was really good heroin.

When being brutal turned boring, he reasoned that the only non-boring thing he could possibly do, the only thing he hadn't ever really done before, was to try being normal for a change. He could just be a regular dude.

This wasn't going to be easy. He had stains from three separate vomits on his shirt. Driving his pinky finger into his belly button, he scraped out a wad of dried shit. Absentmindedly, he stuck his pinky into his mouth and sucked it clean while trying to remember the last time he had dropped a load. He would definitely need to shower. Yes, step one would be to take a shower and get clean clothes.

Technically though, he didn't have a home. Shoving aside the cardboard he had slept under, he looked around the alley. He didn't actually know where he was. His last gig had been in Chicago. A week ago? Two? He was probably still in Chicago. Where was the rest of the band? Fuck them. He didn't need them. If he was going to follow his plan, he couldn't turn to them for help.

They were all fucking nuts anyway. Merle? Dino? They may have had just enough normalcy to hold down places to live, but they were still nuts. Nuts, nuts, nuts. Boring and nuts. "Oh, let's go fuck a prostitute," GG mimicked out loud. "Let's do some coke." The words even tasted fucking boring on his tongue. Fuck the Murder Junkies and their boring, tedious debauchery. Fuck whores. Fuck drugs. He pulled a baggie of dope out of his jockstrap and tossed it in a dumpster. He was on the road to normal now, and it felt so wrong, so gloriously, wonderfully wrong.

He stepped out of the alley. He walked and walked, trying to figure out what he needed to do to fully commit to normality. Unfortunately, even with his heroin haze fading, he couldn't think of any way to complete the transition without engaging in one last boring criminal act. So he walked all the way to the suburbs, and he walked right up to a nice little house with light yellow siding. Not piss yellow, which the old GG would have loved, but a nice, sunny yellow that totally fit the bill for new, normal GG. He went around to the rear and busted open the back door with a surprisingly quiet and perfectly placed kick.

The back door led to the kitchen, where he peeled off his shirt and jockstrap and combat boots and tossed his only three articles of clothing into the garbage. There were three bins: recycling, organic and trash. He looked into the one labeled trash. It barely had anything in it, and what was there looked too clean. He was used to trashcans filled with dirty needles and whiskey bottles stuffed with cigarette butts. But he threw his refuse clothes in there nonetheless. Out with the old.

He found the shower and took a long, steamy soak. The hot water slowly penetrated the layers of shit and vomit and cum and blood. A snake shedding its skin. The detritus pooled in a brown soup around his feet.

Finished, he shaved off his scraggly facial hair. Without it, without the grime, even with the scars and tattoos, he looked surprisingly normal. Innocent. Perhaps even soft. He had never developed the hard lines that most men did, at least not on his face. He had put on some muscle in prison, so he did have some claim to masculinity. Not that he wanted it. He liked the intimidation that came with strength, but he despised the concept of the man's man.

He thought back to his high school days, when he wanted to

be beautiful, when he wore his hair long and flowing, and he knew what to do with makeup. He'd get called a faggot, and he'd take it, even though he knew the label didn't quite fit. In recent years, he still let his inner femininity out whenever he could steal a miniskirt in his size or convince some cunt to paint his nails. Fewer people called him out on it these days.

He found the bedroom. A totally normal bedroom. Off-white walls. Nicely made bed. A shelf full of puppets. He picked up one of the puppets. A blue-skinned humanoid with a burlap eye patch.

Guess this is what normal people have in their pads, he thought, rather than sacks of fertilizer and old drum sets and passed out groupies.

He returned the puppet to the shelf and started digging through closets. He found the wife's clothes first. Dresses. He was tempted to try them on, but he needed to put that behind him. He was going to be a normal man. So he kept digging until he found normal men's clothes. Black slacks. Polo shirts. A perfect fit too. He looked in the mirror. A perfectly normal man in perfectly normal clothes.

But then the front door swung open.

He heard two voices. Two giggling voices. It was time for him to leave. Except he really liked this house, this not-piss-yellow house. He liked the clothes.

So he let the giggling couple find him. He knew he must have had the normal look down just right when, instead of screaming, the couple merely went quiet for a moment and said, "Oh hello, I think you're in the wrong house."

They did, however, scream as soon as GG came at them. He started with the man, delivering a perfect blow between the eyes that caused the man to drop to the floor. The success of the punch excited GG. Was this what fighting was like for normal, not-high people? Blows landing where intended, rather than spiraling out into the ether like defective fireworks? Normal people don't fight, he reminded himself. This is just one last dip into non-normality before he fully committed.

He kicked the woman between the legs and she fell to her knees. He grabbed a picture off the wall and gouged the corner of its heavy wooden frame into her skull, once, twice, three times until she stopped moving and he was sure she wouldn't move anymore. Blood splattered across the shelf full of puppets.

GG got down on hands and knees and sank his teeth into the man's throat. He tore out the adam's apple and chewed on for a minute. It was like putting an entire chicken wing in his mouth. He spat it out quick. This was not how normal people killed each other.

He ran to the bathroom and washed his face.

That night, he buried the couple in the backyard.

The next day, he proactively stopped at each neighbor's house and gave this spiel, using the name his mother had given him, the name he had abandoned so long ago: "Hi, I'm Kevin. I'm David Bannister's, your next-door neighbor's, brother. He and his wife Jill wanted me to stop by today because they didn't have enough time yesterday. They signed on for a five year mission to help in Nepal, rebuilding after the earthquake, and I'm going to be staying in their home while they're over there. If you need anything, let me know. I want to be a good neighbor!"

Each time he delivered the spiel, the voice in his head that said "I bet her cunt tastes like salted deli meat" or "I'd like to lick his scrotum clean" got fainter and fainter. GG Allin's voice got fainter and fainter.

Eventually, Kevin could hardly hear it.

Within a month, he had a job. He had assumed David Bannister's identity for work purposes, which came with a business degree and a pretty solid resume, so he didn't have trouble landing a six figure salary as manager of customer operations of the local branch of a multinational tech corporation. It was very normal. Most of his work entailed sending emails telling people to check with other people to find out what to tell different people to do in order to get something done. It was easy.

There was one situation. One day, one of his underlings came into his office and made a blanket statement about how Kevin AKA David didn't spend enough time coaching his team and helping them be the best they could be. Kevin shattered his coffee mug on the desk and pressed a shard of ceramic against the employee's neck, hard enough to draw blood.

"Be the best you can be or I will peel off your face and use it as a cum rag," Kevin coached.

The employee ran out crying. Thankfully, Kevin had been doing such a good job of being normal, he convinced the board of directors that the confrontation hadn't happened and the employee was trying to frame him. They fired the employee.

Kevin got a nice, normal routine together. A morning run. A stop at the coffee shop. Work. An evening of books and television programs.

During one of his regular pre-work coffee shop stops, he was standing in line when someone tapped him on the shoulder. He had fallen into a daydream about which of the various pastries he should choose: Danish? Donut? And the tap came perfectly timed to pull him out of the daydream just as it shifted into thoughts of shoving these pastries up his asshole.

"It's your turn to order," the voice said, not rude, not angry, almost soothing.

"Thank you," he said, without turning around.

He placed his order and went on his way. As he walked away from the coffee shop, he heard that voice again.

"Excuse me," the voice said.

He turned to see a woman. Early thirties. Light makeup. Glowing skin.

"I've seen you before," she said, with a sly smile.

Kevin's stomach sank. He thought of all the talk show appearances, preaching his vitriol, preaching his truth while clad in a military helmet. He should have known this would happen. He should have known he could not just be normal.

"Yeahhhhhh," he said, shrugging.

"You come here every day, don't you?"

The relief felt wonderful. He would not be torn out of normalcy today. "Yeah, it's my normal pre-work routine."

She offered her hand to shake. "My name is Deb."

Deb. Deb. Deb. Sounded like a drug, he thought. Mainline some Deb. He shook her hand. It was soft. Softer than most girl hands he had touched. No calluses. No cuts. Just a soft, warm hand pressed against his. She smiled when he didn't let go in a reasonable amount of time. He smiled back. "I'm Kevin."

And then a dinner date.

At El Rancho, one of those Mexican restaurants that seemed to have zero Mexicans on staff. Deb lied to the waitress and said it was Kevin's birthday. The waitress brought out the rest of the staff, slapped a sombrero on his head and sang "Happy Birthday" before shoving a bowl of fried ice cream in front of him. He had never seen fried ice cream before. He couldn't even remember the last time he had eaten unfried ice cream. He went at it with his hands and Deb giggled, handing him a spoon. She showed him how to crack the shell and get a good spoonful of fried goodness along with the ice cream hidden within.

And then sex.

After their fourth date, she took him back to her place, a fancy apartment on the edge of downtown. She had vases. Art. She kiss-shoved him all the way to her bedroom and then pushed him onto the bed. She was still wearing her dress suit because they had met up right after work. It made her look powerful. So powerful.

"Punch me in the mouth," he said.

She screwed up her face and raised an eyebrow, but then made a fist and gently rapped her knuckles on his jaw, laughing.

Maybe normal people didn't do that when they fucked. He suddenly became super nervous, wondering what other stuff they didn't usually do. There was only one way to find out. He kicked off his slacks and waited.

Deb said nothing about the size of his penis. He knew it was small. Some girls liked to comment about it. They would say it was cute, or they would belittle him. Deb just dropped her skirt and lunged, face-first. She took it in her mouth and it went hard instantly. Then she climbed on. She rode him.

They maneuvered so he was on top. After she came, he squatted over her chest. He grunted, trying to squeeze a shit onto her boobs, but without his usual pre-fuck laxative, all he got was a turtlehead.

"What are you doing?" she asked, perhaps a little frightened.

That was all he needed to hear to know that shitting on a girl's tits post-sex wasn't the usual thing. "Just kidding," he said. He supposed that meant she wouldn't be shitting in his mouth either. Bummer.

Then he jerked off into her mouth and for some reason she was totally okay with that. Wasn't cum grosser than shit? He was going to have a hard time understanding normal versus abnormal when it came to sexy stuff, he realized. He decided to forego cutting open his scrote for now.

And then marriage.

They dated for nearly a year before he proposed. Although there was still part of him that just wanted to go on an endless fuck-spree, eating up every dick and pussy he could find, he was getting way into this monogamy thing. It was weird, having consistently good sex once or twice a day. It was exciting.

There was also an emotional connection. Deb would ask him questions he had never answered before, like "How was your day?" or "What are you thinking about?" or "What do you want the future to look like?" She seemed to legitimately care, and not in the way that his brother Merle had cared enough to pay for whores and heroin once in a while, but in a sort of normal way that he could barely understand and it made his heart race like he was on speed.

So he proposed and they got married in a small ceremony in Grant Park. He invited a couple co-workers who he had started hanging out with for football games and normal guy stuff, and she invited her sister and mom and a few friends. It was nice. It was so fucking nice.

And then kids.

They moved into Kevin's house, which had remained more or less unchanged since his arrival. Deb liked the exterior color, but required a fresh paint job. She bought a bunch of new furniture too. She made him throw out all the bedroom puppets. Turned out that was actually not super normal.

Deb vaj-blasted out kid number one within a year of tying the knot. It was a boy. A totally healthy and normal boy. Kevin and Deb agreed to name him Grant, after her deceased father who was a veteran. A year later came kid number two, a totally healthy and normal girl who they named Vanessa, because Deb thought that sounded like a model name and Vanessa was so pretty she was going to be a model for sure.

Kevin almost got derailed from normalcy watching Deb shove her milk-tits in the kids' mouths for them to slurp on, but he held it together.

He was good with the kids. He quit his job and became a stay-at-home dad, because Deb's salary was enough and the house was paid for, sort of. Grant's first word was "Daddy," which was about as normal as Kevin could have dreamed.

When they learned to walk, he played games with them in the backyard, trampling over the ground where the rotting corpses of the past homeowners were buried just a few feet deep. He played normal games with them, games like tag and soccer, games that didn't involve any measure of urine or blood. Actually, Vanessa fell and scraped her knee once, and not only did it bleed, but she got so worked up over the wound, she lost control of her bladder and piss shot out of her shorts. It was like old times, but Kevin did not smear any of the fluids on his face or his sex nub. He lovingly took Vanessa inside and washed her off. Grant watched, exclaiming how "Totawy gwoss and awesome" the mess was, because for some reason it's normal for young boys to be excited about that stuff, but not adults.

One sundrenched summer day when Grant was four and his Allin genes started to show through to the point of annoyance, he slapped Vanessa and dragged her by her hair across the backyard because she wouldn't let him play with one of her dolls. Kevin had become strangely protective of his brood, and it actually hurt him a little bit in the pit of his stomach to see either of them injured. The feeling was confusing as hell. One of those unforeseen excitements of normalcy. He tried hard to understand it, and kind of reveled in it. He sent Grant to the basement on time out, because he did that sort of thing now.

When time out was over, Grant emerged from the basement with a massive old garbage bag. Kevin had seen that bag before. He couldn't quite remember though. Had he killed a whore and put her, or him, in there before he had fully committed to normality? Shit, that would explain the smile on Grant's face.

"Daddy! Wook! Wook!" the kid exclaimed.

Vanessa fluttered around him like a butterfly, drawn to the excitement.

"I, uh, have never seen that bag before in my life," Kevin said, as if talking to police officers, although he had never said anything more than, "Fuck off you fucking pig cocksucker motherfuckers" to law enforcement before.

Grant reached into the bag, but instead of pulling out a severed slut limb, he retrieved a puppet—a nappy, blue-felt puppet with a burlap patch over its eye. Kevin remembered the puppets that had been in the bedroom. Deb had hated them. He wondered if she'd be pissed off that they got dragged out, but it made sense to Kevin to let the kids play with them. Shit, less money to spend on new toys.

"Oh yeah, my old puppet collection," he said, swiping One Eye from Grant. He looked closely at the puppet. It didn't look right. In it's one black eye, it held a lot of . . . He wanted to say hate. He wanted to say self-loathing. He wanted to say the stuff he used to see in his own eyes when he looked into the mirror, but that didn't make sense. This was a fucking puppet and that was a goddamn button, not an actual eye, and it couldn't hold emotion any more than the grass below his feet could.

He dropkicked it across the yard as Grant and Vanessa tore into the bag, pulling out dozens of ridiculous puppets. Grant shoved his hand into a furry red one wearing a tinsel boa around its fat neck. The boy held it up to Kevin and said, "This one wants to chew off your ears!"

Vanessa waved around a dragon puppet with a large, cotton-spewing gash across its belly. "This one wants to chew off your penis, Daddy!"

Kevin clenched his teeth. Where was this violent talk coming from all the sudden? He thought of the look in the one puppet's eye. Was it the puppets? Were they influencing the kids somehow? Ridiculous. These kids probably just really did have the Allin family genes. "Don't talk like that, kids. It's not normal."

Grant and Vanessa frowned in tandem for a second before

giggling and going back to the business of sorting through the puppets. Kevin wondered why he hadn't thrown them away. Wait, hadn't he? Well, obviously not.

He left the kids to their mischief and went inside to make supper. Deb was celebrating her work anniversary, so he decided to cook his specialty: spicy sweet potato burritos. They burned so good coming out the back end. But that's not why he loved making them. He loved making them because they tasted delicious, and Deb agreed. And he had bought some brownies from the bakery down the street. It was going to be a really wonderful evening.

"My fingers got ated!" Grant screamed, crashing through the back door with blood spraying out of him as if it desperately needed to be someplace else, like the walls, the floor, all over Kevin's face.

Vanessa followed her brother, the dragon puppet clamped to her shoulder and gnawing deep into her flesh. "Get it off, Daddy!"

Kevin tore the writhing puppet off his daughter. It was strong. He could feel the power of its jaws as they snapped at his face, but he managed to keep the teeth far enough away that he didn't lose his nose.

Cotton spewed out of its gut wound. It squirmed out of Kevin's hands, wrapped its long tail around his torso and squeezed. Kevin felt something. Was it a rib crack? It had been so long since he had felt pain so sweet. He moaned.

But now was not the time to revel in it. With his foot, he flipped the oven door open and threw the dragon puppet inside, onto the cookie sheet full of burritos, completely ruining them. He turned the oven up as hot as it would go. The puppet flapped its wings and collided with the element, catching fire.

Vanessa screeched.

Grant yelled, "Dad, they're coming!"

Kevin looked at the door. One of the puppets had made it inside. Legless, it propelled itself on thin, hollow arms. It looked at the family and cackled through a row of sharpened teeth. Kevin ran at it and kicked it back outside, where it landed on top of its cohorts, who crowd-surfed it to the back of the pack. Kevin slammed the door shut, just as Deb entered through the front.

"I'm hoooo . . . oh my fucking god!" she screamed as she entered the kitchen and saw Grant's bleeding, fingerless hand. He still had his pinky bone, stripped of skin and outstretched daintily, but the rest were gone. Kevin took off his shirt and wrapped it around his son's bleeding mess.

"Puppets. Attacking. Now." That was all Kevin could think to say.

His heart beat so fast. Was it because of the excitement of having blood on his face again? He felt no urge to smear the crimson on his tattooed torso, to trace a bloodstained fingertip over the Live Fast Die logo that was once his motto, which he had now abandoned in favor of Live Slow Happy. No, his heart was beating so fast because he was in danger, because Deb was in danger, because the kids were in danger, because he cared about them. What the fuck?

Deb embraced him. His kids embraced them both. A family hug.

The puppets pounded on the back door. At first, it was cacophonous and undefined. Then it melted into a rhythm. Boom boom pow! Bang rap rap! Boom boom pow! Bang rap rap! And the puppets sang:

Violence now!
Fuck your corpse!
Brutality! Brutality!
Endless warrrrrrrr!

Fuck. Were those his lyrics? Did the puppets know him? Did they know the real him. But this was the real him now: normal father and husband living in a nice house. Those weren't his words. They meant nothing to him. Only his family. These fuckers that had stolen his fucking heart. Fuck them. Let them die. No!

One Eye stared in through the kitchen window, gnawing the head off a squirrel. It used the blood as lube to masturbate a little felt nub that bulged above its puppet hole. It came fast, shooting a neon-pink load all over the glass. It smeared cum and squirrel blood on the window, and then, with its now flaccid puppet dong, wrote the word "Kill."

In a voice like a derailing train, One Eye bellowed, "I'm gonna fuck your fat dead ass. I'm gonna fuck your whole family after I kill them and suck out the goodies from their stomachs!"

Kevin could picture this happening. And he was scared.

Then he thought, why the fuck am I scared? I'm fucking GG Allin! Except he wasn't. Not anymore.

"Kevin, you have to stop them!" Deb pleaded.

But he wasn't a person who could stop them. He had grown pudgy. He had gotten weak. He was a normal, family man, and one thing a normal family man didn't do was fight off packs of cock- and cunt-hungry puppets.

"I'll call the police," he said, reaching for the phone.

"The police? Kevin, there are dozens of those things. They are going to be in here any second now, and they are going to hurt us. You need to stop them."

"I am a normal man," he whined.

"You have to protect your family!" Deb screamed.

He curled his hands into fists. He looked at his scarred knuckles. He could do it. He could open up the floodgates and let GG Allin take over, but then what? GG Allin was powerful. Kevin was not. And Kevin liked this life. It was so sublimely normal, so comfortable. He could live this life forever. Surely the police would be here in time. This was Chicago, after all.

He undid his fists and reached for the phone.

He typed in 911.

He didn't even get past the first ring before the backdoor exploded under the weight of the encroaching puppets. The biggest one led the way, a goat-horned beast with purple fur so tangled it seemed like it was strangling itself, an impression furthered by the way its black tongue dangled from its wide mouth. This puppet had legs, and it moved quickly on them, quickly toward Kevin's family.

It drove its left horn into Vanessa's stomach, ripping through her shirt, ripping through her. She cried out, hands reaching for her mother. A flank of meat hung by her side, where the horn had exited. A little shard of rib jutted out, like a horn of her own. Blood poured out like tar. She lost the strength of her legs, but Deb held her up. Vanessa's eyelids fluttered closed.

Goat Horns clamped down on Deb's leg, but Deb kicked it off

and stomped on it. It seemed impervious to stomping. Just plush and stuffing. There was nothing to break. Nothing to damage. One of its eyeballs popped off and it laughed.

"I'm going to eat your womb, bitch," Goat Horns said as Deb stomped.

A cape-wearing, flesh-colored puppet with a black mask and a plastic pompadour flew at Grant. With surprisingly nimble fingers, it unwrapped the T-shirt from the boy's wound and then wrapped it's mouth around the mutilated hand, slurping up the blood as its massive eyeballs rolled back in ecstasy.

Deb swatted it away. She lifted the two kids off the ground. She kicked and stomped at the army of puppets. She glared at Kevin, who merely stood on the other side of the kitchen, sweating and crying. "Please," she begged.

And he realized he had no choice. His family would die if he didn't help them. They would die and he would die too. But he wanted to die on his own terms. Ideally by his own hand. And while drunk and high. Not by killer fucking puppets.

He spread his arms wide and roared. With both fists, he punched himself in the face, again and again. The old wounds opened up fast, remembering this. Blood poured from his forehead, from his nose. He saw red. He legitimately saw red. The blood framed his vision.

"What are you . . . ? Kevin?" Deb asked, out of breath from the fight.

"I'm not Kevin," he said as he snatched up the already somewhat mangled body of Goat Horns. He bit into its face and tore off a hunk of plush, which he immediately spit to the floor. "I'm GG fucking Allin."

He took another bite. Oily muck oozed out of the puppet's wounds. It tasted like black licorice on GG's tongue. He smiled and it dribbled from the corners of his mouth. He threw the now-limp puppet aside and caught another one, the superhero blood-slurper. He wrapped its cape around its neck, tighter and tighter, until its head popped off and black goo drained from its neck.

GG's cock got hard.

He didn't toss the headless puppet away. Instead, he dropped his slacks and impaled his dick in the inky stump, swabbing his member around inside the still-twitching puppet as the other puppets watched on, suddenly not so tough. He pumped and pumped and quickly ejaculated, so hard his white slime shot out through the thing's empty puppet hole.

Deb gasped. She covered Grant's eyes. Vanessa was passed out from the severity of her wound. Deb said, "Kevin, just . . . just kill them normal?"

"I'm not normal!" he yelled as he grabbed two more puppets by their heads and tore them asunder with his hands, hands already so soaked in cum and blood that they were starting to look familiar, they were starting to look like his hands.

Realizing they had much more of a challenge than they had anticipated, the puppets worked together now. They charged at GG, baring claws, baring teeth, baring horns. GG kicked and punched.

An anus-faced puppet latched onto GG's nipple with little pin-like teeth. Oh, but it felt good. He got hard again as blood poured from his chest wound like electricity, lighting him up. Ripping the puppet free, he got an idea.

He took a squat and, as if all his repressed bowel muscle memory suddenly overcame the self-induced amnesia, he shot a stream of feces so wet and fast it splattered off the kitchen tile and gave his backside an upside down shit shower. He scooped up handfuls and smeared them over the eyes of every puppet he could reach, blinding them and slowing them down enough to give him time to properly execute each and every one of them, which he did, as his wife watched.

When he was done, he stood, breathing heavy, ankle deep in scrap material and black puppet guts. He couldn't keep his hand off his cock.

"Kevin? I don't understand. What are you doing?" Deb asked, as if he was the bad guy, as if he had threatened to kill the family. Well maybe his family deserved to fucking die. Maybe everyone deserved to fucking die.

Before he could address that, Deb pointed to the kitchen window.

That blue-faced, one-eyed fucker was still there, sneering.

GG punched through the glass and grabbed the final puppet by its neck. He squeezed the thing's head, mushing it up and covering it with slick bodily fluids, lubing it up for easy entry. Then he jammed the puppet headfirst up his ass. Groaning, he worked it in and out, using two hands at first, before freeing one up so he could jerk his nub. He realized his wife was still watching.

"Suck my cock," he ordered.

"Wh-what?" she asked.

"Suck my fucking cock, now!"

GG stepped toward her and grabbed her by the back of her head, getting a solid grip on her soft blonde hair. He pushed her to her knees.

Grant dragged his sister to the far side of the kitchen as she blinked back into consciousness. She would die soon. Maybe Grant would too. Who could tell how the rest of the day might go?

The sound of sirens answered that question. The 911 call must have gone through. They must have traced it. Just like the fucking pigs. Too late to help, but just in time to fuck up the party.

They smashed down the front door and charged into the kitchen. Four barrel-chested boys in blue, ready to inflict the law on somebody.

GG tossed his wife aside and threw shit at the pigs.

They were on him fast. He couldn't stop them. They took him down. They cuffed him. They dragged him away in a headlock. Deb ran behind, angry now, but not at the cops. "What's wrong with you?" she screeched.

"This world is what's wrong with me. This fucking world and everything in it. I hate you! You hear me? I love nothing. I love no one. I hate everyone and everything, and I always fucking will, forever and ever until the end of fucking time!"

And then the cops pulled out their nightsticks.

EXPOSED
Monica J. O'Rourke

I stalked him for weeks, as I imagined he'd done with my little girl.

The cops knew who he was, but they kept saying the evidence was circumstantial, that they didn't yet have a case. They had him under constant surveillance, I was told. Yet why did I see him running around on his own, unwatched? I'd see an unmarked cop car in his area, but no one really had tabs on him, which was insanely frustrating. They knew who kidnapped Rebecca—they knew who the guy was!—but what? his civil liberties trumped hers?

You need to stay out of it, they said.

Were they kidding?

I knew where to find him. Right in front of my pickup, as fate (or GPS) would sometimes have it.

I make this sound so easy: He was crossing the street against the light. I waited for him to turn the corner before I cut him off. I slammed on the brakes, and he bounced off the hood and landed on his back, momentarily dazed. I smashed him in the face with my fist—the fist with the roll of quarters in it. I made sure he was out cold before dragging him to the flatbed. I managed to get him in, tied his hands and feet with zip ties, and covered him with a canvas.

No one was around, which is a small miracle in itself—never mind the media and every amateur reporter with a smartphone who also seemed to be following this guy. Isn't that what usually happens? Even more shocking is that the cops weren't around.

An hour later I dragged his sorry ass inside the cabin and tied him to the bed. A quick scan of the woods satisfied my paranoia that I hadn't been followed. Not that it mattered. I would have done anything to save my kid, including give up my freedom. Or my life.

That's how it all started. This part of it anyway.

He started the whole goddamn thing weeks ago.

I build a fire in the fireplace.

Andy's waking up. I found his name on his license. Andy. *Andy*.

His hideous head rolls from side to side, the whites of his eyes flashing, trying to focus.

His eyes pop open. "What—" He sees me. "Are you nuts?"

Well that's an auspicious beginning . . . I pull up a chair and straddle it. "Where is she?" I ask quietly.

He snorts. "What? Who the hell are you? Fuck you! Untie me."

Does that ever work?

My voice gets a little louder. "Where is she?"

He laughs, glints of yellow, nicotine-stained teeth flashing. Smells, like sour mash and cheap tobacco, ooze from his pores. "Go to hell."

What if I told you this was a blue-eyed college kid? No nicotine stains. Smells more like Gray Flannel than old booze. Looks like someone who'd run for state senator.

Ted Bundy was a pretty boy too.

I slowly approach him. These are tricks I've learned from watching every episode of *Law & Order* and *CSI* and *NCIS*. I learned ways to make him nervous (as if being tied to a bed wasn't enough). But none of it seems to be working. It always works on TV. Even when the women are in charge, the skeevy men always cave.

"You're starting to piss me off," he says, licking his lips. "You're making a big mistake. Untie me, you asshole!"

I study his face. Is he panicking? Nervous? Shouldn't he be? But there's no panic. He's just angry.

I have a feeling he thinks I'm bluffing.

I check the bindings on his wrists and ankles, making sure they're solid. He's tied spread-eagle on top of the quilts.

He's not going anywhere.

"You're killing her," he says with a leering sideways glance. "You know that?" His face is solid, tight, the jaw line set. He gnashes his teeth.

Or maybe I'm imagining the bravado. This is a guy who stole my kid. Stole. My. Kid. He looks like a giant slug, riddled with herpes, dripping pus.

I have a hard time reconciling that with the young man lying there . . .

I close my eyes to fight the tears. This isn't easy; this is the hardest thing I've ever done in my life. I don't even know how I'll be able to—

I open them again. "I'm not killing her," I whisper. "I'm saving her."

"I'm the only one who knows where she is." He spits in my face and struggles against the bindings.

I walk into the bathroom to wash the pig's saliva off my cheek. I stare at my reflection in the medicine cabinet mirror. Eyes that haven't rested in weeks stare back. Too many wrinkles on this old face that's really not that old at all. Not until recently. Too many grays where there once were none in a mane full of blonde hair. The pigshit in the bed has done this to me.

He's yelling, cursing at me like something possessed. Screaming for me to untie him. That's laughable. If he were to get away, I'd be dead. I was surprised I could get him in here in the first place, but a rush of adrenaline allowed me the strength. Not that I lifted him over my head or anything; I'm much smaller than him.

I sit in the chair beside him. "Where is she?"

"She's dead!"

I blanche, but I pray he's lying. "Where is she?"

He laughs again, but I can tell he's nervous.

"Look . . ." I say, pulling a bandana out of my back pocket. "It's obvious you won't voluntarily give me the information I want."

"What are you doing?" His eyes bulge.

After twisting the bandana into a long line of fabric, I lay it across his mouth, knotting it near his ear. He shakes his head and tries to avoid me but can't. He tries to head-butt me but doesn't get far.

"We'll try it my way for a while. If you change your mind and want to tell me . . ." I shrug. "Just say something."

Even if he wants to speak, he can't. It's all head games now, you see? It's the only way to make this work. I have no clue what I'm doing, but I hope he doesn't see that. The main reason I gagged him was so I wouldn't have to hear him crying and begging for help.

I grab the scissors off the counter and cut away his clothes. I'm not about to untie him and give him any opportunity to escape. He shakes his head and groans into the bandana. I let him lie in his underpants for a few moments before cutting them off as well. I figure this posturing represents the final act of stripping him of his dignity, and that maybe I can stretch it out. Being naked is one of the most vulnerable states to be in.

He looks up at the ceiling, not at me. I move closer. His eyes are filled with tears and he's trying not to cry. The highest part of his cheeks are tinged a dark pink. He says something into his gag, but of course I can't understand him.

"Are you going to tell me where she is?"

His eyes dart down and he glares at me. Hatred is radiated in that look. He doesn't bother acknowledging my question. I realize a little nudity might embarrass him, but it isn't going to convince him to confess to my baby's kidnapping.

My daughter is twelve. She hasn't lived yet. She hasn't fallen in love, gone to the prom, started the karate and ballet lessons she wants to take. She hasn't had her first kiss or her first date, she hasn't put on makeup, she hasn't traveled. She hasn't learned to drive and hasn't learned to swim. My little girl hasn't lived yet.

He took all that away from her and dangled it over our heads like the Sword of Damocles.

I told my husband I was going to visit my brother, that I had to get away. And while he was pissed that I was leaving him at such an inappropriate time, he told me he understood. Did he believe me? Not likely. But he trusts me.

"Last chance," I whisper, for I truly am afraid of what I must do. "Where is she?"

His Adam's apple bobs and he closes his eyes.

I move over to the fireplace and stoke the embers. Earlier I laid the poker in the smoldering ashes, along with an assortment of knives and sticks.

I wear an oven mitt because the metal poker has become too hot to handle without it.

The way he stares, it looks like he's about to pop a blood vessel.

A poker seems appropriate somehow. I thought it might be effective, but more as a scare tactic. I hope I can use it if I need to. I'd never harmed another human being before today—not intentionally and certainly not physically. Certainly never with a fireplace poker.

It's not easy to think of that pile of cow manure stinking up the bed as anything other than human, but I force myself. I imagine my daughter's face and know I can do this.

But it's something entirely different to inflict pain, even on him.

Still . . . when I close my eyes, I can imagine him doing horrendous things to my innocent child. Suddenly it becomes a little easier to think about inflicting pain.

"Well?" I stand between his feet and glare.

He wildly shakes his head, but I'm not interpreting that as a willingness to confess. More of a begging, a silent "no" screamed into his gag.

I know he can't get away; those ropes are secure and wrapped around every limb and joint in triplicate, but his thrashing won't make this easy.

I lower the poker inches from his chest. His thrashing stops to avoid smashing into it. Instead, he cringes, trying to sink into the mattress.

I swipe the poker across his nipple and quickly pull it back; it dissolves his flesh. It shocks me how devastating that touch was . . . how deeply it sank into his chest, searing the nipple off, the stink of burnt skin and hair making me gag.

His screams are muffled in the bandana and he thrashes again. He smashes into the poker that I held a little too close to his body, and ugly red welts and burn streaks pop up on his skin like a shapeless tattoo.

The smell of burning flesh is new to me. I step back. I want to stop this! But I keep telling myself why I'm doing it. I think what bothers me most is knowing what's still left to come. He can end this now if only he will tell me where he took my daughter!

Sweat pours down his face. The skin on his chest and nipple is raw, oozing pus, severely burnt. It looks horrible.

"Where is she?"

He stares at me, his body quivering, and he slowly nods.

I cut the bandana off and he spits it out of his mouth. A long stream of vomit follows. I hadn't considered that. I have to be sure he doesn't choke to death.

"Stop," he moans. "Please."

"Tell me where she is."

"I can't . . ."

"What?" Not the response I was expecting.

"I'll go to jail."

I tried to figure out his logic. "If you don't tell me where she is, I'll kill you."

"Untie me," he says, his large, insane eyes pleading, now squeezing shut in agony. "I'll take you to her."

I grab the duct tape off the dresser and slap a piece over his mouth. At this point I don't know what to do with him. What will make him talk? I've planned things; I think I've gotten somewhat creative. It scares me that I've thought of these things, but I'll do what I have to, to make him tell me what I want to know.

I remove the chef's knife from the fire. The fireproof handle remains cool enough to touch without an oven mitt.

He sees me coming and shakes his head, squeezing his eyes shut.

I don't bother asking him where my daughter is. He's not ready or willing to tell.

Starting at the bottom of his ribcage, I scrape the white-hot blade across his flesh, searing a message into his stomach. I have to reheat the knife several times to finish burning the words into his skin. In capital letters I write CHILD MOLESTER. Actually, it's not coming out as neat as that. In four rows the message says

CHILD

MO

LES
T E R

Then, under the words, I carve an arrow

↓

pointing to his groin.

His skin is a stippled, bloody ruin. I pour water on his stomach, not to bring him comfort but to wash away the gore so I can see the message.

If I had more time (or the fortitude) I would carve my daughter's image into his forehead so he would see her in his reflection for the rest of his life.

I think he's passed out. I check on him and make sure he's still alive. I know none of my cuts or burns were very deep.

He isn't dead. He's just passed out.

I let him sleep because I don't know what else to do with him. I just want this to be over! I know I'll have to spend time in jail for what I've done, but I don't care. This was the only way I could think of to get my Rebecca back.

But it isn't working.

I set the kettle on the stove to boil water for tea. I hear him moaning again; I guess he's awake. I'd removed the tape a little while ago so he could breathe. I didn't do it out of any sense of empathy but so he didn't drop dead of asphyxiation.

"Help me . . ." he moans, and his pleading makes my blood curdle. "The burns . . . they're bad. Please do something."

Do something? What I'd like to do is throw a heating pad over his stomach.

"You can end this right now," I say. "Don't make me do any more!" I'm near tears, and I hate that. He doesn't deserve one drop of my body fluids. He'll think I'm crying for him.

He tries a new approach. He spews his words at me through puffed cheeks and an agonized grimace. "If you touch me again I'll kill you and that fucking kid!" Spit and vomit flies out of the corner of his mouth. "You hear me?" he screams. "I'll fucking skin her alive!"

"Skin her alive?"

He shuts his mouth, perhaps realizing he's saying way too much, perhaps wondering if he's filling my head with ideas.

But I'm not going to skin him. Tempting as that may be, I don't have the stomach for something like that.

"What have you done to her?" I whisper. "Did you . . . touch her?"

He turns his head, his cheeks flushed, beads of sweat dotting his hairline. And I suddenly know what he's done to her. I think I've always known, but now I see it in his eyes, and I realize the raw stomach carving is an apt description.

I lay a broom handle in the burning embers, knots of red-hot chunks of wood exploding and crashing in on themselves.

"What are you doing?" he asks, wincing in pain. He can't see my movements, and I don't volunteer information.

The broom handle isn't terribly thick—but it's sturdy.

I retrieve a jar from the medicine cabinet and then grab the broom handle from the fireplace.

"What are you doing?" he asks again, this time more nervously, sweat dripping back off his face and onto the pillow. His chest heaves, his breathing shallow and rapid, like a panting dog's.

"Where is she?" I open the jar of Vaseline and slather it on the broom handle, gingerly applying it to avoid burning my fingers. I thought the Vaseline might cool off the treated wood, but it doesn't. The handle remains hot and melts the Vaseline, so I have to use a lot. I decided to use Vaseline, but not out of consideration for him. I figured I'd be able to do more damage with it if I can maneuver the handle better. Without the Vaseline, the wood might stick.

"What are you gonna do with that?" he cries as I approach the bed.

"You can end this right now by telling me where she is!" I don't want to do this! I'm not a bad person, but I'm desperate.

He starts blubbering, twisting on the bed, chafing his wrists and ankles on the ropes.

I rest the handle against the mattress and slap a piece of duct tape over his mouth.

I go back to his feet and pick up the broom handle. I quickly slip on a pair of rubber dishwashing gloves and slather my fingers with Vaseline. I push them inside his ass. He tries to get away but can barely move in any direction. He pushes his groin down into the bed, trying to melt into it. But the pillow I'd shoved under his ass and thighs, just below his tailbone, keeps his pelvis slightly tilted.

I ignore his frantic, spastic movements and muffled screams and force the broom handle into his ass hole and rape him with it.

Tiny hairs sizzle. His skin burns and crackles. I lean on the handle, forcing it further in until I'm sure I'm burning his colon, hoping I'm reaching as far back as his intestines.

Every vein on his head is strained, his arms and legs pulled taut, so tight I thought he would snap right through the bindings. One long, sustained cry comes through his taped mouth, and he throws his head back almost ninety degrees, practically facing the headboard behind him.

Slowly I pull the broom handle out of his anus, blood and shit and burned skin coating the Vaseline-covered wood. I stuff it back inside, jamming it up as far as I can.

I pull it out and lay it in the fireplace. Once again I remove his gag.

His face is ashen, and his eyes roll around in their sockets.

His slow, prodding tongue finds his lips and he licks them. He tries to focus and still hasn't answered my question. He mumbles something, but it isn't words. He'd only succeeding in pissing me off further.

Once more I grab the handle from the fireplace. It's good and hot again, and I shove it back up his ass.

"Where is she?"

"No more!" he shrieks. "God, no more . . ." His eyes are squashed shut, his teeth gritted. "Airport." He's panting, trying to talk through the pain. His skin is chalky. He can barely form the words. "Take it out . . . it's . . . in my stomach . . ."

"Where by the airport?"

Our town's airport isn't very big, and we don't get a lot of traffic there. Still, it's large enough, especially if you don't know where to look.

"South end. In a . . . shed. Small shack." He gasps the words, his face contorted in pain. A spasm seizes him. "A hole in the floor."

"If you're lying, I'll kill you." I'm surprised he's not dead already, to be honest.

I turn away and grab my truck keys off the dresser.

"Wait!" Seeing I'm about to leave seems to rejuvenate him somewhat. "Where are you going? Take it out!"

I leave him screaming and crying as I race out the door.

I rush to the airport, glancing at the clock on the dash. Six hours have passed since I kidnapped Andy. I grab my cell phone to call my husband but get voice mail.

I call the police, leave a quick message with the dispatcher:

"I know where Rebecca is." I give a quick description of the location. "I'm on my way there now!"

"Wait—wait!" the dispatcher yells, but I hang up.

When I arrive I find the shack, but it's padlocked, goddamn him! I look around for a rock or something to use to break the lock, and several police cars come to a screeching halt. Officers stampede toward me, guns drawn.

"Wait!" I cry. "She's inside."

They lower their weapons and shake their heads.

"What are you doing?" one asks.

"Rebecca's inside! But the door's locked."

One laughs, another turns away, a third just looks pissed.

The one who laughed says, "How do you know she's inside?" He removes his cap and scratches his balding head. "Come on, now . . . I thought you promised me you'd see a doctor."

The other officers gather in a small group and watch us.

"I did . . . I didn't like him. I know he was going to have me committed . . ."

"So what did you do, Mary?" Baldy asks. "Crystal ball? Tarot cards?"

"I'm telling you! I've been following him," I snap, grabbing the door handles and violently rattling them. "Rebecca? Answer me!"

An unmarked car quickly pulls up, and Detective Grant steps out. The men quickly fill him in I assume, but I can't hear what they say.

The detective says to me, "What happened? How did you wind up here?"

"I'd rather not say. I don't want to incriminate myself. But you have to believe me. She's in there!"

He shakes his head and sighs but signals to the men to break the lock.

They smash it and throw open the door. Darkness. Flashlight beams lead the way as they step inside the shed. I follow, even though they warn me not to.

I tell them what Andy told me, about her being under the floor. They toss crates and tools and benches until an officer finally yells that he's found something.

A hole in the floor. A trapdoor is opened. More blackness. Blacker than before because down there in the earth there's no source of light to train your eyes on. No windows, nothing to cast shadows.

Flashlight beams slice into the black air. A pair of eyes, terrified eyes, blinks. Rebecca, alive. Terrified.

"Well I'll be goddamned," Baldy says, once again scratching under his cap. "You got one right, Mary."

I quietly sneak away and race home. My heart's pounding. The officer doesn't seem angry, but they didn't last time either, and that didn't end well.

I'm not surprised when I find police cars parked in my driveway.

My husband greets me at the front door. "Let's go, honey," he says, trying to pull me inside.

I chew my lower lip. "But—"

He tries to lead me away, and like an idiot I don't understand what he's trying to do.

An officer grabs one arm, my husband the other. Tightly. They seem ready for tug-of-war.

"Why don't you go inside now?" the officer says, ultimately shoving me. "The county would like to offer their thanks for your help in resolving this matter. Good night."

They never ask me about Andy. Not yet, anyway. I have a feeling that detective will be sniffing around soon.

I overhear two officers talking, pointing at me. Words like *delusional* and *insane* pop up.

Great.

"Come on, honey," my husband says, wrapping his arm around my shoulders. "Before they take you away again."

"But I—" I pull away. "My daughter."

My husband shakes his head and bites his lip. "Please," he mumbles. "Enough with the daughter crap."

Later that evening the eleven o'clock news reports the wonderful story of Rebecca's miraculous rescue. They show the little girl I rescued. My daughter. The one they say isn't my daughter. Ugh . . . guess I'll keep trying to get that right. Don't know how I could have been so mistaken. One day I'll bring my daughter home. Her special bedroom in the basement is waiting for her . . .

Rebecca looks directly into the camera and thanks me.

She could have been mine.

Two days later another one of my daughters is missing, presumed kidnapped, say the police. I need to rescue her somehow. It has to be some other degenerate because this time it can't be Andy.

I really should go untie the guy.

ELEANOR
Jason Parent

Father Stuart Mckenzie had been forgotten. His father was a minister, as his father's father had been before him, serving God while their Church of England broke further away from the tenets of Rome. Stuart shocked his family and friends when he'd converted to Catholicism, and they had shunned him for it, even though they professed to worship the same God Almighty that he did.

And so God had become his only friend. Sent away to a small, West Sussex church in a largely Protestant district, Stuart passed the time writing sermons for the two or three folks who would listen. Even on the weekends when no one attended his mass, he diligently provided his sermons, reasoning that duty required it of him. Mass was an excuse to escape his tiny chamber, a dreary space furnished with nothing but a desk, a dresser, his bed and a few old books, his apathetic companions through the quiet hours of night.

His room sat above the nave. Across the hall was a larger room, with greater space offering greater comfort but requiring less humility. It was grand compared to his confining quarters, but still modest by most standards, adorned only with a bed, a dresser and a desk, much like his. A window was the room's only source of light. It looked out to the garden below, where Stuart alone toiled. It was a room without a soul, barren of life. He had never entered it, not until Eleanor arrived at his door.

Since the day he'd found the baby on his threshold, Stuart had loved her.

At first, he didn't know why he loved her, when all those who should have loved her did not. He didn't know who had placed her there, discarding her without regard for the life it would impact. He wondered if he loved her because she was a gift from God; or perhaps she'd been sent to test him, an offer to prove himself worthy of the Kingdom. More likely, though, Stuart loved her because, like him, she was all alone.

Yes, that was closer to the truth. Stuart loved her because no one else would, and because she was all he had to love.

He had found the child, newly born and starving, outside his tiny parish church's arched wooden doors. He'd opened them expecting to find his delivered groceries, but instead found her sitting in a milk pail. Horrified by her appearance, Stuart retreated, slinking back behind the door. He soon realized that his instant rejection of an innocent child was far more horrifying. Muffled sobs emitted from the steps outside.

He wondered how many people had cast the little girl aside and was ashamed that he'd almost been just like them. His hands hesitant, his mind unsure, Stuart lifted the pail and carried the baby into the warmth of his church and his heart.

She hadn't so much as a blanket to warm her. Naked and abandoned, the child persevered against incredible odds, particularly given her extreme deformities. A young man at the time, Stuart had declared it a miracle and God's wish for him to take in the child.

Someone had tied string around her ankle. Affixed to it was a note that read Eleanor R. Stuart considered that the name might be a pseudonym, but he liked it all the same. Whatever else there was of Eleanor's origins had been buried along with her real name.

That was fifteen years ago. Since then, Stuart had done the best he could by Eleanor. He bled dry his meager congregation to help raise her, and when that wasn't enough, he begged from merchants and passers-by and any charitable sorts he could find, all under the guise of raising money for the church. He sacrificed his own well-being and personal comforts for a baby girl who was not his kin. All the while, he kept her a secret, knowing too well how intolerant the world could be.

Now, fifteen wonderful years later—happy years, he liked to think, for both of them—the world still was not ready for Eleanor.

It would never accept her.

With a heavy sigh, thinking himself more a jailor than a father, Stuart knocked, then opened the door to her chamber. She stood in front of her bed, her back toward the door.

"What mask is it today, Eleanor?"

She turned and faced him. A mask made of stiffened linen, bleached to a fine white, covered her face, a broad smile stretching across it. Stuart had picked up the twin masks of comedy and tragedy on a trip to Greece long before he had parenting responsibilities. Leather straps held the mask in place, hooked into one of the ridges lining the back of her head.

Once, Stuart had given her a whole slew of masks, their expressions marking a full range of human emotion, but variety had led to confusion, and he'd decided to simplify things by ridding them of too many options. Only the original two masks remained: one happy face and one sad. Eleanor always wore one of the two. She kept them on a small table by the door and would put one on whenever she would hear him coming up the stairs. She wore them so often that Stuart hadn't seen her true face in many years.

Not that her face was something he could ever forget.

He struggled with the memory, then remembered his company. A sweet girl, fair-natured Eleanor was undeserving of scorn or ridicule, especially from he who loved her. And when she spun around, all doubt and misgivings vanished. He had raised a wonderful child.

Stuart beamed at the sight of Eleanor in her happy mask. He took her in. Even dressed in a dull brown frock, Eleanor might have passed for a beauty if not for her patchwork, matted hair, her misshapen cranium and that abomination that could not rightfully be called her face because it wasn't a face at all. That hid behind her masks, and Stuart was thankful for it. He had offered her several wigs to hide her remaining deformities, but Eleanor never took to any of them.

For a child who had been given no chance, who by all rights should have died at birth from any number of complications if not from her abandonment, Eleanor had sprouted and grown strong. Tall and lithe like a dancer, she moved with grace, confident in her steps even though she was blind.

She walked a straight line up to Stuart and threw her arms around him. The bag of groceries he carried beneath his arm crinkled. With his free hand, he pulled her closer. Her body seemed to compliment his. Her breasts heaved against his chest.

When did you become a woman? She had grown so much under his watchful eye. Her appearance suggested that Eleanor had come of age, but she was still a child in so many ways. She needed him, and he needed her.

Stuart stared into the empty white eyes of her mask. They, too, were smiling. He hoped that Eleanor was truly smiling behind them, that the life he had provided her was enough and would always be so.

"Give me a moment, dear. Let me put these groceries down." He gently pushed her away, but she resisted and snuggled in closer. He gave in. "Are you hungry? I've brought apples, the kind you like best."

Eleanor's hand slid gently along his side, found the grocery bag and reached inside. When she withdrew her hand, it was holding a plump red apple. Stuart had no doubt that, somehow, she had plucked the finest specimen from the bag. She always did.

"Would you like me to cut it up for you?"

She cocked her head, then scurried into a corner like a dog that thinks its master might take back the treat it had been given. She turned her back to Stuart, her custom when she ate.

Stuart was thankful for that particular quirk of hers. He could never get used to that slit down the front of her neck and how it opened into a cavern when she ate. Somewhere in that hole were teeth and only God knew what else. Eleanor had nearly died the first week in his care before Stuart could summon the nerve to stick a bottle in that hole and see if it would take milk. He shuddered whenever he thought about it.

But Stuart never revealed his repulsion. Eleanor couldn't see it on his face, and he was careful to never let her hear it. He wondered why she hid herself. How could she, a girl who had spent her entire life limited to a single room in the care of one who cherished her, know shame?

Stuart suspected, though he could not understand how, that

Eleanor was tuned in to his emotions. It was almost as if she could sense what he was feeling.

Always.

The face she chose that day and every other day mimicked his mood. Stuart tried his best to be happy as much as possible, for her sake. Eleanor had already suffered her fair share of misfortune.

"What shall I read you tonight?" he asked when she'd finished her apple, core and all. "The Good Book?"

Eleanor faced him. Juice ran down the front of her frock. The mask stared blankly.

Stuart laughed. "I didn't think so. How about Homer?"

Nothing. "Dickens? Yeats?" Eleanor balled up her fists and straightened her arms by her sides. She snapped her head left and right and tapped her foot. Stuart was teasing her now, and she knew it.

He laughed. "Okay. How about Chaucer? Shelley?"

Eleanor raised up on her toes. Stuart didn't believe the Catholic Church approved of either author, but Eleanor seemed to like them. Her head cocked to the side. He knew he had piqued her interest, but she hadn't given him a solid sign of approval.

"Dumas?" Stuart paused, awaiting her reaction but saw none. He sighed. He knew what she wanted. "Swift?"

Eleanor clapped and nodded repeatedly. He figured that was as sure a sign of approval as any.

"Swift it is. One of these days, I hope I will understand your fascination with Gulliver and all those silly Lilliputian fellows."

Eleanor traced the wide smile on her mask with her finger. A gurgle rose from her throat.

"What? Lilliputians? They make you smile?"

Eleanor nodded. She crouched and hovered her hand over the floor.

"Yes, I know. They're small."

Eleanor sprang up. She grabbed the sides of her dress and twirled.

Stuart couldn't help but laugh. Eleanor was good company. She filled all his empty hours, staved off the voracious beast that was loneliness, a constant predator in the life he'd chosen. A twinge of guilt came with the selfish thought. He hoped he offered Eleanor some comfort in return.

And what will she do after I'm gone? Stuart forced the question out of his mind. For now, Eleanor seemed happy. They would face tomorrow when tomorrow came.

"Okay, silly," he said. "Get cleaned up. Dinner will be in one hour, if you didn't just go and spoil it. Afterward, we'll go visit those Lilliputians you like so much."

Eleanor ran to the closet and picked out her nicest dress, a blue one that Stuart had bought her for her thirteenth birthday. It was too big for her then, but she hadn't stopped growing. The last time she wore it, Eleanor had filled it out nicely.

With her mask on, it was sometimes easy to pretend she was pretty. The hole in her neck was barely visible when she closed it. As he looked upon Eleanor, Stuart couldn't help but feel the sin of pride. He had done right by her. He had done right by God.

+ + +

WHEN THE HOUR had passed, Stuart carried Eleanor's dinner—porridge and a bit of leftover lamb from Sunday's supper—up to her room. He set the tray down and knocked on the door, giving her time to make herself decent before entering.

When he opened the door, he jumped, startled to see Eleanor standing just inside it. She wore her blue dress. It clung to her curves, revealing her shapeliness, except where the neckline had been ravaged. Shreds of fabric hung down over her breasts, baring her cleavage.

She wore her sad face.

Stuart frowned. He entered the room and placed the tray on her nightstand, then returned to where Eleanor stood fidgeting. He took her hands in his. "What's wrong, dear?"

Eleanor pinched the front of her dress and pulled it. Her chin dropped, and she shuffled her feet.

"Too tight?" Eleanor nodded slowly. "Couldn't breathe?" Again, she nodded. "Well, there's nothing to be done for it," Stuart said. He released her hands and slapped his own together. "We will just have to buy you a new dress."

Eleanor cocked her head at that, then fell against him, squeezing him tightly. Stuart's fingers drew soothing circles on her back. After a moment, she slipped from the embrace and ran toward the door. She picked up her happy face, then paused.

"Don't worry. I won't look."

And Stuart didn't. He turned away, wanting to believe, wanting to deceive himself that Eleanor was beautiful lest she ever sense from him otherwise.

"You will always be beautiful to me," he muttered. "God's little miracle."

Her happy face on, Eleanor clapped and skipped back over to him. She started to pull her dress over her head, raising the hem high enough for Stuart to glimpse the milky skin of her thigh.

He stopped her.

"Wait a moment. I'm still here, silly goose. Your dinner is on the nightstand. When you're finished, if it pleases you, change into your nightgown and hop into bed. I have to work on next weekend's sermon. I will return with Gulliver as soon as I've finished."

Eleanor nodded and raised her head. She sniffed at the air and bee-lined toward her dinner, but she waited for Stuart to leave before eating. He said goodbye and returned to his room to pen his next homily.

After an hour, Stuart stared down at a blank sheet of paper. He couldn't wipe the image of Eleanor in her blue dress from his mind.

+ + +

Stuart finished reading the last word of the Book of Genesis, then stood to stretch. He slid a finger along the novels on his shelf until he came across a ragged tome. Hello, Gulliver. Eleanor's fondness for the story reassured him. Her body might be growing up, but Eleanor still had the mind and heart of a child.

With the book and a candle in hand, he crossed the hallway to her room. He found her sitting up in bed, waiting in the dark for him. He wondered if she'd been sitting like that since he had left her. She had dolls and toys enough, but had outgrown most of them. What did she do when he left her alone?

He shook his head and paused before stepping into the room. Again, he wished there was more of a life he could offer her. Her room was all she knew, all she would ever know, beyond what he read to her in his paltry collection of books. I will have to ask for more donations soon.

But the worlds in his books were not real. The world outside her window was, and it would destroy Eleanor if given the chance. Out there, happy endings were things the less privileged could only read about.

And with her deformities, Eleanor would end up a toy for the damned.

People fear and hate what they do not understand.

Could Stuart blame them? He had feared her once, too.

He donned a shaky smile and shed the weight from his shoulders. Eleanor clapped as he approached. She slid over on the bed and patted the mattress, offering him a place to sit. Stuart settled in next to her for what would likely be a marathon journey through Swift's work, skipping certain parts he knew would upset her. Eleanor hated when he stopped before the story was complete. He broke the binding and began to read.

Midway through the sixth chapter of Gulliver's exotic journey, a strange purring sound emanated from Eleanor. She had long ago given up on sitting, her head sunk deep into her pillow. At first, Stuart thought she was snoring. He closed the book and rose quietly. That's when he noticed her hand making small circular motions beneath the sheet.

"Eleanor!" Stuart gasped. This was something new, something he had never considered. His face must have spanned every shade of red. He was unprepared. "Are you . . . you can't do that!"

Eleanor didn't stop. Her body and mind seemed locked in a rhythmic trance in tune with the motion of her hand. Her purring turned to moaning. Embarrassed and not knowing what else to do, Stuart ran from the room.

+ + +

OVER THE NEXT SEVERAL DAYS, Stuart couldn't shake Eleanor from his thoughts, his mind endlessly replaying her sinful behavior. Such thoughts were unbecoming of any man, let alone a priest and the girl's guardian. He felt filthy, vile, lowly. He kept his distance from Eleanor, leaving her to her own devices except to deliver her daily meals. Stuart had never been with a woman, and these ungodly visions ruminating in his brain filled him with shame and disgust. He prayed to God every hour on the hour for forgiveness.

Day in and day out, Eleanor wore her sad mask. Did she understand why he kept away? She pawed at Stuart during each brief visit, hugged him tightly, clung to him so that he wouldn't leave her. She'd worn a different dress each time he had brought her a meal. He could tell she was trying desperately to find the one that would please him, make him stay, convince him that she was still beautiful.

Stuart knew all this because he knew Eleanor. Her sadness made him weep. His heart ached with hers. It isn't your fault, Eleanor. He wanted to tell her as much, but how could he explain to her the kind of thoughts that were festering inside him, the feelings they stirred? They were unnatural, ungodly even. If he tried to explain them to her, how would she ever be able to love him again?

At last, he broke down and went to her with wet cheeks. "You know why I have stopped reading to you, don't you?"

Eleanor lowered her chin. The sad, melodramatic frown of her mask, together with the single tear forever emblazoned on its cheek, somehow didn't seem melodramatic at all. It fit Eleanor perfectly. It matched what he felt.

"Well?"

She nodded slowly. "Do you promise never to do it again?" She nodded. "Very well," he said. "I'm sorry we did not have this talk sooner. I was . . . uncomfortable, and I apologize for making you wait and even more so for making you sad. I will come back later and read to you tonight, something other than Swift. Would that please you?"

Eleanor dropped down to her knees and wrapped her arms around Stuart's leg. She rubbed the side of her head, a smooth surface where an ear should have been but where only an open cavern existed, against his thigh.

Stuart stiffened. "Get up." He ripped himself free and stormed out the door, slamming it behind him and no doubt leaving her to contemplate what she had done wrong.

But he kept his promise. That night, he returned to Eleanor's room with a book he selected at random, something by Sophocles. He read, and she listened, and for the moment, they were content. Eleanor even wore her happy face again.

He returned to his room, relieved. Things seemed to be returning to normal—on the surface. But a fire burned within Stuart that no amount of prayer could extinguish. That didn't stop him from trying. He got on his knees and prayed that the Devil would not tempt him again.

His prayers failed him. Temptation had taken residence. It slept across the hall.

+ + +

Months passed. Stuart went about his routine as he always had. But something wasn't right. Life had been difficult, solitary before, but now all joy had left it. The empty space Eleanor had filled had sprung a leak. The contents of his mind and soul spiraled in a whirlpool of doubt and depression. She was still with him the same as she had been, but Stuart had changed, and he didn't know how to change back. So instead, he suppressed his urges toward Eleanor by keeping her at arm's length. The intimacy they once shared had broken.

She must have sensed something was wrong. Though she wore her happy face, it no longer seemed genuine, at odds with body language she'd quickly correct, but not before Stuart took notice. Clinging her arms around her knees while he read, sleeping with a doll again, turning away each time Stuart looked at her with sadness in his heart—Eleanor couldn't hide her feelings from him. At first, Stuart had thought he was only projecting his inner turmoil upon her. But when he visited her this time, Eleanor had on the same frock she'd been wearing for the last three days. Her hygiene suffered, too. A foul odor, faint but persistent like a rotting carcass covered in lye, filled her room. She'd lost her girlish bounce; her energy had gone flat.

"I brought you your favorite," Stuart said, desperate to lessen the rift that had grown between them. He smiled, but his brow furrowed with worry. "It wasn't easy to get them. They're out of season."

Eleanor took two quick steps toward Stuart, then halted. She cocked her head and waited.

"It's okay."

She skulked toward him and reached out her hand. Stuart placed an apple in it.

"Shall I cut it up for you?"

Eleanor started to turn, but pounced back to his side and latched onto his arm. Stuart jumped, but did not pull away. She followed the length of his arm down to his hand, where he held a long, serrated kitchen knife with a dull but effective point.

She snatched it from him. "Now be careful with that—" Eleanor jabbed the knife into the apple near its base and made a horizontal slit through its peel. The apple oozed, bleeding juices from an open wound. Above the line, she dug out two tiny pits roughly level to one another. Then she stabbed the knife at Stuart's face.

He stepped back. He gasped, but was not afraid. He didn't believe Eleanor was trying to harm him, but he didn't immediately understand the message she was trying to convey either. Then it struck him.

"What is it, Eleanor? You gave the apple a face?'

She nodded. She placed the knife and the apple atop her dresser and approached him, standing closer than they had been for months. He could feel the heat of her body against his, the warmth of her breasts and the heart beating behind them. Her breath tickled the hairs on his neck. The sweet scent of ripe fruit entered his nose as her fingers danced across the contours of his face.

"Is it my face, Eleanor? Is that apple supposed to be me?"

Eleanor shook her head and stomped a foot. She poked Stuart's cheek, then ran her fingers across the lines of her mask.

"Eleanor." The word came out as a plea—not to ask the question she had asked too many times before, each time causing Stuart more pain than the last. Some questions were better left unanswered. Others, like this one, couldn't be answered.

She wanted to know why he had a face and she didn't.

His voice fell to a hush. "We've been through this, dear." As a child she had spent hours studying his face, comparing it to her own. She wanted to know why he had a voice and she could only sputter. Ears, nose, eyes: all had been matters that spurred her curiosity. But the answers Stuart had given never seemed to satisfy her.

How does she know that she is the oddity? Maybe I should never have given her the masks.

Eleanor grabbed her mask beneath the chin. The action startled Stuart from his memories and sent his heart racing.

"Leave it on!" he shouted more sternly than he had intended. Eleanor slid her fingers beneath the mask, groping at the disfigurement behind it. Again, she went to take it off.

"Please," Stuart said, grabbing her wrists. "You are stunning with your happy face on. I want to see you happy, always." He faked a smile, not sure if he was trying to reassure himself or the other who could not see it.

Eleanor twisted from his grip, but made no further attempt to remove the mask. A sound akin to a growl emitted from her throat. She pushed past Stuart and stamped her way to the table beside her bedroom door. With her back to him, she ripped the mask from her face and threw it against the wall. She replaced it with her sad face.

"Eleanor, I—"

She stormed past him again, got into her bed and hid beneath the covers, cradling her knees. He walked up to her bed and placed his hand on her back, trying to soothe her. She scooted away.

Stuart winced. A hollow pain stabbed at his stomach. His sadness swallowed him, commanded him to retreat. "I will leave you alone then." His voice fell quiet. "I'm sorry, Eleanor."

He turned and plodded out of her room. His head hanging low, he headed down to the sanctuary where he would pray for God to deliver her the peace he could not.

+ + +

The moon was descending when Stuart finally made his way back upstairs to his room. He stopped at Eleanor's door to check in on her. Her door was open a crack. Had he left it that way earlier? He couldn't recall. Eleanor never left her room, so it seemed the most likely conclusion.

A low moaning came from inside the room. I hope she hasn't injured herself. He moved in closer. He would just have a peek to make sure she was okay.

His eyes widened as he spotted Eleanor atop her bed. Her nightgown circled her waist, everything beneath it exposed. She writhed as if she were feverish, her hand working between her legs with dizzying speed as her moaning intensified.

Stuart began to sweat. His mouth filled with saliva, and he choked it down. He felt his penis stiffening before his mind could register the error in its ways. As he leaned closer, the floorboard creaked with his shifting weight.

All went quiet inside Eleanor's room. Ashamed, he stepped back, and the floor creaked again. He froze, afraid to make even the slightest movement that would alert her to his peeping, his degradation.

After a moment, the moaning resumed. The sin took hold of him. Stuart wanted to walk away but instead found himself leaning in for a second look. He peeked through the crack, unable to resist the perversion.

He could see Eleanor's bed, but she wasn't in it. "Where are you?" he mouthed, barely aware that his hand was rubbing the front of his slacks.

He shrieked when Eleanor sprang out of the darkness, her sad face appearing in the opening inches from his. He fell backward onto his buttocks. She stared at him with false eyes before slamming the door shut.

His face burned with humiliation. Stuart gathered himself and wormed his way into his room. He crawled into bed and laid in silence until his heart and breathing slowed. How he hated himself.

He closed his eyes, begging sleep to come. When at last it did, his dreams were filled with her.

+ + +

Stuart lurched up in bed, sweating profusely. His sheets and pillow were damp. His eyes began to focus. Eleanor's happy mask stared him in the face. Her hand was stroking his penis.

"Eleanor, you must return to bed," he squeaked. "This instant!"

Eleanor didn't listen. She pushed his shoulders down against the mattress, then returned to his pelvis. Stuart swelled inside her hands—hands that shouldn't have been capable of the sins they were committing, that shouldn't have had the skill they seemed to possess. Hands he lacked the strength to remove. They guided his penis inside her.

"Forgive me," Stuart cried and fell victim to her rapture, submitted to his lust.

He climaxed soon after. Eleanor's head rolled back. Her body glistened with sweat in the starlight pouring in through the window. A strange cooing resonated from the hole in her throat as she swayed in time to music only she could hear.

Stuart's pubis and inner thighs were drenched with what he assumed to have been the results of her orgasm. He had never had sex before, but he didn't think it was supposed to be that wet. Concern stifled the guilt blossoming in his mind. For a moment, his thoughts were only on the wetness. He reached between his legs. The liquid he found there was thick and warm.

It felt like blood.

He scrambled out from beneath Eleanor and kicked the sheets away from him. Huddled against his headboard, he inspected his upper legs and saw that they were stained dark. He checked for wounds, but saw none. The blood wasn't his.

Eleanor moved closer. She reached for his flaccid penis, perhaps not understanding why they had stopped. Despite it all, despite the fact that he had just desecrated every vow he held sacred—the vows of his church, the vows of his morality, the vows of a father—a part of Stuart craved more. He felt himself becoming aroused again. He pushed Eleanor away.

Perhaps too fiercely.

She fell off the bed, gasping through the hole in her neck. Had he hurt her? No, not even discouraged her. She rose to her knees, a supplicant reaching out her arms, inviting Stuart into them.

"Get away from me, you demon! You . . . you . . . whore!"

Eleanor cocked her head, and he could see his words were sinking in. She stood, trembling, and reached for the wall, then felt her way back to her room. If she could have cried, Stuart had no doubt she would have. God knew he wanted to. But at that moment, he was sure God wanted nothing to do with him.

He walked to his door and closed and locked it.

What have I done? God forgive me, what have I done?

+ + +

The sun arched high in the sky before Stuart got out of bed the next morning. Dry blood caked his pajamas, flaked off his skin. In the daylight, he could see that it was a lot of blood, more than he imagined could come from a broken hymen. He wondered if Eleanor was menstruating. More blood, still wet where it was at its thickest, painted the sheets. No amount of soap and water would ever wash that blood away. How could she have pushed herself on him like she had?

No, what happened could not be pinned on Eleanor. It was his fault. He had been weak. He knew the connection he and Eleanor shared, yet he'd failed to protect her from passion's poisonous fruit. He had failed to protect her from him.

And worst of all, Stuart had blamed Eleanor for it.

The first thing he needed to do was clean himself up. The second thing, a close second: apologize to Eleanor. After that, he would have to begin the long, arduous process of making himself right again with the girl and the Lord.

After washing and donning a fresh shirt and trousers—he left his collar atop his dresser—Stuart crossed the hall toward her room. I'm a fool. She's just a girl. I've abused her, her trust and the sanctity of our relationship.

"How do I make her understand that this is all my fault?" Stuart asked the question to an empty hallway, hoping God would see fit to place the answer in his mind.

Letting out a deep breath, he raised his hand to knock on Eleanor's door. He stopped when he saw that it was cracked open. This time, he did not peek through the crack.

"Eleanor? It's me. I've come to apologize." When she did not appear, he called again. "Eleanor?" He placed his hand flat against the door. "I'm coming in, Eleanor."

Stuart pushed open the door. The room was in shambles. Eleanor's dresser lay flat across the floor. The contents of her closet were strewn everywhere. She must have made considerable noise causing the disarray. How had he slept through it?

He scanned the room but saw no sign of Eleanor. A soft whimper came from the corner, a spot blockaded on three sides by two walls and Eleanor's bed. That was where he found her.

Her appearance matched that of the room, a disheveled mess. She sat with her back against the wall and her knees tucked against her breasts, her head buried between them. When Stuart approached, she pulled her legs in tighter.

Eleanor appeared to have been in that corner for some time. She still wore her happy face, though it no longer suited her. Blood smeared across its white surface, turning its exuberant grin into something maniacal. Her hands were covered in blood. Her nightgown looked as if it belonged to the victim of a homicide. Blood stained it everywhere, not just between her legs.

Stuart began to weep and rushed to her side. He paused when he saw the knife.

"Where did you get that?"

Eleanor held a long, serrated kitchen knife in her right hand. The blade was red, with little chunks of meat stuck in its grooves. She must have had the knife for several days, weeks even. Stuart could not recall the last time they had red meat.

With her left hand, Eleanor reached behind her back, groping for something hidden there. She pulled out the apple he had given her yesterday and rolled it at his feet. Its carved face stared up at Stuart.

"Here," he said, reaching for her. Eleanor scurried back until she collided with the wall. He had made her like this. He had to fix it. A smile as phony as the one she wore fought to hold up his cheeks. "Let me help you up. We'll get you and this place cleaned up in no time." Even as he filled her ears with calming words, Stuart knew there were some stains he couldn't wash away.

Eleanor shrank deeper into the corner. She slashed at the air between them with her knife. It was a warning, not meant to cut. Stuart heeded it.

Maintaining a safe distance, he tried to pacify her. Tears fell from his eyes. "I'm sorry, Eleanor. Everything that has happened, all of it . . . it's my fault. You did nothing wrong. I was . . ." The words caught in his throat. He pressed on. "I was terrible to you. I have wronged you in so many ways I don't know if I will ever be able to make them right. But I promise you, I'll never stop trying."

Stuart shook and sobbed, fell to his knees. Snot bubbled out of his nose. The backs of his hands rested upon the floor, palms upward, begging forgiveness. From God. From Eleanor. "I am sorry, truly sorry."

Eleanor cocked her head. She's listening, at least. Oh, thank God. It's a start. He wiped his nose with his sleeve and stood. "Let's get you cleaned up, dear. Afterward, I will read you Gulliver's Travels, and we can eat apples, all the apples you want, with the Lilliputians."

Eleanor sat still for a moment, then carefully rose to her feet. Stuart offered his hand. She fumbled in the air until she found it. Her other hand dropped the knife onto her bed.

Stuart pulled her into his arms and held her close. She smelled of old sweat and older blood. He didn't care. Tears filled his eyes. "I'm sorry," he repeated over and over again, smothering the top of her head with kisses. "I never meant to hurt you. I never want to hurt you again."

Eleanor rested her head upon his shoulder. For a while, they stood, holding each other, Stuart never wanting to let her go. He loved her, he knew, in all ways.

But there was only one right way.

Her hand slid down his chest. It slipped down the front of his trousers.

He gently pushed her away, a softer rejection this time. "We can't, Eleanor. It's not right. Do you understand that? It would damn us both."

The whimper Stuart had heard when he had entered her room returned. It came from Eleanor, though he had difficulty believing it. Her purrs, her moans and now that sound were all new to Stuart. She reached for his crotch again. Stuart stepped back.

He straightened. "Eleanor, we can't. I was wrong to permit it the first time. In my weakness, I failed you. I won't fail you again. I'm sorry."

Eleanor grunted. She pointed to her mask. The hole in her neck opened wide. "Boot."

Stuart's mouth dropped open. He was stunned, speechless. Eleanor had made a sound, and he was certain she was trying to speak. "Boot?" He had no idea what it meant, but the joy he felt at the possibility of Eleanor forming her first word made him weep.

"Did you just speak?" Stuart laughed, overwhelmed by the moment. He grabbed her shoulders and pulled her close. "Maybe God has not yet forgotten us. Praise be to our Lord!"

"Boot," Eleanor repeated, a sense of urgency in the way she said it. She pulled away. "Boot." She stomped her foot. A hiss followed by a gurgle spouted from her neck opening. Was she trying to form more words? How long had she been practicing in secret?

"Fell," she said at last.

"Fell? Boot fell?" Stuart stroked his chin. "Are you asking me if I think you are beautiful?"

She nodded and placed a finger on her mask.

"Of course I think you are beautiful. You know that."

Eleanor stomped her feet. A growl emitted from her throat, and she tossed her head frantically left and right. Her fingers walked up Stuart's neck to his chin. They spread wide, curled and dug into his skin. With his face in her hand, Eleanor shook him. When she let go, she did the same to her linen mask.

"Boot . . . fell?"

Stuart thought he understood. She showed a lot of courage asking him what she was asking. She must have known the answer. Stuart hadn't the heart to say it. Hers was the one question that made him dishonest.

"I don't know how to answer—"

"Boot . . . fell!" Eleanor growled. She pounded her fist against his chest and pointed to her mask. "Boot . . . fell?"

"It's a mask, Eleanor. You are beautiful in here." Stuart touched her above her bosom. "And we are all beautiful in the eyes of our Maker."

A stinging ache ran though his cheek. He yelped more in surprise than in pain. He couldn't believe Eleanor had slapped him.

"Boot . . . fell? Boot . . . fell? Boot fell, boot fell." The words were coming easier for her, and she began to chant them, all the while waving her hand at her mask. Spittle splashed from her neck, her voice becoming wet and slithery.

"No," Stuart said. He looked away. "Your mask is not beautiful."

Eleanor clapped. For some odd reason, the answer seemed to please her. She smoothed her dress with her hands and threw her shoulders back, standing tall and proud.

Before Stuart could protest, she tore off her mask. "Boot fell?"

Stuart yelped. He bit down on his knuckle to stifle a scream. His Adam's apple lodged in his throat, and his eyes widened in terror.

"My God, Eleanor. What have you done?"

Eleanor tried to speak. A steady stream of mucus- like plasma oozed from the hole on her neck. It didn't stop until Eleanor said the word she had worked so hard to say. "Fess."

She ran her fingers down her face. Where Stuart remembered a smooth, vacant surface resembling the shell of a brown egg, marked only by two small black circles he had assumed were nostrils, a long gash ran horizontal across a gore-splattered canvas. Pink tendrils of flesh and muscle hung from the carved canyon's ceiling like bats in a cave. Eleanor had removed a section of her face that might have resembled a slice of melon. Stuart couldn't be sure. He didn't know what had happened to that excised flesh, and he didn't want to know.

Above her nostrils were two more incisions, not exactly evenly spaced, but close. Eyes. The contents of Stuart's stomach rumbled. She made eyes. One was slightly higher than the other, tilted at an entirely wrong angle. Blood streaked down from all three wounds.

Eleanor tapped her new face. "Boot . . . fell?"

THE SCAVENGERS
Tony Knighton

"I'll take no less than five a man, Jimmy. I say we stand firm on that." Ace spoke into my right ear, raising his voice to be heard over the engine noise.

I nodded. I didn't want to get into it with him again, not right then. I needed to concentrate on driving. The trail was rutted and we were jouncing badly. Better to let him think what he wanted.

He kept on, though. "That kraut bastard isn't going to rip us off again."

I couldn't tell if it was meant to be a question or a statement of fact. I didn't care. Ace was just letting his nerves show; he'd be okay when the time came. I kept a straight face and said, "Right on, man. Fucking A."

I felt him scowling at me. "Fuck you, too." He turned in the open cab and pointing at me, shouted to Frederick and Joseph, the two Bantus in the back. "All the fucking same, these yanks."

I watched them in the rear-view mirror. They ignored him, but grinned, not able to hear what he said, not really caring. They'd been educated in mission schools; both spoke English along with half-a-dozen other languages, but they feigned ignorance when Ace was on a tear. They knew him well enough to know he was just blowing off steam.

They stood in the truck bed facing outboard in opposite directions scanning the dry grasslands, each with a Kalashnikov slung over his shoulder, muzzle down. It was a tough ride holding on to the tops of the high wooden truck sides, their legs bent at the knees, riding out the bumps.

We weren't on a road; there weren't any roads where we were going. The trail we were on roughly followed a dry streambed that wouldn't see much water until the rains came.

Ace said, "I tell you I need the five. Bello won't wait forever." He took a pouch from his khaki shirt pocket. There were dark sweat-stains under his arms rimmed with a line of dried salt. "It's a beautiful place, Jimmy. Not some slop-shute—a real old-style pub." He chuckled. "Can't you just see me in a barman's white shirt and black trousers?" He unrolled the pouch, grabbed a thick wad of the brown leaf tobacco and shoved it into the side of his mouth.

I *could* see it. Ace looked a lot more like a bartender than what he was. If he'd stayed at home, he might this very moment be happily tapping pints of Smithwicks somewhere along the Falls Road.

It was time to let a little air out of his bubble. "We don't know how big a load we're going to take. We'll have to wait and see." I took up the water jug from the floorboards and drank.

He was quiet for a moment, then sat back. "Ah, you're right. I'm just hoping to see enough from tonight's labors to get out of all this, you know."

His speech lapsed into the rhythms of his youth as he finished the sentence. Over the years he'd worked to rid himself of his brogue, only slipping into it in times like now, when he felt sorry for himself or for comic effect when his mood was up. "I didna' leave the old place soon enough to lose it from me speech, not completely," he liked to say.

He hadn't left soon enough to stay out of the kind of trouble that prevented his return, either. He'd never gone into detail, but considering his heritage and disposition, it was a good bet that some of the boyos from the Royal Ulster Constabulary would like to have a talk with him.

He waved away the water as I offered it.

"This should be a good payday," I said. "Let's do the job and be done with it. We haven't worked all that much lately."

It only got him worked up again. "I'm well aware that we've not worked in recent times. I just can't be as casual about our upcoming transaction as you seem to be. I don't trust the prick. He's selling out his associates just so he can realize a slightly larger profit. What prevents him from treating us in kind?" He gripped the top of the windshield as we rolled over a depression.

I looked back and forth between him and the trail and said, "These aren't his regular guys. Kuhn thinks they're deserters from Botswana—it doesn't matter. He doesn't trust them to play fair. So he decided to take it off them. We can't really expect the same money these guys were going to get. They've been hunting—hiding out for days. We're only looking at a few hours work."

Ace was unconvinced. "I don't like it." He spit over his shoulder and folded his arms across his chest. "I don't like dealing with the kraut. Fucking middle-man."

He was starting to annoy me. I shifted a little in the seat; the .357 I carried on my belt was digging into my hip. "Look, he's doing a job neither of us wants to do—neither of us could. I don't like him either, but we don't have the contacts. Without him we have a truck-load of pretty tusks we can't sell."

I shouldn't have bothered. The worst thing to do to Ace was point out that he was wrong. "I still say I want at least five. Bello won't wait forever." It was his way of ending the conversation.

I'd lived with the man's mood swings since I'd met him in Bahrain fifteen years earlier. The four days it had taken to liberate Kuwait hadn't been enough for me. He'd been looking for someone handy to help him with "a bit of business." We'd been doing this and that together ever since.

I kept my eyes focused on the trail. It gets dark fast in the grasslands and I couldn't use headlights. Our presence in the bush with the hardware we carried would be difficult to explain to any government men that might happen upon us. A pair of Heckler-Koch MP5's was on the seat between us.

In the absence of conversation with Ace, I could hear Frederick jabbering away to Joseph in the bed of the truck. They were pros, in this since they were kids. I knew what they were doing without looking at their reflection in the rear-view mirror. They'd be sharp, eyes open, but Freddy would look at his older comrade from time to time to see if his point had been taken.

Joseph would smile and nod, rarely adding anything of his own. It was his habit to finger a small two-headed ivory carving that hung around his neck on a leather thong and mouth something to himself, a prayer maybe, his lips moving with the recitation of a silent litany. I sensed that Joseph had long ago grown weary of this life but was trapped, knowing nothing else.

I liked the work and the countryside, only going into the cities now and then for a taste of real liquor and a woman who wouldn't give me something that would make my cock fall off.

The sun was well under the horizon and I spotted the moon through the twilight, nearly full, off to my left. There were more and more trees; we were on the edge of the forest.

Frederick called out. I sat up in the seat and looked at his reflection in the mirror. He pointed to our right. About fifty feet off the trail, a pack of wild dogs was making short work of a deer carcass.

Ace shouted at them. A few of the dogs looked up, curious. Their eyes reflected the moonlight and seemed to glow. The animals were lean and vicious. Their ribs stood out, making zebra stripes of shadow across their mangy coats.

They went back to their meal as we rolled by. Ace said, "Some big cat probably took that down and got barely a bite for himself before that lot showed up and chased him off." He spit over the door and turned toward me. "Lousy scavengers. Capitalizing on another's hard work."

His analogous reference to our situation with Kuhn wasn't lost on me, but I was too busy to indulge him in his petulance. He took one more shot, "If you're ever unfortunate enough to be facing down a pack of dogs or a pack of Zulus," he nodded in the direction of the two in the truck bed, "the proper course of action is the same: keep a prayer on your lips and save the last round for yourself." He patted my revolver with the back of his hand.

I drove on, following his directions to the ambush site he'd picked out. It was a natural bottleneck, the trail hemmed in at this point by the tree line and a sharp curve in the dry stream. The bunch we were taking would need to travel miles out of their way to avoid this choke point.

We knew they were heading to meet Kuhn at the outskirts of Tsumeb, the rail junction in this part of the country. They'd come down from ivory poaching in the Kavango region, ranging even into Angola. The big elephants didn't travel this far south in the dry season.

Using the winch mounted on the front of the truck, we dragged a downed tree trunk across the trail on the far side of the curve. Then we hid the truck in the bush and took up positions. And waited. Nightfall revealed a million stars.

They came in two vehicles. I could see that they were green hands, inexperienced—the truck carrying the tusks was following too closely behind the lead vehicle, some Asian version of a Rover.

Ace and I had them flanked on their left side. Joseph and Frederick waited fifty yards up-trail, blocking any possibility of their doubling back.

We fired at the same time, the two of us putting a pair of rounds each into the truck driver's ear, turning his head into oatmeal just as the lead vehicle braked to a stop at our improvised roadblock.

It worked out better than we'd hoped; the truck slammed into the back of the Rover. Steam geysered from the crushed radiator. The driver's headless body fell forward onto the steering wheel and the horn blared. We kept firing, picking them off easily as they scrambled from the damaged vehicles.

Frederick and Joseph did their share, killing the gunmen in the back of the truck before they could recover and return fire.

Only one of the poachers showed any field-craft at all, rolling off the far side of the truck and staying low, firing bursts in our direction to give us something to think about. If they'd all been as good as him we'd have had more of a contest on our hands, but as it was we had him bracketed. Joseph got the angle and ended it.

We approached cautiously, running crouched. Frederick got there first and went among the vanquished poachers, dispensing headshots as insurance.

As I got closer, I saw that they were kids, child soldiers, the oldest not yet twenty. Their clothes were tattered. The insides of their mouths were stained red from chewing khat.

Sub-Saharan armies used kids for clearing minefields and other suicidal tasks. These boys had tired of their roles as cannon fodder and struck out on their own, like Frederick and Joseph had years before. They just hadn't been as lucky.

Ace went straight to the truck, looking into the bed, inspecting the load of tusks. "It's not enough," he shouted over the truck horn. He loosed a stream of tobacco juice onto the parched ground.

Joseph wandered among the dead poachers. He found the last of them, the one he'd killed. The body rested on its side face down. Joseph rolled him onto his back, gently lifting the slain boy's shoulder with the toe of his boot.

The boy appeared to stare off into space, eyes wide with the abruptness of it all. A fly lit on his right pupil.

Ace wrenched open the driver's side door. Grabbing a handful of shirt at the shoulder, he dragged the body out of the cab. It fell in a heap. The horn was silenced.

He reached into the cab and brought out a huge rifle—an elephant gun. "Here's something, anyway." It was double-barreled like a shotgun. He broke it open, hinged at the breech, and looked down the barrels, then inspected the markings on the stock. "It's an old Beretta, Jimmy." He set the rifle across the bench seat in the cab. "Fucking hell." He spat again.

Joseph was still looking at the dead boy. He leaned over to inspect something more closely and started to cough, quietly first, then more violently. I went to see what was wrong.

He looked up at me, the whites of his eyes big and round, freakish-looking in the moonlight. He started jabbering away in Ovambo, shaking and pointing at the boy.

I bent to see what he was talking about but couldn't understand. Frederick came up and looked. "It's Ekwnesu. The talisman. Around his neck, like Joseph's"

I looked again. The dead boy had a figure on a string around his neck like Joseph did, but his was damaged. One of the heads was missing, obliterated by the shot that had killed him.

Frederick said, "One head is Chukwu—God. The other is Ekwnesu—Devil. Joseph shot off the good head, leaving the bad. He's frightened. This upsets the balance of things."

I looked around. Ace was ignoring us, going through the pile of ivory. Joseph was hugging himself, muttering, the fingers of his right hand worrying his own ivory figure. I looked back to Frederick. "What should we do?"

He shrugged. "Don't ask me. I'm a Lutheran."

I looked at him a moment and then started howling. I laughed until tears ran down my cheeks and I was doubled over. Frederick joined me.

I was gasping as I looked back up at Joseph. His face was a horrible thing to see. He stared at us as though we had betrayed him.

I sobered and began to apologize when Ace shouted, "I'm glad you ladies are enjoying yourselves. Anytime you could tear yourselves away I'd fucking appreciate it."

That was when I first noticed the whining of the dogs. They gathered, circling on the edge of the brush.

I looked at Joseph, then Freddy. He said, "Go on. I'll take care of Joe." He went to his friend and put an arm around the man's shoulder, speaking softly.

I walked to the truck. The Buck knife I carried on my left side was slapping against my leg. I put down my rifle and made fast the thong fixed to the scabbard's end—lashed it around my thigh.

I stood and was about to ask Ace what he wanted when I saw the tusks. I put my hand on one of them. "It's good quality stuff, Ace."

The tusk was huge, almost six-feet long—the animal it had come from must have been enormous. In the moonlight it looked creamy and finely grained, and was smooth, very smooth to the touch. It curved, twisting from its rudely hacked stump to the gracefully rounded point. "It's good stuff," I repeated. I heard a yelp; the dogs sounded closer.

"I fucking well know it's good stuff, Jimmy. It's just not enough."

I was still looking at the load but could hear that he'd turned away as he said, "Not split four ways."

It took a moment for that last bit to register. I wheeled around, too late to stop him. I heard his HK speak twice and finished turning in time to see Joseph and Frederick fall.

I'd dragged the .357 out of its holster as I'd spun and was sighting down the barrel at the back of Ace's head. He raised both hands, the rifle still in his right. "Easy, Jimmy." A thin wisp of smoke oozed from the skyward pointed muzzle.

"What the fuck, Ace? What are you thinking?" I glanced at their bodies and repeated, "What the fuck?"

Ace stood very still. "We needed to do that, Jimmy. You know I'm right."

"I don't know that at all. Neither do you." I didn't know what to do. "You're the one that's been crying that we can't trust Kuhn. You just killed the two guys we could trust." I pulled the hammer back on the big revolver. "Why should I trust you?"

"You should trust me because I'm telling you that you can." He turned his head a little bit. "I didn't have anything against those fellows, Jimmy. They just had the misfortune of outliving their use-fulness. I need this money. Bello won't wait—"

I fired a round past his ear to shut him up. "Pat Bello died eight years ago. I'm sick of hearing you go on and on about some dive you're never going to buy. You'll piss this money away like you always do, you fat little prick." I looked over at Frederick and Joseph lying dead. "I'm sick of you." I pulled back the hammer again.

"You have to trust me, Jim-boy." He turned more and faced me. "You have to. What else can you do? Kill me? You'd have to walk away from all that ivory." He gestured in the direction of the truck with his free hand. I kept my eyes glued on him.

He grinned. "You can't bring it in by yourself. Put down the howitzer and let's go get our money." He spat tobacco juice. "Come on, Jimmy. I wouldn't be so stupid as to kill them with you at me back if I wanted you too, would I?"

The hell of it was that he was right. I motioned with the gun barrel. "Put your rifle on the ground and go get the truck."

He smiled. "That's the ticket, Jimmy. I'll be right back." He lowered the weapon and trotted away into the dark. I picked up both of our rifles and kept the pistol in my hand.

I walked over to Joseph's body. The carved ivory piece with two heads was resting on his chest. I reached down and took it, snapping the leather thong. The head on the right was clearly that of the god. The other wore an expression of evil, almost a sneer. The dogs sounded closer still.

I looked up as I heard Ace starting the truck. I looked back at the figure; the god face's eyes were closed. Hadn't they been open?

Ace pulled the truck around. Mentally I shrugged; it was dark— I hadn't looked at the faces carefully. I put the figure away in my shirt pocket.

We brought the trucks back to back and handed the tusks from the poacher's to our own. Emboldened by our lack of concern, a dog reached one of the dead and tore into its body with a snarl. Others joined it. Watching them, my skin hurt. I split my attention between the dogs and Ace.

The truck loaded, I said, "You drive."

Ace smiled. "Good thinking, Jim-boy. That way you can see my hands at all times. Right?"

I didn't say anything else, just moved around to the passenger's side. Before he got into the driver's seat he said, "Be a shame to leave that grand, fine gun. We should take it with us." I stared at him. "Christ, it's yours, okay? I just don't want to see it go to waste, that's all."

"All right. Hurry it up."

He trotted back to the cab of the ruined truck and drew the elephant gun off the seat. He kept the breech broken open as he walked back and put the rifle on the floor of the cab between us. "Got some ammo, too." He handed me five monstrous shells—.50 caliber, more than two-inches long. Nothing smaller would penetrate elephant hide. I put them in the pouch on my belt.

Ace got behind the wheel, put the truck in gear and made a wide sweeping turn. We drove toward Kuhn and the money. Now that his spirits had recovered, he kept up a steady stream of chatter, always coming back to the cash and what he'd do with it. He made no further mention of Mr. Bello's pub.

I ignored the content of his words. I looked forward to taking Kuhn's money and parting ways with Ace forever.

I idly reached into my pocket to finger Joseph's talisman. As I touched it, something pricked my finger. "Shit." It had felt like a bite.

I'd interrupted Ace's monologue. "What?"

"Nothing." I brought the piece out. I reasoned that there must be a sharp edge. I ran my fingers around it; it was as smooth as talc. I was about to put it away when I thought I saw the evil head wink.

Ace heard it first. He let off the gas and cocked his head. Then I heard it too—a rumbling sound and then an angry trumpeting that could only be one thing. I put the figure away and said, "Step on it."

Ace picked up speed—as much as the truck would bear on the uneven trail. We couldn't tell what direction the big animal was coming from, we only knew it was coming. Ace glanced away from the trail to me and then to the big rifle on the floor. "Might do us some good if you were to load that."

I picked up the rifle. It was a monster—it must have weighed twenty pounds.

The great animal trumpeted again, and this time I looked in the right direction and spotted it. He was off to the right, maybe fifty yards away, silhouetted by the moon, a huge bull elephant in full charge. Heading our way. "There he is."

Ace said, "I see him, Jimmy." He gave it more gas, but we were carrying too much weight and bottomed out as we hit a chuckhole.

The elephant wanted us and was gaining. Bellowing, enraged. What was he doing this far south in the dry season?

Ace spun the wheel and we slewed left, angling away from the animal. I dug two of the cartridges from my pouch, thumbed them into the breech and snapped it shut.

Was the creature enraged by thirst? Did it want a female? I didn't know. I did know it was going to catch up with us shortly.

Ace was forced to come back to the right as the creek bed curved toward us. The elephant bore down on us broadside. I stood, my right knee on the seat, and hefted the weapon, bracing it on the wooden truck side. *Was it the tusks?*

I could see the crazed right eye of the behemoth as it galloped, eating up the last few yards of ground that separated us. I struggled to steady myself in the rocking, jouncing truck and drew a bead on that bloodshot eye. I sucked in air and held it. The thing was almost on top of us; I thought I felt its hot, angry breath.

Ace screamed, "Shoot, Jimmy!"

I fired. The rifle kicked like a wild horse. The bullet crashed into the monstrous face, just below the eye. Red exploded. The creature's head snapped back with the impact. It was dead, it just didn't know it yet. Momentum kept it moving forward, its legs still churning, running of their own accord without any command from the now lifeless brain.

It struck us just behind the cab. I hadn't time to drop the rifle and hold on. I was thrown clear of the truck as it was tumbled sideways like a toy. I landed on my back.

In the moonlight I saw a wave, a dark gray tsunami rolling in my direction. Before I could scramble away, the animal's carcass came to rest on top of me, covering my legs.

I couldn't move, of course. The funny thing was, it didn't hurt. At first I thought I must be in shock, but then realized that I'd fallen lengthwise into a depression, a rut, and that neither the fall nor the weight of the dead beast had caused any major injury. I wiggled my toes inside my boots.

I tried to look around. The hairy, gray mass on top of me cut my field of vision to a difficult one-hundred-and-eighty degrees; the only way to see the all of it was to lie back and crane my neck, giving me an upside-down worms-eye view of my limited world.

I looked to my left and saw the truck. It was up-ended, one front tire still spinning. Ace lay half in and out of the cab. He'd been killed outright, his neck broken on impact. His head lolled at a freakish-looking angle. Our tusks, our beautiful tusks, were strewn about as though some giant had dropped a box of toothpicks.

I resigned myself to a long, ugly walk out of the bush and started to scoop at the crusted earth under my ass in an effort to dig my way out from under the dead elephant. The Buck knife on my left leg would have helped the effort, but I couldn't reach it.

I dug with my hands. By the palmful I scooped up dirt, mostly dust. I dug until the tips of my fingers were raw.

I'd been at it a while when I heard the first growl. I stiffened, then hurried my efforts. More joined the first. My hands scratched at the crusty soil, faster, almost frenzied.

Then my fingers found the rock. My leg was wedged between it and the elephant's back. No amount of digging was going to free me.

I heard a snarl and looked over at the truck. Three dogs were pulling Ace's body to pieces, tugging at hunks of flesh and gobbling them whole so as to get back to the body sooner. They were joined by two more.

One ripped the meat from the dead man's upper arm. He carried it away a few steps from the others. Dropping it into the dirt, he held it down with a forepaw and tore at it with his teeth. Another came toward him; he warned it away with a growl.

They'd leave the elephant alone. They knew the hide would be too tough for them until it had lay out in the sun for a few days and rotted, breaking down the meat. They'd go for an easier meal first.

One of them trotted toward me, growling, blinking, its eyes shining in the moonlight. I shouted and tossed a handful of dirt at it. He jumped back a step, then circled.

Frantic, I reached down my right side, pushing my hand between the elephant's hide and the ground. I got a finger on the handle of the .357. I pushed farther down, scraping flesh off the back of my wrist.

The dogs were finishing with the tasty bits of Ace's torso. Two left it and joined the one stalking me. I got my middle and ring fingers around the curve of the handle; my thumb brushed it.

The dogs postured, circling, weaving, barking, now and then coming close then darting back. I tried to face them down as I dug for the gun.

Finally grasping it firmly, I pulled, dragging it farther and farther out of the holster, out from under the mountain of flesh that imprisoned me.

I pulled it all the way loose just as the lead dog sprang. I brought the gun about and fired—the big round caught the canine full in the chest and spun him in the air. He fell still in the dirt six feet in front of me.

The others were on him at once, ripping him apart, slobbering. I saw the blood and pieces of meat and hair stuck between their teeth. Another looked at me. I dropped him where he stood.

That gave the others pause. They jumped back a step, but were joined by still more.

I was enraged. Filthy scavengers. I'd take a few more with me. I shot three in quick succession. That was it.

Save the last round for yourself. I took a deep breath, put the barrel of the big pistol in my mouth and squeezed. Click.

I pulled the trigger again and again. Nothing. I'd forgotten the round I'd shot past Ace's head.

I heard a chuckle. I pulled Joseph's talisman out of my shirt pocket. The god's head was covering his face with his hands. The other was shaking with laughter.

I dropped it as I felt the first bite.

THE MOST IMPORTANT MIRACLE
Scott Emerson

This morning I put ground glass in my wife's pancakes.

Can't really say what prompted me to do it. I was behind the counter, preparing a fresh bowl of batter for the early-morning rush, when the notion came. Without a second thought I dropped a glass onto the floor and stamped my heel onto the milk-clouded shards until they were crushed fine. Then I carefully scooped the glass into my hand and spilled it into the batter.

Like I said, no reason. Just a spur of the moment decision, like choosing a red shirt over a blue one.

All I know for sure was that it was the *right* thing to do.

I went about my business, cooking up orders as they came down the line, the glass-studded batter waiting for when Sally would come and join me for breakfast. In fact, I'd forgotten all about the batter and its contents until the old man stumbled into the diner.

Through the service window I saw him enter, steadying himself against the booths as he weaved toward the counter. He moved like he'd been drinking, or perhaps involved in some sort of accident, jostling a few of the patrons as he went. Nobody seemed to mind or even notice him, even as he spilled their coffee or knocked utensils out of hands.

Once he reached the Formica countertop he ran a hand through his long white hair. Kelly, the morning-shift waitress, walked by without a word; not being rude—she'd dealt with far less savory characters than him, she simply hadn't seen him standing before her. The old man took a biscuit off a plate and bit into it, crumbs gathering in his flowing white beard. He washed it down with a half-empty glass of juice someone had left behind and sauntered behind the counter into the kitchen.

I didn't say anything, just kept on scrambling eggs and tossing bacon on the griddle. The old man watched me for a minute before he spoke. "I know what you did," he said.

"How's that?"

"The pancake batter," he said. "Very sneaky. Clever, almost."

"I'm sorry, I don't follow you."

The old man smiled. He stuck a finger into the batter bowl and swirled it around, plucking free a sliver of glass. It glistened in the fluorescent lighting, like a cheap ring. It was then I remembered breaking the glass. Remembered my wife.

"Hey, look pal, I know how it seems, but I swear to—"

The old man waved me off. "No, you don't understand," he said. "You've nothing to worry about. I approve."

"I don't get you."

He smiled again—*leered*, really, in a way that was almost obscene. "It's an offering, my son. To the God of Breakfast. This morning He is risen, and has called home his flock. Those that have answered, they shall be rewarded in breakfast heaven."

He wrapped his arms around me and drew me into the warmest, most welcoming embrace I've known. His beard smelled of butter and maple syrup. I thought of my grandmother's dining room, her liver-spotted hands smearing orange marmalade over English muffins.

"You are pure of heart, my son. Rejoice, for you're not alone. The God of Breakfast loves you."

Words failed me. I cried into the old man's beard.

"There, there, my son. You've still much work to do."

"What do you ask of me?"

The old man cradled my face in his bacon-scented hands. "I'll be sending someone very soon. You'll know what to do."

"How?"

"It will be just like the glass. You'll know when the moment is right."

And like that he was gone, the smell of butter and syrup lingering behind like a ghost. His absence felt like dying. I'd have given anything to be back in his warm, fragrant embrace.

I went back to work.

Although deeply missing the old man, I found a renewed vigor in myself. I heaped sausage links and stacks of pancakes onto plates with great élan, barely containing my joy as order after order came in. I wanted to sing, to tell all of the diners the good news, but I kept my rapture in check. There would be time for all of that later, and when that moment came they too would know.

All the while the batter for my wife's pancakes sat waiting.

Lost in my bliss, I almost didn't hear the back door creak open. It wasn't until I heard the soft patter of footsteps on tile that I stopped and turned to see.

Before me stood a young man in his early thirties, healthy and glowing, with the same luxuriant beard and mane of hair as the old man's, only his was a rich gleaming brown. His eyes were the same as the old man's too, as was the familiar breakfast that subtly wafted from his being.

The young man smiled beatifically. "My father sent me," he said. "He told me you'd know what to do."

And in that moment I did.

I picked up the meat cleaver and got down to it.

First I cut into his chest, hacking away at the thick layers of bacon beneath the skin. Grease oozed in wet spatters as I shaved meat away from the bone, gathering it onto a plate for later frying. Next I pried open the young man's ribcage to get the plump round ham beating there, nearly dropping it in my ecstatic state. His midsection came next, yard after yard of sausage links unspooling as I pulled them free like a magician's handkerchiefs, slippery and warm. I hacked open his skull and scooped several helpings of hash browns, slit his throat like a slaughterhouse steer and stuck a carafe underneath the gouting wound to collect the orange juice that flowed forth. Grabbing his testicles I squeezed until they cracked like eggshells, the yolks spewing forth to land, spitting, on the griddle; I reached for a spatula and commenced scrambling.

Finally I cut the young man's tongue from his mouth, rolled it in bread crumbs, and tossed it in the deep flyer. This I ate myself, for it carried the God of Breakfast's word.

Renewed, I spent the rest of the morning cooking the young man's bounty. From the kitchen I announced all meals were on the house, and a chorus of approval rose from the diners.

The bell above the door jangled as my wife came in. I caught her eye and she smiled on the way to her booth in the corner.

I took the bowl of glass-spiked batter and proceeded to pour out pancakes.

In the service window waited row after row of plates, each piled high with food harvested from my young visitor. Fishhooks wrapped in bacon. Razorblades nestled in Belgian waffles. Thumbtacks swirled in a soiled toilet and hidden in French toast. Eggs Benedict dusted with bug spray. Glasses of milk and orange juice laced with rat poison.

I thought of all the diners and greasy spoons across this great country of ours, the cooks preparing offerings of their own, of folks sitting down to their own specially prepared meals. I thought of the God of Breakfast looking down with His warm, loving gaze. I thought of what was to come.

It was all I could do not to weep with joy.

I carried a stack of pancakes to my wife. As I placed them in front of her she greeted me with a peck of the cheek. "Hi, honey," she said. "Busy morning?"

"Yes. But a good one."

"I'm glad." She poured maple syrup over her pancakes, slowly, drawing out my anticipation. Then she picked up her fork, cut herself a morsel, and took the first bite of a new age.

HUNGRY FOR CONTROL
Clare de Lune

She liked the stillness of it all, especially when night faded into morning.

But it wasn't like that anymore. Now, it was nothing but blood, death, and a strange, foreboding loneliness.

Lisa watched the young woman coming across the parking lot from her post on the roof of the library. She lowered the barrel of the .22 until the woman was in its crosshairs and concentrated. As the woman got closer, she could see more details: the once-white t-shirt ripped up the middle to show a bloodied bra, a deep slash across her chest that revealed the white gleam of an exposed rib, the matted blonde hair.

Lisa recognized her. It was Sarah, her coworker.

It was like this every morning. She'd wake up to find several of *them* slowly rambling across the parking lot—they'd somehow shambled over the razor wire surrounding the city's administrative complex: a library, a police station with a jailhouse (handy), and a small courthouse. Most of the small town slept quietly, though—but there were enough of *them* around, more than the living, to keep Lisa occupied.

The woman who used to be Sarah came closer and Lisa pulled the trigger. Sarah's head exploded like an overripe fruit. Yes, Lisa had gotten good. And yes, Lisa didn't care anymore. She knew all those hushed moments making out in the stacks with Sarah were a distant memory. If she got near Sarah now, Sarah would devour her in a whole new way.

This was the way things were now. Ever since those outrageous news stories started coming out—"The Dead Have Risen" and "Drug Addicts Turned Cannibal"—nothing remained quiet for long. And if it did, it meant some major shit was about to go down.

One day, she'd take solace in that quiet again. Quiet: just like the library had once been, just like her life had been before the outbreak.

She thought about Sarah with the bloody, ripped t-shirt and her own current routine and how much it deviated from her old one. She used to get up with Jimmy, make coffee, chat over breakfast, see him off to work. Work in the garden before it was time to walk over to the library and start work herself. Sometimes, she and Jimmy would take lunch together, being that he worked just across the way at the police station. And they had a whole hour, which meant plenty of time together.

And that meant crazy hotel room games on the other side of town, ones where he would handcuff her and fuck her hard from behind, or the better ones where she would handcuff him and make him be totally still. Those were the best. She liked stillness. And control. Like she had with the .22 rifle.

She liked being in control for a change. The rifle was like having a cock, but more powerful. Shooting the undead and carrying a rifle had been a nice switch from her day-to-day life with Jimmy. He always insisted on being the one in charge, whether it was by his cop life or by bossing her around. So those times when he gave her control were completely luscious. She felt powerful, God-like, and like she totally owned her sexuality.

Yes, she could make him into a toy during those little rendez-vous—cuffs at the wrists, his belt lassoed around his ankles, her panties in his mouth while she rode his cock and dug her nails into his chest. She made sure she enjoyed herself while she could, because once Jimmy was loose again, there was no telling what he would do. He wasn't a fan of her little games.

Not that she didn't love him. She did. As a matter of fact, she obsessed over him—maybe not him—the idea of him: someone to challenge her, someone to take charge of things and win her over with his dominance and manliness. She sometimes felt a strange need to consume him in her rare moments of domination over him.

But with him, it always ended up the other way around. He'd either free himself from his cuffs or find some way to gain control again, and she'd find herself bound, gagged and taken advantage of.

She never got off with Jimmy. Not once. She knew if she had a chance to keep him completely still, she'd get there.

But now he was either dead or undead—Lisa wasn't sure which.

Lisa reloaded her rifle and her mind tracked back. He had lived for a while after the shit hit the fan. He helped her with target practice, she helped him put up the razor wire around the complex. She remembered him saying they'd make it through, since she was smart and he was a tough cop, right?

But everything was different now.

Where the fuck are you now, Jimmy?

If only he hadn't gone to check on that bus full of refugees . . .

Everyone had gotten in their cars in an attempt to leave, to somehow escape the outbreak, as if it was escapable. Most of those folks who had attempted to escape were now the same ones who always shambled their way over the razor wire. Matter of fact, she recognized a few locals every day—her nosy neighbors, cranky old Mr. and Mrs. Wallace from across the street, her library coworkers, the stoner grocery bagger guy from the market. They all shuffled across the pavement at one time or another, jaws slack and eyes vacant, mindless zombies with an insatiable appetite for flesh and blood.

She always waited for Jimmy to show up, undead and reanimated. He was determined, brave and hardcore, so he was bound to show up, even as his undead self. Right? Lisa always wondered if they retained any remnants of their real selves at all.

She had been working during the outbreak and luckily enough, and of course, brave ole Jimmy came up full force in his F150, blazing through the parking lot to check on her. He'd knocked down a few of the undead then, but they just got right back up (or crawled) and shambled on. That was before they knew you were supposed to go for the headshots. That's what stopped them from getting back up all over again.

Jimmy, so tough and confident. She liked the way his muscles tensed anxiously when she tied him up, as if he was expecting a beating from her, some bloodlust revenge from all the rough sex he'd put her through. She never answered him when he asked if she liked it that way, only moaned and screamed at the right times and bucked her hips back up against his cock when he most needed it. But she never got off that way. She only got off if the roles were reversed, and Jimmy never let her get there.

She supposed she missed him to some degree. And the loneliness and horniness overtook her right about this time, later in the morning after she'd finished shooting all the intruders.

The memories of Jimmy and their power struggle were getting her insanely hot. However, getting herself off was a risk. Leaving the post meant leaving the compound unguarded, and in the throes of an orgasm, anything could happen. She had many nightmares about stroking herself to the edge of climax, only to look up and see the rotting flesh of a starved zombie right above her face. And now, those nightmares had morphed into thoughts much more sinister and taboo, something she'd never dreamt of.

If there were no more healthy humans left on the planet, who would she fuck? She thought it totally preposterous every time it popped into her mind, but this was a nymphomaniac's worst nightmare. Now, her fantasies involved the zombies—if they were totally mindless, that meant they didn't give a fuck what was happening to them.

Lisa's greatest turn on. Total control.

If they were mindless, she could tie them up, fuck them relentlessly, beat them, choke them, punch them, and they wouldn't know the difference. No emotional involvement. No cares. No emotional scars or distressed phone calls the next day, "Lisa, if you said you cared so much, why'd you do that?"

Why? She laughed at the question now. She supposed it had something to do with Jimmy and all the things he'd done to her over the years. Who knew? Some of the people she fucked liked to be taken advantage of. There was one younger girl in the next town who begged to be tied up and brought to screaming orgasm with a little help from Lisa's strap on and various other toys. But some of the men, not so much—except the sissies, and they weren't much of a challenge. Lisa enjoyed dominating and fucking the tough guys . . . guys like Jimmy. Former jocks. Guys who talked a lot of shit about being tied up by a petite woman, yet came like geysers whenever she was finished with them.

Lisa shifted uncomfortably and looked through the rifle's scope again, hoping to find another one of the undead to shoot to distract her from her own horniness. Every day, she thought about what would happen if Jimmy the Undead came slowly shambling over the razor wire. Would she be able to shoot him? Or would she just tie him up and see if he could still pop a boner?

The parking lot was finally quiet, all those forgotten souls dragging their limbs, looking for blood somewhere far away. It was time to go inside and look for something to eat, anything to take her mind off sex.

She'd already raided all the lunches from the refrigerators in all the buildings, had gone through the MREs stashed away in the police station, and had even found a few things inside desk drawers—including an extra .38 special she'd found underneath in the police chief's files. Lisa now doubled back through everything she could think of in search of food, but there was nothing.

That meant it was time to go to the supermarket. Which probably meant facing more of them.

Lisa didn't feel up to it today, but it had to be done. She didn't like leaving the safe confines of the admin complex, its great razor wire teeth protecting her like some loyal pet.

She got the holster for the .38 and put it on, stuck the gun snugly inside and hitched the rifle up on her shoulder. She gulped down the rest of the water, filled her bottle up as much as she could, and headed out of the complex. The sun blazed down from its high noon position in the sky and Lisa's skin crawled. The outbreak was only three months ago, and one of the first things that crossed her mind when it happened was that the worst of it would come in the high heat of the southern summer.

She was sweating by the time she reached the razor wire. Several of the undead snarled and hissed at her, but they weren't going anywhere: they were entangled in the wire. One man in his fifties, fat and balding, had his head firmly stuck in the fence like some overeager dog. A small but muscular woman, probably once an athlete, had impaled herself by a large tendril of fence and wire. Her intestines sprawled across the concrete, blood glistening in the hot sun. Many of the rest of the undead's limbs were deeply caught up in the wire, so Lisa felt a quick sense of safety. And it was best to leave them. Bullets were reserved for the runners.

Those were the ones she hated the most. If only all the zombies shambled. They were only slow if they were a few days changed. The newly turned ones always ran at you.

Lisa turned onto the main road and looked around. All clear so far. She walked carefully, the .38 firmly gripped in her sweaty hands and the .22 rifle bumped comfortingly against the small of her back. A vehicle would have been safer, but the ones left on the complex were either wrecked or out of gas. It was just one more thing on her list: get more gas or find a new vehicle. It would either have to have the keys in it or she'd just have to get lucky. Jimmy never got around to showing her how to hotwire a car.

She came up on the centermost part of town that was scattered with little boutiques and bookshops. She walked in the middle of the street, far away from nooks and crannies of corners and alleys. The grocery store stood at the edge of downtown, and she had quite a few more blocks to go.

The streets looked nothing like she remembered. Plastic bags floated lazily across the pavement. Heaps of trash baked in the hot sun, and a stale and shitty odor hung thick in the air despite the lowly breeze that occasionally touched down. Shops left and right were boarded up, smashed to hell and back or were just completely abandoned. An old bank boasted a red-lettered, spray painted message that read, "Go back now."

The crunching noise made Lisa stop and look around. At first, she couldn't really decipher where it came, but closer inspection told her something was hanging out by the dumpster in the alley between Betty's Books and that newish woo woo shop with the candles and weird figurines.

Usually, the undead were attracted to noise and if you were quiet enough, you could easily sneak by without them even noticing you. Lisa had stopped and stared, hypnotized as if in some trance, her ears tracing the sound of the crunching and rustling from the dumpster.

That's no animal.

It seemed her boots were glued to the hot asphalt and her limbs were locked. One of the undead had its teeth clamped around some poor soul's femur and just then, Lisa's mind whirled ridiculously and she wondered how on earth a body ended up in the dumpster.

The zombie chewed relentlessly, probably trying to crack the bone to get to the delightful marrow inside, crunching and cracking until its own teeth crumbled and fell out of its skull. Its hair had somehow been singed off its skull, so it was difficult to determine its gender.

Lisa stood there too long. If she had ignored the sound and just moved away quietly, the rest never would have happened. She would have been able to secure a few groceries and enough water and would have probably found a car or made it back to the admin complex with no problem.

Maybe she screamed. Maybe it smelled her. Lisa didn't know. It snapped its head around and looked up though, and that's when she knew the shit was about to go down. It snarled and shuffled away from the body, eyeing Lisa like prized prey. Lisa could see its hollowed out chest: it looked like someone had tried to destroy it without realizing they were supposed to go in for the headshot.

Lisa raised the rifle and fired.

Nothing. No jolt, no delightful explosion of brains.

I missed?

The zombie opened its mouth and emitted a guttural scream. Lisa heard shuffling and scrambling, and then it seemed the entire downtown area came alive with the undead. They were everywhere now: mostly shamblers, but she could see runners in the distance, and they were gaining distance at an impressive rate. She fired at the closest one and its head exploded. Then another. Then another. She marveled at how much it looked like red fireworks.

They were coming up fast now, filtering down the alley towards her like rushing water. It was time to run.

Lisa's boots pounded on the asphalt and she squinted at the sun just ahead of her. She bolted as fast as she could—the entrance to the admin complex was just over the horizon.

And she could already see that was not an option. It had become infested with the undead; several of them were meandering across the parking lot towards her.

How the fuck did they get in?

She looked around frantically at the razor wire. One of the undead was face down on it, which provided the perfect safe spot—they had been using the body as a bridge. She made a split second decision to change direction and cut through the woods.

Please don't let there be any in here.

She'd have to be careful. They could be behind trees, hiding behind bushes . . . just about everywhere she turned in the dense woods. It was not quite like walking down an open sidewalk.

The shortcut would take her into the next town eventually. That was the same town she and Jimmy used to visit when they wanted to get away. It was the town where she hooked up with a lot of other people, too.

Wonder who I'll run into.

She ran a good ways before slowing down. Even in the shade, it was hot and sweat ran down Lisa's back in large droplets. She wasn't sure how far she'd have to hike, but it would be a couple of hours before she reached town on foot. And she wasn't sure if it was infested with zombies.

Doves cooed overhead and Lisa's boots sucked hungrily at the mud, but otherwise there was no other noise. She sat down on a dry enough spot on the ground and leaned back into a tree to rest.

How had it all happened so quickly? It had been just another normal day working at the library. She arrived early and Sarah was already there, as usual. They started making out wildly, like they always did before everyone else got to work. On quiet mornings when the book drop was nearly empty, like it had been on the morning of the infestation, they did a lot more than make out—they managed to work in a quickie.

Yes, Lisa was getting wet thinking back on it now. Things had been going as they were supposed to—the morning was quiet, except for Sarah's moans and pants and the occasional whisper of "no one can make me feel like you can" or "you're so good." Sarah definitely didn't get enough of it at home.

Lisa had been on her knees, licking Sarah's slash all the way up and down when the back shipping door buzzer sounded. That meant someone was there early and they had to stop. And that's when Lisa saw and heard sirens.

It was hard to say exactly what happened after that. It was all a blur. There were tons of people outside the library, some smashed up against the windows in the front, and even more people behind them. The whole parking lot seethed with people, and there was lots of screaming and pushing.

It didn't take long before Lisa saw the man's face—or obviously, what used to be a man. His face had been a mask of tortured hunger, so feral and inhuman and downright horrifying. Lisa knew something was terribly wrong, and her mind immediately shifted to Jimmy, but just then, stupid Sarah had opened the door to the library and was pulled outside. Luckily, Lisa was able to snap out of it and lock it behind her. Staying inside, away from those faces, was clearly the best option, and Sarah was quickly consumed by the sea of terrified faces.

For the time being, anyway. You blew her head off this morning.

Lisa got up from the ground and brushed her ass off. There was no need to sit around thinking about the past. What was done was done. She played the memory over too often in her mind anyway, which she assumed was a mixture of survivor's guilt and a bizarre tinge of jealousy. At least Sarah was blissfully unaware of the terrible world that was to come.

She continued trekking through the woods. It would take some time to get to the next town, but Lisa bit her lip in determination.

Gotta get there before nightfall.

At least, she hoped she could. Traveling at night was not an option. Runners could be anywhere, and once they smelled, heard or saw you, you were a goner.

Lisa continued sloshing through the sodden woods, her feet aching. It was humid now and the sun seemed to siphon all the sweat from her body. She scoffed at having only half a bottle of water on her—she thought she'd have either made it to the grocery store or back to the admin complex by now, but that was what she got for being so optimistic.

She finally took a large swig of water when she reached the edge of the woods. She could see the town of Walker just ahead, desolate and depressed just like, she was sure, any other town in the United States these days. Lisa knelt on the wet earth and set her sights through the rifle. She waited and watched.

There were three ramblers just ahead, and they were meandering mindlessly through the theater parking lot. If they were shamblers, she might be safe—she always tried to conserve her bullets. The sound of gunshots usually brought more of the undead around. They were attracted to loud noises like flies on the dead.

Lisa would have to cut through the movie theater parking lot to safety and hopefully, more food and water. The grocery store stood about three blocks away from the theater, but she didn't know if Walker was totally infested with the undead, and these three shamblers just ahead spelled bad news. It was hard to tell what had happened to other cities, towns, communities—the power had gone off completely about two months ago, and the CB radio had been completely silent save for the rare crackle of static.

She stood and trod carefully towards the parking lot, the rifle resting firmly on her shoulder.

Sudden pain ripped into her heel and bloomed all around her foot. The jolting intensity caught her off guard, and so did the yelp that emerged from her mouth. The ramblers down the hill snapped their heads in her direction and began to run towards her.

Lisa only had a split second to lift her foot and take a quick look. A large carpenter's nail rudely protruded from her boot heel. Taking it out felt worse than stepping on it, but she ripped hard, threw the nail and limped back into the woods.

The shamblers seemed to multiply: the three she'd seen earlier somehow exploded to about thirty, and about ten of them were fast. Lisa scrambled up the nearest oak, panting and swearing and oddly wishing for more water. She screamed again when she felt the tug on her foot.

Unbelievable.

She immediately recognized C.J. Riley, the foot fetishist who insisted on giving her money every time they hooked up. Lisa didn't mind the cash, but it did, in a lot of ways, make her feel like a whore for taking it.

"And now you want my foot again? Don't think so," Lisa said out loud, surprising herself. It was strange to hear a coherent voice, even if it was her own. She yanked her foot free and gave him a swift kick in the face. He stumbled back momentarily, but quickly came to and flailed around in an attempt to grab at Lisa's legs.

C.J. Riley, now tenacious and aggressive as a member of the undead, had always been pretty quiet when he was alive. She remembered him being demure, appreciative, and totally willing to please her and submit, and easily embarrassed. Now he was snarling and clawing at the tree bark trying to get at her. Lisa climbed higher, away from the smell of rot and the penetrating glare of the undead's emotionless, feral eyes.

She swallowed and grimaced—it felt like she'd been eating broken glass and her thirst was outrageous. Below, C.J. snapped his jaws hungrily, his mind no longer consumed with dirty thoughts of getting jerked off by pretty, well-manicured feet. Lisa rested her head back against the tree trunk and kept her eyes on the frenzy of ramblers below.

She remembered the last time she'd seen C.J.—that was the time she almost got caught by Jimmy. She had gotten off of work early that day and headed to Walker to see C.J.—she needed cash for new clothes and C.J. always paid her about 300 bucks every time they hooked up, so why not? She sure as hell wasn't getting enough satisfaction at home. She liked being worshipped by C.J., dumb as he was.

C.J. liked it if she'd been sweating in a battered old pair of heels for a good part of the day, so when she arrived, he immediately led Lisa over to the couch, placed her feet in his lap, and slowly slid her heels off. Lisa just watched and casually stroked his hard-on with her feet while he gave her a foot massage.

"Mmm, baby, you look so fine today. That petite little body of yours always looks so good in skirts and those tight little blouses you wear," he'd said with a wink. She thought it charming yet cheesy, but she smirked back at him. It was true: her small but fit frame drew a lot of attention from all kinds of patrons at the library. Lisa had dark skin and curly hair, which made her look incredibly exotic in a small town where most everyone was of the blue-eyed, blonde hair Dresden doll variety. She liked looking different.

"If you like the way I look so much, why don't you shut up and just show me?"

C.J. had been happy to oblige: he obediently unzipped his pants and pulled out an eight-inch cock with a nice curve to it. Lisa licked her lips. After the foot play, he would be all hers. She'd even tied him to his bed and fucked him with her infamous strap-on a time or two. Just as she was thinking she ought to get Sarah to help her tag team C.J., the doorbell rang.

C.J. shot her a weird look and zipped back up. She heard talking. "Lisa?"

It was Jimmy calling for her.

Shit!

A brilliant excuse popped into her head. She just hoped Jimmy would buy it. She slipped her shoes back on and headed for the door.

"Baby! What are you doing out here? I was just on my way back. Mr. Riley here called us to see if we had any books on podiatry. You know how I'm always telling you about Walker's patrons complaining to us that their library's collection is horrible. Nothing on podiatry. Right, Mr. Riley?"

C.J. looked dumbfounded. She doubted he ever read or knew what podiatry was.

Jimmy looked equally baffled. "Right. I saw you pull out of the parking lot early. Wondered where you were off to."

Controlling freak.

That incident had been too close. She hadn't seen or heard from C.J. in months. Now he was nearly scraping his fingernails off trying to claw at the tree. It looked like he had been shot several times: a smattering of bloody holes covered his chest.

Lisa swallowed again and really wished she had brought more water. Her head felt foggy, like her brain was sucking up all the moisture in her body. The shamblers were still snarling and moaning, which was a horrible auditory assault on Lisa's ears. She shut her eyes to distance herself until the moans subsided some.

A strange *thunk* noise roused her. One of the zombies fell over on its face. She looked around.

Thunk.

Another one fell backwards. She steadied herself and looked closely. It had some kind of arrow through its head!

"Who's out there?" She tried to keep her voice hushed.

The thunking noise continued until every shambler's head was speared. Lisa's heart was pounding.

"Who the fuck is out there?"

"It's me."

A figure emerged from the depths of the woods. As it got closer, Lisa felt she had to hold on to the tree branch in a death-grip.

"Jimmy?"

"Come down from there. You're safe."

She slowly clamored down the branches, hands trembling. *I'm hallucinating*, she thought. *I've been up there too long, and I'm imagining all this.*

Jimmy came closer to the tree and Lisa got a better look at him. She had to squint a little; daylight was quickly fading.

"It's really you."

It scared her a little when he didn't say anything. But it was really him. Same cold blue eyes, same square jaw line. He looked pale and wiry, not bulked up and muscular like she'd last seen him.

"You've lost weight."

She wanted to reach out and touch him to make sure he was really real.

"What the fuck happened to you?"

His voice was gruff, different, and had a little too much edge to it. "I'll explain everything at camp. Come on. You're probably hungry and thirsty."

Thirsty. She gulped at the prospect of water.

Camp turned out to be at the other edge of the woods, still near town. Jimmy had a damned military bunker set up out there, tent and everything. It surprised her that he was set up in the woods so close to a town, but apparently, it had been working for him.

She gulped water as he explained.

"When I saw that refugee bus, I ran over to help out."

"I saw. I was covering for you, remember?"

He nodded, his jaw tightening. Lisa knew that look. He usually ground his teeth when he was really pissed off. Lisa kinda liked it. She wanted to throw him to the ground and whip his cock out right then and there. A good old-fashioned wrestling match for power.

"I opened the door to the bus. It was just the driver and some kid in there. I could already tell. The kid had been bitten. He'd already died and was just barely starting to stir again. The bus driver was hysterical. I guess that was his kid, but there was nothing I could do. Shit, best I could do was shoot him."

"Did you?"

"No. It was chaos. They were coming at me from behind and there were too many. I was yelling at the guy to move his ass, but he was totally freaking out. Telling me to help the poor boy. The driver, he grabbed me by the shirt collar," Jimmy said, grabbing his own shirt for emphasis, "and he said, 'you need to help us, save us!' But there was nothing I could do. I couldn't get him to drive and I couldn't get him to move and that kid was about to wake up and become Eddy freakin' Munster, so I went out the emergency exit."

Lisa's mouth fell open. "You have to be fucking kidding me. You left me there?"

"What was I supposed to do? Run back through that crowd of crazed cannibals? Shoot the driver and take off with the bus? Come on. I only had one choice."

He looked at her in that way. Silence fell on the camp as Lisa considered it.

"I knew I'd find you." His voice was barely a whisper.

She hated admitting it, but he did find her and he did save her. She hated being the damsel in distress. And she did the first thing that came to mind to counter it. She put down the water jug, slipped her shoelaces out from her boots, and pushed Jimmy to the ground.

It agitated her to hear him chuckle, almost mockingly. "No, no, my dear. I saved you, isn't that right? We do it my way." He grabbed her wrists and flipped her over onto her back and into the mesh-like folds of the sleeping bags.

That's about when Lisa began to realize she was better off alone. Much better off alone. *Why even be pissed about him leaving me there?*

Jimmy drove his cock into her and grunted in her ear—she could tell he was pleased she was so wet. The helplessness she felt was immense. Jimmy had gotten lean and tough out here in the wilderness. His arms bulged around her neck as he plunged into her from behind. She could not get him off of her, no matter how hard she tried to buck her hips or thrust her knees around under him. He held her in a chokehold and she gasped greedily for air.

"You just wait, you fucker!"

She barely managed to choke it out, but she had to say it. Part of her missed Jimmy and missed the power struggle games and messing with his head, and part of her wanted to kill him.

Jimmy rammed his cock into her much harder now. She could feel her own walls pulling around him, no matter how hard she tried to fight it. It just felt too good and she could no longer hold on to her climax. Jimmy closed in fast, too—he gave her a final thrust and she could feel every detail, every vein and every ridge inside her.

When she finally caught her breath and Jimmy was limp, she shoved him off. She hated that it was amazing, but that didn't really matter.

"What if you get me pregnant? Asshole," she spat. Little waves of defeat coursed through her—it was akin to humiliation. She wished he had left her alone up in that tree. If she tied herself up there she might have been able to leave the next morning.

She thought she'd maybe said it aloud, because Jimmy jerked awake in the middle of his deep dozy state and looked around in a panic.

She looked around too, worried.

"Nothing's here. Chill." She looked at his creased brow, the veins protruding from underneath his skin, a blue and green web-work of real, pulsing, uninfected blood. But he looked terrible. "You must have been through a lot . . ."

"I haven't been sleeping. I kept thinking about leaving you there," Jimmy said as he rubbed his eyes. "Even after all the shit you did. I didn't want to just leave you there alone. I knew there wouldn't be enough food and you'd have to venture out of there and—"

"Look," she cut in, almost offended. "I was handling my own out there. You taught me well. You did what you had to do."

He sighed.

"What are you talking about, 'after all the shit you did.' What the hell?"

"You cheated on me, you bitch!" He was looking squarely at her now, that same intimidating bite in his voice. Now she really noticed how his eyes looked heavy and red-rimmed.

Well, she certainly couldn't deny it. She hung her head, but did not feel the slightest bit guilty. She wondered what the fuck was wrong with her, but she didn't forget. She held his eye contact.

"I was trying to get away from you. You were controlling and demeaning, and you even hit me!" She was getting pissed off now. And that was a good thing. She gritted her teeth and spat the rest out. "I don't want anybody to tell me what to do. I want to do things my way. And that includes sex."

He grinned in that 'aw baby, come on!' way, working his dimples, but she got in a good nose pop before it even worked. Blood immediately gushed under her knuckles and Jimmy made some kind of weird *hrmph* sound. She reached around for the shoelaces and deftly tied his wrists. It was taking a few moments for him to come to—his head bobbed back and forth like one of those car bobble-head dolls, so she snatched her rope from her pants pocket and tied his ankles together while she was at it.

When she was done, she found him blinking rapidly in an attempt to come to. She slapped him so he'd wake the hell up. When he finally did, he groaned a little too loudly. She bit back a smile.

I knocked his ass out!

Lisa slapped him again. "Shut the fuck up!" She said, trying to keep her voice hushed. "We don't want any of those things hearing you. Not with you all tied up, right?" She stuffed her panties into his mouth and wrapped more rope around his head to keep it in place. She backed away from him and admired her work. Yes indeed, she'd gotten plenty of practice tying up half of the town of Walker, and that had come in handy. Jimmy scowled at her. He'd just have to stay like that for a little while, at least until she was able to get her anger under control and figure out what to do with him next.

They were both still naked, exposed in the cooling night air. It struck her how good it felt to be naked in the woods, the darkness of the night unfolding overhead. And Jimmy looked pretty good with his wrists and ankles bound.

"Look at you, tied up and sucking on my panties. You like that?" Lisa sneered as she kicked him teasingly. She was amused to see that he was getting hard again.

"It's been a long time for both of us," she purred as she stood over him. "I'm going to fuck you while you're bound and gagged, and you can't do anything about it." She lowered herself down onto him and enveloped his rigidness.

"I have a right mind to just leave you here and let those freaks eat you alive," she growled, digging her fingernails into his bare chest. Jimmy moaned and struggled, but Lisa just squeezed her thighs around him and held him in place with her razor-sharp nails. "No need to struggle. You're obviously enjoying it. Be still."

Jimmy emitted a loud screech and his eyes bugged. It took her a second to realize he was looking behind her. She stopped and twisted around to see.

Lots of zombies. Maybe thirty or so—but they were barely shuffling. Still, with that many of them, Lisa and Jimmy were as good as fucked, and they were too close—500 feet away and gaining.

Isn't this some shit, she thought. *I finally have him in the perfect position, and now this is happening.*

Lisa had to work quickly to get Jimmy out of his bindings. She clawed at her clothes to find her pocketknife, cut through the rope and stuffed her feet into her boots. She scrambled to pick up the rest of her clothes—she would just have to put them on later. She bolted away from the pack and ran a few hundred yards before she realized Jimmy wasn't behind her. And she had left the .38 and the rifle behind.

She stopped and peered through the dark blanket of the night, her breath coming in huge gasps. She could see him off in the distance, untangling himself from the ropes. "Dammit, you motherfucker! Stand up and run!" Screaming might bring on more, but that was the furthest thing from her mind. *I can't watch him get torn to pieces.*

One of the undead quickened its shuffling when it realized hot, fresh meat was on the ground and helpless. It was a nasty looking thing—as Lisa ran closer, she could see its eye dangling from the socket, and a trail of pus had dried and crystallized on its face and boney chest. Jimmy finally stood and twisted around, but it was too late. The fetid thing reached out its decayed hand and swiped . . .

Time slowed down as Lisa watched the events unfold. The zombie snapped its jaws and its overgrown fingernails ripped into Jimmy's shoulder. He winced but kept moving towards Lisa, and she just reacted: her arm came down on the thing's head, and suddenly it had a knife impaled in its other eye.

"Come on, run!" She said. Her voice was shaking. She knew what would happen next.

Jimmy was blubbering now and Lisa grabbed his arm to lead him through the woods. "I'm fucked, I'm fucked, I'm fucked," he kept saying over and over in a high keening voice, and Lisa wanted to slap him again.

"We're going down into the town. I recognized a few that were wandering around there today. We must have drawn them out of there with all your whining and screaming."

Jimmy stopped and yanked his arm away from hers. "You're going to have to pile drive that knife through my skull. I'm not suffering through this and I'm not gonna become one of *them*!" His brows were furrowed in *that* way, and she knew it would be an Act of Congress to get him to follow her.

She knew it was true. Once you were scratched or bitten, it was over. The fever came next, then the chills, then death. Then you came back as one of them. And it happened rather quickly—she'd seen it before.

She stayed in the library and barricaded herself inside well after the outbreak first hit, knowing that heading back home meant doom. Weeks after Jimmy darted out of the building in an attempt to help the bus of refuges, a lone man, his face hardened by the horrors of the outside world, woke her up one morning by banging on the library's glass windows. She let him in only to discover he'd been bitten, and it wasn't long before she watched him progress and had to put him out of his misery. She knew she'd have to do the same with Jimmy now.

She sighed, noting the hoard of undead just over the dark horizon. "If you stay here, they'll eat you alive. Is that how you want to go down? If we go down there, we can at least find a comfortable place. Then we can talk about pile driving this into your head." She held up the knife and dark, vile blood dripped off of it.

She could see him considering this beyond the cold blue veil of his eyes. His bare muscles twitched in the moonlight, and she could just make out the angry red scratches on his shoulder. The sores were already festering and swelling. He gave her a curt nod and off they went, both still nude except for Lisa in just her boots. Once they gained ground and Walker was near, she stopped and pulled her clothes on.

"We'll get you something once we reach town," she muttered.

Walker was just down the slope and across the highway. They proceeded carefully, but were only greeted by abandoned cars, some burned and some with doors completely ripped off. The smell of death and gasoline was thick in the air, and Lisa could just make out silhouettes of dead bodies slumped in several of the cars. This was as far as she'd ever gone since the outbreak, and she was surprised to see that this many people had tried to escape. Where did they think they would go?

They were closing in on the outskirts of town, which stood beyond the highway like a quiet grey maze of tombstones. The only noise was crickets chirping behind them. No shuffling or moaning.

Lisa led Jimmy through the labyrinth of abandoned cars, through the tree line and on into Walker. She knew there was a drugstore close by. *If I could just get him inside and comfortable, maybe I can find something to take his pain away,* she thought as she searched for the drugstore storefront in the darkness.

The undead, if they were around, were unaware of their presence. Now that they were getting close to the drugstore, Lisa wondered how they would get inside without attracting attention. Breaking a window would cause them to come in swarms, but she couldn't think of another way in.

She walked around the entire building, looking for a way in, Jimmy following her all the while with a hopeless look on his face. She wanted to slap it right off of him, and she wanted to slap herself for being so angry at him. *He saved your life. Even if he always was such an asshole.*

Finally she tried the front door out of sheer last minute frustration, not thinking that it would swing right open. It did. *Fucking hell. All that worrying and the damn front door was unlocked.* She whirled around to look at Jimmy and he just shrugged half-heartedly. She could barely make out his features in the minimal light, but it seemed as though they were fading. His face looked thinner and sallow, and bags were forming underneath his eyes. *He's changing.* She felt her heart lurch and tasted a strong surge of adrenaline on her tongue.

"What are we doing here?" He murmured. He was hugging himself tightly, but the night air was as warm and wet as a sloppy kiss.

"Come inside," she whispered. She let her eyes adjust to the darker interior. Grabbed a blanket for him. Hopped the pharmacy counter. Hoped she was grabbing the right thing—she was pretty sure the labels said Oxycontin, but it was hard to tell in the dark.

She hopped back over the counter, grabbed a warm, expired orange juice out of the mini fridge by the register, and sat next to Jimmy, who was huddled in his blanket in the corner by the reading glasses rack.

She dumped the pills out on the floor. "Start taking these. They'll make you sleepy."

He didn't argue. She supposed he guessed what they were. She shut her eyes. She didn't want to know how many he took. Hopefully it was enough to help him drift far enough away.

Almost as an afterthought, she stood again and headed to the aisle where the ace bandages were located, yanked a few plastic packages off the rack, and sat back beside Jimmy.

"Lie down," she whispered. She couldn't tell if the drugs were already working or if he had just resigned himself to do as he was told, but he spread out on the floor and lay still.

Carefully, almost lovingly, she bound his wrists and ankles with the ace bandage. His eyelids fluttered, but his dick responded well, almost as if it was saying goodbye to her.

The pharmacy was quiet. She climbed on top of him and rode him slowly, enjoying the feel of him, enjoying the control. She could feel an orgasm building from this, a real one, the kind of orgasm she could control. It ripped through her like a languid wave, satisfying and slow. She collapsed with her head on his chest.

His breathing slowed. Stopped. The world was still again.

Quiet.

She wasn't sure if she dozed or not, but when she opened her eyes, the morning light was just beginning to rear its ugly head.

She let her eyes adjust to her surroundings. For now, they were safe and the ace bandages bound Jimmy securely. She heaved herself off of him and pulled her clothes back on, being careful not to make too much noise. Now that the morning light was seeping into the drugstore, she could see the place was a goldmine: blister relief stuff for her feet, water, school backpacks, and even energy bars. She greedily stuffed a child's school backpack with as many supplies as she could fit in there and even smiled to herself a little.

She stopped abruptly when she heard the moan.

Jimmy.

He was still lying on the white tile floor, but he was squirming slowly, like larvae coming to life. His milky eyes rolled in their sockets until they became fixated on her. He emitted a low-pitched sort of *hiss* and she gasped.

This was not like any other zombie she had encountered. Sure, she had run-ins with plenty of other people she knew, but this was different.

Is it because I love him?

She couldn't figure out the answer to this question. The relationship with Jimmy had always been tumultuous in some way—even if things seemed calm on the surface, something was brewing on the horizon. Whether it was stress from his job that built up and contributed to his exploding rages or her own promiscuity, there was always something.

Maybe I hate him.

There it was. Lisa supposed it was a little bit of both. A love/hate relationship.

She had been standing in an aisle that boasted a few basic tools: hammers, screwdrivers, and pliers. She pulled the pliers off the hanger and approached Jimmy slowly, cautiously.

At first, pulling out his teeth and fingernails grossed her out. But soon, she took great delight in it. If Jimmy felt any pain whatsoever, he didn't express it: his untamed eyes were fixated on her and his jaws snapped mechanically, longing for their first bite of unyielding flesh, but he didn't flinch or scream.

She had to chuckle. "You can't hurt me now," she said through her teeth as she yanked the last tooth. "And you'll make a nice pet." She was pleased to see that although he wasn't quite the same Jimmy, his cock could still get nice and hard. Lisa put a dog collar and leash on him and led him out of the drugstore and into the morning sunlight. The sun was just creeping up over the horizon. Night was fading into a new day. She smiled to herself a little as she yanked Jimmy's leash and led him to the outskirts of town, on to a new police station, a new library, a new life where she could have things her way. Yes, there would be blood. There would be plenty of death. But the strange, foreboding loneliness?

No more. She looked back at Jimmy lovingly.

The world around them was still.

And she had total control again. Just the way she liked it.

CLARISSA
Robert Essig & Jack Bantry

Clarissa cried. She cried a lot these days. Her life had been a wealth of tears and now she couldn't feel more helpless and desperate.

She rubbed her belly, bulging beneath a pair of swollen breasts that had become so tender that she wanted to scream into a pillow, but the pain in her breasts was nothing compared to the thoughts that constantly tormented her mind.

Clarissa had lost the urge to escape until recently. She was so tired, but she couldn't stay here and have her child subjected to the same abuse, the repeated rape. A sex toy trapped in a cellar. There was no way she could allow that monster to touch her child. Just the thought sent shudders through her slight frame. She didn't know the last time she had seen daylight. Had no idea how long she had been down there. She had nearly come full term and the length of the pregnancy was just a fraction of her imprisonment.

Clarissa couldn't remember her life before she was trapped in the cellar but she instinctively knew that she had never been a happy girl. The very idea of happiness must have come from some saccharine television sitcom she'd seen in a past that was further depressed in her mind with every dreary morning she woke up in captivity. Now, her mind was filled with dark corners and spider webs, dank, moldering odors mingling with her own sweat and bodily waste when her "bedpan" hadn't been properly disposed of.

Someone unlocked the basement door.

Clarissa wiped away the tears on her face, smearing through grime like cheap mascara.

The door opened. A man, cast in shadow, stood in the doorway.

He was tall and heavy-set. She knew him as the Monster, any details hidden in the darkness.

She looked at him with large, sad eyes. They would have been beautiful had her life not been so tragic.

She rubbed her belly in a circular motion, a reminder that she was surviving for two. She had to get out of there so she could have this child and raise it on her own, away from the Monster.

If she couldn't escape, she wished the child dead, rather than lead a life like this.

The cellar was large but the furniture sparse. The Monster had, at some point, removed anything that could have been used as a weapon. Left her in darkness most of the time.

She had been waiting for the man to bring her food.

Clarissa clutched a hammer behind her back. She'd taken it from the Monster's toolbox when he'd put up a crudely handmade cot for the baby. So far, he hadn't noticed it missing.

She could feel the knot of worry twist her insides.

The baby kicked. That tiny foot reassured her of what she was putting at risk by attempting to escape. She rubbed her belly again with her free hand, soothing her nerves as much as possible. She would have one chance. If her aim was off, the consequences would be dire.

The man walked down the cellar stairs.

Clarissa gasped. Could she go through with it? What if she failed? He would punish her. He'd punish her anyway. That's what he normally did. He'd have rough, painful, degrading sex with her before returning upstairs, like nothing had happened, like she wasn't locked in his cellar.

He truly was a monster.

When he approached he was looking around the cellar, probably admiring his handy work in constructing the cot. She hit him with the hammer and he collapsed like a cow in a slaughterhouse. She scurried up the stairs, towards the light shining down from the room above. Adrenaline surged through her veins. This was her chance. The Monster grabbed hold of her dress and yanked. The light above looked so far away and as she fell backwards, the light seemed to escape. It teased her, forever out of reach. Clarissa shook her head, tears running down her face, her mouth in a trembling rictus.

No!

The scream that erupted as she busted her tailbone on the concrete floor was agonized and shrill. She grabbed her belly, feeling something awful, something like she was going to be sick, only she wasn't going to vomit from her mouth, but from her vagina.

She'd dropped the hammer on the stairs as the Monster yanked her backwards.

He hefted her slack body into a standing position.

Clarissa screamed and flailed.

"Be quiet," he said. His voice was slurred like maybe he was dizzy from the hammer blow.

She felt utterly defeated, destined to be imprisoned in the dark cellar and abused, right up to her dying day.

What had she done to deserve such a fate?

His fist hit her in the belly, hard, the shock and pain enough to cause her to vomit. The man took a step back to avoid the bile spray, laughing at her as if she were some sideshow exhibit for his amusement.

"I said be quiet. You'll wake your mother."

Clarissa's head rose, hair matted to her face with sweat and puke.

Mother?

Anger and hatred wracked her belly, then another. She looked up into the face of the man. The light from above showed her the image of her father. She clutched her abused belly, pain erupting from her womb, into her guts, threatening another bout of vomiting. That would have been a blessing, compared to what happened next.

Her body convulsed. Blood spread across the lower half of her filthy dress.

"I made that cot for nothing, now," he said.

Clarissa acted on impulse. Taking the man off guard, she darted up the stairs towards the taunting light. She slipped and her already traumatized stomach lurched. The slip made her think of the blood running down the insides of her legs. She felt the man—was it really her father?—behind her. His fingernail scratched her calf when he tried to grab her. Instinctively, she kicked backwards and caught the man on the jaw. Looking back over her shoulder, she saw him clatter down the stairs. Relieved, Clarissa turned her body towards him. He lay unmoving. *Her father?* She was confused. Had she blocked it out all these years? Could her dad repeatedly rape her like this monster had? Hesitantly, she moved back down, towards the cellar floor, still no movement from the man. He didn't seem to be breathing. Had he broken his neck? She knelt down and looked him in the face.

It *was* her father.

And mother waited upstairs.

Clarissa turned away and, clutching her pained belly, walked back up the stairs. On her way, she picked up the hammer.

+ + +

The light as she emerged into a house, she only vaguely remembered; seared into eyes that were only used to the dim glow of the solitary bulb hanging from the cellar ceiling. She blinked several times, trying to gain her focus, before proceeding and was startled by a gasp.

"Oh, it's . . . you," came an uneven voice, Clarissa hadn't heard in years. Her mother never had much of a soothing voice, not as far as Clarissa could remember.

Clarissa hefted the hammer above her head, eyes still adjusting. Through a gummy fog, she saw a sickly-thin woman standing in the kitchen. Couldn't make the features out. Clarissa blinked her eyes and things began to come into focus.

Has she been crying?

Emotion flooded through Clarissa. Her mother's face was sunken and sad, as if all the life had been sucked out of her with a vacuum. Her eyes looked too wide, in a head that appeared too large for the fragile frame of her body, hiding beneath a sundress like a dried up corpse beneath a shroud. Did her mother love her, had her father kept her down below against her mother's wishes? She yearned to be touched, embraced. She wanted her mother to make everything better.

Her mother's eyes darted down at the blood on Clarissa's legs. "Oh, my! You didn't hurt the baby did you?"

Her mother completely disregarded the hammer and dashed across the linoleum floor, falling to Clarissa's feet, placing her hands over the protruding belly as if praying to some absurd deity of the flesh.

The hammer wavered in Clarissa's hand. The feeling of this woman's hands on her belly drew attention to the fact that something was terribly wrong. One way or the other, the baby was coming.

"Call an ambulance," said Clarissa, the words coming out in palsied syllables.

"No!" said her mother. "No ambulance, no police. No!"

"B-but . . ." Clarissa was confused.

"Get on the floor. I'll deliver the baby. Your father promised me another baby, you know. It's not yours. It's mine."

Clarissa's face wrinkled in disgust. Was the woman mad? It was *her* baby.

"No," said Clarissa. "I need an ambulance. Please, I need help."

Her mother stood up, the sad, forlorn look wiped away and replaced with one of contempt. She grabbed Clarissa by the arms and threw her to the ground. The impact sent a shockwave of pain through her womb and she knew the baby wouldn't survive. During the fall, the hammer leapt from her hand, hitting the linoleum floor with a dull thud.

With Clarissa's mother crouched over her, pinning her arms, Clarissa realized how weak she had become in the years of confinement. She had little muscle tone and was powerless to defend herself, even from a stick-and-bones, waste of a woman.

"Harold!" her mother called. "Harold, get up here and hold her legs! I want my baby!" Clarissa's mother erupted in tears. "You promised me a baby," she said through rising sobs.

Looking to the left and the right, Clarissa saw where the hammer had landed. Her mother let go of her arms and wrapped them around her belly, placing her ear to the bulge as if hoping to hear a sign of life.

Her mother swallowed hard and became frighteningly lucid. "If you're a boy, I'll name you George. If you're a girl, I'll name you Lilly. It'll be so nice to have a baby in the house again."

Clarissa grabbed the hammer, wrapping her fingers around the grip. When she lifted it, a scraping sound came from the weight of the hammerhead on the floor. Her mother's head popped up. Their eyes made contact as Clarissa swung the hammer. It made contact with her mother's temple. It wasn't much of a blow, but enough to startle the woman and cause her to fall to the side.

Clarissa maneuvered herself into a more compromising position. Pain radiated from her womb. It felt as if she was peeing all over herself, but she knew it was blood. She could feel herself getting weak from the loss of it.

Moaning, with a hand to her head, Clarissa's mother wavered as she attempted to get to her knees. Clarissa didn't allow this to happen. She'd hesitated before, the thought of killing her mother an abstraction that allowed for a disastrous hesitation, but now she realized that this was just a woman. *No, a monster,* just like her father. She smashed the hammer against her mother's head repeatedly before the blood on her hands caused the tool to slip and turn around. The final blow landed the claw end, where it stuck like an axe in a tree stump.

Clarissa screamed. Her eyes darted to the open cellar door and then to her mother's body and back to the door. She felt weak. The smell of blood was so heavy she could taste it. She scuttled out of the kitchen on her hands and knees, coughing and choking on the overwhelming, coppery odor in the room. She wasn't familiar with the house at all, but somewhere in the banished memories of a life lived before captivation, she remembered the numbers 911, emergency numbers to be dialed on the phone.

There was a phone on the littered coffee table in the living room. Clarissa dialed 911, said something unintelligible and then erupted in a fit of crying. The phone lay beside her, the tiny voice of the dispatcher calling for her. She was too weak. Couldn't move. A trail of blood followed her from the linoleum onto the carpeted floor. There was too much blood.

Too much.

She felt dizzy. Her eyes closed and opened again. The world seemed to spin, the red trail from the kitchen along with it.

The baby was dead.

WHERE THE SUN DON'T SHINE
Pete Kahle

SATURDAY MORNING—Gordy Melbourne woke in agony on the couch in his living room with no idea where he was or why his gut hurt so much. With a drawn-out groan, he pulled himself to a seated position, immediately realizing that he was completely naked and covered from head to groin in what appeared to be dried vomit.

"Jesus Friggin' Christ, what did they get me into now?" he moaned under his breath.

By they, he meant his best friends Hector Nieves, Ross McGraw and Seth Mahler—partners in crime since they had all met each other back in 1989 in the same freshman homeroom at Winthrop Crane High School in Stonechurch, MA. Hard to believe that had been over twenty-five years ago since they still acted like foolish teen hooligans whenever they were given the chance to let loose. Gordy was supposedly the responsible one, the one to rein them in when their ideas put them in danger of bodily harm, but from the evidence surrounding him, he had failed miserably this time around.

He leaned forward and rubbed his face vigorously. A flurry of brownish-green puke flakes fell to the stained carpet in a cascade from his whiskered cheeks. Gordy looked around the room, taking in the disaster in all its glory. A trail of mud, gravel and dried leaves led from the front door into the kitchen, before a more recent path meandered into the living room to a spot next to the coffee table. There he had apparently stripped naked, left his filthy clothes in a pile and crawled over to the couch where he had passed out and upchucked on himself in his sleep.

I'm lucky I didn't choke to death on my own vomit, he thought.

I wouldn't have been found for days while I rotted and became a permanent part of the couch.

Gordy shuddered and began to examine himself. Dried vomit and mud were caked like paint in his chest hair leading all the way down to his matted pubes. His arms and legs were covered with bruises and scratches. The nail on his left forefinger appeared to have been ripped off halfway to the cuticle. The sharp pain on his right flank turned out to be a yard-long abrasion from below his hip to his armpit. There were also a couple of large dime-sized puncture wounds there that wept a cloudy sticky liquid as if he had been stabbed by someone and dragged on the pavement. The holes throbbed in time with his heart.

Have I been in a fight? What the hell is going on?

He stood up and almost immediately fell to his knees with a short shriek. His ass and legs burned as if something had torn away a few layers of skin down to the muscle. Sobbing for a moment, Gordy reached far back between his legs and felt raw meat with shreds of torn flesh and hair stuck to the skin with dried blood.

Raw hamburger, he thought. Something ground my ass into Grade A chopped sirloin. He gingerly moved his fingers forward and was relieved to find that, although bloodied and tender, all of his vital male equipment was still intact.

Holding his breath, he whimpered and staggered to his feet. He leaned against the wall for support, leaving a trail of muddy, bloody streaks on the way to the bathroom down the hall.

The harsh fluorescent light revealed a monstrosity in the mirror. He wasn't a handsome man by any stretch of the imagination. At 38, he was the typical American white male. Thinning brown hair, muddy brown eyes, thirty to forty extra pounds that had settled in his gut and ass and the stereotypical goatee that many overweight men of his generation thought would give them back their jawline.

Now, however, he looked even worse than he had imagined, like a ghoul risen from its foul, sodden grave. The sclera of his right eye was suffused with blood from burst capillaries and, below it, his cheek looked like an over-ripe plum, swollen with juices and ready to burst. Gordy touched it lightly and nearly blacked out from the pain.

My cheek is broken, he thought, wondering if he had a concussion or worse. Hematoma. Aneurysm. Brain damage. Whatever it is, I should call 9-1-1, he thought, then instantly forgot the notion when he opened the shower door and stepped under the steaming spray.

He watched, mesmerized by the blood and mud swirling in red and brown spirals down the drain. It reminded him of something but, in his current state, he couldn't retrieve the thought and it slid away into the recesses of his mind.

His ears began ringing, his vision blurred and he had to grab the metal bar on the wall to avoid falling down. Voices chattered and gibbered over and over in his head . . .

. . . thedevilsassholethedevilsassho
lethedevilsassholethedevilsassh
olethedevilsassholethedevilsass
holethedevilsassholethedevilsas
sholethedevilsassholethedevilsa
ssholethedevilsassholethedevils
assholethedevilsassholethedev . . .

. . . twisting his brain into knots. A flood of vomit spewed from his throat covering himself and the glass shower door as he let go of the bar and fell to his knees in a daze.

He sat there on the shower floor sobbing as the spray beat down on his head until he was able to climb to his feet. The puke washed off rather easily, but the dried blood was another matter entirely. It had scabbed and caked all over his lower back and ass crack. He didn't even want to consider what could have caused such an injury or where it might have happened. For all he knew, he had been gang-raped by a family of inbred hillbillies Deliverance-style out in the woods.

Squeal like a pig, boy! C'mon, squeal! Yew shore got a purty mouth!

Unable to scrub away the dried blood as hard as he would have liked, he simply let the water dissolve the clumps as best as possible, and let the heat of the spray soothe his pain as he tried to remember what the hell had happened to him over the past few days.

+ + +

SATURDAY AFTERNOON—He was feeling slightly more human after the shower and two Percocets that he had left over from
when he had his wisdom teeth pulled last year. On second thought,
he took four. He wasn't ready to venture out of his apartment,
though—didn't want to leave his house at all—not even to see a
doctor. The pain was still present, but not so bad that he couldn't
think things through.

After his shower, Gordy changed into fresh boxers and a thread-
bare shirt that said Jesus Hates the Yankees! He collapsed once again
on the couch (after flipping the cushions over so he didn't sit on the
stains) and turned on the television when he realized that he didn't
even know what day it was.

"Saturday?" he muttered when he saw the date listed on the
channel guide. "What the . . . ?"

As far as Gordy could tell, he had lost nearly four days of memories. His last recollection, foggy though it may have been, was from
Tuesday morning when he had woken up at the crack of dawn to
go meet the guys and head out . . . somewhere. And that was the
problem. His memories simply ended there when he left the apartment complex in his beat-up Honda Civic.

In retrospect, he probably shouldn't have taken that many Percocets. His pain had been numbed, especially in his nether regions,
but his concentration was shot to hell now. It was only after zoning
out and watching twenty minutes of a documentary on the mating
habits of African hyenas that he came to his senses and realized that
the phone was still in his grip and he had yet to make any calls to
see how the other guys were doing. Perhaps they could shed some
light on his injuries and what they had been up to in the interim.

He called Ross first. Like Gordy, Ross was "between relation-
ships" and he had much more free time than the others. Unlike
Gordy, however, Ross did not have a job, nor did he live on his own.

He lived in his parents' house in the basement.

Of course, Ross would argue with anyone who described his living
situation that way. According to him, it was much more than that.

His room in the basement was technically called a mother-in-law apartment due to the fact that it had a separate entrance around back and he could come and go as he wanted (as long as he was quiet). But there were a number of other factors that complicated his claim.

For instance, he only had a half bathroom in what was actually a cramped converted closet, so he had to take showers upstairs. The washer and dryer for the entire family was just off of his living room, and although he did have a refrigerator, it was filled with beer, ice cream and microwave burritos. His place smelled of beans and drier sheets. Accordingly, he ended up eating most meals with his mom, dad, and sixteen year-old twin sisters upstairs.

And then there was the fact that he didn't have his own phone line downstairs.

One of the twins answered on the first ring.

"Hi Katie. Put Ross on the phone."

"I'm sorry. Who is this?" she answered in a saccharine tone.

"Gimme a break for once, Katie. You know it's me—Gordy. Can you please get him to come the phone? It's very important."

"This isn't Katie." Gordy could hear the sneer linger in the silence that followed. The twins didn't particularly like him that much.

"Kirstie . . . sorry," he sighed and corrected himself. "Can you get him? It's really urgent."

"I go by Kit now . . . and, just so you know, Katie wants to be called Kat."

Jesus Christ. Give me a break . . .

"Ok, Kat—I mean Kit—I'll remember that from now on. Can you please get him? Seriously. It's kinda important."

Kit paused, apparently enjoying the act of stringing him along for a few seconds, before relenting. "He's not here."

"What? Do you know where he is?"

"I dunno, Gordoooo," she dragged out his nickname in disdain. "You were with him last, weren't you? I haven't seen him since you dipshits left on your trip last week. I thought you weren't coming back until tomorrow, anyway."

"Wait . . . what trip?"

"Don't play stupid, Gordo. You know what trip. The one you all were planning so you could get back to nature and do some primitive "male bonding". That's what we heard you say when you thought we weren't listening. I thought it was your idea in the first place."

< B L I N K !>

Gordy gasped as a light flashed behind his eyes and a sudden rush of vertigo overwhelmed him. His guts clenched and he became lightheaded as a torrent of mental images overwhelmed him, flooding his senses. His eyes rolled back and he fell back, slumping over the stained arm of the couch, telephone falling from his grasp to the floor.

+ + +

TUESDAY AFTERNOON—Gray clouds obscured the sun. A steady drizzle of rain leaked from the sky as the four men hiked up the beaten dirt path. They all wore large backpacks filled with the essentials for a few nights away from civilization—including a significant amount of alcohol—but it was obvious that none of them had been camping in quite a while.

"Gordo—where the fuck are we?" bitched Hector as he stumbled on a small tree limb in his path. "Do you even know where this lake is? This was a completely stupid idea—camping at this time of year."

"Almost there," he responded. "You'll like it. I swear."

"We'd better," grumbled Hector again. "My shoes are ruined now."

"No one told you to wear your Jordans, man. We all knew it would be wet. Don't you have any boots?"

Hector just muttered unintelligibly in response.

No snow had fallen yet this year, but the perpetual gloom and the smell of rotting, wet leaves hung in the air. The trees had only a few orange and yellow stragglers left clinging to the branches. The last time he had been up to the lake was over two years ago when his parents were still alive. Winter was only weeks away and Gordy realized that this was probably not his best idea, but he wasn't about to turn back now. The guys would never let him live it down. He resolved to persevere and keep marching onward.

A dog or coyote yipped in the distance and Hector let out a whimper, eliciting taunts from the rest that he sounded like a little girl. Seth lagged behind as usual, staying out of the conversation and surreptitiously sucking on a lit cigarette like it was his mother's tit. Ross was the only one who seemed unbothered by the weather, probably because he was already well on his way to getting shit-faced, taking a swig every few minutes from a scarred pewter flask. Big surprise there, huh? What was actually astonishing was that he hadn't already sparked up a joint. He was probably saving that for after their arrival.

Ross wasn't the only one who had started drinking. For most of the hike, Gordy had been nursing a PBR tallboy in one hand while gripping a sturdy branch he had appropriated as his walking stick. He already regretted coming along on the trip, but he could never admit that to the guys. He had been the one who had planned it and talked it up over their misgivings. And now, of course, he was sick. The possibility that he would catch a bug had never even crossed his mind, but here he was, wheezing and coughing like an asthmatic schoolboy.

The first hour of the hike hadn't been too bad. The incline had been gradual and the path was easy to follow, but once they took the trail that led up the mountain to the lake and the elevation increased, his friends began to whine and complain. Especially Hector. Up ahead, the mountain rose sharply on a sheer grade to a cliff face at least fifty feet tall. The trail hugged the face before disappearing around the bend. Worst of all, debris littered the forest floor. Branches, tree limbs, and in some cases even entire trees, had fallen across their route, roots thrust out of the ground as if a moody giant had torn them free. Part of the dirt path even appeared to have been washed away. As they continued up the incline, evidence increased that something had scarred the land in the recent past.

"I guess there actually was an earthquake," grunted Seth.

"Huh?" Ross said, looking back. "What the hell are you talking about? I didn't feel anything."

"Not today, dipshit."

Gordy intervened, "Wait . . . was that the one on the news a couple of months ago? I think I heard about it."

"Yeah. That's the one. It wasn't very big, but supposedly the epicenter was right around here."

Gordy looked around. "Probably why all these trees are up-rooted, huh?"

"Ya think?" Seth rolled his eyes and took another drag on his cancer stick. Ross and Hector snorted at his comment. Gordy held back a retort and continued up the mountain. After a few more minutes, though, Gordy was finally on the verge of calling it quits. He was just about to suggest that they turn back and head down the mountain when nature intervened and the light rain transformed into a torrential downpour.

"Are you kidding me?" yelled Hector at the sky. "Are you seriously kidding me? Just what we fucking needed!"

Yelling in frustration, they were soaked to the bone within seconds. The drumming of the rain on the land around them was deafening. Ross hollered, pointing out a mammoth, twisted maple tree half a football field away that had planted roots in the cracks at the base of the cliff face. Seeing no other shelter remotely close to its size, the four men raced to the meager cover beneath its sagging branches.

"Damn it, Gordy," cursed Hector.

"Oh, give me a break. Like I had anything to do with this."

"You could've checked the weather report," muttered Seth as he pressed against the mossy trunk of the tree, vainly covering his eyes to avoid some of the more powerful squalls.

Gordy was about to retort again when Ross blurted out, "Guys, there's a cave here!"

On the cliff face behind the tree, one of the cracks in which the roots were growing was large enough for a full-grown man to squeeze through. Even with his bulky backpack, Ross, who was not a small man, could obviously wriggle through the gap.

"That won't fit all of us," argued Gordy. "It looks dangerous."

"Screw that. If you're not going in, I will," Hector said, rushing forward. He ripped away the foliage that had camouflaged the entrance and leaned in, illuminating the interior with the flashlight app on his phone. Lightning flashed and a crash of thunder sounded close behind them. He laughed and took off his backpack. "It gets a lot wider after a few feet. Big enough for all of us! I'm going in."

"Wait . . ." Before Gordy could protest, Hector wriggled past the narrow opening into the wider passage beyond. Ross and Seth ducked in after him. Gordy let out a string of profanity and, seconds later, followed his friends into the crevasse.

+ + +

Gordy was shitting fire into a hole in his backyard when he came out of his fog. A guttural howl escaped him as what felt like a torrent of molten lead laced with shards of glass streamed in a brown arc from his ravaged colon. He was leaning forward on his knees, straddled over a foot-deep hollow that, based on the grass and mud caked beneath his fingernails, he had recently excavated with his bare hands. Each spasm of his guts released another steaming discharge into the hole, so painful that he nearly blacked out in agony again. He couldn't even think.

Finally, after he had apparently emptied the entire contents of his body cavity, Gordy fell forward sobbing and curled into a ball. He lay there in the afternoon sun and moaned for a few minutes before crawling to his feet and looking himself over. He was naked from the waist down. Red and brown streaks ran down his thighs. A few feet away, the remnants of his boxers lay torn to shreds, stained with blood and fecal matter in a ball at the foot of his porch.

"What the fuck is going on?" he blubbered. Something was seriously wrong with him. First, he had lost four days of memories and now this? Who knew what he had done in the lost four days? Gordy didn't even want to think of what could have happened while he was blacked out. Maybe he had a concussion. Some type of head injury had to be causing these blackouts. The alternative was not something he even wanted to consider.

And then there was the river of shit that was pouring out of him. He didn't know if it was a disease or some sort of bizarre intestinal infection, but he knew that he had to see a doctor as soon as possible. That was an unmistakable fact. It just wasn't normal to crap like a fire hose, especially with what felt like enough force to perforate his intestines. He did not want to consider why he was doing it in a hole in his backyard.

Gordy normally hated doctors—in fact, he couldn't remember

the last time he had gone in for a physical—but this time there was no other alternative. He would have to suck it up and seek some help, but first he needed to get clean. Again. He pulled himself slowly to his feet and staggered toward the hose attached to the spigot on the side of his house.

Thankfully, he lived in a relatively wooded area. The Tumasovs, his closest neighbors, couldn't have seen him doing his business unless they walked through a few yards of brambles that separated their two properties. They were an old antisocial Russian couple with at least ten quasi-feral cats and dogs that used his and other yards in the neighborhood as their own personal toilet. He had waved to them a few times when he first moved in, but when it became obvious that they didn't want to be friendly, he gave up and left them alone.

He hoped they had at least had their windows closed because he had been screaming pretty loudly and, based upon the pain in his throat and the hoarse quality of his voice, it had been going on for quite some time. Perhaps he was lucky and they weren't home.

Each step he took induced another wave of burning agony in his nether regions, but he eventually made it to the faucet and gingerly turned it on. He gasped as the water hit him. It was so cold, but the initial shock gave way to relief as the icy flow numbed his raw wounds. Closing his eyes, Gordy let the open hose run freely over his bloody hindquarters, rinsing away the stains and the chunks. The pain was still there, but at least it had subsided to the point where he could think again.

Blearily, he examined his hands. His fingers were raw and swollen, his nails torn and bloody. Dirt stained his pores. Dozens of fresh cuts and abrasions scarred his palms and knuckles. It looked like he had been digging with his bare hands for hours, and when he looked around the yard he realized that might be closer to the truth than seemed possible.

In addition to the open hole he had recently occupied, there were at least five—no, make that six—similarly-sized mounds of torn-up grass and earth. Odds were that he had also made a deposit in those holes as well. That settled it—he needed to get to a doctor ASAP. Whatever was going on was much more than an intestinal bug or food poisoning. Neither caused people to black out or go into a fugue state, did they? It needed to be taken care of immediately, but before he could do that, however, Gordy had to change his clothes . . . yet again.

He climbed the back steps and reentered the house, hobbling like an arthritic old man. Remarkably, other than the fact that the screen was wide open and his cell phone had been left unattended in the middle of the kitchen floor, there was no sign that anything else had happened inside the house since his blackout.

He finished cleaning up in the shower, and pulled on a t-shirt and the baggiest pair of sweatpants he owned. His stomach gurgled and he felt pressure in his lower abdomen. Goddamn, I'm bloated. Feels like I swallowed a bowling ball, he thought. Please let this be over soon. I don't think my ass can take this anymore. He was deciding whether to go to the ER, or to see if his primary physician had any open appointment soon, when a series of thoughts occurred to him. How did I get home? Why can't I remember driving? Is my car even in the driveway? Heading to look out the window facing the street, Gordy racked his brain for any hint of what had happened since they had hidden in the cave—if that was even an actual memory rather than the remnants of a nightmare.

Thankfully, his fears were unfounded. His beat-up Honda Civic was parked out front, half on the driveway and half on the piebald turf that he pretended was a front lawn. It was undeniable that it was a dreadful parking job, but otherwise the vehicle had emerged unscathed.

A barrage of barks and growls filled the air. He turned around, wincing at the agony in his ass, and realized that the animal sounds were coming from his backyard. The growls became louder. Peppered with wailing and intermittent yips, the baying was coming through the window over the kitchen sink. Gordy limped over and peered out. One of the neighbors' dog was in his yard, going psycho barking at something on the ground. Right around where he had left his droppings.

"What fresh hell is this?"

+ + +

TUESDAY EVENING—Ross started drinking first. In other words, as they all had known, he had been drinking the whole while, but now that they were stranded for the duration of the storm—and it looked like it would be a continuous downpour all night—he made the executive decision to salvage the day and make sure everyone got utterly shitfaced like him. Ross loved to drink, but he preferred that others drank with him. It was easier to deny that he had an alcohol dependency that way.

Gordy initially took it easy with the alcohol intake. He had the thought in his head that the rain would stop soon and he could get them to the cabin where they would start a fire, dry off, and get thoroughly obliterated in front of a campfire. Soon, however, he realized that they would probably be sleeping in the cave and it quickly became apparent that he would never live this down, so he might as well have some fun.

They had all brought some beer, but without a stream in which to refrigerate the cans, it was piss warm, so they started on the hard stuff right away. Gordy and Hector had each brought a couple bottles of cheap rum, Seth had his usual bottle of scotch, and Ross had filled his Camelbak canteen with Kool-Aid and a generous amount of grain alcohol.

Things got stupid rather quickly after that.

After several hours of drinking and praying for the storm to subside, the guys grew restless. The four of them huddled in various stages of undress, waiting for their clothes to dry. Even though there was still at least an hour of daylight remaining before sunset, the rain clouds outside obscured the sun and the illumination inside the cave was little more than a dim glow from the entrance, muted and gray. Gordy did have a couple of flashlights, but he only used them sparingly in order to conserve the batteries on the chance they would be here through the night, namely when they were searching their backpacks for alcohol. During those brief moments of light, they saw that the cave became funnel-shaped, narrower towards the back wall where a small waist-high opening led into darkness.

The howling wind blowing across the cave entrance produced a continuous haunting sigh that hissed off the walls like the final gasps of dying men. A mutual chill traveled up their spines at the sound. Conversation had ceased earlier. Listening to the rain, they had come to the obvious conclusion that they would be staying the night. Hector had already unrolled his sleeping bag and passed out. Gordy had changed out his wet clothes and now sulked next to him in his pajamas until they dried off. Seth sat near the entrance, smoking another cigarette and watching the rain pound the earth mere feet away, while Ross paced around in a nervous circle like a dog waiting by the door to go outside.

"I'm bored, guys." he said, slurring his words. "This seriously sucks."

"I said I was sorry, dude. I should've known better," Gordy replied. "Next time we'll go to Foxwoods and play the slots."

"Foxwoods?" I'd rather go to a Pats game and tailgate. We could watch them stomp the other team"

"And be home sleeping in our own beds," interjected Seth.

"Anything would be better", he said. "Hey Gordo, let me borrow that flashlight for a bit."

"What for?"

"Just want to walk around the cave a bit and see if we missed anything."

"Fine," Gordy said, handing over the SureFire. "Don't use it for too long. It's expensive and we may need it later."

He nodded and flicked on the beam, immediately blinding Gordy, who cursed as he covered his face and stumbled back into the wall. Ross ignored his friend's pain and walked away, waving the light in a back-and-forth pattern along the walls and floor.

Other than the debris of the past few months—branches, stones and leaves mainly—nothing seemed to stick out and spark his interest, until the flashlight beam washed over the hole on the far wall. He looked in the opening with the light and immediately realized that the small tunnel curved down into a narrow chimney. Aiming the beam down the shaft, he realized something immediately.

"Holy crap, this is deep," he exclaimed. "I can't even see a bottom." To prove his observation, he picked a baseball-sized stone from the floor and dropped it down the hole. Nearly ten seconds later, the sound of it hitting bottom echoed up to them.

Seth looked up sharply and walked over with a curious look on his face.

"Try that again," he said.

Ross repeated his action and Seth counted the seconds.

"Nine," he reported.

"Wow . . . that must be like a football field."

"Try five of them. It would have to travel a few hundred yards to take that long to hit bottom."

Ross shook his head in bewilderment. "How do you even remember that? We took Physics over a decade ago."

"You might still know it too if you didn't spend your high school years stoned off your ass," blurted Gordy from the other side of the cave.

Seth laughed as Ross grumbled under his breath. He seemed about to respond with a when he cocked his head and frowned. "Do you hear that?" he said as he stuck his head back in the hole.

"Hear what?" Gordy said. "All I hear is the rain."

"Ross, give it a rest," Seth added with a sigh.

"Shhh, shut up! Just shut up! Stop talking and listen!"

Seth and Gordy exchanged worried glances. They had been friends with Ross for a long time. He had a severe inferiority complex and they were well aware that he had a short fuse when he felt he was being mocked, especially when he was drunk. Sometimes it was fun to needle him until he did something that he would regret the next morning, but now was not the time for him to have a meltdown. Neither of them would put it past him to rush out into the night and get lost in the storm where he would probably get struck by a falling limb from a tree or maybe die of hypothermia. That was definitely something they did not want to deal with at that moment.

So they held their tongues and shut up . . . and, surprisingly, they heard the noise, too.

A slick, rustling sound came directly from the hole in the wall. Hearing it painted a picture in Gordy's mind of someone crumpling a large amount of cellophane at the bottom of a well. Crackling and echoing up the twisting stone chimney, the noise sounded like a chorus of whispers that moved with an organic ebb and flow.

Ross, grinning at the looks on their faces, proclaimed, "I told you I heard something!"

Seth walked back into the cave to take a look. "It's gotta be an echo. Some trick of the acoustics warping the sounds of the storm."

"Maybe an underground stream?" suggested Gordy.

Ross shook his head. "Nah, it seems like something's moving down there. Up and down the sides of the hole."

"Shine the flashlight at it."

"No shit, Sherlock. I've already tried that, but it's too friggin' deep. The light can't reach that far down."

"Let me try looking," interrupted Seth. Ross handed him the flashlight and he looked down the shaft, carefully aiming for the center of the darkness. Nothing. Shadows and stone walls extending down. That was all.

"Sounds like a giant bowl of Rice Krispies down there, but I still can't see shit," he admitted. "It's black as hell down there."

An updraft of warm air hit him in the face and he pulled his head out coughing as he tried not to vomit. The smell of rot and methane filled the chamber, so thick they could taste it on their tongues. Hector woke screaming. "Aaauuggh! What is that? It smells like the Devil's asshole!" He ducked back into his sleeping bag and covered his head. The others covered their faces with their sleeves and alternated between holding their breath and trying not to fall down laughing as he spewed forth a barrage of muffled Spanish profanity.

Seth began shouting in a fake Speedy Gonzalez accent, "Andale! Andale! Es el Culo del Diablo!"

Normally Gordy would have sighed in disapproval when Seth or Ross blurted out an ignorant comment like that, but now he couldn't even catch his breath. He was already feeling a bit sick from the amount of rum he had drank and the stench was more than he could handle. Sinking to his knees, he attempted to filter it out by breathing through the fabric of his sweatshirt.

Behind them, Ross was on a mission. He ran to his backpack and pulled out a long thin object wrapped in plastic. He peeled the wrapper off, revealing a bundle of long, thin, brightly-colored cardboard tubes—roman candles left over from the 4th of July. He had planned to light them one night at the cabin, but now seemed more appropriate.

"This'll light things up," he laughed as he separated. "I'm gonna shoot this down where the sun don't shine—right down the Devil's Asshole." Pulling out his lighter, he walked to the opening and stuck his head in once more to check if anything had changed.

The smell of decay was even stronger and the beam from the flashlight still could not penetrate the stygian depths of the shaft. "This is gonna be awesome," he muttered to himself. He flicked the lighter and held the flame to the wick.

Back behind him, both Seth and Gordy were watching. Hector was still huddled in his sleeping bag. Seth was somewhat confused. Gordy, on the other hand, felt nervous when Ross pulled out the fireworks, but he couldn't think clearly.

"Ross—" he said. "What are you—?"

The wick sparked and ignited. Ross pointed it down the hole and prepared for the pyrotechnics to begin. All at once, the pieces all clicked together and Gordy knew what was wrong.

Methane.

Fire.

"Stooooopppppp!" Gordy screamed, but it was far too late. The gas ignited and a plume of fire exploded into the main cave.

+   +   +

Something was making the dog lose its mind. It straddled the edge of the shit pit in the center of the yard and howled so loud that it seemed its throat would rupture. Gordy recognized it as the one he considered the alpha male of the Timusovs' pack of untamed mutts. He didn't know its name, but since one of its favorite activities during the winter was to scour Gordy's yard for frozen poopsicles for a midday snack, he liked to think of it as the Unholy Ravenous Turdmonster.

The Turdmonster was an extremely large dog. Scratch that—it was freaking humongous. There was obviously some St. Bernard blood in its bloodline, or perhaps a Bull Mastiff, or some breed that regularly gets mistaken for a horse or a baby mammoth. Gordy also thought that there might be some poodle in its lineage since its hair, though matted, overgrown and filthy, was on the curly side. If it weighed anything less than two hundred pounds, Gordy would eat his hat.

Though it could have intimidated anyone who was unfamiliar with it, Turdmonster had never bothered Gordy or scared him. Before today, he had only heard his canine neighbor bark a few times, and those instances were in response to other dogs yapping down the street. To be honest, Gordy's backyard would have been much more unsanitary if it hadn't been regularly looking for some snacks. Whenever Gordy came out during one of its frozen feces foraging missions, it just gave him a look that said Okay, okay, hold your horses, buddy. I'm outta here, and then he slunk into the woods between the yards. The unspoken agreement between them had always been that neither one of them would deny the other passage through the backyard. It was an amicable truce.

As its booming barks echoed through his and the neighbors' yards, Gordy went to look out the screen door to see what was causing the canine meltdown. The Turdmonster was thoroughly enraged by something in the hole where Gordy had had his unfortunate accident earlier. Quietly, he stepped out onto his back deck, careful to avoid the boards that creaked, and leaned against the wooden railing to get a closer look.

Now that he was closer, he heard a whisper of something in the air in the few moments between the barks and growls. Bubble wrap, he thought. Sounds like someone is popping bubble wrap. A shitload of it. The weird noise was coming directly from the makeshift toilet. He wanted to go investigate, but, with the Turdmonster in a mindless frenzy less than ten yards away, he realized that the idea was ill-advised.

Seconds later, the opportunity presented itself. Turdmonster leaned forward sniffing and whining at what he saw in the hollow. The big dog appeared confused and frightened. A hole filled with shit wasn't something it found every day, but it seemed to sense that something was off kilter. The bubble wrap noise seemed to increase in pitch and a flash of movement lashed at Turdmonster's muzzle. He reared backwards with a sharp yelp of pain. The dog scrambled frantically away from the hole and turned tail, yipping in panic as it ran away, blood leaking from a deep circular wound that had been ripped from its nose by whatever had attacked it.

What the hell just happened here? Gordy thought to himself. He looked around but the Turdmonster was long gone, having run off into the trees.

Did something attack the dog? What the hell is in that hole? He would rather not see the contents, considering where they had come from, but he had to see what had scared the dog away.

Taking the wooden stairs gingerly, Gordy stepped down to his lawn and walked to the edge of the hole, wincing with every movement. He still heard the popping bubble wrap sounds and they were growing louder as he came closer. Reaching the hole, he peered in and immediately staggered back, nauseated by what he saw.

He had expected to see the remnants of a soup of blood and feces soaking into the earth. Not pleasant at all, but instead the pit revealed a mass of worms writhing and churning in the stew. No, not worms—worms didn't have scarlet pincers and mandibles and dozens of small, thorny, chitinous limbs. Worms weren't translucent and their innards weren't visible—at least Gordy didn't think so. He could see clumps of the most recent meal they had eaten (and he was pretty certain he knew what had been on the menu) passing through their abdomens.

Again, Gordy felt sick to his stomach and more than a little afraid. Did he really crap those things out, and were any still inside him? He steeled himself and peeked over the edge again to get a second look. This time, he forced himself to take note of the details, regardless of how disgusting they were. If more of these worms/grubs/larvae were actually still inside him, he would need to be able to describe them to the doctor. They could be some type of exotic parasite that he had picked up in the woods. Who knew what diseases he could have now?

The larvae swam in the pool of waste, rolling over each other in a slimy tangle. Their constant motion and chittering mandibles were the source of the bubble wrap sounds. Gordy realized now that he couldn't delay any longer. He had to go to the ER immediately, and he needed to bring a sample of the larvae so they could quickly identify what they were. To do that, he needed some tools.

A not-so-quick trip to the kitchen later, he was back at the hole with New England Patriots souvenir cup (that Hector had left in his sink last week), and a plastic ladle (which he would toss in the trash as soon as he was finished with it).

"Ugh, this is vile," he muttered as he skimmed a couple of the smaller larvae from the surface of the pool into the cup. Each were about an inch long and they began wriggling furiously as soon as they were pulled away from the warm comfort of the pit. Violently, even. As if they were calling for help . . .

Gordy secured the lid of the cup and turned to walk back into the house and call for a ride to the ER when something jabbed his left ankle. All strength in that leg was gone, and he fell to his knees. A sensation of burning acid spread past his knee into his thigh. He looked back to see what had attacked him. One of the larvae was attached to his leg, but this one was much larger than the ones in the cup. By a factor of ten, at least, perhaps as much as twenty times larger. It was the size of his forearm with serrated pincers larger than his thumb buried in the meat of his left calf. The larva squeezed the pincers again, cutting deeper into the meat. Through the jelly-like flesh, Gordy could see a gland beneath each of the pincers pumping the acidic venom into his muscle.

With each squeeze, the burning crimson liquid seared inside him, cauterizing his pain receptors and gradually numbing his lower leg, but Gordy was too shocked to care. The sight of the giant gelatinous larva had triggered a critical synapse in his brain, opening the floodgates, and he remembered the missing days.

He remembered every horrible second.

+ + +

The explosion was instantaneous. A blinding white radiance filled the cave, followed milliseconds later by an equally powerful swell of scorching heat that had the three of them diving for the cave floor to escape it. And then, as soon as it happened, it was over.

The cave smelled like burning hair and ozone. A high-pitched ringing muffled their screams. Hector whimpered in panic from

270 WHERE THE SUN DON'T SHINE

inside his sleeping bag; Seth and Gordy were sprawled on the cave floor, amazed that they were still alive; and Ross leaned against the wall, moaning in pain. Even in the dim light of the cave, it was apparent that he had taken the brunt of the explosion in the face. His hair and eyebrows were singed and the skin on his face was bright red as if he had been sunbathing without any sunblock for hours.

"Asshole!" screamed Seth, losing his usual cool composure, "You stupid, braindead burnout asshole! What the fuck were you thinking, Ross? Have you killed every single brain cell in your skull?"

"Dude," muttered Ross. "I'm sorry. I made a mistake."

"It was a mistake that could have gotten us all killed, man," said Gordy. "You gotta tone it down with the 'crazy and unpredictable' act. It's old."

"Man, I said I was sorry! We wouldn't have been here if you had . . ."

"Gimme a break, Ross. That's beside the point. My mistake has no connection to your decision to shoot a roman candle off at all."

Hector sat up suddenly and cocked his ear. "Guys, is it me or is that weird noise getting a lot louder?"

"What?"

"That noise," he said, pointing toward the opposite wall with the hole where the fire. He was right. In the minute since Ross' adventures with gunpowder, the sounds echoing from the hole had steadily increased in volume until it could easily be heard from every area of the cave. Needing a distraction to calm his nerves, Seth walked over to the gap in the wall and stuck his head in to look down the shaft.

Seconds later, he was engulfed by a crawling, slithering mass of pincers and claws.

+ + +

The plastic ladle was not an optimal weapon at all. Gordy whacked the giant larva over the head three or four times, but it just bounced off the rubbery flesh like a spoon bouncing off of a Jell-O mold. The greasy foot-long grub let out a few clicks and hisses, but it wouldn't release its grip. By then, his left leg had the worst case of pins and needles he had ever experienced, rendering it thoroughly numb and useless.

He reversed the ladle and tried to pry the thing off him by inserting the handle between the pincers and levering it out of his leg, but the handle was too flimsy. It snapped in half and all that remained of the handle was a jagged six-inch stump.

"Goddamnit!" Cursing, Gordy desperately stabbed it over and over until he finally cut through the rubbery skin and it popped like an old blister. A cloudy foul-smelling sludge slopped from the wound onto the ground as the larva froze in death and slid off his leg. Scooting backwards a few feet, he began to sob in great heaving gasps.

Everything from the past few days was now fresh in his mind as if it had just happened within the hour. The wounds on his ankle matched the two swollen holes in his armpit, only smaller and closer together. He rolled over onto his stomach and began to drag himself around the side of his house toward the garage. He still had to get to a hospital, but before he could think of that, he had to take care of this and other nests. These creatures could not be allowed to live.

+ + +

A tide of twisting mouths and slime poured from the breach in the cave wall, swarming over Seth and flowing into the cave. The sounds resembling bubbles popping and thousands of claws scraping against the stone deafened them. The wormy mass was so heavy that the ones on the bottom were crushed; their vile innards coated the cave floor with a slick layer of viscous sludge.

Ross was the next to be overwhelmed. Holding his burnt face in his hands, he never had time to recognize the threat coming for him. The worms flowed up his legs and torso, biting and stinging their way into his nose and mouth. He fell to the floor choking on them and soon was lost from sight.

Gordy was closest to the entrance. He screamed at Hector, exhorting him to get out of the cave. Hector was in a panic, trying to pull his way out of his sleeping bag, screaming for help when the zipper became stuck.

"Gordy! I can't get out," he begged. "Please!"

Without thinking, Gordy ran forward and yanked on the zipper tab. It was thoroughly jammed; a folded bit of nylon was caught between the slider and the teeth. There was no time to work it loose.

"Fuck the zipper," he yelled. "Rip it open. Pull yourself out!"

Hector's eyes widened. Looking back into the recesses of the cave, he wailed, "GORDY!"

Gordy turned around. The crawling sea of grubs was nearly to them, but the monstrosity beyond them was what caught his eye. A massive specimen was pulling itself out of the shaft through the hole in the wall. The grubs flowing across the floor ranged in size from half an inch to three inches long. This one was the size of a full-grown man.

Anyone who had watched as many Animal Planet documentaries as Gordy had could identify it as the Queen.

Pushing the last of her bulk out of the gap, she flopped to the floor, crushing hundreds of her spawn as she landed. A flurry of wet squelches sounded as each of her two dozen legs emerged from muculent cavities in her sides, unfolding to gain purchase on the slippery floor. She rose up and faced the two remaining friends across the cave, snapping her blood-red clapperclaws together like a chef sharpening her knives. Scarlet venom leaked from the tips. Though Gordy couldn't see any eyes along her flanks, it was dreadfully apparent that she was looking directly at him. She began to drag her immense bulk in his direction.

With a hoarse desperate cry, he dropped Hector's sleeping bag, turned toward the narrow entrance of the cave, and ran blindly for his life. Behind him, Hector's screams of terror were quickly muffled as the worms reached him and filled his mouth.

+ + +

Gordy pulled himself up on his good leg and dragged himself around the corner of his house by leaning against the vinyl siding for support. His other leg was completely useless from the paralyzing venom that the grub had injected, but he still managed to shuffle along with his three good limbs.

I let my friends get slaughtered by those things. It's my fault we were even in that goddamned cave. The horror of what had happened repeated itself in his mind over and over again. He saw his friends' dying faces again and was overwhelmed with nearly crippling guilt. Even if their actions may have slightly contributed to the situation, ultimately Gordy knew that he was at fault.

He turned the corner and, as he had expected, found the garage wide open. At the back, covered by an oil-stained tarpaulin, his old riding mower sat in the corner. He hadn't used it in nearly two years, ever since he had begun paying an entrepreneurial neighborhood teen to mow it twice a month. He crossed his fingers that it would start. Otherwise, he was out of options.

Ten minutes later, after an effort so draining that he had vomited on the garage floor, he sat on the mower and managed to start the ignition on only the third try. At his feet, on the mower deck, sat a 5 gallon jug of gasoline. It was only about half full, but he didn't have anything else that was flammable, so that would have to be enough for the job he was about to do.

Driving with his left hand, Gordy held a propane grill lighter in his right ready to ignite the gasoline and fry those vermin. He exited the garage, leg limply splayed out to the side, and turned the corner into his back yard where the churning holes remained. The sound of the mower drowned out the noise coming from the original hole, but he could still see the frothing, churning soup of grubs ahead of him. He drove the mower to the open hole and poured a few splashes onto the surface. Immediately, the grubs began writhing and jumping out of the gory sludge. One flick of the lighter and the hole was filled with dancing flames. Gordy smiled to himself as the grubs sizzled and popped. He continued around his yard, soaking the five other mounds where he had left a deposit with gasoline. Once all six holes were burning, he sat there to make certain that the contents were thoroughly burnt to cinders.

As he watched the six plumes of black smoke rise in the sky, he felt some discomfort and nausea as the burning shit stench filled the air and blew back in his face. Disgusted, he retched on the opposite side so violently that his upper abdomen spasmed and he doubled over the steering wheel as more violent convulsions rippled through him. He fell off the mower holding his gut as another sharp pain hit him. It felt as if someone was stabbing him . . . from the inside.

Gordy rolled onto his back screaming. He pulled up his t-shirt and confirmed what he had feared. A large bulge in his abdomen had pushed his navel inside out, and a two inch long pincer covered in blood and gore was slowing digging its way out of the umbilical cavity.

+ + +

Freedom was less than ten feet away when the Queen caught Gordy and slammed him to the cave floor. He wailed as she climbed his back and pinned him beneath her mass clamping her pincers on his right flank. The jagged barbs pierced the flesh directly beneath his armpit and the paralytic venom pumped into his body. Within a minute, he was unable to move more than with the slightest of tremors.

Circulation and breathing slowed as he was dragged back into the dark cave. He was still conscious but his perception was altered to the point where sounds echoed and everything he saw faded in and out in a slow-motion strobe effect.

Thankfully he was numb, feeling no pain and only the slightest of pressure.

Once the Queen had pulled him back into the main cavern, she left him on his side on a layer of bodies of her crushed and scorched spawn. He could see now that she had been injured by the roman candle. A foot-long burn mark like molten glass scarred her upper flank and a pungent ooze leaked from the wound.

Hours passed.

Thousands upon thousands of her children crawled along the floor and flowed up the wall in the dim glow of the flashlight that still cast its beam from where it had fallen. A few even walked along the ceiling, sometimes dropping to the floor and bursting with a wet impact. Many of them climbed his frozen body as if he were only an outcropping of stone around which they needed to maneuver. Across his arms, legs, mouth and eyes, he felt their sharp feet scratch along his skin. None of them, however, attempted to crawl inside his mouth or other orifices, nor did they feed upon him.

His friends were not so lucky.

Little remained of Seth. He had been consumed down to his bloody bones. Even his clothes had been eaten, except for his wrist-watch, the eyelets of his boots and his beloved Captain America belt buckle that he wore when he could be certain that no one of the opposite sex was likely to see him.

From his vantage point, Gordy could only see the upper half of Ross, but what he saw would have made him scream in terror if he was able to make a sound. The grubs had crawled inside his body like the carcass of a wild animal left to decompose on an African veldt. Gases had bloated his face and torso to twice their size and the constant motion of the creatures feeding on his interior caused his skin to ripple like the ocean tide. Hector seemed to have suffered the same fate as Ross, but since he was still stuck inside the sleeping bag, all Gordy could see was the seething flow of grubs entering his body through the eye sockets.

More time passed. Despite his paralysis, Gordy became quite hungry and desperately thirsty. The Queen had been out of sight since he had been tossed aside, but he could hear her massive bulk slide around the cave from time to time.

Suddenly, the grubs began flowing in his direction and surrounding him. A subsonic humming vibrated the cave and tingled the surface of his skin. The cave seemed to get warmer and a smell like horse piss tainted the air.

Something was obviously different about her as she slithered into Gordy's view. She seemed larger and her skin was awash with a pinkish mucus. She circled him three times in an ever-tightening spiral. As she rolled by on the final pass, the heat radiating off her body was palpable.

It was at that point that he saw the ovipositor.

Gordy knew what that horrible thing was the second he saw it (Yet another benefit of watching too many Animal Planet documentaries). He understood that an ovipositor is an egg-laying organ generally located on the tail end of an insect's abdomen. In this case, it was a foot long with a fleshy sheath surrounding a black segmented organ that protruded from the butt end of the Queen.

All signs pointed to the unequivocal fact that the Queen was going to stick a Humongous Monster Insect Dick inside of him and plant a few hundred thousand eggs. Technically "dick" was not the correct term since she was a female, but for all intents and purposes, it performed the same basic function as a penis did. It penetrated.

Gordy gibbered and screamed in his mind as the reality of what was going to happen crystallized in his mind. Covered in warm, glutinous, reproductive mucus, the Queen slid on top of his frozen body like a nightmare lover. As she rolled him over, some of the mucus filled his mouth and nose. For a few long seconds, he couldn't breathe. His sight began to blur, his ears began to ring, and he was momentarily thankful that this mouthful of bug sludge was going to kill him before the Queen could consummate their union. Unfortunately, however, his involuntary survival instinct was in full effect. His gag reflex was triggered and he vomited out the sludge just as the Queen spread his legs and struck.

The pain of the impalement was so great that he immediately passed out.

+ + +

Another pincer tore through the flesh of his belly and a grub equal in size to the one he had already stabbed to death emerged through the wound wrapped in the shredded remnants of Gordy's intestines.

This was it.

This was the end

This was how he would finally die.

After all he had survived in the cave, with the ghosts of his friends haunting him, now he was going to perish wallowing in a pool of his own blood and shit in his own backyard. Somehow it didn't seem fair at all.

Another grub poked its head through the bloody gash and he felt more of them—dozens more—writhing inside him.

+ + +

FRIDAY, JUST BEFORE DAWN—Gordy woke to the smell of his friends' rotting bodies. It was darker inside the cave, with only the fading light of the flashlight, which had been kicked to the opposite wall and now cast a meager glow on the surrounding rocks. Silence hung over the stone chamber like a bloody shroud. Shadowy mounds littered the floor around him, unrecognizable in the blackness. A vile, feculent taste filled his mouth; he spat several times and gingerly lifted his head off the floor. Gummy residue on his cheeks stuck his skin to the stone until he peeled it away.

Gordy tried to move his arms and legs and cried out, shattering the stillness. He tried again and slowly managed to pull himself to his knees, biting his lip to keep from screaming out. Running his hands up and down his body, he noted that he only wore tattered remnants of his pajamas. Other than that, his entire body felt as if it were throbbing in time with his heart. Every spot was tender. He must look like one giant bruise.

Gradually, as his eyes adjusted to the low light, flashes of memory came back in fractured shadowy images . . . the storm . . . the explosion . . . the Queen . . . the death of his friends . . . NO! The rest was lost to him in a blur of remembered pain and terror. He knew now what the mounds most likely were and he began to sob again. He cried for a number of minutes, then realized something astonishing. He was alone.

The cave was silent, except for his own voice, and he realized that the Queen and her brood must have left, returning to their lair down the shaft in the wall.

Only one thing was on his mind. He staggered over and grabbed the failing flashlight. Nearly dead, it had enough of a light to find his backpack lying in a dried pool of grub slime. In the outer pocket, amazingly, he found his car keys. Gordy did not look back. He hobbled out the entrance, forgetting everything in his fugue state. All he wanted to do was escape.

+ + +

After Gordy fell sideways off the riding mower, it lurched left and the gas can toppled off. It landed upside down next to him, soaking the grass and ground around him with the last few pints of gasoline. Rolling for a few more feet, it stopped when a wheel fell into one of the burning holes and sat there with the blades spinning through the flaming worm shit stew. Sparks and burning crap sprayed through the air.

Gordy saw none of this. He was too busy screaming, blinded by the pure agony of his abdomen being torn open. He was on his way out to a much better place. There was no way he could come back from these injuries, and he only hoped it would be quick. The grubs writhed in the open wound, covered in blood, shit, and a number of other body fluids. Arcs of arterial blood spouted past them onto the ground. The reek of gasoline filled the air. Gordy tried to grab the larger of the two grubs, but it just wriggled through his fingers and started crawling out of his gut-hole. It slithered up his chest toward his mouth, aiming to burrow back into him from the opposite end. Gordy shrieked and prayed to die before it reached him.

Ten feet away, the mower's front wheel sank lower in the fiery trench, pulling the spinning blade deeper into the blazing waste and changing the trajectory of the splatter. Left and right, burning clumps landed around Gordy from head to toe. One especially large flaming shit patty fell smack dab in the center of the gasoline-soaked grass and instantly ignited the entire area. The flames jumped to Gordy just as the grub reared back, and engulfed him and the grubs in a cleansing inferno. As he died, his screams sounded a lot like laughter.

+   +   +

Sergei Tumasov stood on his back porch drinking his evening tea and staring through the wall of smoke hanging in the air above the trees. A host of flashing red and blue lights lit the evening sky. He finished the last sip, grumbled, and went inside his house.

"What is it?" asked his wife Sofia. "Did you see anything?"

"That boy has finally gotten into trouble, Sofi," he answered. "I knew he was a problem waiting to happen. There are firemen, at least five or six policemen and an ambulance."

"Stop it," she admonished him. "You say that about all of our neighbors. How are we to make friends if you think that all of them are criminals?"

"I was right about him. I'll bet he blew up a meth lab"

"You have been watching that show about that science teacher too much. Not everyone makes drugs in their basement. Maybe there's a medical emergency."

"You are too trusting, dear. Most Americans are selfish assholes."

Sofia laughed, "Should I remind you that we are now citizens? Do I fit that category now?" she said, giving him a warning glance.

"Of course not, my kroshka," he said, using her pet name to hopefully mollify her. He looked around absentmindedly. "Where are the boys?"

"In the den. All of them. I think Yuri got into a fight. He has a cut on his nose and he smelled horrible when he came home. I cleaned him up a bit and put some salve on it, but we may need to take him to the vet to check it out."

"Hmmm . . . I'll check on him and see how he looks." He left her in the kitchen and walked down to the basement. A flurry of barks greeted him when he entered. Their boys, ten dogs they had rescued over the past few years, were as happy as always to see him. Mischa, the terrier mix, greeted him by racing in circles around his feet and peeing a bit in excitement. The others, varying in size and age, were content to mill around and nuzzle his hands. All except for one.

Yuri, the largest dog by far, was lying on his chosen pile of blankets in the corner looking miserable. Immediately, Sergei was concerned. Yuri had been with them the longest—over six years—and, though he wouldn't have admitted it out loud, the giant mutt was his favorite, even if he had the disgusting habit of eating his own week-old turds.

Sergei kneeled down next to Yuri and patted him on the flank.

"You've got yourself into a mess. Huh, boy?" he soothed the dog. "What was it? A skunk? A raccoon? You need to be careful, my boy."

The big beast flopped his tail against the blanket and whimpered in distress. He gagged, shook his head and tried to blow air out of his nostrils.

"Are you okay, boy?" Sergei was becoming concerned. Nothing usually bothered Yuri. One time he had even been struck a glancing blow by a car and Yuri had just walked away with a bruise. The car's door panel, on the other hand, had a dent the size of Yuri's head in it.

Yuri began whining frantically. He stood up, walked a few steps and began retching in the middle of the concrete floor.

"That's it, boy. We're taking you to the doctor," said Sergei. He walked to the stairwell and yelled up, "Sofi! Call the vet. I have to take Yuri in immediately!"

He turned back just in time to see his dog vomit up a softball-sized lump of pinkish pudding and collapse to the floor. Sergei ran to Yuri to gather him up in his arms, but once he saw what had come of Yuri's throat, he stopped and stared.

The object seemed to be a shredded piece of one of Yuri's internal organs. It smelled like death, and it was crawling with hundreds of grubs. Their pincers were the color of blood.

BLACKBIRD LULLABY
George Cotronis

*And He asked him, "What is thy name?" And he answered,
saying, "My name is Legion: for we are many."*
—Gospel of Mark 5:9

I'm lying in bed, alone. My arm extends over the side of the bed, wrist resting on the night table. I move my fingers and I can feel the tendons in my arm pulling them like puppets on a string. My middle and last finger are stripped of flesh down to the second knuckle, leaving the bone visible. The blackbird makes two small jumps and comes closer, disturbed by my sudden movement. I stop moving and it starts to peck at my flesh again. I watch it for a while. There is no pain. When I get bored, I shoo it away and it takes flight across the room to join its murder. His buddies are everywhere in the room, perched on furniture and lamps. They seem to be waiting for something.

The bed is full of trash, pieces of fabric and twigs, plastic bottle caps and paper. The blackbirds have turned it into a nest. I get up and find myself bleeding from several different places on my body. They've been eating me in my sleep again. My clothes are stained with blood and full of holes. Most of the blood is old, because I haven't changed in a week. All my shirts have holes now.

In the bathroom, I wrap my fingers with gauze, trying to make them look even, as if there's still meat underneath the white cloth. I consider using some antiseptic, but don't see the point. I throw the bottle in the trash bin.

I catch a glimpse of myself in the mirror.

Gaunt. Tired. Broken.

There are black circles around my eyes, my lips are dried and split, my face swollen and puffy. One of the ravens took out a small piece of flesh right under my eye. The blood runs down the side of my face, like the streak of a red tear. I wash up and put on a clean shirt. I feel almost human again. I look at my watch. I'm gonna be late.

Out on the street, people avoid me. Little girls clutch their father's hand and hide their face. They cry. I guess the clean clothes didn't help. Head down, hood up, I try to look more like a thug, a guy you shouldn't mess with, instead of the monster that I really am. It seems to work better. In the subway, a blackbird finds its way to me. It watches from the seat across from me, like it's the most normal thing in the world. No one seems to notice or care.

Me, I'm used to it. I look down my nose at it and hold its stare. Not that it gives a shit. It hops down to the floor and comes closer. It picks at my shoelaces. I look at my face in the reflection in the window. I'm bleeding again. I feel no pain in my fingers or the myriad of smaller wounds I carry, but my head is killing me. I used to wonder how I can still be alive, but these days there's a lot of things I don't think about. I just don't care. The extent to which I do not care would shock you.

I get off at my stop and head for the old church up the hill. There was a fire a few years back they never repaired the building, but it is still in decent condition. You just have to get creative about entering it. Around back, where the fence put up by the city has a human-sized hole in it, I enter the churchyard. One of the doors, the one closest to the fence, is unlocked. When it's not, they key is behind one of the loose bricks in the wall beside it.

Inside, Meg and Jonathan are already waiting. Meg is a tall woman, thin, used to be pretty. She's wearing a summer dress that's two sizes larger than it should be. I suspect it used to fit her once. One of her nipples is showing but she's too out of it to notice. Her dead eyes stare straight ahead. She doesn't see me.

Jonathan is holding her hand. He turns his head to me when I come in, but then turns to her again. They met here two years ago. Meg is near the end now, Jonathan still going strong.

Two blackbirds fly in from the broken window and land on the rubble strewn about in the church. Most of the roof is gone, but the little corner we have set up here keeps dry even when it rains. Winters are tough; then again we rarely meet like this. Usually it's just desperate phone calls in the middle of the night and unexpected visits. A circle of pews stands in the middle of all the trash and junk. I take my seat across from the couple and say nothing.

Welcome to Damned Anonymous. Living with things that are killing you from the inside. "Getting well—not really, we're just dying—together."

Our little support group. When Meg first started growing tumors that got up and walked around in the night, she figured a support group for cancer survivors wasn't going to be that helpful. When Jonathan woke up to find himself chewing on his little daughter's arm, Alcoholics Anonymous just wasn't an option for him anymore.

But they tried. And in those endless support group meetings, we found each other. Maybe it was the desperation that we saw in each other's eyes. The fear of something worse than death, which we recognized. Meg found me in a depression support group. I was saying I feel empty, numb, dead inside. After the meeting, over stale coffee and even staler donuts, she came over and said: "You're not really afraid you're gonna kill yourself, are you? You're here for something else." Maybe she saw the birds, perching on the windowsill. Maybe she noticed the bloodstains. So we started our own group. A few of us sometimes visit A.A. and groups like that. We recruit the demonically possessed.

Brennan walks in and takes me out of my little trip down memory lane. He's looking a bit better than last time. It probably means he fed again. One of those hookers downtown didn't wake up today and right now she's floating in the river, face down in the water, bloated like a balloon. If she's lucky some poor fisherman is gonna snag her in his nets and she'll get a burial.

He looks ashamed, but in this little crowd, no one gives a fuck if he ate some girl's heart and dumped her over the bridge. We're too involved in our own misery. I wave to him and he sits down. The room slowly fills up with the rest of the monsters and the stench gets progressively worse. The blackbirds have flooded the church, but they're quiet today, so I'm not gonna get in trouble with Jennifer, our group leader. Jennifer has a mouth full of razor-sharp teeth, each one filed to a point. When she cries, she cries blood. A Catholic, she tried to get an exorcism a year ago. It didn't work. I'm pretty sure she killed them, but she says she didn't. I think I read it in the papers, two priests missing around the same time. She looks like she's been crying.

Today, there is a new girl. Short black dress, ripped in some places and dirty with what looks to be ashes, heavy black make up, her eyes unblinking and taking in everything at once. She's gorgeous and deep within me I feel something slither, like Leviathan at the bottom of the ocean.

Her name is Magdalene.

There's a rat gnawing at her ankle.

I think my heart has stopped.

We go around the circle, telling our story for the umpteenth time, pouring salt on our wounds again, to try and *center ourselves*, get in touch with the *reality of our situation, understand and accept* what we can't change.

When it's Brennan's turn, he confirms my suspicions.

"I fed again. I couldn't help it. I was looking at my wife and thinking about eating her heart. I had to do something." He pauses and looks at the floor between his legs. Crocodile tears.

"I drove downtown and picked up a streetwalker. Young thing. I just picked up the first that came up to my car. I held it off until we reached the hills and then I killed her. I ate her heart and buried her up there, in the woods."

He's almost gone, he just doesn't know it yet. He's talking about this girl and crying, but I can see he's also salivating. I see him smile when he says the word "heart."

He breaks down and between sobs he keeps repeating "I'm so sorry . . . so sorry."

Jennifer consoles him with a hug while I roll my eyes. Fucking poser.

Meg is too out of it to share today. Jonathan says he's okay, he's controlling the cravings. I'm trying not to fall asleep. I'm waiting to hear *her* story. I think I know what she's going to say, but I want to hear her voice.

She will say:

"One day I saw them watching me on the street. I saw them again the very next day and the day after that. They watched from the alleys and under cars and from the roofs of buildings. They followed me around, they came into my house, they watched me sleep. No matter what I did, they found a way in, they killed themselves in their attempts to come to me, and in the end, they always found me. There was no way to stop them. No poison or weapon would keep them away. So, they became a part of me. They live with me. They are everywhere, always. I have no friends, because the last time I went for a cup of coffee, the little freaks attacked the waiter and I had to run out of the place with them after me, always after me. They are eating me alive."

Me, blackbirds.

Her, rats.

We have so much in common.

After *sharing* I walk up to her and say, "Nice dress."

She turns around and gives me the once-over. She seems unimpressed.

"Nice scabs." She smirks, but doesn't turn away.

"There's a rat trying to climb up your dress." I smile.

She looks down and then catches herself.

"Made you look," I say.

"Funny," she says, angry but laughing.

"Do you want to go someplace?" I ask.

"I don't really go out in public." She motions with her head towards the two rats gnawing on donuts on the table. "But you could come to my place."

A blackbird lands on my shoulder, tries to pluck out my eye. I slap it and it flies away, back up to the rafters.

"Where do you live?"

"Parkside," she says.

"Too far. Too many birds out there. How about my place?" I ask.

She agrees to come to my apartment tomorrow, to see my record collection. She's into *The Smiths* but who the fuck cares; we both know she doesn't give a shit about my records or anything else in my shitty apartment. Except me. She wants me.

On the subway ride home, I feel almost human again. I'd celebrate, but I haven't eaten or had a drink in weeks. I go home and I sleep on my bed made out of blood and black feathers.

She's at my place exactly on time. I put on a relatively clean shirt, my skin itchy all over from the feathers and the bird shit that's been irritating it. I open the door. She's cute in her flower pattern dress, with fresh little wounds at the top of her breasts. A bit of her scalp is missing over her left ear and she uses a flower to hide it.

"Hey."

"Hey."

She walks into my apartment, which is covered in black feathers and dirt, birds taking flight with every step she takes. I feel like a teenager. A teenager slowly turning into something else, but still. Nervous.

I drop the *The Smiths* record on her lap. She pretends to be interested for a bit but ultimately discards it on the coffee table. She pats the place beside her on the couch, and I obey.

"How are you doing with *them?*" I ask.

"Okay. I think I'm getting close."

I nod. I've felt the same lately. There will be a tipping point and then, the transformation will be complete. Our demons will consume us.

"You?" She picks at a scab on her knee. It's cute.

I shrug. "Who knows? I don't think about it," I lie.

I get up and bring out the wine and the glasses. She looks excited. We finish the bottle off in half an hour flat and when we're done with the boring chit chat, we make out on the couch. Our wounds open and we bleed into each other, feathers and coarse brown hair sticking to our bodies. It's painful and awkward and sometimes I feel like I will faint from the blood loss, but there are moments when I forget that my body is rotting and my heart is dead and hell is waiting for me.

We stumble to the bedroom and fuck in a drunken stupor, with the rats and the blackbirds watching.

I wake up and I feel empty, hollow. I reach into my chest and I touch a crow nesting there. Its coat is slick with my blood but it's not afraid. It feels safe inside of me. I feel safe too.

She's still here, her arm resting on my chest. A rat is peeking from under her dress. I wake her with a kiss and her little rat teeth gnaw at my lips. She draws blood and immediately I'm hard. I climb on top of her and then we are one, and the blackbirds and the rats are clawing and biting, and we flow into one another, and as monsters we are reborn.

ABOUT THE AUTHORS

JACK BANTRY is the editor of *Splatterpunk Zine*. His debut novel, *The Lucky Ones Died First*, will be published this summer by Deadite Press. He works as a postman and resides in a small town at the edge of the North York Moors.

THE BEHRG is the author of dark literary works ranging from screenplays to 'to-do' lists. His debut novel, *Housebroken*, was a First-Round Kindle Scout Selection, and semi-finalist in the 2015 Kindle Book Awards. He has had several short stories published in both print and digital anthologies and is the author of The Creation Series, with books two and three scheduled for a 2016 release. His 'to-do' list should be completed by 2017 … (though his wife is hoping for a little sooner). Discover why he writes as "The Behrg" at his website: TheBehrg.com

ADAM CESARE is a New Yorker who lives in Philadelphia. His books include *Mercy House, Video Night, The Summer Job*, and *Tribesmen*. His work has been praised by Fangoria, Rue Morgue, Publishers Weekly, Bloody Disgusting, and more. His titles have appeared on "Year's Best" lists from outlets like Complex and FearNet. He writes a monthly column for Cemetery Dance Online.

GEORGE CONTRONIS lives in the wilderness of Northern Sweden. He makes a living designing book covers. He sometimes writes. His stories have appeared in *XIII, Big Pulp* and *Vignettes from the End of the World*.

CLARE de LUNE, also known as Clare Castleberry, is a librarian who writes weird stuff: erotica, horror, sci-fi, transgressive and bizarro fiction. When she's not traveling to strange lands, she lives with her beloved boyfriend and cat in New Orleans. Clare has been published in *The Big Book of Bizarro* Anthology, *Necronomicum* Magazine and with Zombiegasm Press and is a member of the Horror Writers Association.

SCOTT EMERSON: Perhaps best known for his blog 365 Days of the Dead (in which he watched and reviewed a zombie movie every day for a year), Scott Emerson has recently appeared in the anthologies *Destroy All Robots, Diner Stories: Off the Menu, Westward Hoes*, and *The Big Book of Bizarro*. Currently he serves as facilitator for Morgantown Poets.

ROBERT ESSIG began writing as a result of his fascination with everything horror—books, magazines, movies, etc. He is the author of the novels *People of the Ethereal Realm* and *Through the In Between, Hell Awaits*. He has published over 40 short stories and two novellas. Robert lives in Southern California with his wife and son. Find out what he's been up to at robertessig.blogspot.com

MICHAEL PAUL GONZALEZ is the author of the novels *Angel Falls* and *Miss Massacre's Guide To Murder And Vengeance*. A member of the Horror Writers Association, his short stories have appeared in print and online, including *Gothic Fantasy: Chilling Horror Stories, 18 Wheels of Horror*, the Booked Podcast Anthology, HeavyMetal.com, and the *Appalachian Undead* Anthology. He resides in Los Angeles, a place full of wonders and monsters far stranger than any that live in the imagination. You can visit him online at MichaelPaulGonzalez.com

ADAM HOWE writes the twisted fiction your mother warned you about. A British writer of fiction and screenplays, he lives in Greater London with his partner and their hellhound, Gino. Writing as

Garrett Addams, his short story "Jumper" was chosen by Stephen King as the winner of the *On Writing* contest, and published in the paperback/Kindle editions of SK's book; he was also granted an audience with The King, where they mostly discussed slow vs. fast zombies. His fiction has appeared in *Nightmare Magazine*, *Thuglit*, *The Horror Library*, *Mythic Delirium*, *Plan B Magazine*, and *One Buck Horror*. He is the author of two collections, *Black Cat Mojo* and *Die Dog or Eat the Hatchet*, plus the eBook single, *Gator Bait*. Future works include *Tijuana Donkey Showdown*, *One Tough Bastard*, and a crime/horror collaboration with Adam Tribesmen Cesare.

MP JOHNSON is the Wonderland Book Award-winning author of *Dungeons & Drag Queens*. His most recent books include *Cattle Cult! Kill! Kill!* and *Sick Pack*. He is the creator of Freak Tension zine, a B-movie extra and an amateur drag queen AKA Maddy Manslaughter. Learn more at www.freaktension.com.

PETE KAHLE is the author of the award-winning scifi/horror epic *The Specimen*. In April 2015, he founded Bloodshot Books, a small press dedicated to cross-genre fiction that mixes the best of horror, science fiction, mystery and thrillers. In October of that year, the anthology *Not Your Average Monster* was unleashed to universally excellent reviews. Volume 2 was released five months later to equally positive accolades. In addition to original fiction, Bloodshot Books will be launching Second Sight, an imprint dedicated to reprinting a number of classic horror novels from past decades that deserve wider exposure. Pete's current project is *Blood Mother*, a stand-alone vampiric novel --without vampires--due out this summer, followed by the second and third books in the *Specimen* saga.

DAVID JAMES KEATON'S work has appeared in over 50 publications. His first collection, *Fish Bites Cop! Stories to Bash Authorities*, was named the 2013 Short Story Collection of the Year by *This Is Horror*, and his second collection of short fiction, *Stealing Propeller Hats from the Dead* (PMMP), recently received a Starred Review from Publishers Weekly, who said, "Decay, both existential and physical, has never looked so good." He has also been nominated for the Pushcunt Prize. He lives in California.

TONY KNIGHTON published the novella and story collection *Happy Hour and Other Philadelphia Cruelties* with Crime Wave Press. His story "The Scavengers" will be included in the upcoming anthology *Shocklines: Fresh Voices in Terror,* published by Cemetery Dance, and his story "Sunrise" is included in the anthology *Equilibrium Overturned*, published by Grey Matter Press. He has also published short fiction in *Crime Factory, Static Movement Online,* and *Dark Reveries*. He is a lieutenant in the Philadelphia Fire Department.

LILITH MORGAN Lilith Morgan is a horror writer (and definitely not a serial killer) who makes her home in Brooklyn, New York, with a summer residency in your nightmares. "Drama aside, my goal is to scare people. To get under their skin, to make them uncomfortable, but above all: to tell good stories."

CHARLES AUSTIN MUIR is a horror author, freelance writer and chiropractic assistant who lives in Portland, Oregon. He was an obituary writer and humor writer for The Oregonian. His fiction has appeared in many small press publications, including Cthulhu Sex Magazine, Morpheus Tales and the Bram Stoker Award-nominated anthologies *Hell Comes to Hollywood* and *Dark Visions: Vol. One*. His latest short story, "Party Monster," appears in *Peel Back the Skin*, an anthology from Grey Matter Press. He is known to lurk and blog at charlesaustinmuir.weebly.com.

MONICA J. O'ROURKE has published more than one hundred short stories in magazines such as *Postscripts, Nasty Piece of Work, Fangoria, Flesh & Blood, Nemonymous,* and *Brutarian* and anthologies such as *Horror for Good, The Mammoth Book of the Kama Sutra,* and *Eulogies II*. She is the author of *Poisoning Eros* I and II, written with Wrath James White, *Suffer the Flesh*, and the collection *In the End, Only Darkness*. Her latest novel, *What Happens in the Darkness,* is available from Sinister Grin Press. She works as a freelance editor, writer, and book coach. Find her on www.facebook.com/MonicaJORourke.

JORGE PALACIOS is the author of *Procreation of the Wicked* and numerous short stories. He is a writer, self-publisher, and zinester who writes anything, from horror and erotica to essays and reviews. He's interested in extremes, and more importantly, creating them.

JASON PARENT: In his head, Jason lives in many places, but in the real world, he calls New England his home. The region offers an abundance of settings for his writing and many wonderful places in which to write them. He currently resides in Southeastern Massachusetts with his cuddly corgi named Calypso. He is the author of the novels *Seeing Evil, What Hides Within* and many published short stories.

JEFF STRAND is the author of a bunch of demented books, including *Pressure, Dweller, A Bad Day For Voodoo, Wolf Hunt, Single White Psychopath Seeks Same, Benjamin's Parasite, Fangboy, The Sinister Mr. Corpse,* and lots of others. Three-time Bram Stoker Award finalist. Three-time Bram Stoker Award loser. Four-time Bram Stoker Award Master of Ceremonies.

KRISTOPHER TRIANA is the author of the novels *The Ruin Season* and *Body Art,* as well as the short story collection *Growing Dark,* which Rue Morgue Magazine called "a must read". His short fiction has appeared in countless anthologies and magazines, and some of it has been translated into Russian. He works as a professional dog trainer and lives in North Carolina with his wife. Visit his website at kristophertriana.com